FEMICIDE

PASCAL ENGMAN

Translated by Michael Gallagher

Legend Press Ltd, 51 Gower Street, London, WC1E 6HJ
info@legendpress.co.uk | www.legendpress.co.uk

Contents © Pascal Engman 2022
The right of the above author to be identified as the author of this work has
been asserted in accordance with the Copyright, Designs and Patents Act
1988. British Library Cataloguing in Publication Data available.

Print ISBN 978-1-91505-4-432
Ebook ISBN 978-1-91505-4-449
Set in Times.
Cover design by David Grogan | www.headdesign.co.uk

Translated from Swedish by Michael Gallagher

First published in Sweden in 2019 by Bookmark förlag, Sweden
Published by arrangement with Nordin Agency AB, Sweden

Printed and bound by CPI Group (UK) Ltd, Croydon CR0 4YY

Pascal Engman's debut novel *The Patriots* was published in 2017, and he has since become the best-selling Swedish crime novelist of his generation. He has been acclaimed by Camilla Läckberg, David Lagercrantz, The Swedish Crime Writers' Academy and others as a rising star of Swedish crime fiction. Engman, who resides in his native Stockholm, was born to a Swedish mother and a Chilean father. Engman was a journalist at Swedish evening newspaper *Expressen*.

For Linnea

One wants to be loved, in lack thereof admired, in lack thereof feared, in lack thereof loathed and despised. One wants to instil some sort of emotion in people. The soul trembles before emptiness and desires contact at any price.

From *Doctor Glas* by Hjalmar Söderberg.

PROLOGUE

A PLASTIC BAG had got stuck in the wire fence that surrounded Åkersberga Prison. Twenty-five-year-old Emelie Rydén turned the key in the ignition of her green Kia and the engine fell silent. She leaned forward, rested her head on the wheel.

Two years earlier, she had given birth to their daughter, Nova. Now she was here to end it with Karim, the man she had thought was the love of her life.

Emelie was scared. She straightened her back, raised her top lip and examined herself in the rear-view mirror. The bottom half of one of her front teeth was yellow. Four years before, Karim had flung her into a radiator during an argument. Emelie had fainted. When she came round, he had gone. Forty-eight hours later, he'd come home, stinking of bars and sweat, and asked for forgiveness with bloodshot eyes.

Emelie opened the car door and put her foot down in a puddle that had formed in a pothole. She had to bring this to an end. For Nova's sake. Her daughter didn't deserve to grow up with her father behind bars. Even if Karim was going to be released in three months' time, Emelie was certain that he would be back. Sooner or later. Probably sooner.

She walked with long strides towards the visitor entrance, pressed the bell and was let in. For three years, with only a few exceptions, she'd been here every week. Nova had been conceived in one of the visiting rooms. Some of the prison officers showed empathy, others thinly veiled contempt.

Over the years, she'd done all she could to keep her head held high, to walk the corridors with her back straight. She recognised the officer in reception. He was quiet, seemed shy. Despite them having met on several occasions, he gave no indication of knowing who she was.

"I'm going to see Karim Laimani," said Emelie.

The officer nodded.

"Could I borrow a pen?"

He kept his eyes fixed on the screen as he handed over a biro. Emelie unfolded Nova's drawing and added the date in the top right-hand corner.

The procedure after that was the same as always: jacket, bag, mobile phone and keys were locked in a cabinet. She was then led over to the metal detector and searched. Emelie held out her arms and let the officer pat her down.

"Follow me," he said mechanically as he pushed an access card against the reader. They walked down the corridor, then off to the right. The officer first, Emelie behind him with Nova's folded drawing in her hand. He stopped in front of a white door with a round glass window. Emelie peered in. Karim was sitting there with his hands on the tabletop. The hood on his grey sweatshirt was up. The door was pushed open and Emelie stepped into the little room. She took a deep breath. Her hands and legs were shaking. She rehearsed everything she was about to say as the door was pulled to behind her.

Karim stood up. It was as if the words she'd learned by rote had been blown away. He pulled her towards him, grabbing hold of her breast.

"Karim, stop..."

He pretended not to hear her, instead pressing his groin against hers and pushing his tongue into her mouth. She pushed him away.

"What the fuck is up with you?" he said.

Karim stared at her angrily for a couple of seconds, turned around and sat down on the chair. Emelie placed Nova's drawing on the table in front of him. He glanced at it impassively.

"You've put weight on. You're not up the duff again, are you?"

Emelie straightened a lock of hair that had fallen out of place. She opened her mouth, but her throat was dry. Once she had said those words, she would no longer be his girlfriend, but an enemy. In Karim's world, everything was black and white. Those words could never be unsaid. She cleared her throat and tried to keep her voice steady.

"I don't want us to be together any more."

Karim raised his eyebrows. His fingers made a scratching sound as he pushed them through his dark stubble.

"Stop it."

"It can't work," she said. Her voice cracked. She cleared her throat once more. "I can't take any more."

Karim's eyes narrowed. The chair legs scraped across the floor as he slowly got to his feet, his jaws grinding as he moved towards her.

"Do you think that's up to you?"

He was almost touching her. Emelie braced herself.

"Please…" she whispered as her eyes welled up. She closed them. Swallowed. "Can't you just let me go? You can see Nova when you come out."

"Are you fucking someone?"

"No."

Karim's face stopped ten centimetres or so from hers. He sniffed the air. "Oh yes, you've always been shit at lying. Have you been running around town opening your legs? You stupid. Fucking. Whore."

Emelie turned around, reaching for the door handle. Karim got there first and grabbed hold of her.

"You won't get away with it. If I find out you've been opening your cunt for anyone else, I will kill you."

The prison officer flung open the door. Karim let go and held up his palms. Emelie pulled her arm in and rubbed her wrist.

The next second, the visiting room echoed with Karim's voice.

"I will kill you. Just you wait. You are going to regret this," he roared.

The officer stepped in between them.

"Calm down."

Karim stared at Emelie over the guard's shoulder. As he backed away, he smiled.

PART I

We are people too. We just want to be loved for who we are. Our hopelessness does not come out of nowhere. I am pleased that you have never felt this way, but I hope you can sympathise. You bully us, belittle us. Everywhere. Instead, you ought to ask yourselves what it is that has made us feel this way. There is often a story that has brought us here. If you heard our stories, you might be more sympathetic to our situation, which, after all, is involuntary.

An anonymous man.

1

A STRING OF PURPLE fairy lights hung from the spruce tree in Monica Zetterlund Park. Detective Inspector Vanessa Frank was wearing a dark-blue coat. Underneath, she wore dark suit trousers and a newly ironed white shirt.

She ran the tip of her tongue across her gums. For the first time in her life, Vanessa had made a New Year's resolution: to stop using snus tobacco. She had put it off all winter. Now it was April. The snow was gone. Forty-eight hours earlier she had finished her last tin and the abstinence was causing her whole body to itch.

In Hassan's Phone Shop, which, despite the name, sold all sorts, the lights were still on.

The doorbell rang. Hassan smiled when he saw it was Vanessa.

"Sheriff Frank," he greeted her in thickly accented Swedish and bowed half-heartedly. "I hope you're not here to buy snus?"

"Give over, I'm forty-three. Give me a tin."

"Two days ago, you were standing exactly there when you forbade me to sell you snus."

"Either you sell me a tin, or I'll rob you."

Hassan moved quickly to shield the tobacco fridge with his body. "E-cigarettes, less dangerous, keep you busy," he said, pointing to a glass display cabinet. "I mean it, Vanessa. You made me promise. I intend to keep it."

Vanessa sighed and straightened her shirt collar. She appreciated people who kept their promises.

"Okay, okay, give me that shit then. But Hassan, careful you don't scratch the floor."

Bemused, he looked at her, then down at his feet.

"Eh?"

"Yeah, with that stick you've got shoved up your backside."

On the corner by Odengatan, Vanessa stopped, got the vape going, took a drag and then thoughtfully studied the white steam dissipating into the spring night sky. She walked in the direction of Sveavägen. The restaurants' outdoor terraces had opened. People were drinking beer with blankets draped across their shoulders, hunched over rickety wooden tables.

Vanessa's life was being renegotiated. In December, Natasha – the sixteen-year-old Syrian girl who Vanessa had had living with her – had received a phone call from her father. He had survived the war, crippled but alive. On Christmas Day, as the snow fell heavily, Vanessa had waved Natasha off and watched the taxi's rear lights disappear up Surbrunnsgatan. The brake lights had flickered. Made Vanessa hope, for a second, that Natasha would tear herself out, dragging her suitcase with her, and rush over to Vanessa as she explained it had all been a misunderstanding. Four months had passed, and still the loneliness felt like a rusty brown bike chain against her ribcage every single day.

On Sveavägen, the vintage cars cruised back and forth, carrying enthusiasts in vests and checked shirts singing along to Eddie Meduza and Bruce Springsteen. Petrol fumes. Confederate flags. A man pushed his anaemic arse cheeks against the rear windscreen of a passing white Chevrolet. Vanessa had planned to turn right, taking the route home through Vanadis Park – but just ahead, a huge scaffold towered over the pavement. She hated walking underneath them; they looked like they might collapse at any second. Instead, she crossed Odengatan and continued parallel to the bus stop.

As she passed Storstad bar, she caught a glimpse of a face she recognised – theatre director Svante Lidén's. They had been married for twelve years, until she found out that he'd got a young actress pregnant. Vanessa didn't flinch, just kept walking. She hadn't got more than a couple of metres when she heard her name being called.

"You can at least say hello?"

"Hi."

She turned on her heels. Svante rushed over and placed a gentle hand on her shoulder.

"Can't you come in for a little bit?"

He gave her a pleading look. The alternative was going home, flopping onto the sofa and watching Animal Planet.

"Okay."

Svante held the door and asked what she would like to drink. Vanessa asked for a gin and tonic and took a seat by the window. She glanced towards the space between the bar and the tables, where inebriated people were trying it on with one another.

Us humans are just wild mammals in colourful clothes, she thought to herself. In a hundred years from now, everyone in this room will be dead. White bones and dust, buried six feet under. No one will know that they shared these hours together. The realisation made her feel bleak.

"You look fantastic," Svante said, putting the drink down on the table between them.

Vanessa raised her glass towards him.

"You look like you died in 2003."

"Cheers!" Svante responded, untroubled. "How are things?"

Vanessa took a gulp. Now she was here, she might as well be nice. For old times' sake. In spite of everything, she was pleased to see Svante.

Those years she had lived with him had been good ones. The fact that he would shag anything with a pulse, she had learned to live with. What had wounded her was that he denied her a child. When Vanessa had become pregnant, a while before the divorce, he had persuaded her to have an abortion. And now it was too late.

"I've got a new job."

"Have you left the police?"

Vanessa shook her head.

"New division. I left NOVA and I'm an investigator for the National Homicide Unit now."

He put an ice cube in his mouth and crushed it between his teeth.

"*Riksmord?*"

'Piano Man' streamed from the speakers. Vanessa leaned in to be heard above Billy Joel.

"I travel around the country, helping colleagues in murder investigations."

"A business traveller for murders, then. That would make a good film title. And plenty of work at the moment, if the papers are anything to go by?"

An hour and three G&Ts later, Vanessa felt intoxicated. She didn't want to go home. In many ways, Svante was a boil, a poor excuse for a man, but she liked him. They still hadn't touched upon the subject of Johanna Ek, the actress who Svante now lived with. Nor had they raised the subject of the couple's child. Vanessa was afraid of ruining the moment, but in the end, she could not hold back any longer.

In the middle of a question, she raised her palm towards Svante.

"How's the kid then? The one-year-old, I mean, not the one you left me for."

Svante opened his mouth to respond, but Vanessa cut in again. "What did you christen her? Yasuragi Lidén?"

"Yasuragi? That spa? Why would we…"

"I found a hotel bill in one of your jackets, paid nine months before she was born. You celebs usually name your kids after where they were conceived, don't you?"

Svante scratched his cheek.

"Granted, I didn't handle that very well," he said. "I'm sorry."

They stared into each other's eyes for a couple of seconds until Vanessa waved her hand.

"Don't be."

She looked at his brown eyes, continued upwards to his spiky fringe. He was greyer than last time she saw him, almost completely, in fact.

Vanessa let her eyes wander to his big hands, his chewed nails. She missed his humour. The security. That way he bit his bottom lip if he was reading something he didn't agree with in the paper. How he grabbed hold of her. Decisively. Proprietorially. His poorly disguised jealousy when he noticed she was attracted to someone else.

"Are you happy with her?"

His chin was resting in his cupped hand.

"It's different. Easier, somehow."

"Do you have to be so bloody honest?"

A man bumped into Vanessa's back. She moved her chair closer to Svante's. "Do you know what gets to me most?" she asked.

"No?"

"That you turned me into a cliché."

Svante raised his eyebrows. Vanessa grabbed hold of his hand and moved it inside her unbuttoned jacket, to her breast. She had had surgery six months before. "A walking fucking cliché of the ageing, jilted woman."

He laughed and withdrew his hand. A bit too slowly for Vanessa not to notice. Why did she want Svante to want her? Why did he have that effect on her? She was fine. She didn't need him. He had made his choice.

Did she want revenge on Johanna? Was it that simple?

"Say it."

"Say what, Vanessa?"

She leaned in, could smell his aftershave.

"That you still want me."

2

JASMINA KOVAC TOOK off her round-rimmed glasses and the editorial office of *Kvällspressen* immediately became a fuzzy haze. She felt inside her rucksack, which was hanging on her chair. Once she'd found the case, she pulled out the little blue cloth and rubbed it over the glass expertly.

She put her glasses back on her nose. Chairs, people and computer screens regained their sharp edges.

Jasmina often thought that if she'd been unfortunate enough to have been born before spectacles were invented, she would never have been able to live for twenty-eight years and would probably have ended up as wolf food a long time before that.

She tittered out loud at the thought of herself in a loincloth, and her colleague Max Lewenhaupt, sitting at the desk next to hers, turned towards her.

"What's so funny?" he asked disapprovingly, peering over at Jasmina's screen.

"Oh, nothing," she replied, feeling the blush spreading across her cheeks.

Max opened his mouth to reply but was interrupted by a voice behind them. "Are you youngsters having coffee?"

Hans Hoffman, a senior reporter who occasionally came in to cover evenings and weekends, popped his head above his screen. Max rolled his eyes and mimed the word "mess". Jasmina felt sorry for Hoffman.

"Great," she said and stood up.

They walked past row after row of desks, past the Editor-in-Chief's glazed office. The coffee machine coughed out a weak brown liquid.

"You're from Småland region, aren't you?"

Jasmina nodded. "Växjö."

"And Kovac. Croatian?"

"Bosnian."

Jasmina prepared to return to the computer to finish off the evening's final article – a piece about a cat in the remote northern town of Ånge who had come home after having been missing for two years. Hoffman, though, gestured to her to stay.

"You're going to have to start coming up with a few ideas of your own if you want to stay at this paper. Otherwise, the likes of him will eat you up," Hoffman said, nodding in Max Lewenhaupt's direction.

"I know. I've got something good about William Bergstrand. You know, the MP?"

"Good. Best foot forward, kiddo. That's what you have to do. You're good, you've read what you're supposed to. That piece on unsolved murders of women was fantastic, but you need to broaden your scope. Hold the politicians to account."

Jasmina glanced at the desk where news editor Bengt 'the Bun' Svensson was sitting with his feet up. His laptop was resting on his tummy. Jasmina plucked up courage. She walked back to her computer and opened the investigation. Earlier that week, she had requested copies of Social Democrat politician William Bergstrand's receipts from the parliamentary administration. He had recently been to Paris, and among his receipts were two restaurant bills for five thousand crowns apiece, luxury hotels and shopping. All paid for with the parliamentary card. What was even more embarrassing for Bergstrand – who had been tipped for a great future in the party – was that he had been accompanied by fellow MP Annie Källman. She, however – according to her Instagram – had been in Sundsvall at the time.

"Where are you off to now then?" asked Max.

"I'm just going to get a print-out."

"Stop talking so quietly. I can't hear what you're saying," said Max. He mimed a telephone with his fingers and put it to his ear. "What have you printed out?"

"I'm working on something." She hesitated, sat down at her desk again and leaned towards Max. He was good. She gave a quick account of what she'd discovered from Bergstrand's receipts. "But I can't get hold of him. He's ducking me. Do you want to help me?"

Max nodded slowly. Jasmina noticed that he was reluctantly impressed. She was pleased.

As the printer whirred away, Jasmina looked at the classic headlines and news bills that adorned the walls. VJ Day 1945, the hostage drama at Norrmalmstorg 1973, the bombing of the West German Embassy in 1975, the MS *Estonia* disaster 1994, the attack on the Twin Towers, 2001.

She went and stood behind Bengt. He carried on staring at his screen.

"Yes?" he said, scratching his ear.

"I thought I'd ask if you'd… Have you got a few minutes? There's this thing I've been working on."

Bengt looked at his finger in disgust and then wiped it on his thigh, leaving a yellowy fleck on his jeans. "Jessica, I don't know…"

"Jasmina."

She smiled nervously.

"Jasmina," Bengt said with a sigh. "I don't know how it works in Norrköping or where…"

"Växjö. I'm from Växjö."

Bengt was busy with his other ear.

"Whatever," he said. The only piece I want from you is three columns about that fucking cat that turned up, wherever the hell that was again, Haparanda?"

"Ånge."

"Yes. Is it done?"

"Basically, yes, but…"

"No buts," Bengt grunted irritably. "Shuffle on back to your desk and do as you're told. That's how things work here at *Kvällspressen*. It's been a winning concept since the paper was founded in 1944. I'm sure whatever you've come up with is a lovely idea, but I don't have time."

An hour later, Jasmina Kovac left *Kvällspressen*'s offices and took a seat right at the back of the number one bus. It was only when they got to Fridhemsplan that other passengers got on board. An ambulance flew past at high speed. It was a chilly Friday night, and Kungsholmen was bathed in a yellowish light that ran from the street lamps. Freezing people congregated outside the bars. Rough sleepers sought shelter in stairwells and under awnings. They slept huddled together, like starving, frozen animals.

Stockholm was Jasmina's dream city. She'd wanted to be a journalist for as long as she could remember, just like her father had been until war came to Yugoslavia.

A couple of months before, as a reporter on local paper *Smålandsposten*, Jasmina had investigated a number of unsolved murders of women. In some cases, she had been able to demonstrate that the police's mistakes had led to the murders going unsolved. The article had had a big impact and been picked up by syndicated news agency TT and both of the main tabloids. Two hours after publication, *Kvällspressen*'s editor-in-chief had phoned her to offer her a temporary role.

So far, though, nothing was going her way. "Tomorrow is a new day," she muttered.

3

THEY WERE TEARING each other's clothes off as soon as they got into the hall. Svante pushed Vanessa against the wall, changed his mind, pushed her in front of him over towards the sofa, bent her over and entered her from behind. Animalistic. Rough. Desperate. The way she wanted it, the way she'd always wanted it.

Afterwards, Vanessa produced a bottle of red wine. She handed him the wine and a corkscrew while she turned on the vape.

She stared at the ceiling through the white vapour.

"I haven't been screwed that well since..." Vanessa muttered to herself before realising and going quiet.

"Since when?"

"I was going to say, 'since I had a very passionate romance with my high-school teacher,' but I thought that might hurt your feelings."

"Did you sleep with your teacher?"

"Have I never told you about Jacob? He was twenty-eight and was a maths supply teacher. I was seventeen and pretty pissed off at most things in life. We used to..."

"That'll do, won't it?"

Svante gave her the bottle.

"By the way, what's going on with the windows?" he asked. They were covered with white plastic sheeting.

"The frontage is being restored."

"You can't even tell if it's dark out there."

"No, this really is an environment to lose your mind in."

She wished he could say something meaningful. That life was boring without her. Instead, he started telling a story from a rehearsal that she'd already heard. Vanessa listened with one ear while stroking the inside of his thigh. It's weird, she thought, what time can do with feelings. Svante was finding it increasingly difficult to deliver his anecdote as her hand wandered further and further up his thigh. His breathing became strained. She straddled him. He closed his eyes, mouth half-open. Vanessa imagined that he was thinking of Johanna, and she gave him a slap. Svante jolted his eyes open in surprise. For a second she thought he was going to return the blow, but he laughed and closed his eyes again. She pushed herself harder against him, felt him getting deeper and deeper inside her as she rode him with slow, rolling movements.

When she came, she clasped her fingernails into his hairy chest, and he batted them away.

It was half two in the morning when Svante mumbled that he was going to have to go home. He gathered up his clothes. Vanessa followed, with the blanket wrapped around her body.

"How are you going to explain the scratches?"

He stared down at his black shirt as he was buttoning it and shrugged.

"Are you angry?" she asked.

"No."

Vanessa pressed her lips together to physically stifle the question of whether he could stay. They kissed before she gave him a light shove. "See you later," said Svante.

"I suppose you will," she replied, closing the door.

4

THE EDITORIAL OFFICE at *Kvällspressen* was in a state of sleepy Saturday morning calm. Jasmina Kovac was on her way to the canteen to grab herself a stale pasty when Bengt called out. She assumed it was about an error in the cat piece and prepared herself for a ticking off.

"I need a big piece. For the Monday edition."

"Sure," Jasmina said, struggling to hide her surprise. "What were you thinking?"

"A double-page spread."

Jasmina was actually supposed to have finished her shift. They had attempted to contact MP William Bergstrand, who was still avoiding their calls. Max and Jasmina had decided that they were going to try and get hold of him when they got off work in the middle of next week. She planned to go to Växjö, to visit her mum. She'd already booked the tickets. But it couldn't be helped. The opportunity to write an in-depth piece was a chance she had to take.

"Of course. What's it about?"

"A summary of the latest on #metoo. Hoffman was busy and he put forward your name when I asked him if he could do it. You know I'm really not sure you're ready, so don't leave me disappointed."

Jasmina couldn't supress a smile as she returned to her desk. Hoffman came walking towards her with that day's paper opened out in front of him.

She bounded over and gave him a hug. "Thank you," she whispered.

"For what? I'm too old to be up all night writing copy," he said. "But if you're going to manage it, you'd better get started. Go home. If they see you here, they'll dump more work on you."

Jasmina realised that Hoffman was right. The article could be her ticket to bigger things, but she was going to need to work undisturbed. She gathered her things, squeezed her laptop into her backpack and hurriedly said goodbye to the other reporters.

Mum was going to be disappointed. Jasmina was her whole life. She had read every little notice Jasmina had ever written, cut out the pages and saved them in boxes that she kept under the bed.

"Hi, Mum."

"Are you here already? I thought you were coming tonight?"

"I have to stay here. They want me to do a big article. It needs to be ready by tomorrow."

Despite Jasmina's best efforts to hide the fact, her mum had understood that things hadn't gone according to plan so far in Stockholm.

"That's great," her mum exclaimed. "Of course you have to do that."

"Are you sure? I miss you. You do know that I want to see you?"

"I miss you too, my little girl, but you'll have to come next time you're off instead."

Jasmina got off the bus at Stureplan. She had always produced her best writing while surrounded by people, and she found it hard to concentrate when she was alone. The gloomy studio flat she was renting on Valhallavägen did not appeal. She walked over the pelican crossing and into the Hotel Anglais. The lobby was half-empty. Perfect, she thought to herself as she ordered a mineral water and a coffee.

She asked for the Wi-Fi password, sat down on one of the sofas near the window and got out her laptop.

Before she got started, she felt a wave of pride wash through her body. Here she was, sitting in a hotel bar, writing a piece for Sweden's biggest tabloid. Living the dream.

The next time Jasmina looked up from her screen, the lobby was full. Her glass was empty, and her coffee was cold. She could barely see the bar for all the people. A DJ was standing by the decks.

Her eyes were stinging, and her body was stiff. She straightened her back and decided to take a break. A man a little way away was staring at her. She looked away and closed her laptop. Jasmina assumed he'd misread the situation, because he then made a beeline for her.

"Would you like a cocktail?" he asked.

He looked to be about thirty-five. Black shirt. Handsome, in a rough-hewn way. Jasmina pointed at her laptop.

"I'm working, so I'm on alcohol-free tonight," she said with a smile. "Thanks though."

He squeezed in alongside Jasmina.

"Come on. One cocktail. It's Saturday."

She figured she did need a break after all. Every sentence in that article needed to be perfect and if she was going to keep her concentration up, she'd have to focus on something else for a while.

"A coffee?" she said. "Then I have to go home and carry on with it."

"My name is Thomas," he said, standing up. After shaking her hand, he moved it to his mouth, the stubble on his chin prickling against the thin skin on the back of her hand.

A while later and the coffee was drunk. During the conversation, Thomas had moved closer and closer. He'd asked a load of questions without seeming particularly interested in the answers. His eyes stared at her body, settling with increasing frequency on her breasts. Jasmina thought he was creepy. She felt dozy and tired.

She excused herself, explaining that she needed to go to the toilet and freshen up.

The room started spinning, her legs folded, and she grabbed hold of the table. Thomas caught her. Where was her backpack? The computer?

"Thanks," she heard herself slur. Her voice sounded metallic, as if she was talking into a can.

He held her by one arm, with his other arm around her waist. Her jaw felt slack, her eyelids heavy – she could barely keep them open. Jasmina tried to protest as he led her through the throng, but no sound emerged from her lips.

Suddenly, they were outside. She could see the pavement beneath her feet and could feel his strong hand on her shoulder. Blinding headlights. Jasmina closed her eyes. Her head slumped onto his shoulder. A car door opened, someone laughed. She was lifted into the back seat. The engine started and the car moved off. Thomas' face appeared, over her own. Jasmina tried to say something, but the only thing to come out was nonsense. Even more laughter. She tried to turn her head, but that didn't work either.

How many of them were there? Where were they taking her? A hand pushed under her top, felt its way across her stomach and grabbed hold of her breast. Another hand sought its way between her legs. The car picked up speed, the streetlights disappeared, and Jasmina lost consciousness.

5

EMELIE RYDÉN LOOKED around the empty two-bed apartment on Åkerbyvägen in Täby. Although she would never say as much, it was nice not having to look after Nova sometimes. She and Ilan had been supposed to spend the weekend together; that was why she'd asked her parents to look after her daughter.

Ilan, though, had had to go to Malmö for work.

He had promised to call her from the hotel room after he'd had dinner with his bosses, who he'd gone to meet. It was now 10.32 pm and he still hadn't rung.

Emelie flicked on the telly and zapped between channels.

For a second she imagined that Karim had somehow found out about their relationship, gone to Malmö and hurt Ilan.

It had been three weeks since she'd visited Karim in prison for the last time. He could have got parole without her knowing about it. Since there were only two months left of his sentence, he would be completely unsupervised if that was the case.

Emelie had met Ilan four months earlier, when she had four large crates of product delivered to her salon. The courier shook his head when she'd asked him to carry them inside.

Ilan, who had happened to be walking past, spotted Emelie and the crates and asked if she needed any help.

He'd rolled up his sleeves, carried the crates inside and then disappeared. The following day, Ilan had returned, and

Emelie – much to her surprise – had discovered that she was pleased to see him and invited him in for a coffee. A week after that meeting, they slept with each other for the first time.

Her phone rang, and Ilan's face appeared on the display.

"Sorry it took so long," he opened. "They wouldn't stop drinking."

"Are you drunk?" she asked, taking a gulp of her tea.

"Not at all. I stopped drinking early."

Emelie put the cup on the coffee table and lay down with her head on the armrest.

"I'm sorry it turned out like this," said Ilan. "I really was looking forward to seeing you this weekend."

"It's okay. We'll make up for it next week."

"I've got something I have to tell you," said Ilan.

Emelie heard a sound outside the window and looked towards it. Probably just a branch blowing against the window in the wind.

"I lied to you. The reason I came down here is because they've offered me a job. Here in Malmö."

Part of her felt relieved, another part of her felt grief. He was going to take the job and leave her. And she couldn't fault him. They had just met. Obviously he wasn't keen on dragging a kid around that wasn't his. And even if she hadn't told him everything about Karim, she presumed he had his suspicions.

"I understand."

"I know it's early, but I am just so fond of you and Nova. I might be mad, but I was wondering whether you'd like to move with me?"

Emelie laughed with astonishment. "Are you being serious?"

"Yes."

Emelie closed her eyes.

"Of course we would."

She could see his thin, lanky body in front of her. Those kind, dark eyes. She wished he was there. With her. When they moved to Malmö, she wouldn't need to long for him any more.

A movement outside the window made Emelie jump. Ilan

was still talking, but Emelie had stopped listening. She stood up slowly, with the phone glued to her ear, and peered out into the gloom.

She moved closer to the window, put her head against the cold pane and looked one way and then the other. Nothing. Just the dark, deserted courtyard where Nova loved to play with the neighbours' kids.

"What did you say?"

"That I'm happy," said Ilan. "Today I walked past a unit that would make the perfect skincare salon. Not that there's any rush. I'll be getting a hefty rise, so you really don't need to feel like you have to start working straight away."

Emelie crossed the living room, went out into the hall and checked that the front door was locked.

"I thought you were going to say that you'd slept with someone else."

Ilan laughed. A loud, liberating laugh.

Emelie peered out at the stairwell through the peephole. Empty. She relaxed. If Karim was on parole, and he turned up, she was going to call the police. But she didn't want Ilan to understand what was going on. She had told him about Karim but held back on the details. Said he was living overseas.

Emelie lay down on the sofa again, but she couldn't relax and concentrate on what Ilan was saying. She really hated living on the ground floor.

As they said goodbye, she could hear the entrance door opening, and she rushed to hang up. She didn't want Ilan to start asking questions if there was suddenly banging at the door.

Emelie stood up again and listened to the footsteps in the hallway.

She closed her eyes, hoping that the person out there would walk past her door and that the lift machinery would start. Just when she thought she'd heard the familiar rumble from the lift shaft, there was a ring on the doorbell.

6

JASMINA REGAINED CONSCIOUSNESS with a hard slap. She was lying on a bed in a dark room. Her head was pounding, she felt nauseous. Another slap struck her cheek. Where was she?

"Time to wake up."

She remembered the bar, and Thomas. Jasmina grabbed her waistband and tried to resist. Her hands felt weak, the fabric slipped between her fingers. Her trousers came off. He stood over her and tore off her knickers.

"No," she croaked.

She could hear voices. She squinted, trying to understand what or who was around her. But everything was blurred. On the right was a wardrobe with a mirrored door. She could make out movement in it. There were several people in the room.

They pulled her jumper off, ripped her bra apart.

"Please stop," Jasmina pleaded.

The panic was rising, and she lunged back and forth, kicking her legs. A blow struck her stomach, and her body was emptied of air. Wheezing and coughing, she gasped for oxygen.

"If you make a fuss, we'll have to get the knife out, and you don't want that," said Thomas. His hand glanced her cheek. "That would be a shame, on such a pretty face." His breath was moist and sour.

"She's not as shy as she's making out. Look at this," he added, grabbing her nipple ring and tugging at it curiously. "You are a right little whore after all, aren't you?"

"Please, let me go," she whispered, blinking.

"Little whores like you like this, even if you pretend you don't."

He stroked her cheek and then unbuckled his belt. Strong arms turned Jasmina onto her stomach and pinned her down. Someone pushed her face into the mattress. Breathing became difficult. She tried to struggle free. Her screams were drowned in the feathers.

Thomas groaned as he pushed into her. It hurt like hell. She felt powerless. Small. The movements got harder, hurt more and more. Jasmina screamed straight into the mattress.

"Fuck, it's been a while. A real tight little cunt she's got. Maybe she's younger than we thought?"

"Or else no one's ever fucked her properly. Look how she's enjoying it."

New laughs.

They took turns, turning her over, prising her legs apart when she tried to resist. She caught a glimpse of their naked bodies in the mirror. She turned her eyes away. Forced herself to stare up at the ceiling. It was like her body was paralysed. They didn't need to hold her down any more. There was nowhere to escape. She fell in and out of consciousness until one of them tore out her ring. She screamed. A large hand slammed over her mouth.

"Shut up."

She was struggling to breath, wheezing. She flailed her arms in blind panic. She could see a shiny, blurred face.

"Open your legs."

They kept groaning, egging each other on, humiliating her.

Eventually they tired of it. Stood up and disappeared. A moment's peace. Jasmina lay perfectly still and moved her hand down between her legs, then held up her fingers. She was bleeding.

Muffled, hoarse voices and cigarette smoke found their way

under the door. Jasmina lay on her side, feeling for her glasses. She couldn't find them. She was shaking with cold. Then she touched her breast. The blood stuck between her fingers.

Hearing footsteps, she curled into a ball, turned to face the wall and closed her eyes. She could take no more. Not again.

"You're out."

Thomas sat down on the edge of the bed and forced her to turn around. He leaned over her.

"If you tell anyone about this, we will kill you, Jasmina Kovac."

He grabbed her hair, turned her face to his, held up her driving licence a couple of centimetres from her face and read out all her information.

She started crying.

"Hear that, you little slut? We'll get hold of you, and next time we won't be so nice."

He threw her clothes at her. Jasmina managed to get her trousers on. It was stinging and throbbing between her legs. She could see the outline of Thomas' unshaven face out of the corner of her eye. He dragged her to her feet and shoved her ahead of him. Jasmina stumbled into the living room. She waddled as she walked. Each step was painful.

"You look like you've had a good time," said a voice.

They led her out into the stairwell, down some stairs and foisted her into the back seat of a car.

The car started. The men seemed tired, didn't say much. The sun was about to come up. Jasmina tried to read the signs to work out where she was.

"Here will do," one of them said to the driver.

They pulled into the kerb and the door swung open. Someone beeped. "Remember what I said, Jasmina Kovac – we'll find you, and kill you."

She put her feet down onto the ground.

"Out, now, fuck's sake."

She felt a shove, almost tripped but managed to stay upright.

7

VANESSA PICKED UP that day's copy of *Dagens Nyheter* from the doormat. The paper edition was old-fashioned and a strain on the already hard-pushed environment, but the world was unavoidably going to pot anyway. And while it did, Vanessa could entertain herself by staying abreast of the latest political scandals, Brexit and the American president's tweets. The world was getting weirder all the time, and she felt less and less at home in it. For the first time in human history, more people were dying from overeating than malnutrition. Old age was killing more people than infectious diseases. And above all: more people were taking their own lives than deaths caused by war, violent crime and terrorism. Yet people were more scared than ever before.

She put the paper on the kitchen island, switched on the coffee machine and caught herself missing Svante. The television hummed in the background.

"Three men have been found dead in Frihamnen. *TV4 News* understands that the men were shot in the head. All three were known to the police."

Vanessa turned up the volume.

Another gangland revenge attack.

Stockholm was flooded with firearms, and young men were prepared to use them to gain a share of the cocaine market or to take revenge for some perceived slight. Automatic Kalashnikov weapons were being sold on the streets for twenty-five thousand crowns. A pistol cost ten. A hand grenade could be obtained for about a thousand, unless there was a major conflict in progress, in which case the dealers raised the price to two thousand five hundred.

The executions in Frihamnen were probably to do with drug deals, but anything was possible – the criminals were even more easily offended than Donald Trump, whose angry little eyes were staring out at her from *DN*'s front page.

After leaving what had been known as NOVA, but after reorganisation was renamed *Investigations Unit, Surveillance Group 5 & 6*, Vanessa was at least able to avoid having to get involved in those gang attacks which were so tough to crack, ones in which neither witnesses nor those directly involved wanted to talk to the police. She had spent the previous week in Kalmar, where a house party had got out of control and one of the guests had been found stabbed to death with a pair of scissors.

Vanessa poured some coffee and prepared to return to the sofa when her work phone rang.

"Good morning," said Mikael Kask, director of *Riksmord*, chirpily. "How are things?"

"I'm halfway through my breakfast."

"Anything nice?"

"Coffee and a vape. Breakfast of champions."

"Sounds healthy."

Presumably Mikael had been on a management course where he'd learned to use a familiar tone with his subordinates.

On TV, the piece about the triple murder was over, replaced by a panel discussion on children's parties.

Mikael cleared his throat. Enough small talk.

"I know you are off today, but Serious Crimes have been in touch. They need help."

"The triple murder in Frihamnen."

"No, although that is eating up their resources. A young woman was found dead in Täby this morning. They don't have enough detectives. Can you get down there? Forensics are already at the scene."

Although perhaps it was wrong of her to feel that way, Vanessa was always more upset by women falling victim to violence than when gang members were found shot dead. Perhaps that was because she'd lost her own daughter Adeline when she was younger. Maybe it wasn't the women's deaths themselves that affected her, but the parents' loss. Vanessa knew what kind of a life they were being sentenced to.

"Sure."

Mikael gave her the address. Vanessa jumped in the shower, then got dressed – suit trousers and a shirt. She stopped by the mirror and studied her face. After that, she punched in the code to open the gun safe and stuffed her Sig Sauer in its holster.

After smashing the Södertälje Network a couple of years earlier, Vanessa had been given permission to store weapons at home. In recent years, the threat faced by police had grown significantly. Yet the main reason Vanessa kept her weapon at home was not one her bosses knew about.

A little over a year earlier, she had been involved in an investigation into a criminal organisation that called itself 'The Legion'. During a deal in a safe house north of Stockholm, Vanessa and Nicolas Paredes, a former elite soldier, had shot dead four members of the group. The Legion had – aside from supplying Greater Stockholm with large volumes of high-quality cocaine – kidnapped refugee children and sent them to South America.

A police officer and the witness who lived in the house were already dead when Nicolas and Vanessa arrived at the scene.

The air felt fresh and dry as Vanessa stepped out onto Odengatan. A pale sun struggled to climb above the tall buildings. People at leisure picking their way between the puddles to get to the cafés and vegan bars. A muscular man with green-blue tattoos sticking out over his collar walked past the garage. His head was shaved. With one arm, he was steadying a white-haired woman. She looked tiny by his side, leaning into him almost.

His mother? He walked slowly, cautiously, so that she could keep up. Vanessa thought about how, forty years ago, he would have been the one hanging onto her.

Down in the garage, her phone bleeped again. The murdered woman's name was Emelie Rydén.

8

THIRTY-YEAR-OLD NICOLAS PAREDES waited for the kettle to finish its job before he got up from the sofa, picked out a mug, poured a spoonful of Nescafé into the bottom and drowned it in boiling water. He opened the balcony door and shielded his eyes against the sunlight with his hand.

On the next-door balcony, a girl with long green hair was sitting on the railing. Her legs were dangling way above the ground.

"*Hej*, Nicolas," she said cheerfully without turning her head. He raised his cup towards her but didn't say anything. "Want a toke?" she asked.

He shook his head.

"How old are you, Celine?"

"Twelve."

"Jesus."

"Scrambled eggs then?" she continued, untroubled.

Nicolas gave her a weary glance and noticed that she had a fresh black eye. Probably her dad's doing. Or a classmate. Nicolas ought to have a word with the dad or at least call social services, but he could not get involved in anything that might attract the interest of the authorities.

"Do you never cook anything other than scrambled eggs?"

"I can boil them too, if you prefer?"

"You cook whatever you like, but don't sit like that – you

know it makes me nervous. If I eat the eggs, do you promise not to get stoned then?"

Celine nodded, jumped down from the railing and disappeared into the flat. From inside his own flat, Nicolas heard the letter box opening and something landing on the parquet floor. He walked in, bent down and picked up a brown envelope. His name and address were written in childish handwriting. Nicolas took the letter with him back out onto the balcony – at the same time as Celine reappeared holding a frying pan. He used the spoon from his coffee cup and took a taste. Celine looked at him expectantly. As usual, they were far too salty.

"Nice."

Nicolas ate hungrily; he hadn't had any breakfast yet. "Thanks," he said, wiping his mouth and handing back the frying pan.

Celine put it down on the floor. She leaned forward, arms resting on the railing, and looked miserable.

"I know that neither of us have got a particularly good day ahead of us. Do you want to hear our horoscope?"

Without waiting for a reply, she picked up the newspaper from the balcony floor and started reading aloud. Nicolas tore open the envelope.

The message was short and written in the middle of a sheet of A4.

Need to speak to you. Ivan.

"Looks like it's going to be a really shitty day," Nicolas said as he crumpled the paper into a ball.

"Told you so."

9

THE APARTMENT BLOCKS were three storeys high, and the spaces between them were filled with lawns and playgrounds. Vanessa approached the uniformed officer who had been posted by the cordon, showed her ID and lifted the blue-and-white tape.

The front door was open.

"Hello?"

While she was waiting for someone to come and get her, she studied the lock. No signs of forced entry. On the other hand, the apartment was on the ground floor – it would hardly take an acrobat to get in through an open window. A female technician in a white overall poked her head out.

Vanessa pulled on the overall, shoe protectors and plastic gloves that the woman passed her, then put her feet where she was directed. In the living room was another technician, kneeling down with a camera and filming the body.

Emelie Rydén was lying in a pool of blood on the parquet floor. Her torso and throat were perforated with knife wounds. Her eyes stared blankly, and her mouth was wide open, giving her a surprised expression. Vanessa walked in an arc around the body and turned to the female technician who had shown her in. Above the face mask, Vanessa could make out a pair of dark eyes and a light brown complexion.

"What do we know?"

The woman gestured with her thumb that they should go to

the kitchen. By the worktop counter, she pulled off her hood. Beneath it, a hairnet strained to keep her thick – probably long – hair in place.

She looked to be around thirty. Vanessa guessed that she was of Indian origin.

"Her mother found her this morning, when she came to hand over her granddaughter who she'd been looking after for the weekend," the woman said, with a Norwegian accent. "More than twenty stab wounds to the abdomen and neck. She was twenty-five years old. She made a living from skincare, and she had a salon in a basement unit near here."

"Did the neighbours hear anything?"

The woman shrugged.

"Don't know. Your colleagues are doing house-to-house."

Vanessa took a shine to her. She was sharp, expressed herself clearly and concisely, and didn't bother with unnecessary detail. "Mobile phone?"

"Password protected. The IT technician has just packed it away to be sent to technical investigations."

"How much more time are you going to need here?" Vanessa asked.

"If there's nothing else, we'll be done soon."

Vanessa heard the sound of an engine and turned her head towards it. Outside the window, a first call vehicle pulled up to collect the corpse. As two men mechanically lifted in the bloody body that only hours before had been a living person with dreams, childhood memories and emotions, Vanessa went into the bedroom.

The double bed in the middle of the room had been made. She opened the wardrobe. The clothes were either neatly folded or hung on coat hangers. She turned around and walked over to a dresser, on top of which stood three framed photographs.

Flanked by four friends, a teenaged Emelie Rydén was depicted making the sign of the horns with her tongue out. Her hair was platinum blonde, heavy eye make-up, and the teeth in her top jaw were adorned with a shining rail. She was wearing a T-shirt emblazoned with the words *Tokio Hotel*.

Vanessa found it hard to look at pictures of people who were now dead. *One day, when I'm dead, someone will be looking at photos of me.*

She put the picture back and walked to the other bedroom.

There was a cot by the window. Translucent plastic boxes stood stacked on top of each other, full of toys. Vanessa sniffed the air, thought she could detect a faint smell of detergent. Two photos in Disney frames stood on the window sill. One of them, taken on a beach, showed Emelie Rydén lifting her daughter high in the air. Behind the mother and daughter, the sun was setting. The girl appeared to be squealing with laughter.

Vanessa glanced at the other photograph. It was black and white, taken in a hospital. A muscular man with a shaved head holding a newborn baby wrapped in a blanket. He was studying the baby with loving intensity. His straining arms were covered in tattoos.

"It can't be," she muttered.

The sound of someone clearing their throat came from behind her, and Vanessa spun around, still holding the photo. Standing in the doorway was a man of about forty-five with short red hair, wearing a green long-sleeve T-shirt over a paunch.

"Vanessa Frank?"

They shook each other's gloved hands.

"Ove Dahlberg. Serious Crime Unit."

Vanessa held up the frame towards her colleague and pointed to the man in the picture.

"Do you know who this is?"

He squinted at the image before shaking his head.

"Not from Adam, but if I might allow myself to be judgemental, he doesn't look like the local bible salesman."

"Karim Laimani. Member of the Sätra Network. Convicted of GBH, drugs offences, weapons offences and domestic abuse. He is the father of the victim's baby."

"Where is he?"

"In Åkersberga Prison, if I remember rightly."

10

JASMINA STUMBLED OVER to the bedside table and took out the spare glasses she kept in the top drawer. Her hands were shaking. Her body shuddered as if she was fitting.

The events of the last few hours played again on her retinas. The blows, the pain. The men's laughter, the smell of alcohol. The film rewound. Played again. Jasmina lay in the recovery position on the bed and pressed her hands against her ears. Clamped her jaws together. Her teeth squeaked; she was hyperventilating. She closed her eyes. Tried to get the film to stop, to get the blurry figures to dissolve.

The sounds that came out of her were not human. They sounded as if they came from an injured, stressed animal.

She put the pillow over her head. She lay down on her back, pushing the soft fabric against her face, and screamed out loud. She screamed like she'd never screamed before, with her whole body.

As Jasmina turned onto her side and carefully put her feet on the floor, she didn't know how long she'd been lying on the bed. Whether she'd been awake or sleeping. Her glasses were skew-whiff, and she straightened them out. She reached past the photo of her father and turned the alarm clock to face her. The red digits showed 13.47. She got to her feet, found her phone on the worktop in the kitchenette and saw that she had nineteen missed calls, all from *Kvällspressen* numbers. One number belonged to Hans Hoffman; the other was Bengt's.

She'd missed the meeting, and the piece was not ready.

Jasmina leaned against the cooker, holding her hand to her mouth as she pondered.

How many reports and articles had she written about rape victims? Her Dictaphone had recorded lots of police quotes that always said the same thing: *Report it.*

Jasmina had always been convinced that if she was ever raped, she would not hesitate to do just that. To stand up for herself. But, if she did report it to the police, everyone would find out. Every one of her colleagues. She would always be 'that reporter who got raped'. Worst of all, her mother would find out. Poor Mum. She could not subject her to that. Anything but that.

Besides, she couldn't face talking to anyone, having to answer questions, remember and explain. At least not for now.

Jasmina opened the cupboard and took out a carrier bag. She removed her clothes and underwear and stuffed them in. Slowly, she walked into the bathroom, stood with legs apart on the cold tiles and carefully inserted a cotton bud inside herself. Moved it around. Picked up another and repeated the procedure. She put them in a plastic lunchbox, wrapped it in clingfilm and threw it into the empty fridge.

The phone rang. She reached for it, expecting the call to be from Bengt or someone else at the paper – but it was her mum.

"Hello, darling. I didn't want to bother you, but I am so curious. How did it go, with the piece?"

Jasmina closed her eyes.

"Hello?"

She clenched her fists, forced herself to speak, tried to seem normal.

"There won't be an article," she said grimly.

A moment of confused silence followed. Jasmina stared into space.

"What's happened?" said her mum.

Jasmina knew that she was trying to remain calm, not to seem too anxious, too mumsy.

"Nothing. Everything's fine. They just didn't need the piece any more. There was something else that was more important."

"Are you upset, love?"

"These things happen."

"Yes, exactly. If you want, you can send me the article. I'd love to read it."

"My work computer is in the office."

Jasmina smiled ruefully. She hated lying.

"What a shame. What are you going to do tonight then?" her mum asked.

"I'm going to meet a few colleagues for a beer."

"Oh good." Her mother went quiet, searched for words. "If anything happens, you can call me. I love you, my little girl."

"Wait," Jasmina said quickly. She took a deep breath.

"Yes?"

"What are you doing tonight?"

"Don't you worry about me. I'll think of something."

After the call, Jasmina was left standing there with her phone in her hand. She took a couple of steps forward and ended up in front of the full-length mirror.

Her right nipple had been reduced to a big sticky gash. She had a purple bruise over her ribs. She photographed herself from various angles and sent the pictures to her Gmail address before she deleted them so they wouldn't be on her work phone.

Finally she pushed the bag of clothes under her bed. The next second, she changed her mind. She grabbed the bag and pushed it into the bin.

She was going to forget. Move on. That night had never happened. She got into the shower, let the warm water rinse away the smell of the men. She was scared that they would track her down and hurt her.

"I am a fucking hypocrite," she muttered.

11

"SO THAT BASTARD was on parole?" said Ove.

Vanessa nodded, without taking her eyes off the motorway's dark tarmac. It was a grey day, heavy with rain. Vanessa pulled out into the fast lane to overtake a lorry.

"And he presented himself this morning, as if nothing had happened?" Ove said disbelievingly.

"That was what the prisoner governor claimed."

He had sounded nervous when Vanessa called and explained her task. She could see why. If Karim Laimani had stabbed Emelie Rydén to death during unsupervised parole, there would be hell to pay.

"Un-fucking-believable."

Vanessa turned the wheel and headed towards Åkersberga. She drove past a golf course on the right, straight over a roundabout and arrived at the district centre. By the train station, Ove pointed at a hotdog stand.

"I didn't have time to eat. Can you stop by that place?"

"Sure."

A sign announced that the fast-food place was open around the clock. Vanessa felt an instinctive and immediate affection for everything that was always accessible. Hotels, hospitals, kebab shops, 7-Eleven shops. They helped her feel calm.

They each ordered a wrap from a man with flour on his hairy arms and then got back in the car.

Ove ran his finger along the BMW's walnut panels.

"So, Frank. You were married to that director. Is it true that you're loaded?"

Vanessa took a bite, swallowed, and wiped some mayonnaise off her cheek. She nodded slowly.

"Filthy rich," she said.

Ove pointed at her chest. The Sig Sauer was poking out from an opening in her blue coat.

"Did you manage to pick your gun up before you went to Täby?"

"I have mine at home."

"How come?"

"Risk of abduction."

Ove raised an eyebrow.

"Seriously? Are you *that* rich?"

"No. I worked for NOVA. There were a couple of guys in Södertälje who were less than delighted about our efforts."

A prawn fell from Ove's mouth, down onto his trousers and disappeared. He swore. Vanessa passed him a serviette.

"Thanks. Are you scared?" he asked as he attempted to locate the prawn on the car floor.

"Only of sharks and tax demands."

Ove snorted. At that moment, his phone started ringing. He looked at the display and held up an apologetic finger towards Vanessa.

"Hello, darling," he said. His voice was gentle and amenable. Vanessa put her hand over her mouth and looked away. "Eating? Yes, love, a banana. And a protein shake. Quite the bodybuilder."

He pounded his chest.

Vanessa wiped her hands on a napkin, started the engine and slowly drove out onto the road.

"I don't know when I'll be home. I got called in this morning and I'm on my way to an interview. But I miss you."

Vanessa liked the way he spoke to his wife. Despite having lied about what he was eating, there was a clear warmth there. She hated men who treated their women like troublesome appendages.

Once he'd hung up with a "mwah, I love you," he revealed his upper arm by pulling his top down. There was a little white box attached to it.

"Diabetes," he muttered. "I was diagnosed six months ago. She watches me like a hawk. Which I appreciate, of course. But jeez, sometimes you just want to plunder a hotdog stand, eat a wrap, throw it up and then eat another one."

"Don't you worry, Ove. As long as you don't throw up in the car, I won't tell anyone."

At Åkersberga Prison, they handed in their weapons and phones. They were searched and shown into a visiting room. Just like every other prison in the country, it was overcrowded.

There was a waiting list to be imprisoned. After their trials, some criminals went on holiday to South East Asia for months at a time before returning, tanned and rested, to Sweden to serve their sentences. That was the best-case scenario. Sometimes they continued committing crimes.

Vanessa and Ove sat down to wait, and after a couple of minutes the door opened, and Karim Laimani was escorted in by two burly prison guards. He sat down without looking at them. Instead, he kept his eyes focused on a point just to the left of Vanessa's head.

"We want to know your whereabouts last night," said Ove.

Karim Laimani tipped his head to one side so his neck cracked. He then repeated the procedure on the other side.

"Read my parole application," he said.

"You have a daughter with Emelie Rydén. Did you meet her?"

Karim let his eyes run over Vanessa's body before settling on her chest. He licked his lips.

"So?" Ove said impatiently.

"Why would I be meeting that whore?"

He crossed his arms and leaned backwards, running the tip of his tongue over his gums. Snus tobacco peeked out from his top lip. Vanessa could feel the abstinence dancing around her body.

"She was found this morning," said Ove. "Stabbed to death."

Karim raised an eyebrow and studied their faces. He seemed genuinely surprised. "Are you winding me up?"

Vanessa rolled her eyes.

"Yes, Karim," she said. "We are two clowns who decided to come down here and lift the mood. We came straight here from the children's hospital. Answer the question now; where were you last night?"

"I was at a mate's."

His voice was no longer as self-assured. Vanessa pointed to a paper that was lying in a plastic wallet on the table.

"According to what's in there, you threatened to kill her three weeks ago, when she was here visiting."

Vanessa read aloud from the incident report. Silence. Karim studied the back of his hands.

"What were you rowing about?" Ove asked.

"None of your fucking business, fatman. And it doesn't matter. I haven't touched her."

"It wouldn't be the first time you had a go at a woman," Vanessa chipped in. "Looks like one of your specialities."

Karim burped out loud.

"You little cop-whore. I'm not saying another word until my lawyer gets here."

12

NICOLAS JUMPED ON the metro's red line towards Vårberg to go and visit his sister Maria. Just two and a half years earlier, he had been a full-time soldier. However, after a failed rescue attempt in Nigeria, he had had to leave the Special Operations Group – the army's most elite unit.

To find his feet again, he had – along with childhood friend Ivan Tomic – robbed Bågenhielms, an exclusive watch retailer on Biblioteksgatan. The target was not the expensive watches, but the list of customers featuring the addresses of some of Sweden's wealthiest individuals.

The plan was to kidnap three businessmen, blackmail their relatives for a ransom and then leave Sweden.

Everything, though, had gone wrong.

Ivan had told The Legion's leadership about the existence of the list. He had sold Nicolas out. If Vanessa Frank had not intervened, Nicolas would have been dead or at least behind bars. As a thank you, he had accompanied Vanessa to southern Chile to save Natasha, the Syrian refugee who had been taken there by The Legion.

And Ivan was in Åkersberga Prison. What did he want with Nicolas?

Even if the police didn't have his name and really ought to be busy with other things, he was still careful. In the apartment was a sports bag containing almost fifty thousand crowns in cash and an illegal firearm.

Stockholm had changed since he was growing up. Become tougher. Young guys who had barely finished school were seduced by fast cash. The gangs were job centres, open around the clock, where no one asked about grades or previous experience.

Above all, they were looking for the respect that society had never given them. In a way, he could understand that. Nicolas had grown up with the same hatred and distrust of authority.

In his teens, he had committed petty crimes with Ivan, until his parents intervened and forced him to apply for a scholarship to the elite Sigtuna School. He got in. His time boarding there had changed Nicolas' life and put him on the path that would eventually lead to the army.

He got off the metro, walked slowly along the platform and through the deserted precinct. He knocked on Maria's balcony door. Through the glass, Nicolas could see the back of her head over the top of the sofa. As always, she was watching *Friends*. He knocked again, a bit harder. Nicolas grimaced, cocked his head to one side and pushed his nose and lips against the glass.

Maria laughed and hauled herself up. She had been born with a hip condition that meant she dragged her right leg. A wave of tenderness washed over him as she hobbled over towards him and pushed open the door.

"Hi, sis," he said as he gave her a hug.

"Hiya," she said, extricating herself. "Are you hungry?"

"Yes."

"Shall we go and get you a burger?"

They walked side by side along the footpath. Lone figures walked in the opposite direction, from the metro station, towards the illuminated housing estate.

Nicolas noted that Maria was moving more awkwardly than usual.

"Does it hurt?" he asked, being careful to sound unfazed. Maria hated him coddling her.

"Yes."

"Shall I put you on my back?" he asked.

She gave him an angry stare. Nicolas stuck his tongue out and she realised he was joking.

"Blockhead," she laughed, but her expression soon became serious. "You have to promise not to get cross," Maria said cautiously.

"Do I ever get cross with you?"

"Dad is in Sweden. He wants to meet you."

Nicolas went quiet. He could see their father, Eduardo Paredes, in front of him. He had left Sweden when their mother died. Gone back to Chile, in mourning. But also after a row with Nicolas. Eduardo, who had left at the time of the military coup in 1973, had never been able to accept that Nicolas had become a soldier.

"Are you going to talk to him?"

Nicolas put his arm around Maria's shoulders.

"I don't know. Would that make you happy?"

"Yes."

They bought a burger from the fast-food kiosk. Maria ate hungrily. Sauce and lettuce got stuck in the corners of her mouth and on her cheeks. Nicolas asked for a napkin and wiped her face as Maria chewed and swallowed.

13

BENGT STARED ANGRILY at Jasmina. When she called from Hotel Anglais, having searched in vain for her backpack with the laptop in, and explained that the text wasn't ready, he had demanded that she come in to the newsroom to explain herself. He had deliberately made her wait half an hour before bringing her into the glass-walled room that was next to the Editor-in-Chief's office.

Jasmina told him that the bag had been stolen.

"This is completely fucking unacceptable."

Bengt got to his feet and put his hands on his hips. Jasmina glanced down quickly at her thick jumper; she'd stuffed paper underneath it so that the blood from the torn-out piercing wouldn't seep through.

"I haven't seen this kind of incompetence in a very long time," he said bitterly. "You didn't manage to get the piece together and the paper's computer is gone? Why didn't you call?"

"I…"

He held his palm out. Took a couple of steps to one side and peered out, through the glass, across the newsroom.

"That's enough. I'll be raising this with the editor. You've got a few rest days now, haven't you?"

Jasmina nodded quickly.

"Good. We'll be in touch. I hope you understand that we need reporters we can trust."

"I can stay and work tonight, if you want," she ventured.

Bengt sniggered. "Get out of here. Now."

Max Lewenhaupt walked past the glass room. Bengt knocked on the pane and waved him in. Jasmina avoided making eye contact with Max as they passed each other in the doorway.

Her body was shaking, and she had a painful pulsating sensation between her legs. She strained to walk upright and look normal.

Hans Hoffman gave her a troubled look, stood up from his desk and walked over to her.

"I'll walk you out," he said.

"There's no need," whispered Jasmina.

"I will anyway."

They walked through the newsroom, past the canteen and stopped at the glass doors. Reception was unstaffed at weekends. "What happened?"

"I didn't have time to finish the text. And my computer got stolen on the bus. I'm sorry if I've messed things up for you."

Jasmina could feel the tears welling up. Hoffman was the person on the paper who had been kindest to her. He had stood up for her in suggesting to Bengt that she should write the piece about #metoo.

"Why didn't you get in touch earlier so that they could adjust their plans?"

"I don't know."

It was obvious that he was bewildered and didn't believe her. She was grateful that he wasn't pushing her. "What did Bengt say?"

Jasmina cleared her dry throat.

"That they would be in touch."

She pressed a button and the lock on the door clicked.

"Jasmina, you've got a lot more talent than most of the people who've come here over the last few years. Believe me. I wish you could tell me what happened. But if you don't want to, you don't want to. And then I can't help you."

She felt choked. Just wanted to get out of there. On the way down in the lift, the tears came.

It was over.

At best, someone from *Kvällspressen* would call tomorrow and explain that she needn't go back. She could hardly blame them. The story she'd given them didn't stack up. Every reporter knows that if there's a risk that a piece won't be finished on time, they should contact the editor straight away. Jasmina, though, just had not had the energy to invent another explanation.

In the worst-case scenario, she'd end up frozen out. That would mean staying on for the remainder of her contract but being demoted to the crossword section or one of the gossip supplements.

Jasmina longed to go home to Växjö. To her mother and the sleepy but comradely atmosphere of *Smålandsposten*'s editorial team.

14

EVEN BEFORE THE lift doors had slid open, Nicolas
could hear that someone was on his floor.

Celine was half-lying outside her front door with a blue
cap on her head and her mobile in hand. Her face lit up when
she spotted him.

"I'm locked out. Thank God you came."

Nicolas climbed over her outstretched legs, stopped outside his door and unlocked it. He felt sorry for her but couldn't
possibly have a twelve-year-old girl in his apartment.

Besides, Celine's babbling would drive him mad. He
needed some peace and quiet, to think over how he was going
to deal with his father.

"Nicolas?" Celine said pitiably. "They took my keys. I
didn't forget them, I promise."

He closed the door and hung his coat up in the hall, then sat
down on the sofa. The doorbell rang. Nicolas tipped his head
back. Closed his eyes. A few seconds' silence passed before
it rang again. The letter box creaked open.

"Let me in. Come on. It's so boring out here."

"Go out and wait in the courtyard."

"It's raining."

Celine kept ringing the bell at increasingly short intervals.
After a minute, Nicolas understood that she wasn't going to
give up. He stood up to open the door.

"Thanks," she said and slunk in.

Nicolas returned to the sofa while Celine was taking her shoes off. When she got into the living room, she stopped, put her hand over her mouth and giggled. He looked at her, surprised.

"What's up?"

"Your TV. It's one of those fat TVs."

"What about it?"

"I've only seen them in films," she said and sat down next to him. "Where's the remote?"

She stank of sour sweat. Nicolas edged away.

"If you want to watch it, go over and press the button. But you have to keep the volume down. I need peace and quiet."

"I can cook something instead," she said, heading for the fridge. "Dad says that you Muslims hit your women and let them do all the chores."

"First of all, that's not true. Secondly, I'm not Muslim. My dad is from Chile, where most people are Catholic. Thirdly, your dad hits you."

Celine opened the fridge door.

"And I'm the only one who cooks and cleans at home too," Celine said, closing it again. "Give me some money." She held her hand out.

"I'm going to buy eggs. And oil."

Nicolas was hungry. If she just held the salt, scrambled eggs might be nice. He went out to the hall, got out a hundred crowns and stared at her as she pulled on her coat.

"I'll put the salt in. And if you buy anything else with that money, you'll be sitting out in the stairwell again. Eggs and oil. That's it."

"I swear on our friendship," Celine said, crossing herself.

Nicolas chuckled.

She had almost pulled the door to when he called out her name. The door swung open again and she stuck her head in. "Yes?"

"Buy some deodorant too."

"Why?"

"Because you stink. That's why the others are horrible to you at school."

"You think?"

"No, I know. It smells like a tiny animal has crawled into your armpit and died."

She giggled, pulled down the zip on her coat, sniffed her armpit and grimaced. "Yes, it does actually."

When Celine returned, Nicolas sent her into the bathroom with the deodorant and told her to wash her armpits before putting it on. They ate in silence, hunched towards the telly with their plates in their laps. Every now and then, Celine lifted her arm and sniffed contentedly.

"Do you want a sniff?"

"I'm fine, thanks," Nicolas smirked.

He wondered why Celine's dad was away so much. He obviously had a drink problem; it was difficult to see how he could be holding down a job. But Nicolas didn't want to ask – if she started talking, there was no stopping her. Eventually the plates were empty, and he put them in the dishwasher while Celine stretched out on the sofa.

"Can I change channel?"

"As long as you don't turn it up."

"Shall we play a game?"

"No."

A pounding on the door.

"I think that's Dad," whispered Celine, her eyes gleaming with fear.

He recognised that look. He knew what it felt like to be little and vulnerable. The banging grew in intensity. Nicolas put his hand on Celine's shoulder. He could not let her dad carry on abusing her. She was a child. A lonely child. He felt shame at not having acted earlier. Because of his ego.

"I'll talk to him," said Nicolas.

"Open the door, you fucking kiddyfucker," Celine's father screamed through the letter box.

Nicolas opened the door. A clenched fist heading for the door stopped and pulled back.

"What the fuck are you doing with my daughter in your flat, you nasty fucking Arab? I know what people like you want, what you do to little girls," the man roared.

He studied Nicolas with contempt. His mouth hung open, hair all over the place. Nicolas calmly stayed where he was.

"Move."

Celine's dad tried to force his way into the flat. Nicolas placed his hand on his chest and shoved him backwards, out of the door. He didn't want Celine to see what was happening, so he pulled the door shut behind him.

"Don't touch me, you nasty wog."

The man clenched his fist and lined up a punch. Nicolas took one step towards him, grabbing his arm. He twisted it. Pushed the man's face against the wall, whilst simultaneously feeling rage and the urge to hurt flare up inside him.

"You should take better care of your daughter if you don't want her hanging around here," he said.

The man tried to twist himself free.

"Let me go," he screamed.

Nicolas pushed his arm upwards. Celine's dad snorted with pain and his face turned red. "If I hear her crying at night one more time, I'll jump over the balcony, smash the window and strangle you. Got that?"

The man was breathing heavily, apparently having realised that resistance was futile. He nodded, with his jaws clenched. Nicolas let go and he straightened out his top. Celine was standing in the hall, with her rucksack hanging over her shoulder.

"I think I should go now," she said.

She walked past him with her eyes down. "Celine?"

She turned towards him.

"Yes?"

Nicolas smiled.

"The deodorant?"

"In my bag."

15

VANESSA BROUGHT THE PAPER with her – she hadn't had time to read it that morning – to McLarens bar on Surbrunnsgatan. She said hi to the owner, Kjell-Arne, asked for her usual cheeseburger and sat down at a window table.

"We have introduced a vegan dish to the menu – bean pasta with tomato sauce," Kjell-Arne said proudly.

Vanessa looked up from the newspaper and studied the menu that the Norwegian had just placed on the table.

"Have the customers been asking for that?"

"No, but I say the same as Henry Ford. If I'd asked my customers what they wanted, they'd have said 'faster horses'."

Vanessa was sympathetic to Kjell-Arne's efforts to modernise McLarens, even if she didn't believe that anyone was going to order the vegan bean pasta. Most of the clientele were semi-alcoholic benefit recipients and long-term sick, clinging onto the few remaining rental apartments Vasastan had to offer. They went to McLarens to drink beer and wait for their apartments to be put on the market and to be forced into moving out to peripheral estates. The place had probably smelt better before the smoking ban came in.

"It's your bar. You do what you like."

"Wanna try it? You'd be the first customer in McLarens history to order something vegan."

Vanessa smirked. She liked Kjell-Arne. If her eating his vegan pasta made him happy, it was worth it.

"Go for it."

Kjell-Arne clenched his fists in the air, picked up the menu and hurried to the kitchen.

"You won't regret it," he called over his shoulder. "If you like it, your next portion is on the house."

Since Karim Laimani had been unable to give police a proper alibi, they had called in forensic technicians to go through his cell. Vanessa didn't hold out much hope that that would lead anywhere. Karim Laimani was a career criminal; he knew plenty about police work and forensic evidence. If he had murdered Emelie, he would hardly have presented himself at the prison in the same clothes he'd been wearing for the murder.

What he did have was a motive. Emelie had left him for someone else. Vanessa and Ove were going to meet Ilan, the new boyfriend, on Monday afternoon.

Vanessa struggled to concentrate on the newspaper and contemplated writing to Natasha to see if she was okay. She couldn't bring herself to do it, though. If the girl was going to succeed in starting from scratch once again, she'd have to cut all ties with Vanessa. Yet Vanessa still couldn't help feeling abandoned. She knew she was being unreasonable. You couldn't blame a teenage girl for wanting to return home when it turned out her father was still alive.

She turned her phone face down, drilled her eyes into the newspaper and tried to banish thoughts of Natasha and Emelie Rydén.

Her phone buzzed.

"Hey, Frank," said Ove. Children's voices could be heard in the background.

"Hello there."

"I just spoke to the technicians," Ove began but was interrupted by a woman.

"And… wait… no, I'm not having a single bite of Falukorv, darling. I'm frying it up for the kids."

Ove's wife embarked on a tirade that was drowned out by the cooker hood fan.

"Well then, Liam got it wrong, I put the sausage between my teeth to check it was done. I'm well aware that I'll be having salad tonight."

Vanessa smirked.

"Sorry. It's like Stasi surveillance here. You can't trust anyone any more. Guess what they found on the soles of the shoes Karim was wearing when he returned from parole? Blood. And a long strand of hair that could potentially be Emelie's."

"That complete shit," muttered Vanessa.

"The tabloids will go crazy if it does turn out to be him. At least National Forensics Centre have promised to hurry it along. The results should come back as early as tomorrow."

The statistics pointed to it being Karim. In Sweden the previous year, twenty-two women were murdered by their male partners or exes. And as a rule, three in four women had previously sought help from the police, a hospital or social services.

On two occasions, Emelie had sought medical attention as a result of Laimani's assaults.

An infamous, violent gangster killing his ex-girlfriend while out on parole – three weeks after they split – *was* a scandal.

Kjell-Arne emerged from the kitchen with a plate in his hand. His face lit up with pride as if it was his firstborn he was presenting to the world.

"Thanks for calling, Ove. I'm going to eat now too. See you tomorrow."

"What you having?"

"Bye, Ove, see you tomorrow," she said and hung up.

Kjell-Arne carefully placed the plate down in front of Vanessa. "*Voilà!*"

"It looks tasty," she said approvingly.

Kjell-Arne observed her expectantly. She realised that he wasn't planning to go anywhere until she'd given her verdict.

She reached slowly for the cutlery, twirled the spaghetti onto the fork, blew on it gently and popped it into her mouth.

It tasted delicious.

"Very nice."

"Yes!" Kjell-Arne pumped his fist. "I told you. Give me a shout if you'd like some more."

16

MINISCULE RAINDROPS FELL from grey skies. Nicolas walked along with his hood up and his hands stuffed in the pockets of his black bomber jacket. Two young men held onto each other as they swished past on an electric scooter.

On the right was Nybro Bay. Half-empty tourist boats disappeared towards the archipelago. Nicolas had spent his Monday off wandering around an empty Djurgården. Trying to work out how to deal with Ivan and his father. But the rainy circuits hadn't made any difference either way.

As he crossed at the pedestrian crossing outside the Royal Dramatic Theatre to make his way to the metro and head home, a man in a dark-blue trench coat stopped alongside him.

"Nicolas?"

Magnus Örn was one of Nicolas' officers in his first years in the Special Operations Group. An ordinary but brusque man of about fifty, who had spent all of his life in the Swedish military. Nicolas supressed the urge to put his hand to his brow and salute, instead offering it to Magnus, who shook it heartily.

"I heard you're not in Karlsborg any more," said Magnus, referring to the little town where the SOG were based.

"That's right."

"And now? What are you up to?"

"Removal firm."

Even if Magnus Örn was surprised, he disguised it well.

"AOS Risk Group," he said, pulling off his leather glove and fishing out a business card in an elegant movement and placing it in Nicolas' hand. "London. The change of scene did me good. The salary is nuts. You should give it some thought. Someone with your experience and training would be useful to say the least. Give me a bell. Unless you like lugging furniture around, of course. Nothing wrong with that. I expect it can be a bit therapeutic."

Nicolas watched Magnus Örn's back disappear from view. He stuffed the card in his jeans pocket, put his hood up and carried on towards the metro station. Just a hundred metres or so away, on Biblioteksgatan, was Bågenhielms, where he'd got hold of the exclusive watchmaker's customer register – which he had failed to report to the police for fear of losing face.

Vanessa Frank, however, had sussed out what was going on. Almost arrested Nicolas. Then persuaded him to change sides instead. He had her to thank for the fact that he wasn't doing time in Åkersberga right now, like Ivan. Not a day went past without him thinking grateful thoughts about Vanessa. He could not contact her though. It was too much of a risk. She was a police officer, after all.

Nicolas had no place in Sweden.

London, on the other hand… He wouldn't be more than a few hours from Maria. He'd been looking for a purpose ever since being thrown out of the SOG. He knew nothing about AOS Risk Group, but he knew that it was one of many private security firms in the British capital.

He would no longer have to keep looking over his shoulder. Wouldn't have to move furniture. And if the money was as good as Magnus Örn was making out, he'd have money left over to send back to Maria.

It was definitely an avenue worth exploring.

On the escalator down to the platform, his phone rang. "This is your father," said a voice he hadn't heard in more than ten years, in Spanish.

How many nights had he spent lying awake fantasising

about this moment? Known exactly what he was going to say, what arguments, how he'd ask his father to leave him in peace and explain to him that he'd made his choice when he left Nicolas and Maria alone after their mother's death. Yet it was as if all those well-rehearsed lines had been blown away.

"Nicolas," his father said impatiently. "Are you there?"

"Yes."

"I know things haven't been good between us. But I'm in Sweden, for your sake and Maria's, and I want to see you. We need to talk."

"Now?"

"I can't right now. Maybe…"

"I mean that now, after all these years, you want to meet and talk?"

The train hurtled into the station. He swapped platforms.

"Nicolas, I really want to talk to you. It would mean a lot to me."

Nicolas ran his hand over his cropped hair in the nape of his neck. "I'll think about it," he muttered. His voice was guttural and thin.

"Come on. I'm your father."

"I said I'll think about it."

He hung up. Clutching his phone, he sat down on a bench and stared into space. Maybe his father was ill? And the illness had brought him to his senses? Two trains had stopped, filled with passengers and rolled away by the time Nicolas got to his feet.

For Maria's sake, he thought. For Maria, and no one else. He fired off a text to his father: *See you tomorrow at Café Giovanni at Central Station, two o'clock.*

17

ILAN MODIRI'S STUDIO apartment was on Wollmar Yxkullsgatan, in Stockholm's Södermalm district. No previous convictions, a computer programmer without so much as an unpaid parking ticket to his name. Vanessa thought he had a sympathetic-looking face, with dense black stubble and kindly brown eyes. His body was tall and trim, bordering on thin.

It was plain to see he'd been crying – the whites of his eyes were bloodshot. "Excuse my clothes," he said, gesturing towards his grey track pants.

He showed them into a sparsely furnished room, with a kitchenette and an alcove for the bed. The only thing on the walls was a film poster from *The Matrix*. There was a stuffy smell in there. Vanessa had to stifle the urge to walk over to the window and push it open. Ilan pointed to the sofa, grabbed a desk chair for himself and sat down on it.

Ove explained to Ilan that it was a routine interview, and he was not under suspicion.

"No, it looks pretty obvious who did this," he said bitterly.

"Who?" said Ove and Vanessa in unison.

"Karim."

"What did she tell you about him?" Vanessa asked.

Ilan put his hands in his lap and sighed.

"Not much. She said he lived abroad. But I knew there was something off about the guy, so I checked the electoral roll. And then… I'm ashamed of it now. Shit. But one morning when she was in the shower, I checked her phone. She'd got a load of threats from him."

"Weren't you scared?"

Ilan gave them a crooked, sad smile.

"Course I fucking was. That's why I asked my bosses if there were any jobs going in Malmö."

"Were you planning to leave her?"

Ilan stared at them in confusion before quickly shaking his head. "No, of course not. I was going to take her and Nova with me. We talked about it the night she was murdered."

"Did she want to go?"

"Yes."

"Did she seem worried or upset?" asked Ove.

Ilan thought about that for a moment.

"She was just happy. Obviously she was surprised when I asked her. We hadn't been seeing each other very long, but I immediately felt that there was something special about her." He briefly went quiet. "Or rather, about me, when I was with her."

After a further half hour, they made their way out. Just as Ilan was about to pull the door to, he stopped himself.

"I just need to ask. How's Nova, and where is she?"

Vanessa glanced at Ove.

"She's with her grandparents, from what I've heard. I don't think she really understands what's happened."

Ilan smiled. Then his expression turned serious.

"A while back, I read about men who'd murdered their partners but still got custody of their children. Could it turn out like that with Nova?"

Ove's Ford was parked outside Hotel Rival on Mariatorget. Outside, people were running for shelter from the rain that had suddenly started pelting down. Ove put the key in the ignition and was just about to turn it, but then stopped himself and patted his breast pocket instead.

He pulled out his phone, looked at the screen, answered and handed it over to Vanessa.

"This is Trude Hovland," said a woman with a Norwegian accent. Vanessa realised that it was the forensic technician from Emelie's apartment.

"Yes, hi," said Vanessa. "Ove's driving. This is Vanessa Frank."

Ove crawled towards Hornsgatan while the car's windscreen wipers worked flat out.

"Oh right. Hi." Trude sounded surprised but composed herself quickly. "Yes, I've got a reply from NFC. The blood on Karim's shoe is Emelie's."

Vanessa glanced at Ove and nodded. "And the hair?"

"Hers."

"Thanks. I'll ring the prosecutor then." Vanessa hung up and turned to Ove.

"I heard," he said, pulling off towards the waterfront and Söder Mälarstrand.

Vanessa handed back the phone. She thought about the photo of Emelie she'd seen in the apartment. That lovely, healthy smile. Gone. Forever. And somewhere out there were her mum and dad – grieving and in shock.

Every night, Vanessa had leaned in towards Adeline's peaceful, sleeping face and promised to protect her from everything. Vanessa had failed though, and Emelie's parents had too. Karim Laimani had murdered their daughter. At the same time, he had also taken their lives from them.

People only have one life, but parents can die twice.

The rain whipped onto the dark waters, the roar of traffic lost in a crack of thunder. Ove laughed.

"What are you laughing at?" asked Vanessa.

"Those bloody idiots who wandered up here a few thousand years ago – to this cold bastard place – and thought it was a good place to settle!"

18

NICOLAS STOPPED IN the doorway. Eduardo Paredes was sitting with his back to Café Giovanni's entrance. The décor looked like it had been taken from a 1950s film. A zinc counter ran along one wall; the wooden furniture was dark and heavy. White-clad waiters with slicked-back hair lined up, waiting for guests to serve.

He could still turn around. Behind him, Stockholm Central Station was full of people rushing through, suitcase in hand. But instead he took a few steps forward.

"My son." His father smiled.

Eduardo Paredes got up and rushed to embrace Nicolas. His body felt smaller, more feeble than Nicolas remembered. The few hugs he'd got as a boy were like hugs from a giant. A giant who could erupt into screams at any moment. Kicking chairs so they smashed into the wall, roaring and slamming his fist on the table, getting up and promptly disappearing and staying away for a few days.

Eduardo Paredes gestured towards the empty chair on the far side of the table. Nicolas sat down.

"It was what… ten years ago we last met?" said Eduardo.

"Eleven."

Nicolas looked away as he remembered the last time, in the apartment in Sollentuna. His mother had died only weeks before. Nicolas was doing his national service as a coastal ranger at the time, and he told his father he was planning to stay in the military.

Traidor, Eduardo had said. Traitor. Turned his back. He'd then held the door open, and Nicolas had left the apartment. Sometime later, Nicolas heard that his father had moved to Chile. He would never be able to forgive him for abandoning Maria.

It was for his sister's sake that he was there now. She wanted the remnants of their family to make peace. For Nicolas, an explanation would be enough. He was surprised how imposing his father's presence was. How it affected him, made him into a defenceless boy once again.

A 'sorry'. That was all that was needed. *Sorry for leaving you and your sister alone here after your mother had died. You were only eighteen and nineteen. It was wrong of me.* At the same time, he couldn't shake off the thought that his father was seriously ill.

That was why he'd looked him up. He anxiously studied his father's face, looking for signs of ill health.

"Are you still a soldier?"

Nicolas shook his head. A waiter came over. Nicolas ordered coffee. Black.

"I am pleased. Either way, I have forgiven you. I need your help with something."

Eduardo reached for his cup and took a sip. Let the tip of his tongue feel for an escaped crumb in the corner of his mouth.

"It's a silly little thing really, but I'm in trouble," said Eduardo Paredes in Spanish.

"A friend of mine in Sweden had power of attorney over Maria. Easy money, you know. A few thousand a month, money I needed down in Chile. Now though, that friend is in a spot of bother. I need someone to vouch for him having taken care of Maria. And to persuade her to go along with it. It would mean a lot to me."

Out of his inside pocket, Eduardo Paredes pulled out a piece of paper, put it on the table and spun it around.

Nicolas could feel his hands shaking. He pushed them underneath the table.

"Is that why you got in touch with her?"

"I haven't said anything to Maria yet. It would be best if you spoke to her. As I said, Nicolas, I have problems. This is a chance for you and me to start again – to put things right. All you need to do is sign here."

He pointed at the dotted line at the bottom of the sheet. The waiter returned with the coffee. It chinked as he put it down in front of Nicolas, who was staring at the A4 page on the table.

Why couldn't he say anything? Why was he sitting there as if he were frozen solid? His father was trying to get him to commit a crime. Throughout all those years Eduardo had been gone, he'd been picking up money thanks to Maria. Exploiting her condition.

Nicolas cleared his throat.

"This is why you got in touch?" he asked again and pointed at the page. "For this?" His voice sounded unfamiliar. Strained. His father nodded. Nicolas took a deep breath. He clenched his fists so hard that his fingernails cut into his palms.

"Stay away from us. Never contact me or my sister again."

Nicolas grabbed his coffee cup and poured its contents over the paper. Stood up and left.

PART II

I'm almost thirty years old. My best years will soon be behind me, and I have never even been anywhere near a woman – not as a boyfriend, not as a one-night stand. They don't want me. They make it very obvious too. They might not hate me, but they treat me with contempt, which is worse.

An anonymous man.

1

GRIMALDI PIZZERIA WAS not far from Bredäng metro station. The premises contained nine tables, covered with red-and-white tablecloths, a glass counter with a bowl of the Balkan cabbage salad ubiquitous in Swedish pizza restaurants, as well as little pots of sauce. The walls were covered in red brick wallpaper, which was in turn plastered with football and boxing posters, most of which depicted Zlatan Ibrahimović and Muhammad Ali.

It was a quarter past five when Nicolas ordered a Vesuvius to take away and sat down at an empty table near the toilet. He'd been up since five that morning. Picked up the lorry. Lugged furniture up and down from an apartment on Kungsholmen. He was done in. Desperate for bed. For another life. He couldn't carry on like this. Looking over his shoulder, worrying about getting arrested for his part in the kidnappings.

Nicolas picked up the business card he'd been given by Magnus Örn and dialled the number on his phone.

"Nicolas," said Magnus when he realised who he was talking to. "I'm really glad you called."

"I'd like to meet."

"How about next week?"

"In London?"

"No, no. I'm in Stockholm then. I'll get back to you in the next few days and we'll book a time."

The bell on the door chimed.

Two men and a woman – all around twenty-five – walked in. The men looked high. Their eyes were glaring. Untrustworthy. Nicolas' thoughts turned immediately to Ivan. He had decided not to meet him. No good could come of it. He wasn't interested in what he had to say. Nicolas glanced at the woman. She was beautiful, and her brown curls fell halfway down her back. Shimmering blue eyes. She was holding one of the men by the hand.

"Eat in?" asked the pizza maker.

"Yes."

They filled their plates with cabbage salad, took a can each from the fridge and sat in one of the booths in the far corner.

The conversation with his father was playing over and over in his head, even though it had been two days. It was pointless telling Maria. It would hurt her. Make her feel stupid, since she'd wanted Nicolas to meet him.

After a while, one of the men stood up, walked past Nicolas and disappeared into the toilet. Through the thin door, Nicolas could hear the toilet seat being put down and the man muttering something before a loud snort.

After that he sniffed loudly, flushed the toilet and opened the door.

At the moment he was walking past, Nicolas turned towards the door because the bell had tinkled once again.

A guy dressed in black, wearing a cap and with a scarf wrapped around his face, walked in. He kept his arm hidden by his side. When he was within half a metre of the man who had just left the toilet, he raised his arm and fired a shot. The man was hit in the back of the head and thrown over an empty board, flipping it over.

The other customers took cover under the tables. The pizza maker rushed into the back. One woman was lying on her front, holding her hands above her head and hyperventilating.

The shooter continued into the restaurant, towards the couple curled up in the booth. Nicolas stayed put, looking at the dead man. Blood and brain tissue were running out of the back of his head across the shiny lino floor.

As he fell, the dead man's jumper had ridden up, revealing a black Glock handgun sticking out of his jeans.

Nicolas found himself two metres away from the weapon. He peered over towards the black-clad man who had his back towards him. Outside the window, sitting on a moped, a second black-clad man was waiting, his stare fixed on the pizzeria.

Nicolas understood that this was some kind of criminal feud. The shooter was to finish the job, shoot the other man, leave the premises and jump on the back of the moped. Drugs. Women. A perceived lack of respect. All manner of things could have led to this. There was nothing Nicolas could do. If he intervened, the police would become aware of him, and if he was unlucky, make the connection with the kidnappings the year before. He could not risk them conducting a house search. A bag containing the last fifty thousand and a revolver was still in the flat. Maria had no one, except Nicolas. She needed him more than ever.

The couple in the booth held their hands up.

The shooter approached with his weapon raised, in no hurry. The acrid smell of gunpowder hung in the air.

Nicolas kept his eyes on the woman. Her face was pale. She opened her mouth to speak, but nothing came out. Nicolas really felt for her.

She probably wasn't involved but had just had the poor judgement to fall in love with the wrong guy.

The man in the booth stood up defiantly. Then, suddenly, it was as if the mask cracked, and he realised that he was about to die. Nicolas looked away. He had seen enough bloodshed. Here. And previously.

The shot rang out and Nicolas instinctively looked up. It had hit the man in the chest, throwing him backwards. He was lying there, his body in spasm. The woman looked back and forth between the weapon and her wounded boyfriend. The shooter stood over him, legs apart, and put another bullet in his chest.

The woman was wailing loudly.

"It will be over soon," Nicolas muttered, glancing out of the window. He thought that the shooter was about to turn around and leave the restaurant, but instead he pointed his weapon towards the woman's head.

"No!" she screamed. "No, please!"

She pushed herself against the wall, making herself small, holding her hands above her head and pleading for her life.

Nicolas stared at the first victim's Glock, which was sticking out of his waistband.

He had a clear aim, less than ten metres to his target, and he knew he would never miss from that range.

He had to make up his mind.

2

TOM LINDBECK WAS alone in the auditorium at the Grand as the credits rolled up the silver screen.

Why couldn't people have some respect for those who'd made the film? Only when the last name had disappeared did he get to his feet. Popcorn crunched beneath his soles and his trainers kicked a soft-drink cup. Tom bent over and then carried it to the bin by the exit.

In the foyer, the cinema-goers were putting their coats on, standing in little huddles, or making their way out into the April air. Tom's twenty-one-year-old niece studied him impatiently. The cinema trip had been her thirty-third birthday present to him.

"Shall we go to a bar and grab a beer?" she asked.

"Well, just one. I'm going to the gym later."

Outside on Sveavägen, the rain was falling in miniscule droplets. Tom put on his coat, pulled the zip up to his Adam's apple and threw his kitbag over his shoulder. They crossed the road and headed towards Sergels Torg. By the commemorative plaque at the spot where Olof Palme was murdered, Tom slowed down and looked over towards the steps. He visualised the prime minister's assassin rushing towards Malmskillnadsgatan. Disappearing. As a boy, Tom had dreamt of inventing a time machine, travelling back to the night of the murder and catching the perpetrator. Becoming a feted hero.

They found an Irish pub on Kungsgatan, Galway's. The place was half-empty. Low ceilings. Wooden panelling.

Booths, with green leather benches. TV screens. The Pogues on the jukebox. The leather cushion creaked as Tom manoeuvred himself in. He pulled out his phone, as he always did when visiting somewhere new. Partly because he was curious, partly because it gave him a feeling of control. The pub's homepage boasted that several staff members were real live Irishmen and that the bar itself was one of Stockholm's longest.

Katja returned and slid a glass of iced water across the table to Tom. She took a big gulp of her beer and then wiped the foam from her top lip.

"Would you like to hear some gossip?"

She leaned in and lowered her voice.

"You know who Rakel's sleeping with?"

Tom ignored the absurdity of the suggestion that he could possibly know that and shook his head. Katja's friend appeared in his mind's eye. A ten-pointer. Out of reach for ordinary guys.

"The TV presenter Oscar Sjölander, you know, the one from TV4. So fucked up. He's married, with two daughters."

Katja reclined and waited for Tom's reaction. None was forthcoming. Tom wasn't surprised. Oscar Sjölander was one of those guys that all women wanted.

"Rakel thinks he's going to leave his wife for her. She's a bit fucking thick. Have you read what people write about him on *flashback.org*?"

Tom shook his head as he raised his glass of water to his lips.

"Apparently he almost got caught up in #metoo," said Katja. "He just can't keep it in his pants. And he hits his wife. It's surely just a matter of time before he starts beating Rakel too. That's if he doesn't tire of her and dump her first."

That didn't surprise Tom either. Women didn't care whether men were decent. It was the other things: money, career. What kind of car they drove. What clothes they wore. Tom was ugly, even if he had managed – through furious and regular workouts – to improve his appearance somewhat. Unfortunately, that had never helped with women. They had never liked him. They wanted men like Oscar Sjölander. Rich, famous and self-assured. The kind that treat everyone around them like shit. Katja could pretend to be upset, but the sad truth was that she too would have spread her legs for the presenter, given the chance.

"Are you seeing anyone?" Katja asked.

"Yes."

Katja seemed surprised, and she wound her finger, gesturing for him to continue.

"Her name is Henrietta."

"That's great," Katja exclaimed. "Did you meet on Tinder?"

A couple of months earlier, Katja had set up a Tinder profile for Tom. His niece, though, had set the age range from twenty-seven to forty. Divorcees. Rejects. Tom preferred young women. Just like all men, even if some didn't admit it in public. Not that it mattered – not even the divorced horror shows were interested.

"No, at the gym," said Tom.

He stood up to go to the toilet, mostly to avoid Katja's questioning.

At one of the tables close to the toilet queue sat three young girls. Ordinary women, not exactly beauties. Tom looked hopefully in their direction, and one of them gave a look of distaste in return, leant over to her friend and whispered something. Grimaces. Sniggers. He felt a stabbing in his stomach and thought to himself that he could no longer tell if it was down to rage or arousal.

The difference was hard to pin down.

Shortly after Tom returned, they finished up. Katja was heading home. She lived in Blackeberg. Tom was planning to go to the gym, and he offered to walk her to the station at Fridhemsplan.

"All sorts of shit happens nowadays. I don't want you getting in trouble," he said.

"Thanks," replied Katja. "Since Mum died, you've been the only one who has really been there for me."

3

NICOLAS COULD NOT WATCH the young woman being executed. She was young, with her whole life in front of her. The men whose blood was pouring across the floor were hardened criminals who'd known what they were getting themselves into.

Nicolas grabbed the dead man's weapon from his waist. As soon as his fingers closed around the barrel, his brain went onto autopilot. He stood up and shot as he exhaled.

The bullet hit the gunman's neck, continued out the other side and struck the wall. Instinctively, he had aimed high – to kill – like he was trained to do.

The man fell forwards, and the stream of blood hit the woman's face. She screamed, probably believing she'd been shot herself.

Nicolas spun around. The driver of the moped raised an automatic weapon. "Down," roared Nicolas as he threw himself prone onto the floor. The window pane shattered; glass splinters rained down. Nicolas crawled towards the exit, shards of glass pushing into his forearms and thighs. He felt the bullets whistling above his head. His body knew where it was going, what was expected of it to survive. He reached the doorway, knelt up and steadied his weapon. He was just about to poke his head out and locate the target when the shooting stopped. The next second, the moped tore off and the man's back disappeared in the direction of the E4 motorway.

Nicolas surveyed the devastation.

The restaurant guests were still lying under the tables, curled up with their hands above their heads. To his relief, he was able to ascertain that none of them appeared to be injured.

The woman had the shooter's blood on her face, hair and clothes, but was she unhurt? Nicolas hauled the black-clad body out of the way and helped her to sit up with her back against the wall.

"Are you all right?"

She nodded and looked around in a daze.

"What's your name?"

"Molly."

A weak wheezing sound was coming from her boyfriend. Nicolas dropped to his knees and examined the bullet holes, put the pistol down and pushed both hands down on one of the wounds.

From the corner of his eye, he could see that the other guests were crawling out and carefully getting to their feet. Someone was crying. Nicolas contemplated leaving before the police arrived but decided that that would attract more suspicion than staying put.

He had acted in self-defence and saved her life.

"Go to the kitchen, get some napkins or towels. We need to stop the bleeding," he said to Molly as he tore off her boyfriend's shirt.

The first police car pulled up outside the pizzeria three minutes later. Two officers – a man and a woman – turned off the sirens but left the blue lights on. Curious passers-by gathered outside the shot-out window and documented the chaotic scene with their mobile phones.

The police officers roared at them to back away. Nicolas was kneeling over Molly's boyfriend, pushing towels against his chest. The man was in shock. His pulse was racing, and his body temperature was falling rapidly. His body had started to shut down, focusing on basic functions and not simply switching off and dying. Nicolas didn't expect him to survive.

"We need an ambulance!" Nicolas shouted over his shoulder.

"On its way," replied the female officer. She leaned over Nicolas to inspect the man.

"Shit," she muttered, then walked over to her colleague and whispered something to him.

Nicolas realised that she'd recognised the shooter. The police put out a call on the radio. Two medics in neon-yellow jackets crouched down at the man's side. With some effort, Nicolas got to his feet. More police arrived. Cordoned the place off. Screamed at people to keep their distance. *Fucking pigs!* screamed someone. Nicolas stayed in the back of the restaurant to avoid being captured in any of the film clips that would doubtless be uploaded to social media.

He righted a chair that had been knocked over and sat down heavily. His chest, hands and forearms were sticky with blood, both his own and that of the man he'd shot. He pulled out a few splinters of glass while his glazed eyes followed the organised chaos that was now unfolding.

The medics had put the casualty onto a stretcher and disappeared. Three police officers were taking witness statements from the customers. The police were talking to a man who was pointing in Nicolas' direction.

"I must ask you to come with us out to the car."

Nicolas stood up slowly. The policewoman had her hand resting on her weapon, and the look on her face was serious and alert.

"Do you have any ID?"

Nicolas reached slowly for the driving licence he had in his trouser pocket. He was told to wait in the car, and he scraped the nail on his index finger across the black upholstery. Whatever happened, it was out of his control. His actions had been morally right; if he had not intervened, the woman could have been dead. She had got another chance, a chance to grow old.

Outside the car's window, a man in plain clothes was talking to the police who'd been first at the scene. The man was around forty, and almost two metres tall. He was wearing a trench coat and his head was shaved.

After a while, he got into the front seat and turned his large frame around.

"Nicolas Paredes," he read from the licence and then looked up. "Can you tell me what happened in there?"

Nicolas took his time. He explained thoroughly and dispassionately, almost as he had explained to his superiors in years past. He avoided embellishing or altering details that might prove inconvenient for him. The policeman nodded and chipped in a question every now and then. To Nicolas' relief, he didn't seem hostile.

"How could you be so sure of hitting your target? That was a distance of, what, maybe twelve, thirteen metres?"

"Ten. I'm a soldier. Well, I was."

"Not any more?"

Nicolas shook his head. Molly was sitting with a blanket over her shoulders, talking to a medic. She had washed her face, but her brown hair was still caked in dried blood.

"May I ask why?" the policeman enquired.

Nicolas shook his head.

"I'm afraid I can't tell you. Not without a lawyer."

The man muttered, shifted his position and moved his long legs. If he decided to do a house search at Nicolas' place, they would find the money and the revolver. He needed to cooperate, not give them any reason to search his flat.

"When can I leave?" Nicolas ventured.

"Not for a while yet."

"Am I a suspect for something?"

"For the time being – no. But you have just shot someone dead. So you'll be taken to the station for further questioning."

4

VANESSA TOOK HER shoes off, leaned back and put her feet up on the desk. The offices of the National Homicide Unit were empty. Her colleagues had gone home to their families, pets and hobbies. She, meanwhile, had spent the past hour re-reading Karim Laimani's criminal CV.

Laimani was an archetypal violent criminal. His first brush with the law had come early, at fourteen, when he assaulted a boy the same age. Drugs, weapons dealing, serious assault, armed robbery. He had been incarcerated on a total of four separate occasions.

In his cell at Åkersberga, the technicians had found a pair of shoes with Emelie's blood on the soles. The prison's CCTV clearly showed that they were the same shoes Karim had had on when he reported back from parole. On top of that, a strand of her hair had been found on the jumper he'd been wearing. Karim and his lawyer had attempted to argue that the hair had ended up there on a previous occasion, but Emelie had had her hair dyed in a salon the week before.

They could not explain the blood, but Karim continued to maintain that he had not been in Täby at all during his parole.

A motive and forensic evidence pointed towards Karim Laimani. She scrolled through to Ove's number and pressed call as she stood up to go to the coffee machine.

"Are you busy?" she asked.

"I'm playing ice hockey."

"Don't you do that in the winter?"

"Videogame. With my son."

Vanessa thought to herself that, in spite of everything, things were moving forward. Fatherhood, at least. It was impossible to imagine her own father, the director, playing games with them or even showing the slightest interest in their lives.

The sound of a boy celebrating in the background.

"And now I conceded."

"I'm going through Karim's track record," said Vanessa. "He's violent, nasty, he does drugs, and he hits women."

"Yes?"

"But he's not stupid."

"He's hardly a potential Nobel Prize winner." Ove chuckled.

"He's a career criminal. He probably knows as much about investigations and forensics as you and I. Yet he forgets to change his shoes after the murder and heads back to prison. Not only that. He wears the same jumper."

"She'd left him. For someone else. He was wounded. Fuck the consequences. It's not exactly the first time some caveman has done in his ex or his girlfriend."

Vanessa stopped by the coffee machine.

"But shouldn't he have tried to escape? He must have known that the first thing we'd do would be to check out men with previous in her immediate surroundings?"

She pressed the button, the machine stirred into life, and steaming black coffee poured into her cup.

"Listen, Vanessa. I don't know how these clowns' brains work. But the forensic evidence speaks for itself. As do the statistics. Karim Laimani killed Emelie because she'd left him."

Vanessa returned to the desk, moved the mouse and went onto *Kvällspressen*'s homepage. The tabloid was leading with a new shooting. This time in the Stockholm neighbourhood of Bredäng. Two dead, one seriously injured. The grainy images showed forensic technicians on their way into a pizzeria, a shot-up window and grim-looking uniformed officers. A nightly postcard from gangland Stockholm.

Before locking Karim's file back in the document safe, Vanessa took one last look at the pictures of Emelie Rydén's lifeless body.

Vanessa stepped out of the lift and walked past the long rows of parked police vehicles in the station's garage. Men like Karim Laimani lacked self-control. That was all that set them apart from ordinary citizens. Every single setback was an affront. They turned all their hate outwards, never examined themselves.

The garage doors opened, and a patrol car drove in.

The car swung into a space in front of her, the engine fell silent, and the doors opened. Officers climbed out and raised their hands to acknowledge her. Vanessa walked towards them.

"Southern District's cells are full, so we had to bring him here." She tried to see into the back seat.

"The shooting in Bredäng?"

The male officer nodded. He was pale, seemed shaken.

"What did it look like?"

"Fucking terrible," he quickly replied. "Two dead. A third is probably dying as we speak. Blood and glass everywhere."

The policewoman opened the back door. The man who climbed out of the back seat had his back to Vanessa, yet she still realised immediately that there was something familiar about him.

His white T-shirt was flecked with blood, his underarms wrapped in bandages. The policewoman walked him around the car, past Vanessa and over towards the lifts. Nicolas and Vanessa stared at one another for half a second. Neither showed so much as a flicker of recognition. Vanessa turned to her male colleague and gave him a pat on the shoulder.

"I hope the rest of the evening is a bit calmer."

"So do I," he said, following Nicolas and the policewoman.

Vanessa watched them walking away. How was Nicolas involved in the Bredäng shooting? Was he the one who'd carried out the execution in the pizzeria? He was intelligent, reserved and calm – and loving and tender towards his sister. Yet there was another side to him. Vanessa had never met anyone with a greater capacity for assassination than Nicolas Paredes. The Ministry of Defence had ploughed millions into his training. As an operative within SOG, he was trained to kill. Quickly, efficiently, unsentimentally.

Could he have been recruited by a street gang?

No, that didn't fit with Vanessa's idea of him. Nicolas had morals; he didn't get involved in meaningless violence. He was not like Karim.

If he'd got into trouble, Vanessa was honour-bound to help him – he had risked his life for her sake many times the year before. He had accompanied her to South America's southern tip to find Natasha. Without him, neither she nor Natasha would be alive.

The least she could do was to find out what had happened. She rushed back towards the lifts.

5

TOM STROLLED ALONG S:t Eriksgatan with his training
holdall over his shoulder. He opened the door of the gym, said
hi to the guy on reception and held his membership card to
the reader.

Women in leggings and thin sports vests or crop tops
sweated breathlessly on the cross-trainers and the treadmills.
Beefy men lifted weights, grunted quietly, tensed their muscles.

Tom found an empty locker and got changed.

He put his track pants on first, did a lap past the mirror
and inspected his upper body. The testosterone injections
had made him broad-shouldered; his facial hair was denser
despite him shaving carefully every morning. He was a
gentleman, not some scruff. He spun around to study his
back; it was covered in red zits and blemishes. One of his
colleagues who'd seen him getting changed had asked him
if he'd been sleeping on a cheese grater. The others had all
laughed. Even if he was used to it, Tom despised it when
they had a laugh at his expense.

The door opened, and the sound of a barbell hitting the
floor found its way into the changing room. A muscular
immigrant man with a granite jaw, white wrestling vest and
rippling, sweaty biceps walked in.

Tom moved away from the mirror. He didn't want to seem
vain and weak.

He put his top on while surreptitiously observing the

newcomer, who had sat down and pulled out a tin of tuna. He had the look of a small-time criminal. He probably had a pretty blonde girlfriend with a beautiful body. She was probably here at the gym too. Would they go home later? Shower together?

The guy paid no attention to Tom, burped loudly and peeled off his vest.

On Facebook, there were groups intended for women. Male-free zones, as they were called. They hosted discussions about sex, menstruation and dating. Tom, thanks to a fake profile, was a member of several of them. Wimpy, clumsy men that the women had had one-night stands with were mercilessly mocked. Some women wrote that they wanted to be 'properly shafted' by 'real men'. They discussed penis size and criticised men who had been unable to satisfy them in bed. How did that fit with all the talk of equality? Tom couldn't get his head around it. He used to ask the women questions, inventing all kinds of conditions that his alter ego was suffering from. It felt intimate, and it turned him on. In reality, none of them would ever even speak to him.

He bent over and tied his shoelaces.

The other man had finished his tuna fish and was lining up a throw. The tin arced through the air, missing the bin, hitting the wall and falling to the floor. The guy left it there.

Tom was pumping his chest, lying on his back on a bench. Eight lots of four reps. Twenty-six kilos on each dumbbell. He was stronger than ever, and his muscles glistened and rippled beneath his pale skin.

The thin, bird-like creature he had been a few years earlier was gone. He wiped his glasses on a towel and put them back on. Just behind him, a girl of about twenty was deadlifting. Her ash blonde hair was gathered in a tight bun on top of her head. He couldn't help himself; while he caught his breath, he turned around to look at her. She seemed annoyed and stared daggers back at him. Henrietta had not turned up. He checked her Instagram to see what she was up to, but she hadn't updated all day.

Tom lay back down on the bench, grabbed the dumbbells and set to work again. Towards the end, he closed his eyes and was grunting through clenched teeth. They squeaked under the strain. The lactic acid was flowing. He let the dumbbells fall to the floor and slumped there, panting. To his surprise, he noticed that the girl was now standing over him.

"Stop staring," she said. "Otherwise I'm going to tell reception."

Tom straightened his back. The other men were looking at him with disgust. He stood up, placed the weights back on the stand by the mirror before wandering over to the treadmill. What difference did it make that he'd spent years building up his body, working it to its very limits, pumping it full of testosterone? Something made women hate him. He was tired of their contempt. Tom was intelligent – he could solve a Rubik's cube in under a minute. Admittedly that was a long way off the world record of 4.73 seconds. If, though, he had been rich, a star athlete or TV personality, women would have been swarming around him.

But he was ugly and poor. A loser. He lived alone, was going to die alone and no one besides Katja could care less. He programmed the treadmill and ran for a couple of uninspired minutes before wiping himself with a paper towel.

In the mirror, on the way back to the changing room, he saw two women making disgusted faces behind his back. He realised that he'd forgotten to wash his gym kit. He probably stank. Tom didn't care any more and decided to change gyms for the fourth time in six months. He might be able to meet Henrietta anyway. He got changed without showering, put on his jeans, top and jacket and then pulled a cap onto his head.

His clothes were sticky against his body. He felt the hatred flaring up, stronger than it ever had before. Or was it grief? At being alone, rejected, always turned away? By everything and everyone.

6

BEFORE ARRESTEES WERE taken to the custody cells on the seventh floor, they were brought to the Officer in Charge, three floors down. Vanessa stepped out of the lift and wiped her palms on her trouser legs. Nicolas was sitting on a wooden bench with his head slumped and his elbows propped against his thighs. He didn't look up. Behind a plexiglass screen, the policeman who Vanessa had spoken to in the garage was filling in an arrest report. Vanessa assumed that his female colleague was explaining to the Officer in Charge why Nicolas had been brought to Kungsholmen instead of the cells in Flemingsberg, given that the shooting had taken place in Bredäng.

Vanessa walked past Nicolas, who still hadn't seen her, and over to her colleague and tapped on the plexiglass screen.

The policeman looked up in surprise.

"Yes?"

"I've realised that I recognise him from another case," she said, pointing to Nicolas. "Why is he here?"

"From what we understand, he shot dead one of the men. It's a bit messy. According to witnesses, he did so to save a woman. We're going to keep him here overnight and then do a house search to rule out him being a member of one of the gangs."

He picked up his pen again. Vanessa gulped. He mustn't get suspicious. "Can I talk to him?"

Her colleague gave her a quizzical look.

"Why?"

"As I said, he's involved in another case and I need answers to a few questions," said Vanessa.

The policeman shrugged.

"Do it. But Serious Crime South are coming any minute to interrogate him, so it'll have to be quick."

Vanessa went over and stood by the bench, next to Nicolas, and turned her back to the policeman.

"I'm going to try and help you, but first I need you to answer a question. What are you doing here?" she asked in a hushed tone.

"He was going to shoot the woman too," Nicolas muttered.

"Who was?"

"The man who shot the others, in the pizzeria. He was going to execute her as well. I grabbed the first victim's weapon and killed him."

Vanessa quickly decided that he was telling the truth. She felt relieved.

"Do you have anything compromising at home?"

Nicolas looked at her with surprise.

"Why do you ask?"

"Because there's going to be a house search soon."

Nicolas closed his eyes and clenched his jaws.

"Behind the bathtub is a black bag full of cash. And a weapon."

"And the money comes from the kidnappings?"

Nicolas nodded slowly. Vanessa consulted with herself for a second. He was her friend, at least one of the few people she really cared about. He had risked his life for her and Natasha in Chile. If it hadn't been for Nicolas, Vanessa would've been rotting in a mass grave in Colonia Rhein.

She had to help him, even if that meant breaking the law. She would be risking her whole career. Without it, she had nothing. But if she did not do what she could for Nicolas, she would be disloyal. That was worse, she decided.

"Address? And how do I get in?"

The sound of voices came from the other side of the room. The officer was walking towards them with the Officer in Charge, who was going to ask Nicolas if he knew why he'd been taken there, enquire about possible injuries or illness and whether he had any requests for a specific defence lawyer.

"Ålgrytevägen 14C, in Bredäng," Nicolas hissed. "The code is 1132. Fourth floor. Knock on the flat next door – it has the name 'Wood' on the door. Celine will help you in."

Vanessa studied the satnav and turned off the motorway. A while later, at low speed, she passed Bredäng shopping precinct, where a dozen or so passers-by were still hanging around the cordon. She hoped that interviewing the witnesses was going to take time, that the detectives weren't already in Nicolas' apartment. For once, she felt like the shortage of detectives was actually a good thing. Vanessa continued up Ålgrytevägen and parked a hundred metres or so from the entrance to Nicolas' block.

There was no sign of any police cars. She tapped in the code and took the stairs up to the fourth floor. The lock showed no signs of forced entry. Now she just had to get this Celine to hand over the spare key.

Vanessa rang the bell.

The next second, she was standing eyeball-to-eyeball with a girl wearing a faded T-shirt bearing the word *Feminazi*.

"Yes?" said the girl, measuring up Vanessa belligerently.

"I'm looking for Celine," said Vanessa, peering over the girl's shoulder into the apartment.

"Who's asking?"

"Me."

The girl raised an eyebrow.

"Are you from social services?"

"No."

"Do you want to recruit me into some sect?"

"No."

"What do you want then? Are you a cop or what? In that case, I want a lawyer."

"I am a cop, but you don't need a lawyer. I'm here for Nicolas' sake."

"I don't know any Nicolas." Celine huffed and attempted to close the door. Vanessa managed to wedge her foot in the opening.

"He's run into some difficulties. I need to get into his flat. Quickly. He said I should talk to Celine and that she'd help me."

Celine sniggered. "You think I was born yesterday, or what? Go and trick some pensioner or something."

"I'm serious. Nicolas sent me. I know him."

"Prove it."

"How can I do that?"

Celine shrugged. "That's up to you."

"I'll give you five hundred crowns."

"You think I'd sell out a friend for that?"

"A thousand then?"

Biting her lip, Celine slowly shook her head.

"I'm sorry, but I can't be bought."

Vanessa glanced behind her, down the corridor. Time was starting to run out. Her colleagues could appear at any moment.

"Celine, I understand that you like Nicolas. I do too. That's why I'm here. I need to get into his flat, and he gave me your name, didn't he? That means he trusts you, just like he trusts me. Now let me in so that we can help him."

Celine looked at Vanessa, nodded and took a step backwards. Just as Vanessa was going to enter, the girl held up her index finger.

"If you're tricking me, you're going to regret it."

Celine spun on her heels and used the same outstretched finger to signal to Vanessa to follow her. They walked through the flat and Celine slid open the balcony door.

"You just climb over."

Vanessa looked at the girl, then at Nicolas' balcony door,

which stood open, and realised that she'd misunderstood Nicolas. There was no spare key. She walked over to the railing and rested her hands on it. It was half a metre between the balconies. Unsettling, but doable.

"Do you have any gloves?"

While Celine disappeared into the flat, Vanessa climbed up onto the railing and carefully hauled herself over. She was left standing on Nicolas' side while she waited for Celine to return. If her colleagues came across the bag of cash, it would be difficult to explain what Vanessa's fingerprints were doing on it.

Celine chucked over a pair of black gloves and Vanessa pulled them on.

She blinked a few times in the gloom of the flat. It felt weird being in Nicolas' home, even if she was there to help him. In many ways, he was still a mystery to her, despite everything they'd been through together. She couldn't resist stopping for a second to look into the bedroom. The bed was neatly made.

In the bathroom, she knelt down on the grey tiles and looked underneath the tub. A black holdall was squashed in against the wall. Vanessa got to her feet, bent over and tipped the bathtub, releasing the bag. As she passed the bedroom for a second time, she heard voices and footsteps from the stairwell.

The next moment, someone pushed the door handle of the front door.

7

"TUVA WANTS A word with you," Bengt said to Jasmina.

"Now?"

"Yes."

It was her first day in the newsroom since Sunday, when Bengt had scolded Jasmina for missing her deadline. On Monday, he'd called to say that she could come in on Thursday, without explaining what was happening then.

Jasmina had kept herself indoors throughout her time off. Lived on sandwiches. Stared at the wall. She'd tried watching Netflix, but every violent or sexual scene made her want to vomit. The only time she'd left that apartment was to buy crispbread and sandwich fillings. On her way home, a man had called to her to hold the door and then joined her in the lift. She'd trembled throughout its ascent. On her floor, she had rushed out of the lift, pulled the grille shut and then quickly locked the door behind her. Any unknown man was a potential assailant who could hurt her.

Jasmina knocked on the door of Editor-in-Chief Tuva Algotsson. When she saw Jasmina, she waved her in and stood up. Tuva was dressed in a blue pinstriped trouser suit that seemed to add a couple of centimetres to her already impressive height. Jasmina had never been alone with the big boss. All she knew about the woman who had brought her to the paper was the stuff that appeared in industry journals where Tuva would fleetingly address publicity issues. Her private life was shrouded in mystery. Jasmina didn't even know whether she had a family.

"Could you close the door behind you," said Tuva. "We're waiting for one more person. I'll ring and say that you're here."

She pulled out her phone and waited as it rang. "You can come now," she said curtly.

Tuva sat down behind her desk and pushed off her high-heeled shoes, threw them to the floor and started massaging the balls of her feet with a pained expression.

Jasmina stayed standing. She discretely wiped her hands on her jeans.

"This isn't the military, Jasmina. You don't have to wait for me to ask you to sit down."

Jasmina rushed to take a seat. Sitting down was still painful, but she gritted her teeth.

"You can read this article while you're waiting," Tuva said, sliding over a copy of *Kvällspressen* that was lying on the desk. "Read from page fourteen onwards."

"Okay," said Jasmina.

She picked up the newspaper and flipped through to the page Tuva had directed her to.

Leading Social Democrat's luxury foreign trips with his wife – at the taxpayer's expense. In the accompanying picture, William Bergstrand was grinning broadly. According to expenses claims, the trip was to attend a party congress. There had been no congress, however. Instead, he had been living a life of luxury and eating at expensive restaurants with his wife.

From the byline, Max Lewenhaupt stared out at her. Tuva watched carefully, giving nothing away as to what she might have been thinking or feeling. There was a knock at the door, and Hans Hoffman entered the room. He pulled a chair over and placed it next to Jasmina, opposite Tuva. He looked sullen, almost enraged.

Jasmina folded up the paper and left it sitting in her lap.

"Good piece, right? News bills nationwide. Sales up everywhere," Tuva said, looking calmly at Jasmina. "Haven't you seen it?"

"No, I've just been at home," Jasmina said quietly.

Hans Hoffman turned to her.

"The receipts. The hotel stays. The restaurants. That was your thing. How come it's Lewen*pratt* grinning in the byline?"

8

VANESSA RAN THROUGH the living room, pulled the balcony door shut and chucked the bag over. Celine was waving eagerly to get her to hurry up.

Vanessa climbed up onto the railing, pushed off and flew through the air.

She slammed her knee into the opposite railing with a loud bang, clung on and, with a gargantuan effort, managed to haul herself over. From inside the apartment, she could hear someone approaching quickly. Vanessa pressed herself onto the floor, hidden by the metal screen that enclosed Celine's balcony.

Celine stayed put, standing calmly with the bag at her feet, pretending to admire the view.

"Were you in here just now?"

As Vanessa lay curled up on the floor of the balcony, peering under the railing, she could see a pair of black shoes on Nicolas' side.

"Are you sure you weren't in there? It sounded like someone jumped across."

His voice was suspicious. Celine kicked the railing.

"Did it sound like that?" she asked. "I tend to hit things when I think about stuff that makes me angry. Dad says I mustn't, so I make the most of it when he's not home."

"There's no one else there?" asked the policeman.

"No, just me and my demons," Celine said with a theatrical sigh. A moment's silence followed.

"Alright, have a good evening then."

"Same to you."

The policeman walked back into Nicolas' apartment and the balcony door was pushed closed. Vanessa liked this defiant, strange girl. She crawled along the floor, pushing the bag in front of her, over the threshold and into the combined kitchen/living room.

Vanessa sat on the sofa, grimacing as she studied her painful knee. It was only then she noticed how run-down the flat was. Big cracks in the ceiling. Missing wallpaper. Worn-out furniture. Dark stains on the sofa upholstery.

Celine closed the balcony door.

"What shall we do now then?" she asked indifferently. "I suppose I'm going to have to stay put for a while."

"Is that okay?"

"Sure. Do you want some scrambled eggs?"

"Okay."

"Nicolas always says I put too much salt in."

"He's a wimp."

Celine nodded approvingly. "That's exactly what I usually say." She got out a frying pan, opened the fridge and took out a few eggs. While she had her back turned, Vanessa quickly checked that the money and revolver were indeed in the bag.

"Where are your parents?"

"Mum's dead. Cancer. Dad is probably out getting pissed. He's English. From Hull. You know what that place gets called?"

Vanessa shook her head.

"The armpit of England."

Vanessa smiled. She looked around and noticed for the first time that the flat – despite being run-down – didn't smell bad. On the contrary, it smelt of clean floors. She guessed that was Celine's doing, that the girl did what she could to keep the stench – poverty's foremost hallmark – at bay.

"Do you want to watch Netflix while I do the cooking?"

asked Celine. "Dad hasn't paid the bills for a couple of months, so I've been using Nicolas' Wi-Fi."

"We can just take it easy for a while, can't we? How did you get hold of his password?"

"He usually leaves the balcony door open, so I hopped over and looked under the router and there it was. Don't tell him that though. I don't think he'd be very impressed."

"I promise."

"How do you know Nicolas?" asked Celine as she poured some oil into the frying pan and put it on the stove.

Vanessa leaned back on the sofa. The sound of voices and footsteps could be heard from next door. She suddenly realised she was still wearing the gloves. She took them off and put her coat over the arm of the sofa.

"He helped me with something a while back."

Celine cracked an egg into a mixing bowl and raised her eyebrows teasingly. "Are you in love with him?"

Vanessa laughed.

"No."

Silence followed. Celine whisked the eggs with her tongue resting against her top lip.

"Are *you* in love with him?" Vanessa asked tentatively.

"I don't think so, but I have always had a thing for older men," Celine said as she poured the eggs into the pan.

"Me too." Vanessa sighed.

PART III

Society hates us and we are men. No one cares about us. We have to turn to violence, to force society to help us.

An anonymous man.

1

THE WIND WHIPPED and tore at the dark-green tarpaulin. Fifty-one-year-old Börje Rohdén held Eva Lind to his body to warm her. Despite being wrapped up in double sleeping bags and several layers of clothes, their teeth were chattering. The dark forest towered around them in all directions.

"At least we've got each other," she said with a smile.

They said that a lot. Half seriously, half in jest.

"Whether we like it or not," Börje said, turning his head so that his beard wouldn't tickle her. "I think we've frozen solid."

Börje loved Eva's laugh and was always trying to coax it out. She was missing two teeth in her upper jaw, but for Börje, that laugh was his single biggest reason to keep on living.

A few hours earlier, they had been moved on from a doorway in Södermalm and then caught the bus out to Tyresö and *Junibacken*, as they had christened the shack they had built the summer before.

"I'm going to try and get the fire going again," Börje said, wriggling out of the sleeping bags. "You stay put."

Between the tree trunks, further up the hill, a light was on in the window of a red-painted cottage. Last summer, and that autumn, the owner of the summer cottage had taken every opportunity to throw their stuff into the water, accuse them of stealing gardening tools and doing drugs around his children.

"Is that such a good idea? What if he sees that we're here?"

Börje could see Oscar Sjölander's face in front of him. "You can't treat people any way you feel like, just because you're on TV. And if we don't get the fire going, we're going to freeze to death."

Eva sighed.

"I wish he'd leave us alone."

"I promise I'm not going to let him hurt you again."

In September the previous year, Eva had arrived at Junibacken before Börje. The presenter had appeared and screamed at her. When she refused to leave, he had grabbed her by the neck.

"I don't understand why he's so angry. He's got a lovely house, two sweet kids, a nice, beautiful wife."

A broad, orange flame rose from the damp wood and its heat struck Börje's face. Eva stood up, grabbed two slices of bread and rushed over to the fire.

"Look," she whispered. "He's back."

A grey tabby cat stroked itself against her legs and purred.

"Was it Gustaf we christened you last summer?" She lifted the cat into her arms. "Yes, that's right. Gustaf the cat."

With Gustaf pressed against her chest, she walked over to one of the black refuse sacks and untied the food bag.

"Let's have a look and see if we've got something tasty for you."

Eva took out a tin of tuna. Börje wanted to object. They only had two left. He bit his tongue though.

"We'll share it," Eva said, burying her nose in the cat's fur. "He's hungry too."

Börje held up his palms and Eva chucked the tin over. While he opened it, she stroked the cat tenderly between its ears. The smell of fish made her stomach rumble. Börje was just about to stuff a bit in his mouth when he glanced over at Eva. It had been a cold, ruthless winter. Her face was pale. Her skin was stretched taut over her cheekbones. He changed his mind and passed her the tuna.

"Aren't you having any?" she asked in surprise.

"I'm not that hungry. I got some fruit before we met up," Börje lied. "Eat now, my dear."

Eva ate with a hearty appetite while feeding the cat at the same time. Börje could feel the calm. The cat made Eva happy. So that meant he liked the little rascal too.

Eva had been clean for two months. With a fool's stubbornness, he hoped that she was going to be forever. But she'd had good periods before. Disappeared one day. Fallen back into it. And then he would find her sitting on a bench with dead eyes and a slack jaw. He couldn't be everything she needed. Every day, he worried that she would be taken from him. That she would overdose and be found without a pulse on some shitty toilet with a needle in her arm.

Eventually the tin was emptied, Eva put it on the ground, and the cat licked up the residue.

They snuggled down in the sleeping bags under the tarp, all three of them. Gustaf squeezed in between them. His coat tickled Börje's nose and he sneezed. He thought about Oscar Sjölander, hoped that he'd stay away. He wanted to smack him in the face, tell him to leave Eva in peace, but that would only make everything worse. That time he had found out about what Sjölander had done to Eva, he hadn't been able to hold back. He'd gone straight up to the house, knocked on the door and given him what for. Oscar Sjölander had called him a filthy tramp and slammed the door in his face. A few years ago, Börje would've smacked him in the face without hesitating, and without a second thought about the consequences. Börje, though, had sworn never to hurt another human being. His time in prison had left him a changed man.

"You know what I think about quite a lot?" asked Eva.

Börje shook his head.

"How I wish that we'd met before… before everything. I could have got dressed up for you, not been ugly like I am now. Could've smelled nice. Had a house. Gone on holiday."

Börje closed his eyes. He knew that Eva had never been out of the country.

"No," he said.

"Wouldn't you have wanted all that with me?" Eva asked, taken aback.

"It would never have worked. I wasn't a good man before. I was selfish, nasty, and cold. A bit like that TV personality up there."

2

VANESSA WALKED DOWN to McLarens, ordered a hamburger from Kjell-Arne and sat down at a window table. On one wall was a new black-and-white photograph of a boxer.

"Who is that?" asked Vanessa.

Kjell-Arne clapped his hands together, took down the frame and brought it over to Vanessa.

"Johan Trollmann. He won the light heavyweight title in Germany in 1933, but it was taken away from him a few days later. Why? Because he was Sinti, a Romany. Ahead of the next match, he was instructed to fight like a German. That basically entailed standing still and exchanging blows. Do you know what he did then?"

Vanessa shook her head.

"He dyed his hair and dusted his body white, with flour. A caricature of an Aryan."

"Did he win the fight?"

"No, he lost. With dignity. And bravely. Then he fought for Hitler until 1942, when he was sent to a concentration camp. The camp commander recognised him and had him training SS soldiers at night. Sometime later, he was beaten to death in the camp, by some criminal with a shovel."

Vanessa sighed. "Nice story."

"There's light in the darkness. In 2003, he was given justice.

The German Boxing Federation posthumously awarded him that 1933 title fight."

"He must be delighted," she said.

Vanessa felt that the wish for honour and praise after death was a typically male desire. Wondering who might visit her grave tormented her then, but she knew that she would stop worrying about that the moment she drew her last breath.

A forgotten copy of *Kvällsposten* lay on the window sill.

The paper had got wind of the fact that Karim Laimani was suspected of murdering his ex-girlfriend while out on parole. Thus far, neither Karim's nor Emelie's name had been mentioned, referred to instead only as *the thirty-five-year-old gangster* and *the young woman*. Somehow, the reporter had also managed to get hold of information about Karim threatening to kill Emelie on her last visit to the prison. In the article, Karim's convictions were listed along with a number of quotes from politicians and experts. All demanding tougher restrictions on parole. The article concluded with details of a vigil for the dead woman, to be held at Sergels Torg the next day, Sunday.

Vanessa put the paper down and stared out of the window. A second later, her phone started ringing.

"Hi, how's it going?" asked Ove Dahlberg.

"Good, thanks."

"I'm well too," Ove said chirpily. "Thanks for asking."

In the background, there was the sound of someone nagging about sweets. Ove asked the kid to calm down, was ignored, then gave up and swapped rooms.

"I'm calling about Emelie Rydén. I should've done this yesterday, but…"

Vanessa took a gulp and waited while Ove hauled the kid, who'd followed him in, out of the room.

"Anyway, we've got the results back from the other stuff in her apartment that was sent for analysis. In the inside pocket of the jacket that was hanging in the hall, there was a pen."

Vanessa searched her memory in vain as she tried to understand what he was talking about.

"You asked me to send the jacket in because it matched the description of what she'd been wearing the last time she visited Karim."

"Okay?"

"You know what was on the pen?"

"No, Ove, I don't know what was on the pen."

"A fingerprint matching the presumed perpetrator in a five-year-old unsolved attempted rape case in Rålambshov Park."

"What sort of pen?"

"An ordinary blue biro. From Rosersbergs Slotts Hotel."

3

PEOPLE RUSHED PAST Börje Rohdén in Farsta Centrum. He stopped by a bin and rooted around. Nothing of value.

A woman looked at him with distaste. Börje was used to people grimacing at the sight of him. At least he no longer felt tormented, as he had during his first days on the streets. Then he'd walked around huddled over, with his eyes fixed to the ground, so that no one would recognise him.

Börje plodded over to the next bin, found a deposit bottle and put it in his carrier bag. Dug deeper. Felt the familiar, cold clump and pulled out his hand. A brown sludge had attached itself to his hand. Dog shit.

"Fuck," he mumbled.

He held up his hand and looked for somewhere to wipe it. There was a crumpled serviette lying by a bench and he cleaned his hand with the last drops from the bottle.

Börje picked up a copy of a free newspaper. He never used to care about the weather, except during his holidays. Now the weather forecast was the first thing he checked whenever he got hold of a paper. An improvement in the weather over the coming days was promised. Sunshine, fifteen degrees. No rain. The warm weather seemed to be here to stay. Life was pretty good, all in all. He and Eva had survived their second winter together and he was going to surprise her with an almost-whole Big Mac that he'd found outside McDonald's.

Börje got the deposits back on the bottles and cans he'd

managed to gather, put the twelve crowns in his pocket and got the escalator up to the metro platform. The view from there had led the alkies who would gather on the benches and drink beer to call the spot 'the Sky Bar'.

Just then, the bar had only a single guest: one-armed Elvis Redling, on his mobility scooter emblazoned with Hammarby football stickers.

"Börje," Elvis called out when he caught sight of him, then revved up the scooter and raised his stump. "Give me five."

Elvis had grown up in Farsta. He was born here and had stayed here.

The accident had occurred on the very same platform, in the summer of 1994. Elvis, who'd just been sacked from his job as a joiner, had been heading into town to celebrate Sweden's win over Romania in the World Cup. A friend barged into him, and he fell onto the tracks. Three carriages thundered over him. Fleshy ribbons were all that was left of his left arm.

Börje peered into the basket on Elvis' scooter. Inside lay a bottle of vodka and a couple of beers. Åbro, 7.3%. Since his mother's death, a month and a half earlier, Elvis had stuck to beer and tablets. Now, though, it was time to get back on the vodka.

"How's it going?" Börje asked as he sat down on the bench.

Elvis had a tormented look in his eyes. "Jeez, Börje, I don't know if I'm going to get over Mum. This is the worst nightmare I've ever had. The other day I phoned her up and wondered why she wasn't answering. Oh, that's right, she's dead. I haven't grasped it yet."

Börje didn't know what to say. Elvis reached over and grabbed an Åbro. A train pulled in. A school class got off and the kids peered at them. Elvis hid his beer in his lap until they'd gone past. He always did.

"*Ach, you don't drink in front of kids. That's how I was brought up,*" he'd replied when Börje had asked him early on in their friendship.

Two security guards waddled towards them. Börje recognised them. Nasty bastards. Especially the bigger one, whose name was Jörgen. He had a shaved head and a beer gut, and close-set eyes. It was plain that he enjoyed demonstrating his power. The other one was average height, normal build.

Jörgen went and stood in front of them. The other one hung back a step and placed his hand on his baton as he scanned the platform.

"You know you can't sit here," Jörgen said, taking a firm grip of his belt. "People get scared."

"Be reasonable," Börje said calmly.

"You can keep your mouth shut." Jörgen grinned mockingly, then lowered his voice. "Freaks. If you'd had any honour in that horrible body of yours, you'd have done yourself in."

The smaller of the guards nodded his agreement.

Börje put his hand on Elvis' shoulder. "Come on, there's no point staying here and squabbling."

"Nasty rats. You're parasites. Should be exterminated," Jörgen hissed through a smile.

Börje and Elvis took the lift down to the ground level in silence and did a lap of Farsta Centrum before returning to the platform.

It wasn't until a few hours later that Eva arrived. Börje got up and went over to greet her. He buried his nose in her hair, which smelt freshly washed.

"Get a room," Elvis shouted. "Oh yeah, that's exactly what you can't do."

Elvis rolled off back to his place, and Börje and Eva waited for the metro. Resting her head against his shoulder, she seemed sad and withdrawn.

"It's going to get warmer in the next few days," he said encouragingly. "With a bit of luck, we can move out to Junibacken permanently now."

"That would be lovely, my big old bear."

Her voice sounded hollow, and the angst multiplied like

needle-pricks in the gut. Then Börje remembered the Big Mac. He dug in his coat. It felt paltry, but it was all he had to offer.

"Close your eyes," he said.

Börje put the box down on the bench and lifted the burger towards Eva's mouth. She sniffed.

"Open up."

Her mouth closed around the bun and meat, and she opened her eyes. She swallowed and closed them again. She took the burger in her hand and ate it with her eyes half-closed. Small bites, so that it would last longer. Börje loved seeing her eat. If Eva wanted to still her hunger, she wanted to live.

An hour and a half later, they arrived at Junibacken. But Börje and Eva realised straight away that they were not alone. Someone was rooting around in their stuff.

"Wait here, Madame," Börje whispered and then moved towards their camp.

4

TOM WAS ZAPPING through TV channels, then settled on a docusoap. *Paradise Hotel*. For a while, a couple of years earlier, Tom had engaged with the programme almost like an academic. That was before he woke up, while he was still trying to understand what it was that made certain men irresistible to women.

On the screen, three guys were standing by the outdoor gym, talking. Two of them were tanned, muscular and tattooed. The third was obese, probably cast as some sort of comedy character. The two alphas were lifting weights, grunting and pumping. The fat one looked on, drinking from a cola can. His stomach hung over his shorts as he sat there on the bottom step.

"Have you thought about becoming a bodybuilder?" one of the alpha males asked the other.

"The thing about bodybuilding is that as soon as they give up the gym, they become obese. They end up with a body like Henke," the other one replied, nodding towards the fat man.

All three of them burst out laughing. Women, Tom thought to himself, would never be able to say things like that to each other. There would be arguments. Tears. Men are used to joking and being made fun of. Women, however, you weren't allowed to say a bad word about. Especially not about their bodies.

Tom yawned, pulled out his phone and opened Instagram to see whether Henrietta had posted.

She'd uploaded a picture, twenty-seven minutes earlier. Tom straightened up and moved the screen towards his face.

These things happen, it read. The picture was tagged with Danderyd Hospital, A&E.

Tom bit his lip while he typed the name of her boyfriend, Douglas, into the search bar. He was overseas. This was Tom's big chance to talk to her. Show her what she meant to him. It would take some sacrifices, but it was a price he was prepared to pay.

Tom stood up. He put on his favourite jumper, rolled deodorant in his armpits with his back to the mirror to avoid having to see his own face.

He went and stood by the kitchen worktop, opened one of the drawers and took out a knife. He caught sight of his reflection in the kitchen window. He checked to make sure he had a roll of kitchen towel close at hand. He ran the blade across his fingertips. It was going to hurt, but hopefully not too much. The scar would help him to look manly. He could invent a good story about it. A fight? A dog bite? Maybe he'd got it saving a girl from a gang of robbers.

Tom dialled the taxi firm, and an automated message informed him that he was in a queue and asked him to wait.

He grasped the handle with his right hand, steeled himself, closed his eyes and sliced across his palm. He groaned.

The phone crackled.

"Taxi Stockholm, this is Linda."

The blood poured onto the work surface, down onto the floor. Tom clenched his jaw. He was a real man who could take pain. "Hello?"

He studied the wound with fascination, reached for the kitchen roll and wound it around his bleeding hand.

"I need a car from Essinge Brogata," Tom said grimly. "As soon as possible."

By the time Tom walked into Danderyd Hospital's A&E department, the paper was red, and the blood had stained his top and jeans.

The room was bathed in a cold, white light. In the middle was an oval counter where he was registered while a nurse ascertained that it would need stitches. Medics were running back and forth. Behind the woman's head was a row of eight beds, each containing a patient. One of them a terrified geriatric, who another nurse was attempting to soothe.

Tom craned his neck and saw that Henrietta was lying three beds down from the confused old man. She wasn't wearing any make-up, and she looked younger than she usually did. More beautiful, too, thought Tom. There was an empty bed next to hers. How close could he get? What would happen if she recognised him from the gym? No, that wasn't going to happen. He was a shadow, and she probably didn't even remember him at all.

"I feel really weak," Tom said and looked pleadingly at the nurse. "Is it okay if I lie down for a while? I think I might faint otherwise."

He pretended to stumble and held himself up against the counter with his good hand.

"Come with me," she said. Holding one arm, she led him towards the empty bed. Henrietta didn't even look up. "You wait here, and someone will be along to take care of you."

There was a screen between the beds, which meant that Tom couldn't see what Henrietta was up to. He was starting to regret having come. What was he going to achieve? Half an hour passed. A screaming man was rolled past on a stretcher. His arm was twisted at a bizarre angle. Tom closed his eyes, listened to the sounds, fantasised about being a Second World War hero injured on a secret mission.

An hour. No one came to examine him. The wound in his hand was pulsating and becoming increasingly painful. The confused old man padded off down the corridor, only to be led back moments later by one of the nurses.

Tom tried to attract the attention of a nurse as she flapped past. He wanted to know whether he'd be getting sewn soon, but she ignored him.

"Excuse me," he heard from Henrietta's bed. "Could I please have some water?" No one cared about her either.

Carefully, Tom put his feet down on the floor. He pulled the curtain to one side. Henrietta stared at him. Did she recognise him? "Yes?"

He had to say something. "You wanted... I heard... should I get you some water?"

She smiled gratefully and pointed to her heavily bandaged foot. Despite being prepared for it, he was still a bit saddened that she hadn't recognised him. But maybe that was just as well? Now he could start afresh. Be someone else.

"That would be very kind."

5

BÖRJE CREPT TOWARDS the sound alone and peered out from behind a tree trunk. A light was jumping around in the darkness, and he saw a man picking up the stones from the fireplace and throwing them into the woods. Afterwards, the figure walked over to the black bin bags, tore them open and strewed their contents around. Despite not having caught a glimpse of his face, Börje knew it was TV presenter Oscar Sjölander.

He glanced anxiously towards Eva. He didn't want her getting scared or upset.

Börje stepped out of his hiding place. The presenter froze, mid-movement, straightened his back and rushed towards him.

"You've stolen my son's bike," he roared.

"No, we haven't. As you can see, it's not here," Börje said as calmly as he could. Oscar Sjölander turned the torch beam straight towards him. Börje squinted and raised his hand to shield himself. He stayed calm. For Eva's sake. If he touched a hair on that idiot's head, the police would move them on.

"Well then you must've sold it to buy booze. I've told you I don't want you here."

"That isn't up to you. We live here. Can you point that somewhere else?"

Börje heard a noise behind him. Eva. Oscar pointed the torch beam at her. She was shaken.

"I'm calling the police," Oscar Sjölander screamed.

"Enough's enough, isn't it?"

"What do you junkies cost us taxpayers? If this country had been in any sort of order, we'd have lined up the likes of you against the wall and pulled the trigger. Take your toothless junkie hag with you and disappear!"

"No."

Oscar Sjölander took a step towards Börje. Their faces met at the same height, about ten centimetres apart. A couple of seconds passed, and the TV presenter realised he could do no more. He kicked one of the black bin bags and disappeared into the woods in the direction of his house.

"It's over now," Börje said and smiled at Eva. "Are you okay?"

She nodded slowly and peered out at their possessions that were strewn across the damp ground. Börje gathered the stones and placed them in a circle to protect the fire while Eva picked clothes up and hung them on a washing line.

While Börje was hanging the tarp, his foot knocked against something hard. The remains of his Walkman. Trampled to bits.

"Fuck," he exclaimed.

Eva, who was crouched down picking up the pieces of their two plates, looked up. "He's broken the cassette player."

"Maybe Elvis or one of the boys have got one spare."

Eva always referred to the haggard figures in the Sky Bar as *the boys*. Börje thought there was something nice about that.

"No, let's eat now, Madame. I am starving."

Börje chucked some more branches on the fire, and they snuggled up close to each other. Eva was full after her hamburger, and she was happy to make do with a slice of bread. He smeared tuna onto his bread and ate hungrily. When the fish was finished, he dipped the bread in the brine, rubbed it around and popped it in his mouth.

"You seem a bit sad," he said hesitantly. "We can't let

people like Oscar Sjölander ruin things for us. You know that, right?"

Eva stared into the fire.

"It's not that. I saw Nina today, with a pushchair. She got off the train in Älvsjö. At first I thought I was lucky. I'd had a shower, smelt good, probably didn't look too bad. But she pretended not to see me. I was so happy for her sake. I wish I dared to go over and have a look at the kid, or at least see if it's a boy or a girl. I nearly did a few times."

She bit her lip.

"Might be just as well. I was a dreadful mother. I probably wouldn't have been much of a grandmother either."

Börje put his arm around her. He wanted to comfort her, tell her that everything was going to be okay, but he couldn't lie. Nina had cut all ties with Eva. There was nothing to suggest that was about to change.

"She's the one missing out on the world's best granny for her child," he said, and he meant it.

When they went to bed half an hour later, Börje could hear Eva crying. He held her tight but didn't know what to say to comfort her.

6

TOM LEFT THE curtain that separated their beds drawn while he looked around. On the far side of the reception desk was a transparent water butt on a stand. Tom walked over, filled a paper cup with water and walked back again. The senile old fellow followed his movements with a glazed look in his eyes. He gave Henrietta the mug; she took it and drank thirstily. A trickle found its way down her chin, along her neck and disappeared towards her breasts. She sighed and put down the empty cup.

"Thanks," she said.

"What happened?" asked Tom.

He felt surprisingly self-assured. He'd given her water. And she hadn't turned her nose up at him. If he was going to get a chance in life to become her lover, it was now.

"I injured myself while I was working out," said Henrietta. "God, I'm so clumsy."

Tom sat down on her bed.

"How did you end up here?" she said and pointed to his hand.

Tom repeated the story he'd told the nurse.

"I cut myself cooking."

Why hadn't he lied? If he was going to have a chance, he needed to show he was interesting and energetic. He had to make up for that mistake.

The conversation was flowing though, Tom thought to

himself. He was talking to Henrietta, without being nervous. Without stammering. She hadn't pulled any faces. Or pointed out that he was staring or smelt bad.

He licked his lips.

"What do you do for a living?"

"I'm a project manager at a PR bureau."

She still hadn't said anything about the boyfriend. That had to mean something. Maybe it was as Tom suspected, that she was mostly with Douglas because it meant somewhere to live. She was younger and more attractive than him.

Tom could hear her talking but was distracted by thoughts of how many men had pushed themselves inside her. On the forum he visited regularly, he had read that the average twenty-two-year-old in the Western world had had around one hundred sexual partners. Henrietta was older. She'd be turning twenty-five on the 18th of May. Two hundred men? His penis started swelling inside his trousers, straining against the fabric of his underpants.

Henrietta waved.

"Hello?" She laughed. "I asked you what you do for a living."

"I am a police officer," he said.

The lie came instinctively. And he regretted it immediately. Not that he'd lied, but the job he'd chosen. It was, after all, a good, masculine job. They didn't make much money though. Women wanted to be supported and taken care of. Maybe he should have said that he was a stockbroker? It was too late now. He leaned in, glanced around and lowered his voice, conspiratorially.

"I'm in surveillance. Sometimes I work as a bodyguard."

She studied him; he looked away. He'd always struggled with eye contact. Did she suspect he was lying? He had to avoid feeling unsure. She was actually talking to him. In his mind's eye, he could see them sitting at a kitchen table, eating dinner. Two blond boys, each sitting on a chair. The kitchen was bright and clean, straight out of a makeover magazine. He was going to take care of Henrietta, and their sons. Do everything for them. A new scene. Henrietta straddling him. Her full breasts bouncing as she rode him and whimpered his name. She climbed off, and moved down, maintaining eye contact throughout as she prepared to take his organ in her mouth.

"I was lying before," he heard himself saying. "I didn't cut myself cooking. There was a girl who was about to get raped. The assailant had a knife. He cut my hand while I was disarming him. The girl is fine now; he didn't get the chance to hurt her. He'll probably do time."

Henrietta opened her mouth to reply but then turned her head and looked to his left. A nurse was standing at the foot of his bed.

"Tom Lindbeck, if you'd like to follow me, you can see a doctor now."

Twenty minutes later, the wound had been washed, closed with three stitches and the hand bandaged. Tom said goodbye to the doctor and hurried into the corridor, half-jogging back to the place where he'd left Henrietta. The bed she'd been lying in was empty. He walked over to the desk, interrupted a young man and leaned in towards the nurse who'd admitted him.

"Where is Henrietta?"

"Excuse me?"

"The woman who was lying in the bed next to me," Tom said feverishly, pointing at the empty bed. "Where is she?"

The nurse wiped drops of Tom's saliva from her top lip.

"She just left."

Tom turned around and dashed down the corridor that led to the exit. He called the lift. Changed his mind, punched the wall and ran down the stairs instead. Outside, it was dark. He stepped out and looked around. Empty, silent. A swishing sound came from behind him as the sliding doors opened.

Henrietta hopped out onto the street with a crutch in each hand. At the same time, a taxi drove round the corner. The headlights came closer, causing their shadows to grow like giants against the wall of the hospital.

"You take it," said Tom.

"Thanks."

The car slowed to a halt and Tom opened the door. Henrietta passed him the crutches and laughed as she fumbled her way into the back seat. "Where do you live?"

Tom passed her the crutches and leaned forward. "Lilla Essingen."

"Get in then," said Henrietta. "I live by S:t Eriksplan."

7

IT WAS HALF-PAST ten on Sunday evening when Vanessa heard a sharp knock at the door. She got up, pulled on her jeans and a T-shirt and opened it, after checking the peephole.

Nicolas walked in. In the living room, he gestured towards the cushion and the rolled-up blanket on the sofa.

"You've got three bedrooms, and yet you insist on sleeping there?"

"I take it you made sure no one was following you."

"I just came to thank you for what you did last Thursday. I realise that it wasn't easy for you."

"Would you like a drink?"

"I'll have what you're having."

Vanessa went and got a bottle of whisky, put out two glasses and poured. They sat down on the sofa. She studied him calmly.

"How did you manage to get involved in the shooting?"

Nicolas put the whisky down.

"I couldn't let him kill her. If I hadn't got involved, then he would have shot her too. The first man to get shot was armed – I took his weapon, had a clear sight of the target and shot."

Vanessa thought to herself that he sounded like a soldier giving a report. Concise. Factual. With no regret. Just another soldier carrying out his duty, neutralising the enemy. Yet she knew Nicolas well enough to know that he was tormented by having shot another man dead.

"How's Natasha?"

Vanessa didn't reply. Nicolas looked like he regretted having asked the question.

"At the end of last year, she found out that her father was still alive," said Vanessa. "She's with him now, in Syria."

"How's she doing?"

Vanessa shrugged.

"You haven't spoken to her?"

"She needs to build a life there. I don't want her thinking that I'm going to…"

"She worships you. You don't even believe that yourself, Vanessa."

"No, I know," she said.

She leaned back, emptied the whisky and reached for the bottle. After serving herself, she pointed to Nicolas' glass, but he put his hand over it.

She couldn't pretend. Nicolas had come into their life just after Vanessa had met Natasha in the care home and taken her in. He had seen how Vanessa had risked her life, her career, for the girl.

"Truth be told, I can't face talking to her. I miss her too much." Nicolas gave her a friendly tap on the knee. He stood up.

"Are you leaving?"

"I assume you've got work tomorrow?"

"Can't you stay a little while longer?" Vanessa got to her feet. "Or get going, if you've got stuff to do."

Nicolas looked at her.

"I'll stay for a while," he said, refilling his glass. "Ivan contacted me. He wants to meet."

"Why?"

"I don't know. He's in Åkersberga Prison."

"Weird. I was there last Sunday, in connection with a murder investigation. A young woman was killed. Her ex, Karim Laimani, was on parole. The next day, he wandered into prison with her blood on the soles of his shoes. Imagine that rage, at being left."

"Is that what he says?"

"No, he's denying it. The remand hearing is tomorrow, and I think he'll be charged before long. What are you going to do about Ivan?"

"I don't know." Nicolas' mouth stayed open, but the remainder of what he was saying was left hanging in the air. He shook his head. "Shit, I really don't know."

Vanessa recalled Ivan's face. His short, powerful body. His non-existent neck and staring eyes. His insecurity. His hatred. It beggared belief that Ivan and Nicolas had been best friends. It would be hard to find two people less alike.

"I've been offered a job," said Nicolas. "At least I think I have. I ran into one of my old officers. He works for a security firm in London. He said that I'd... fit in."

Vanessa realised that she didn't want him to go. She wanted him in Stockholm. Close to her. That was selfish. They didn't even socialise. Perhaps it was their shared memories of Natasha. That they were keeping her alive.

"What do you think?"

She couldn't ask him to stay. Not for her sake.

"You need a purpose. Otherwise you'll go under. I saw you in Colonia Rhein; you were a different person. I think some people need something to fight for. You've experienced things that have left you ill-prepared for an ordinary life."

"I have tried," said Nicolas.

She patted him twice on the thigh.

"I know."

They raised their glasses and let them meet. There was something about Nicolas that she'd found attractive from their very first meeting. It flared up. Itched. Tickled. Physically, he was one of the most attractive people she had ever seen. Strikingly handsome. Tall and muscular. Masculine without being macho. Nicolas was soft. Contemplative. But inside, he had a primal strength, which the Swedish military had invested significant resources in polishing. Taught him to convert it into controlled, efficient violence.

She suspected that he was attracted to her too. She knew, however, that if anything was going to happen between them, she would have to make the move. There was a boundary between them, a wordless agreement that she would have to break. And she wasn't sure that she wanted to. Because if she did cross the line they'd drawn, their relationship would change forever.

"What are you thinking about?" asked Nicolas.

"Nothing," replied Vanessa.

8

MOST OF THE reporters, editors and sales people were out in the meagre selection of lunch restaurants around Marieberg. Bengt, as usual, was eating a microwave pasty at his desk.

"What would you like me to do today?" asked Jasmina.

Bengt put the pasty to one side and finished chewing. A bit of mince shone reddish-brown between his front teeth.

Since Max stole her article, Bengt had been more pleasant, and entrusted her with more. Tuva must have told him what happened. And Bengt was, of course, grateful that Jasmina hadn't mentioned the fact that he'd turned down the same proposal when it had come from her. She didn't want any more enemies in the newsroom.

"In the middle of April, a woman was murdered in Täby, perhaps you heard about that? The one found stabbed to death in her apartment. We haven't released the name, but I can tell you it was Emelie Rydén."

"Yes?"

Bengt scraped the mincemeat off his teeth with his index finger, studied it briefly before popping it into his mouth with a sucking sound.

"Her ex, Karim Laimani, will have his remand hearing today. That bastard was on parole. Get down to the courthouse and follow the hearing."

Jasmina walked over to her desk. Max Lewenhaupt's spot had been conspicuously empty since Hans Hoffman revealed his plagiarism. His future with the paper was uncertain. Officially, he was on leave for personal reasons. Tuva had asked Jasmina not to say anything to her colleagues until she had made a decision.

Although it was nice not to have to deal with his unpleasant manner and conceited comments, she did feel sorry for him. Stealing another reporter's idea was crossing every line. But *Kvällspressen* was a lesser paper without Max. In a short time, he had built up a stable of informants within the police. It was going to be difficult for Tuva Algotsson to replace him.

Jasmina gathered her things and headed for the exit. She took the stairs to avoid ending up in the lift with someone she didn't know. She passed the revolving door and the reception on the ground floor. Outside, she sat down on a bench to wait for her taxi.

A car pulled into the loading bay. Tuva climbed out, pushed a large pair of sunglasses from the top of her head onto her face and moved towards the entrance.

"Jasmina, there you are. Are you off somewhere?"

"The courthouse."

"Have you got a minute?" Tuva glanced around, making sure that no one could overhear. "It's about Max."

Jasmina nodded. Tuva pushed her sunglasses to the tip of her nose and peered over them.

"I'm inclined to keep him on. If you don't object?"

Jasmina opened her mouth to reply, but Tuva hadn't finished.

"Of course he needs to apologise to you. If anything like that happens again, he'll be out on his ear. But I can't afford to lose another good reporter."

Jasmina thought about it for a couple of seconds. She didn't want to cause trouble. Her future at the paper was still up in the air. But what did Tuva mean by 'another'? Had someone else been fired?

"Sounds good."

"If you like, I can put you on different shifts so you don't have to see each other?"

Jasmina shook her head.

"No need for that."

Tuva seemed content with her response. Loyalty to the paper was everything. One way of demonstrating it was to always answer when the bosses called, whatever time of day or night it was and regardless of what plans you might have. Another was not talking about *Kvällspressen*'s internal issues.

"Great. So that's what we'll do. And if you have any ideas for articles that Bengt turns down, come to me."

9

BÖRJE TILTED HIS head upwards, looking up at the grey frontage and feeling the butterflies fluttering in his stomach.

He had never seen Nina, Eva's daughter, except in the photo that Eva always carried with her.

When he woke that morning, Eva had gone, and he was beside himself with worry. To avoid wasting time travelling between Tyresö and town, Börje hadn't gone back to Junibacken, but had instead spent the night in a stairwell in Södermalm.

How could someone he had only known for two years affect him like Eva did? That meeting with her, on a cold autumn evening in the Sky Bar, had changed his life.

Börje had two children. Sure, he loved them, but his love for them had always been complicated. Parents' evenings, picking them up, football training, putting them to bed. He had not been prepared to give up himself and his life for them.

Perhaps that was the difference? When he met Eva, he'd had nothing to sacrifice. Destitute and addicted. After his prison sentence, his family had turned their backs on him. He was without a home and refused to take help from the authorities. He had spent his days waiting for death, vodka in hand, in the Sky Bar. On Sundays, he would lie there shaking with withdrawal in some little woodland or stairwell.

Eva and Börje had raised each other up and loved each other violently, unconditionally and without distractions, because that love was all they'd had to give.

For the first time in his life, he was vulnerable. Scared. He knew that without Eva, he would disintegrate, fall down without being able to stand up again. He needed Eva not just for who she was, but for the person she made *him*.

If something had happened to Eva, an accident or an overdose that left her in hospital, Börje would never find out. They weren't married. In the eyes of the authorities, their love was non-existent. In Börje's world, however, it was the most important thing that had ever happened. He closed his eyes and tried to keep her safe with the power of his mind. At the same time, he knew what he had to do to get answers, and maybe to find Eva.

Börje studied his own face in the window next to the entrance. He usually avoided mirrors. It felt strange and unfamiliar to see himself dirty and unkempt. His complexion was yellowish; he looked ill. He stared at the reflection, wondered whether his kids and ex-wife would have recognised him. He wished that he'd been able to meet Nina under different circumstances. That she could forgive Eva or at least not hate her. At the same time, he did understand her, just as he could understand his own children.

With clumsy fingers, he pushed a couple of strands of hair into place. He straightened the collar on his careworn shirt, tried to scrape off the worst of the stains with his fingernails before dusting off his trouser legs. That would have to do. The important thing was to find out whether anyone had called Nina about Eva. At the same time, that was precisely what he was afraid of: that Nina had been told that her mother was dead.

Börje waited for someone to come out through the door, stepped inside and studied the list of names on the wall.

Nina lived on the third floor. Voices, television sets and laughter met him as he worked his way up the stairs. Sounds that you don't think about until you don't have anywhere to sleep. He closed his eyes and listened to children crying.

Please, let it be okay, he thought to himself. Outside Nina's door, he smoothed his hair one last time before he rang the bell. Maybe it was unfair to both Nina and Eva, turning up like this, but what could he do?

He could not stand the uncertainty any longer.

Börje heard footsteps. He stared straight into the peephole and tried to give an air of trustworthiness. The door opened and his heart skipped a beat. He hadn't expected Nina to be quite so like her mother.

"Yes?" she said suspiciously, letting her eyes wander over his ragged, dirty clothes.

"My name is Börje," he said, attempting a smile. "I am a friend of your mother's. The look on Nina's face changed from one of suspicion to one of rage.

"I haven't got a mother," she said.

The door had almost closed by the time Börje wedged his foot in the opening. "What the hell are you doing?" she hissed. "Get out of here, otherwise I'm calling the police."

"You have to listen to me, please, Nina," Börje pleaded. "Your mother has disappeared. I don't know where she is."

"When I was little, I often used to wonder where she was too," said Nina.

"I know she hasn't been a good mother. And so does she. But she's sorry; she has changed. She might not look like much, but she's the kindest person I know. Please. Help me."

Nina laughed sarcastically. She poked her head around the door and aimed her index finger at Börje.

"How can you say she's changed, when she's just disappeared without letting you know? I've had enough of her. Get out of here, now!"

She slammed the door.

The courtyard outside was empty. Börje sniffled, wiped away a tear and covered his mouth with his hand. If it had been Eva looking for him, his children would have reacted in the same way. The worst part was, he couldn't blame them.

Eva was the only person on earth that he hadn't let down, hurt, or deceived. She was the proof that he was still able to get some things right. She counted on him; she needed him. As long as she was still breathing, Börje still had a right to exist and his own place in the universe.

10

JASMINA JUMPED OUT of the cab outside the courthouse and hurried up its stone steps. Before she pushed open the door, she looked up at the pale blue sky. The weathermen had been talking about temperatures over twenty degrees. It looked like summer was properly getting underway with two days left until May.

The remand hearing was to be heard in Court 22.

Outside, journalists from *SVT*, *SR* and *Aftonposten* jostled with each other. A couple of female activists were there with homemade placards, one read *Woman-killer*, the other *Woman-hater*. Social media was boiling over. Even if the establishment media hadn't named Karim Laimani, Jasmina had read that there were both pictures and personal information on Facebook and *flashback.org*. A male professor of law had called for calm in an opinion piece, reminding them that no judgement had been passed. He immediately received death threats and was accused of cosying up to murderers and rapists.

The judge – who would single-handedly decide whether Karim Laimani should be remanded into custody – had to be aware of the pressure, Jasmina thought. That was only human.

If Laimani did end up on remand, then the tabloids at least would consider publishing his name and photo. While they would usually hold back until after a conviction, in this case there was forensic evidence and huge public interest – not least given the fact that Sweden was still in turmoil in the wake of #metoo. Jasmina was a strong opponent of exposing identities, especially before a conviction, but thankfully the difficult call was not hers to make. Whatever Tuva Algotsson and the other editors decided, they would be faced with criticism.

While Jasmina waited for the courtroom to be unlocked, she went over the conversation with Tuva in her head. Sure, meeting Max again would be nerve-wracking, but everyone deserves a second chance. Tuva had clearly demonstrated that she had noticed her.

There was a jangling from the doors and the journalists' scrum began to move. Jasmina was the last one in, and she sat down on a bench at the very back.

She felt nervous, because this was the first time she'd been present at a remand hearing in a murder case. Jasmina put her Dictaphone on her lap, pressed rec and opened her laptop.

The judge, a red-haired woman in her fifties, entered the room. The murmuring from the journalists died down immediately. Before she sat down in her seat, she reminded the spectators not to interrupt proceedings.

Jasmina felt the nerves and the tension rising. Another door opened and when she turned to look, the whole room started spinning. The Dictaphone fell to the floor with a crash. Jasmina hurried to pick it up.

The man entering the courtroom was the man who had raped her.

11

A DARK-RED FORD Scorpio slowed as it drove down Surbrunnsgatan. In the back seat, two blonde kids had their faces pressed to the glass as they glared at Vanessa.

Ove stepped out of the car and said something to the kids before coming towards Vanessa. Behind him, the boy and girl started bashing each other.

"Cute, eh? I forgot the leads, otherwise I could've walked them on the lawn," Ove said, pointing to the park across the road.

Vanessa grinned.

"I've got to get going soon. Liam's got football practice and Sara is doing a ballet performance."

"Your wife?"

"She's deserted. Temporarily, I hope. She's having a post-work drink with a friend."

"Deserted," Vanessa repeated. "At least you're not one of those men who calls his wife 'the government'?"

"Lenin," Ove said with a grin. "But that can be explained by the fact that her name is Lena. Here's the file of what I unearthed about the attempted rape."

The boy took off his seatbelt and threw himself onto the horn. Both Vanessa and Ove jumped.

"Ceasefire's broken down. I must get back to the front," said Ove.

Vanessa was left standing outside the entrance with the

folder under her arm. It was a nice afternoon. The sky was pale blue, and a surprisingly warm wind blew through the streets.

She decided she might as well treat herself to a coffee on an outdoor terrace.

Outside Café Nestro, she found an empty table and ordered a coffee. A young woman walked past, pushing a pushchair. Vanessa watched her pass. She swallowed. Probably a first-time mum. At the moment Vanessa had become a mother, everything else paled into insignificance. From that instant, she was a parent, above all. When Adeline died, there was no one to be a mother to. The screaming baby she had given birth to, shaped in her womb, nourished at her breast, was gone. Eliminated from the surface of the planet. The pain was still a physical one. Vanessa didn't even know where in Cuba she was buried, if she even was buried. She'd gone straight to the airport, bought a ticket for the first available flight to Europe, and gone home to Sweden. She had never told anyone, not even Svante. Maybe she should have told him. Perhaps then he wouldn't have persuaded her to have an abortion all those years later.

"Fuck you, Svante."

Vanessa pulled her sunglasses out of her blazer pocket, pushed them onto her nose and dived into the file.

The attempted rape in Rålambshov Park had taken place at around half-past two in the morning on the night of the 14th of May 2014. The victim's name was Klara Möller, a twenty-year-old medical student on her way home from a night out. The assailant had approached her from behind, put a knife to her throat and forced her into a bush. The detective had asked Klara Möller how she could be sure it was a matter of attempted rape.

Because he said so. He said: I'm going to fuck you like you've never been fucked, you stupid whore, she had explained.

She also described the man's build as slight, even if it was a guess that he was just under one hundred and eighty centimetres tall. He had bald patches on his head, small rectangular glasses and close-set eyes. She thought he was about twenty-five, and ethnically Swedish.

Vanessa took out the picture of the pen.

It was an ordinary ballpoint pen, with blue ink. *Rosersbergs Slottshotell*, read the letters on the shaft. Where had Emelie Rydén come across it? At the salon?

Vanessa was going to ask the technicians to go through the salon's appointment system, to see if anyone of the perpetrator's age had been there recently. She also decided that as soon as she had time, she was going to visit Rosersbergs and look for a connection to Emelie Rydén. That would have to be soon. If Karim Laimani was remanded, Mikael Kask would send her off to some little town to rescue the local detectives.

Vanessa put the papers back in the folder and asked for a refill.

12

THE JUDGE ORDERED Karim Laimani be remanded into custody, on suspicion of murdering Emelie Rydén. Jasmina gathered her stuff together and rushed out of the courtroom.

She ran down the stone-floored hallway and into the toilet, closed the cubicle door, fell to her knees and puked into the bowl.

Her body shaking, Jasmina closed the lid, flushed, and pulled out her phone.

She read *Kvällsposten*'s coverage of the murder. According to the police, Emelie Rydén's life had been taken at around midnight between the 20th and 21st of April.

"No," she whispered.

Jasmina shook her head. That was impossible. She had met Thomas – Karim, she corrected herself – at around eight that night. For the next few hours, he and the other two had raped her. Or had she got it wrong? Everything pointed to Karim having murdered Emelie Rydén. They had even found her blood under the shoe he was wearing while he was out on parole. Was she going mad? She rocked back and forth, trying to stop the mental images from the rape from getting stuck.

She tore open the door and was met by her own reflection, at the same time as one of the two female activists walked in. She glared at Jasmina.

"Are you a journalist?" she asked.

Jasmina nodded. The girl sneered.

"I don't get why you don't name that bastard. Cowardly

fucks. You let them get away with it. He'll get a couple of years in prison, at best. In the worst-case scenario, he'll be acquitted. What'll happen to the next woman who leaves him?"

Jasmina didn't respond. She tried to walk past the second woman, but she took a step to the side, blocking her path.

"As a woman, you should be ashamed. Next time it could be you or a friend who falls victim to a man like that."

Jasmina left the toilet and could feel the activist staring at her.

She headed for the exit, where disappointed muttering journalist colleagues had hung around in the hope of getting something to pad out their articles or TV segments with. Karim Laimani's lawyer did not want to make any comment. The prosecutor had also avoided the press pack.

Jasmina decided to walk back to the newsroom so she could sort out the chaos in her head. She had never hated another human being as violently as she hated Karim. She wanted to physically hurt him.

She was faced with a dilemma. If she kept quiet about the rape, there was a risk of a murderer going free. But if Karim Laimani was convicted of murder rather than rape, the sentence would be much harsher. With his record, he could be looking at life imprisonment. The chances of a conviction were also higher than with rape. Through her silence, Jasmina could get him away from society.

But the moral aspect? Could Jasmina allow a person – a disgusting person who absolutely deserved to be locked up – be convicted of a crime he hadn't committed? If she was the one to provide him with an alibi and Karim Laimani was later acquitted of the rape charges? Then released? And then he attacked another woman? Didn't Jasmina have a duty as a citizen, above all as a woman, to keep men like Karim Laimani as far away from society as possible?

13

TOM WAS STANDING on the corner of Rörstrandsgatan and Norrbackagatan, with a view of the entrance to Henrietta's block. On the way there, he'd bought new clothes at Dressmann. He was so pleased with them that he'd asked the shop assistant to cut the labels off, put on the new shirt and trousers and stuffed the old ones in the carrier bag.

In the two hours he'd found himself there, he'd been flung between hope and despair. He wondered whether her boyfriend was in there, and whether he took care of her. Whether he was kind. Caring. Would that spoil what Tom and Henrietta had built up at the hospital and on the enchanting taxi ride home through the Stockholm night? The next minute, Tom convinced himself that Henrietta was in love with him. That she was just waiting for him to ring the doorbell, to tear off her clothes and to submit to him.

Last Saturday they'd said goodbye outside the entrance. Tom had been quiet all the way from the hospital. He'd spent most of the journey looking out the window. He could not remember ever having been so happy – so close to another human being who was not treating him with contempt. Henrietta hadn't talked an awful lot, but she had offered to share a ride. Despite the journey being paid for by the hospital, the journey felt like a token of love.

Henrietta was his last hope. Ever since puberty, he had felt a desperate thirst to get close to a woman's sex. To be seen as worthy of entering it. He had never come close. No one had found him sufficiently attractive to spread their legs. Give themselves up. At the age of thirty-three, he was still a virgin.

The door opened and Henrietta struggled out. She was wearing light jeans, a white vest top, and she had her hair up in a bun.

Tom stifled the urge to rush over and offer to help. Henrietta put her crutches to the ground and hopped off in the direction of S:t Eriksgatan. Tom slowly followed. It was frustratingly slow. Several times he had to stop, force himself to stand still, to avoid catching up with her. On the wall ahead of him was a poster.

Love. Sisterhood. Music.

A male-free festival.

Eventually Tom couldn't stand it any more, and instead he began half-jogging across the street, ran for a hundred metres before switching pavements again so that he was walking straight towards Henrietta. Should he stare straight ahead, not look at her, so that she was the one who saw him first? If she didn't see him, or didn't bother to say hi, then everything would have been in vain. He would have to start again. With a dozen or so metres to go, Tom turned towards a shop window, and saw her profile in the reflection.

"Oh, look who it is!" said Henrietta.

Tom spun around, pretending not to have seen her until now.

"Are you going to buy anything?" Henrietta said, nodding towards the window. Tom hadn't noticed that it was a shop selling lingerie. Long-limbed mannequins in provocative get-up watched over the street with dead stares. He wanted the ground to swallow him up.

"How's your foot?" he mumbled.

"It hurts."

"Where are you going?"

She raised a crutch in the direction of Västermalm shopping mall.

"I'm meeting a friend for coffee, but I'm well early. It's

hard to know how long it's going to take to get anywhere on these things. How's your hand?"

Tom ran a finger over the bandages.

"Better. I'm off for a coffee too," said Tom. "I'm waiting for a colleague."

Henrietta smiled, seemingly unaware that he wanted to join her.

"Must get going," she said.

Tom was stricken with panic. Was she going to leave him now? What had he done wrong? They'd started out so well. Henrietta had stopped, said hi, made small talk. Been friendly.

"I'll join you until your friend turns up," he said.

Henrietta raised an eyebrow, pressed her lips together and nodded. "Okay."

In the café outside H&M in the mall, Tom bought two coffees. He had never drunk coffee anywhere other than at home, and he had no idea it could be so expensive. Sixty crowns, for two cups. He pulled out his chair, put the mugs on the table and sat down.

"Thanks."

Should he ask whether she was waiting for a man or a woman? No. He'd find out soon enough. He felt pleased that she still hadn't said anything about her boyfriend. That had to mean something. Perhaps that happy façade that she displayed on social media was just that. Tom had seen through it. He had understood that she was, in fact, deeply unhappy.

He peered in her direction.

Was he imagining it, or was she being a bit reserved? He quickly ran through what had happened since they met on the street. Apart from it having been a lingerie shop he'd been staring into, he hadn't done anything wrong.

Yet he felt paralysed. Incapable of finding a subject of conversation.

Tom took a sip of the tasteless coffee, which burnt his tongue. His eyes watered. "Hot," he said.

Henrietta glanced at her watch.

"Is it boring, sitting at home?" he asked.

"Yes."

"I'd be more than happy to keep you company. We could watch films? I could cook for you. Or we could order something, my treat. Do you like burgers?"

Time was running out. Soon the person she was waiting for would arrive and Tom did not know when they might get the chance to meet again. Henrietta turned her wrist once again to check the time. Tom could feel the desperation pulsating through him.

"Would you like that? Tonight, maybe?"

"I've got plans."

Tom moistened his lips.

"What kind of pl… tomorrow?"

Henrietta looked up, and Tom turned his head. Behind him was a brown-haired woman, about Henrietta's age. Chubby. Fat thighs packed in denim. The relief washed over him. It wasn't Douglas or some other man. Besides, it was hardly surprising that she couldn't meet up with Tom at such short notice. As her friend reached over to hug Henrietta, he pushed the shortcut to start recording on his mobile, got to his feet and put the phone in the bag of clothes.

He introduced himself.

"Julia," the friend said as she shook his hand.

"Could you keep an eye on my stuff while I nip to the loo?" said Tom.

They nodded and Julia sat herself down on Tom's empty chair. While he looked for the toilet, he wondered whether they would ask him to stay. He hoped so. He washed his hands, avoiding, as always, his own reflection in the mirror, then opened the door and returned to the table.

Tom went and stood next to them, waiting for one of them to suggest he grab a chair and join them. Nothing happened. Just a thick silence. He grasped the bag. Waited another second.

"Bye then," he mumbled, turned around, and left.

14

JASMINA WAS STILL in the newsroom, despite long-since having finished the three-thousand-word article about the prosecutor's decision to remand Karim Laimani on suspicion of having murdered his ex-girlfriend Emelie Rydén.

She felt restless and was struggling to concentrate.

Jasmina's hatred of Karim Laimani was in direct conflict with her ethics and her task as a journalist. She was supposed to seek the truth. And the truth was that Karim Laimani was guilty of rape, which therefore meant it was impossible for him to have murdered Emelie, since the crimes occurred at the same time.

She could not withhold information from the police, and in so doing let Emelie's murderer go free. If, however, she gave Karim Laimani an alibi, then the story of the rape would unavoidably come out. She would have 'rape' stamped on her forehead for the rest of her life. But perhaps there was another way?

She pulled out her phone and wrote a message to Hans Hoffman, asking where he was.

At my local, came the immediate reply. Jasmina packed the spare computer into the temporary cover she'd been given and left the newsroom.

Hans Hoffman's local, Little Bollywood, turned out to be an Indian restaurant in Fredhäll, a couple of hundred metres from *Kvällspressen*'s newsroom. The place was empty.

Hoffman was sitting at a table near the entrance, reading *Aftonposten* and drinking a bottle of Singha.

"Hungry?" he asked.

"No, thanks," Jasmina said as she placed the laptop case on the empty chair next to her. "Do you live round here?"

Hoffman raised a finger and pointed up at the ceiling.

"Third floor."

Jasmina recalled a conversation she'd overheard in one of her first weeks with the paper. An editor had complained that Hoffman wasn't answering his mobile. One of the bosses had asked the editor to ring the head waiter at 'The Indian' and try and reach him there. Fifteen minutes later, Hoffman had ambled into the newsroom.

"Is the food good here?" Jasmina asked, mainly to fill the silence.

"Not really. But it's better than the microwave meals I used to eat in the early years after my divorce."

"I'm sorry."

"You needn't be. My wife is a paramedic; she saved some man's life after a road accident. Married him a year later. They're happy. The kind of story you'd think was nice, if it wasn't about you."

Jasmina knew that Hoffman, who had previously been one of the paper's star reporters, had had to leave *Kvällspressen* for a time. Now she realised that it had probably had to do with the divorce. And his alcohol consumption, which probably correlated with the break-up. He had later returned to cover evenings and weekends.

Hoffman tore a bit of the label off his bottle.

"Don't feel sorry for me, Jasmina. Life changes. I used to sit in the bars around Stureplan. Riche, Teatergrillen, Sturehof, Prinsen. Now I'm sitting here. People who used to say hello, lick my arse, want to have dinner, now pretend not to see me. I call and they never call back. No one wants to employ me. I kill time here, and that's okay. You learn to live with that too. So tell me why you're here instead?"

"I need your help. If you've got time, and you want to?"

Hoffman raised his bottle, which Jasmina took as a yes.

"You've got the best police sources on the paper, and I want to know which detectives are on the Karim Laimani case."

He scratched his stubble. "Why?"

"Bit of research, that's all."

"Don't they teach you how to lie at journalism college any more?"

Jasmina opened her mouth to reply but fell silent when Hoffman raised his hands towards her, laughing.

"I'll sort it, kiddo. Off you pop for now. I'll call you later."

15

TOM WAS LYING on the living room floor. The apartment was in thick darkness. The motorway hummed. The rats squeaked and ran across the floor on their sharp claws over in the study. He felt around for his phone. Pressed play. Why was he tormenting himself – he'd heard the conversation at least twenty times, knew it off by heart.

Who was that?

Just some guy. I met him at the hospital.

He's a creep. I promise. I saw that straight away. And his halitosis!

Julia gurgled, made a vomiting sound. Henrietta giggled.

I know. I'll steer clear, but he seemed kind. Lonely.

Stop it, Henri, he was nasty. And did you see his clothes? What the fuck was he wearing? You've got to be clearer with the likes of him. Otherwise you're going to get fished out of the harbour and put in a body bag.

Henrietta and Julia started talking about Douglas, and Tom switched it off.

Women were disgusting. Tom had done nothing wrong, but they only cared about looks. And money. Tom would never get anywhere near a woman's sex, would never be seen as fit to spread his seed, to reproduce.

He got to his feet and tore off his new clothes. He kicked them under the sofa. He didn't want to look at them, to be reminded. He was ashamed. How could he have convinced himself that Henrietta was interested in him? She was just like all the others.

Tom hobbled into the bathroom and turned on the light. He started tearing at the bandage, felt trapped in his own body. He screamed. He stared into his repugnant, ugly face and roared. He clenched his injured fist and whacked the mirror. An explosion of pain. Blood pouring down his arm. He ought to go round to her flat and humiliate her.

Tom slumped down onto the bathroom floor and buried his head in his hands. He was sobbing. Gasping. The meeting with Henrietta, the sudden fantasies of a life without loneliness as its defining trait, had changed nothing. He was amputated from the body of society forever. An appendix, not necessary.

16

A WHITE FAN, placed in one corner of the room, was working flat out.

Ivan Tomic got to his feet when Nicolas appeared in the doorway. He was wearing white tracksuit bottoms and a grey shirt. On his feet, Adidas sandals. His head was shaved, the scars on his scalp clearly visible. Dark tattoos climbed above his round collar, covering his thick neck.

Ivan had a bruise on his forehead. He pushed his index finger against it. "Handbags. About an egg. Some bloke thought I'd pinched his."

"Had you?"

Ivan smirked. Then nodded.

The last time they'd met, Nicolas had violently forced him to reveal The Legion's plan to strike the safe house in which Melina Davidson, wife of one of the kidnapped financiers, was being protected by police. Ivan had deliberately waited. Until it was too late. When Nicolas and Vanessa did get there, Melina was already dead.

"What do you want?" Nicolas asked and pulled out a chair to sit down. Ivan took his time. Sat down and stared at Nicolas.

"To say sorry."

"I can never forgive you."

"The junk made me forget what was important. I let my best friend down. Jeez, you've only ever protected me. Tried to put me on the right track." Ivan looked down at his hands, which were now interlaced on the tabletop. "I'm clean now, never going to touch that shit again. Prison changes you. You get me? You have time to think. About growing up, childhood, shit like that."

Nicolas considered getting up and leaving. Coming here had been a mistake. What's done is done. Even if Ivan had changed, Nicolas didn't want him in his life. Too much had happened.

"Dad's dead. Cancer. Of the pancreas."

Nicolas pictured Ivan's father Milos in front of him. The man was authoritarian. Nasty. Beat Ivan black and blue, forever screaming and wailing. A man from another generation. Not unlike Eduardo Paredes.

"I'm sorry for your loss."

"He always liked you. I think he wished you were his son. Good at school, well-liked. You know, everything I never was."

"Did you get to see each other before... he died?"

Ivan's mouth was smiling, but his eyes were mournful. He shook his head.

"He wrote to me when he got sick, saying that he didn't want me at his funeral and that I was his biggest mistake. The bane of his life. You're my first visitor. No, second." Ivan rested his elbow on the table and ran his hand over his shaved scalp.

Nicolas was curious. Ivan had no friends. Never had done. At school, Ivan had been called 'Nicolas' puppy'. For a second he thought that it was Maria that Ivan had managed to trick into coming.

"Who came to visit you?"

"Just a bloke I got to know in here. Eyup. When he got out, he stabbed his girlfriend to death. But he was freed, lack of evidence."

Nicolas felt his irritation increasing. A murderer. Of course. Ivan couldn't change. High or not. In his desperate search for respect and belonging, he would make common cause with anyone. Men who killed women, gangsters, rapists.

"And you? How are you?" Ivan asked.

"I can take care of myself."

The fan whirred, doing its best to stir the stale air into motion.

"I know. I was just trying to be sociable."

Nicolas pushed his chair back.

"This is the last time we'll see each other. I just needed closure. Don't ever contact me again."

17

LORRY AFTER LORRY passed by, causing the concrete bridge to vibrate. Eva clung onto the railing and watched them pass. As a girl, she had dreamt of becoming a lorry driver. There was something about the size of the chassis that felt safe – if you were the biggest, no one could hurt you. Following the road, out into Europe and the world.

Eva let go of the railing and carried on.

After having left Börje two days before, she had laid low and slept in places where he wouldn't look. She had avoided all the places she usually ended up when she had a relapse.

Ahead, the forest towered above her. Even if she couldn't see through the trees, she knew that Lake Insjön was glittering behind them. *Like a window into the earth*, as poet Tomas Tranströmer once wrote. Eva loved poems. She had attempted to write a couple herself, but they ended up being pompous and silly. She had never shown them to anyone, not even Börje.

Beneath her feet, the tarmac turned to soil. It smelled of damp and leaves. Rays of sunshine picked their way through the canopy. The rumble of heavy traffic grew increasingly distant, until in the end it was just a whisper.

The lake was smaller than Eva remembered it. It was often like that. Things that felt impressive and vast to a child shrunk and became manageable.

She found a recess in the rocks, sank down and let herself be immersed.

When had she come here for the first time? It must've been 1980, when she was eleven, and her stepfather Kjell had raped her.

After several hours' hiking, she thought she'd reached the sea, and that it was Finland on the far side. She'd eaten up her meagre supplies and read *The Brothers Lionheart* by the light of the torch she'd got for her birthday.

The next morning, an elderly couple had spotted her, asked where her parents were and taken her with them to the police station.

Kjell picked her up, hugged her and thanked the police for their hard work in getting his beloved stepdaughter home. On the way home, he pulled off the road into a deserted car park, threw her into the back seat and raped her again.

Eva pushed a lock of hair off her face and stared out across the lake. Why was she remembering the hard stuff, the stuff that had brought her here?

She ought to be remembering all the good things, things that had kept her away from here.

Nina being born, the first six years of her daughter's life, when Eva was still coping. When she stayed off the streets, away from the pimps and the punters. Poor, difficult years. But she'd made sure that Nina was clean and respectable. Had a job in a supermarket. Read Astrid Lindgren stories and played. Then she got the sack and could see no way out other than to start working the streets again.

She preferred to get down on her knees in front of clients than in front of the authorities. At least the men who bought sex weren't making any bones about what they wanted.

In the years that followed, she started using heroin, injecting what she could to numb the pain. Nina was taken away from her. The void in her chest grew bigger and bigger, the darkness darker still. Men who hit her, told her how worthless she was, the filthy flats, the STDs.

In the end, she was just waiting for death. She had come close a few times. Overdosed, been beaten unconscious, raped in stairwells by other junkies or dealers. But she had always survived, scraped by.

And then she'd met Börje in the Sky Bar.

She immediately noticed how clumsy and awkward he became in her presence. He was so unlike all the men she'd met before. He never expected anything from her, never told her what she *should* be like. She dared to laugh without hiding her mouth, never even thought about it. He could make her laugh at the misery so much that on one occasion she had wet herself. Even then, she had not felt ashamed. Instead, they had waded out naked into the water in front of Junibacken, then floated around on their backs, looking at the stars.

Deep down, she had always known that the time with Börje was borrowed time. The relapses became more frequent, dragging Börje down. She could not keep hurting him. He wouldn't have the strength to carry her forever. If he was ever going to get back on his feet, then Eva was going to have to die.

Eva pulled out the syringe and put it on the stone next to her, along with her lighter. She hoped that someone would find her soon, so that Börje didn't have to wonder, so that her body didn't deteriorate too much.

In her bag were the three farewell letters she had written. One to Börje, one to Nina and one to the grandchild she would never meet. She prepared the needle, located a vein in her arm and shot up, reciting her favourite poem, by Yvonne Domeij, as she did so.

The poem was for her dead son, Torbjörn. Once he was buried, Yvonne became obsessed with checking the weather. Not for her own sake, but for her son's.

I walk the beach collecting stones and seashells I plan to give to you. You're welcome to laugh if you like, but that is all I can give you.

In poverty there is no beauty, let alone love. You're welcome to laugh if you like, but I love you nonetheless.

Eva thought to herself that Börje would probably keep an eye on the weather, for her sake.

PART IV

I don't regard women as people. All they are, or should be, is slaves for men. Cooking, cleaning and spreading their legs when they're told.

An anonymous man.

1

FORTY-TWO-YEAR-OLD OSCAR SJÖLANDER was walking with his wife Therese on his arm, up the red carpet that led into the sponsors' room. After being stopped by photographers from both the tabloids and a gossip mag, he thanked them and found a standing-height table close to the buffet.

Around three dozen specially invited guests were on the premises.

People, young and old, men and women, formed a steady stream of those wanting to take selfies. He agreed to all of them with a smile. Therese kept up appearances. She knew it was part of his job.

She picked up two wine glasses and waited obediently a little way away.

"I still think it's unsettling," Therese whispered when they found themselves alone.

"Kids imagine things. You know that." Oscar nodded at a passing colleague.

"Josephine doesn't usually lie."

He pictured their five-year-old daughter. Her angelic face, ruffled blonde hair and the little nose that creased with laughter when he 'made things disappear'.

"She was dreaming then. We live in Bromma, not Baghdad. Why would anyone break in and then not take anything? Just stand there looking at her?"

"I don't know," said Therese. "But I'm going home after

the broadcast." She went quiet and looked across at him. Oscar knew she was waiting for confirmation that he would go with her. He wasn't about to give it to her. Didn't want to promise that. Who knew where this night might end up?

A female dancer walked past them, her body tightly wrapped in a short lace dress, her beautiful, tanned legs wrapped in shimmering nylon. She swung her hips invitingly.

Hadn't she sucked him off at a Christmas do a few years earlier? What was her name? Mikaela? Misha?

An hour to go until broadcast. These days, he hated this kind of event. He was perfectly uninterested in seeing half a dozen sun-drenched, desperate B-list celebrities trying to dance. Pathetic. But then a PR girl at his channel had called and asked him to go along and sit in the crowd. Besides, Therese liked the show.

Oscar was from Växjö, and he'd started his career as a sports reporter on TV4. Worked day and night. Covered the football World Cup, the ice hockey world championships, handball and then finally the Olympics. He progressed to becoming a sports anchor.

He was young, popular, and good-looking. Women loved him. The channel's management spotted his potential and moved him away from sports. He did a few years on the breakfast sofa, got to take over a Friday evening light entertainment show, and was then honoured with a talk show of his own.

Oscar won Male TV Presenter of the Year, was named the 'celebrity Swedes would most like to live next door to' and was voted the man most Swedish women would like to have an affair with.

He'd met Therese twelve years earlier. In a bar. She was blonde, with a beautiful, contagious smile. They'd gone home together and got married a year later. She worked as a nurse back then, but now she was the one who took care of his accounts, booked appearances and interviews. In between that, she looked after their children.

Someone tapped him on the shoulder. Shit. Rakel. Holding a can of Coke in her hand.

"Hi, Oscar."

His palms started sweating and Oscar wiped them discreetly on his trousers. How did she have the nerve to show up here? She was mad.

Therese beat Oscar to it, stretched out her hand and introduced herself.

"We're colleagues," said Rakel. "Oscar and I worked together on the production of his talk show a couple of years back."

Rakel made him feel young. Younger, at least. Recently, he'd been wondering whether he was falling in love with her. He never missed a chance to see her. Couldn't get enough.

"Oh great." Therese smiled coolly at Rakel.

Oscar knew that she hated him working with younger women. She saw them, correctly, as a threat. She knew he had problems resisting temptation. Oscar had noticed a correlation between the intensity of Therese's workouts and whether or not he was involved in a production with a lot of young women at the time. It was sad. Sure, he felt sorry for Therese, but he couldn't help it.

The truth was that if Oscar had had time, he could've been bedding young production assistants all day long. After #metoo, though, the rules had changed. He had come alarmingly close to getting sacked. In the industry, talk of his extramarital affairs and conquests had been rife for years. Not only that. A thread on *flashback.org* accused him of assaulting Therese.

What had been gossip before #metoo was now, with the tabloids beginning to abandon fact-checking and publishing names all over the place, something more, and his employer's whole attitude had changed completely. Sensationalist reporters had called both him and Therese to ask uncomfortable, insinuating questions.

Yes, he'd assaulted her. Three times it had gone black.

Overflowed. But he wasn't a wicked person. He even voted for Feminist Initiative and had joined their May Day parade the other year.

Once though, drunk, he had gone way too far. They'd been arguing, and he'd punched Therese and made her black out. He drove her to hospital, terrified that he'd killed her.

She had of course lied, protected him, said that she'd fallen down the stairs. And he was so ashamed afterwards, promised her that it would never happen again.

At the time #metoo was breaking, he had spent hours calling various women who had reasons to talk to the papers. Some he had pleaded with, others he had screamed at and threatened. It worked. With the exception of a little article in the industry organ – about an anonymous TV4 presenter who was said to have exploited his position in order to sleep with younger women – he got away with it.

"Lovely to meet you," Therese said to Rakel, then turned to Oscar. "Shall we go and find our seats, darling?"

2

VANESSA GOT OUT of the car, and she looked over at Rosersbergs Slotts Hotel. The frontage was illuminated by floodlights, while flickering lanterns lined a path through the gravel. Judging by the sound, there was some kind of party going on. Probably a works do, where people were getting too drunk, being unfaithful, getting into fights and generally embarrassing themselves. The gravel crunched gratifyingly underfoot.

Vanessa wanted to find out how the pen that Ove Dahlberg had called about, with the fingerprint matching the five-year-old attempted rape in Rålambshov Park, had ended up in Emelie's jacket. She hadn't managed to get away before now, because she'd been busy with a shooting in Linköping.

Her boss, Mikael Kask, had called to explain that she was going to be sent to Halmstad next week to assist her colleagues there with inquiries into a two-year-old murder in a hair salon.

Vanessa could have rung, but then the receptionist would have had to make a call to check her identity. And – according to Vanessa's previous experience – become less inclined to be helpful.

She pushed open the door and stepped into a large hall, illuminated by candelabras. A narrow, green carpet led to a reception desk from behind which a woman in a black blazer was smiling at Vanessa.

"Good evening," said the woman. "Do you have a reservation?"

Vanessa held up her police badge. The smile disappeared.

"I need your help," said Vanessa, moving her focus to the woman's name badge on her lapel. Charlotta. "Have you had a guest here by the name of Emelie Rydén?"

"I don't know if I..."

On the desk was a bowl full of pens identical to the one that had been found at Emelie's.

"Well, as you can see, I'm a police officer."

The woman glanced at her ID once more, then moved her hands to the keyboard and started typing with her index fingers. Vanessa remembered how her father used to handle typewriters in the same way.

"No, no Emelie Rydén," Charlotta said eventually.

A side door opened. Two men stumbled in. Their noisy laughter echoed between the stone walls before they disappeared up the stairs.

"Conference guests?" Vanessa asked.

"Yes."

Vanessa picked a pen out of the bowl and spun it around. Someone, with a connection to Emelie, had stood exactly where she was standing now. Picked up a pen, taken it with them. Perhaps even talked to the same receptionist.

"I need a list of the companies that have been here over the past six months. Christmas dos, conferences. Everything."

Charlotta's eyes widened.

"Now?"

"If possible."

"It could take a while to collate. Our system..."

"Could you have it ready by tomorrow?" Vanessa interrupted.

Vanessa parked in her usual place in the garage under Norra Real. It was a warm evening; she hung her coat over her arm and opened the door.

From the school playground came the sound of voices

and bouncing balls. A few youngsters playing basketball and drinking beer. How old could they be? Sixteen? Seventeen? Vanessa hung back. She listened to the laughter, the hoarse, happy voices drowned out every now and then by a taxi or a bus rushing by.

As she walked home, she was filled with the familiar nagging loneliness that had been her companion since she lost Adeline. When Adeline was just a couple of months old, she had fallen ill. Vanessa took her to hospital, where the doctors declared that she had been infected by a bacteria that was impossible to treat. All they could do was manage her pain while she wasted away. Adeline drew her last breath with Vanessa at her side.

What stopped Vanessa from jumping off a bridge? Or, like just now, when she'd been driving on the motorway, just veering into the path of an oncoming truck? Vanessa didn't know. She didn't much like being alive. The people she had cared about were gone. Adeline. Natasha. She didn't include Svante amongst those she had loved, and she found it sad that she had never truly loved the man she had spent more than a decade with.

And now? All she had left was her job. And the question was whether she actually really cared about the murder victims whose final hours of life she was attempting to cast some light on. Or was it more about herself? That she didn't want to be outwitted by a suspect. Punish those who played God, who caused pain and suffering. Bring order. Gain control.

She thought about Nicolas, and how, sadly enough, he was the closest thing she'd had to a friend in the past few years. She missed him. For the first time in a long time, Vanessa felt like drinking. Not a few glasses, but proper drinking. Numb the body. Lose control. Die a little. She pulled out her other phone, the one she'd used with her informants during her time at Nova, and dialled the number she'd got from Nicolas when he was at her place.

3

FORMER REALITY TV star Paso Doble danced across the shiny studio floor with a beautiful brunette. Oscar Sjölander stifled a yawn while trying to spot Rakel in the audience on the other side.

The reality star froze to ice with the dancer in his arms, and the next second rapturous applause broke out. Behind him, one man was wolf-whistling so loudly that Oscar's ears were ringing. Paso Doble reached towards the heavens, displaying his phosphorous-white teeth.

The audience stood up and cheered. Oscar applauded mechanically and could feel his phone vibrating in his pocket. He realised it was Rakel, and glanced at Therese, who was waiting on tenterhooks for the jury's verdict.

See you later?

Oscar thought about it. He was going to take their oldest daughter Laura to a tournament at eleven tomorrow morning. After that, the whole family were going to spend Saturday evening in their summer cottage. He didn't like deceiving Therese, but any man in his shoes would have done the same. Anyone who claimed differently was gay or didn't understand what these women would do to shag a celeb. Oscar was a realist, had no illusions. Sure, he was good-looking, hadn't had problems attracting women even before he became a presenter, but clearly celebrity had multiplied his attractiveness by a factor of thousands. There was something special about Rakel. She wasn't like the others.

It was more than just sex.

Recently, he had often wondered what life would be like with her, if he were to leave Therese. He loved his wife and his daughters, but he needed this too. For now, this was enough – meeting Rakel in a hotel room or her little apartment. Drink wine, fuck, do a line of coke, talk about stuff he and Therese didn't talk about any more.

But what about in a month's time? Six? Divorce had become the norm. The kids would suffer more from being in a broken marriage. He wouldn't be absent; he'd still take them to football practice, parties and museums, just like before.

"Darling," he whispered, lovingly stroking Therese's thigh. "I'm heading out to the cottage when this is over. The heating's been playing up again. I'll drop you home first though."

An hour later, he picked Rakel up from Frihamnen, where she'd hung around the VIP area while he dropped Therese in Bromma.

Some of the crowd were still there, waiting for transport. Taxis shuttled back and forth, and he parked his Mercedes SUV a little way from the studio to avoid unwanted attention.

Rakel opened the passenger door and sat in the seat where his wife had been sitting fifteen minutes earlier. She leaned over and pushed her mint-scented tongue into his mouth and swirled it around.

"Drive now," she said, connecting her phone to the car's Bluetooth. "I'll put our playlist on."

They left the cranes and containers of Frihamnen behind them to the tones of Ron Sexsmith's 'In a Flash'. Rakel babbled on, telling him about how one of the male dancers had tried it on with her during an interval. Oscar laughed. He didn't understand men who got jealous. He used to think it would be weird if no one wanted to sleep with his woman. Rakel was a fantastic storyteller. Apart from the obvious – her amazing looks – it was probably the one thing he'd noticed when working with her.

She hadn't been as straightforward as the other girls on the production. Not given him the same appreciative looks and slightly submissive behaviour. On the contrary. She had been fearless, joked harshly with him and given him digs. Got him to laugh at himself.

Right from the start, Rakel had been clear that she wasn't looking for anything serious. 'The celebrity shag', she had jokingly called him, and she'd hooked up with him in hotel rooms after his pub crawls. For once, Oscar had been the one nagging and pestering. Eventually he had reluctantly accepted that he was probably in love with her, even if he would never admit it, for fear of losing her. Over the last few months, she had softened. Sometimes she could treat him with something approaching tenderness. Sure, she still joked with him, about how vain he was, his pedantic way of dressing, but behind the happy tone, he suspected that she too was starting to see their relationship as something more than just sex.

"Hungry?" he asked.

"Fucking starving."

"McDonald's," they chorused, laughing.

Life with Rakel was uncomplicated. Ron Sexsmith. Takeaways. Pub stories. Alcohol. A line or two of coke. He knew he wasn't being fair to Therese, that their life had also been like that once, but that they now had two kids, which was why they had other things to talk about. The girls. The parents' evenings. The school run. Schedules.

Just before Tyresö, Oscar swung off towards the hamburger chain.

As always, they chose the drive-through – partly because they didn't want to be seen together, but mostly because they liked eating in peace and quiet at the summer house.

Rakel lit some candles while Oscar unpacked the food. The calm was a godsend. Not having to deal with the kids' rain gear. Or sending them off to the bathroom to wash their hands and telling them not to play with the food. After they'd eaten, they took a bottle of wine, two glasses and headed for the outdoor jacuzzi. Steam rose from the water, climbing towards the clear night sky. Rakel's naked, trim body lured him towards the illuminated surface of the water.

Oscar thought about the rough sleepers. The bastards who'd built a shack just two hundred metres from his summer cottage, littered, drunk and done drugs around his kids. Right now, he didn't even hate them.

He looked at Rakel, who was resting her head on the edge of the tub, as she closed her eyes and enjoyed the bubbles. Would he choose her over his family? The thought was tempting; he wouldn't have to sneak around any more. He wasn't a bad man. He would pay Therese proper maintenance and let her keep the house. No one would want for anything. For Oscar, seeing the girls every other weekend was enough. He could take them on outings and trips in the holidays. He could move in with Rakel, to an apartment in town, maybe persuade her that they should have an open relationship. Do things right, from the start this time so that he wouldn't have to go around with his guilty conscience holding him back.

You only got one life, and he wanted to get as much out of his as possible. As a young, spotty sports reporter on *Smålandsposten*, he could never have dreamed of the position he had today. He had struggled, slogged, elbowed his way forward.

He noticed that Rakel hadn't drunk any of the wine, and he reached for the glass and placed it in her hand.

She put it down on the edge of the tub.

"There's something I need to talk to you about," she said.

She looked pained, almost nervous. She cupped her hand, filled it with water and splashed it on her face.

"Don't go having a heart attack and dying on me now, but I'm pregnant."

4

VANESSA FELT LIKE a teenager as she stuffed two bottles of whisky into the pockets of her coat and rushed down to the waiting taxi. They proceeded down Karlavägen. At Karlaplan, the driver turned right onto Narvavägen.

It was in these wealthy, auspicious neighbourhoods that she had grown up. A feeling of being an outsider was deep-rooted in Vanessa, never left her, regardless of circumstance. It was only at certain times, with people who were themselves outsiders, that she could feel a sense of belonging. Perhaps that was why she felt kinship with Nicolas? The guy from the mean estate who had been sent to the elite school against his will. His own relationship with his father was at least as problematic as hers.

The taxi bounced its way up Djurgårds Bridge, waking Vanessa from her thoughts. The driver slowed outside the enormous stone frontage of the Nordic Museum. She walked slowly across the lawn behind Josefina's, the outdoor restaurant, sat down on a bench and waited.

Twenty minutes later, Nicolas arrived. He sat down alongside her without much of a greeting. He had more of a beard than the last time they met, which she quickly decided was a good look for him. He was wearing a black bomber jacket, grey hoody and black jeans.

Along the quay on the other side of the bay, car headlights edged forward. Somewhere out there was the sound of a boat engine whirring.

Vanessa handed over one of the bottles of whisky. Nicolas lifted it into the light of the street lamp, unscrewed the top and put it to his lips. He raised his hand and pointed to the right, towards Strandvägen.

"In high school, my little sister Monica went out with a guy who lived there. She caught him getting off with someone else. Every day for a week, we came down here and threw eggs at his window."

Two ducks walked up from the water's edge, shook the water from their feathers and waddled off towards a bush. Vanessa took a sip of whisky.

"Then there was the time Monica didn't dare dump some boyfriend of hers. She went quiet for a week, wandered around worrying about it. Eventually, I managed to get out of her what it was that was bothering her. Our voices sound alike, so in the end, I rang and pretended to be her. Afterwards we carried on like that. We'd call and dump people on each other's behalf."

Nicolas raised his bottle. Vanessa did the same. They chinked.

"Great. Here's to you."

"Cheers."

They tipped their heads back and drank in unison.

"I feel like drinking myself back to the Neanderthal stage," said Vanessa.

"Why?"

She shrugged.

"Maybe because it's Adeline's birthday. Maybe it's just the time of year. Everyone around me is getting themselves ready for the summer, planning trips, time off with the kids. I don't have any of that. Shit – I've got millions in the bank and no one to go on holiday with."

"That sounds sad."

She never talked about Adeline. There was something about Nicolas, though, that made her take her guard down. Did she want to explain why she was sometimes so difficult to be around?

"Being a parent means you can die twice over. When Adeline died, so did I. Do you understand? I'm dead, even though I'm breathing. That's why…"

Her voice died away. Vanessa took a healthy slurp. She could feel the spirit warming her throat and her stomach.

"Adeline is buried in Cuba. My adopted daughter – or whatever you'd call Natasha – is in Syria. I will probably never see either of them again. Why do we spend so much time thinking about the people who are gone instead of the people we have around us?"

Nicolas pondered that for a while.

"It's only when they go that we take stock, and we see who they really were. When we write their bottom line, we take the time to understand them. To judge them. Or free them. That's when we can finally say, 'he was like this, she was like that.' Things are much simpler that way. You know, you can never be proved wrong."

"Your mum?"

"What about her?"

"You've talked about your dad, but never a word about your mum. Wasn't she important to you?"

Vanessa felt the booze numbing her tongue and making her slur.

"It hurts too much to talk about it. It's like I carry her death around with me, on my back, the whole time. A bit like Adeline's for you."

It felt strange to hear someone else uttering her daughter's name. "It's not…"

He realised he had upset her. He held up his palm apologetically. "The same. No, it is not."

They went quiet. Stared out over the dark waters and illuminated city.

Vanessa felt that she was dangerously close to crossing that line. She liked the feeling of being thin-skinned that she got around Nicolas. How she revealed herself, peeling off one layer at a time. Around others, she wanted to be invincible, regarded every word as a potential ambush – but with Nicolas, it was so obvious that he did not wish her any ill.

She stretched out her hand, clasped his and held it. He looked at her in surprise. What would he say if she asked him to go back to her place?

Glancing over at him, she could see he was distracted, and she knew him well enough to know that something was weighing on his mind.

"What is it, Nicolas?"

"That job in London I was talking about. I took it."

Vanessa withdrew her hand. She tried to digest the fact that he was going to disappear. London was only a matter of hours away, but now that he was finally back in her life, it was too far. It was best for Nicolas though. He was more than ten years younger than her.

"Congratulations," she said flatly.

"I survived the shooting in the pizzeria by a hair's breadth. Your colleagues are going to find me sooner or later and understand my role in the kidnappings. And if they do, they'll see the connection to you."

"So this is farewell?"

"I'm leaving next weekend." He looked her straight in the eye, smiled, and tipped his head to one side. "Can you check in on Celine every now and then? She needs a friend."

Who doesn't? Vanessa thought bitterly. She pressed her lips together, not wanting to reveal how much he'd hurt her. She stood up.

"See you," she said, and started walking towards Djurgårds Bridge.

5

RAKEL SJÖDIN LAY in bed as the sound of the engine disappeared. She closed her eyes. Revelled in the solitude. As usual, she wanted to wait a while before calling the taxi. The silence out here was almost exotic for her, city child that she was.

There was something forbidden and titillating about being alone in another family's home. If it did really end up being her and Oscar, she was going to spend as much time as possible in the summer place. Before they met, she'd dreamt of a big apartment in town, but for a while now her internet property searches had been for houses.

She rolled onto her side and stared up at the beautiful beams in the ceiling.

I. Am. Pregnant. After saying those three terrifying, wonderful words to Oscar yesterday, she had closed her eyes. Worried about how he would react. And boy had he looked shocked. If he asked her to have an abortion, she would. She wasn't a psycho. The type of girls you see on telly who hold onto the baby to keep the father in their life. She wasn't about to bring a child into the world against someone's wishes. That wouldn't be good for anyone. Least of all the child. Or Rakel's career.

She put her sockless feet onto the white wooden floor. Stood up. She could feel Oscar's sperm running down the inside of her thighs. Maybe she was imagining it, but when he rolled her over as usual this morning, started running his hands over those parts of her body that made her wet and then fucked her, it had been different. In some strange way, he'd felt more serious. Rakel liked that. Not to say that she hadn't liked the other ways too. But this was... different.

Rakel passed the large window next to the bedroom door. She stopped. Turned side-on. You couldn't see she was carrying a child. Not yet. She had the same neat figure and flat tummy. No, it wasn't a *mombod*. Things were going to change though; she had to be prepared for that. But she wasn't going to become one of those mums who only talks about their kid, who after a few hours on the maternity ward were no longer able to conduct themselves in polite society. Who were nothing but *mum*. Sacrificed their entire identity. That was the most depressing thing she could think of.

Rakel walked out into the kitchen-living room. There was a strong smell of freshly brewed coffee. She grabbed a cup and filled it. Pulled on Oscar's Ralph Lauren dressing gown that he'd hung out for her and sat down on the sofa, then put her legs up on the coffee table.

She wasn't going to end up like Oscar's wife. Rakel did feel sorry for Therese. And for his daughters, who were now going to have to go through that. Rakel was herself a child of divorce and knew what a difficult adjustment it was. She promised herself to always be kind to Oscar's daughters, to treat them just as well as the child growing inside her.

She thought about getting her phone out to call Katja. Her friend knew that Rakel was going to tell Oscar and would surely be wondering how it went.

Rakel yawned. That could wait. She'd call from the taxi on her way into town instead. Suggest going for a coffee by Nytorget. She was looking forward to telling Katja, who had been against their relationship.

With tightly pressed lips, Rakel had clicked through to the discussion thread about Oscar on *flashback.org*. Wife-beater, they called him. Rakel shook her head. She would have to get used to that kind of gossip from now on.

She heard footsteps from the decking outside and looked over at the door. What if it was Therese? Perhaps they'd come out early, without saying anything to Oscar? But the next second, the doorbell rang. Then it couldn't be Therese, surely. She had her own keys. Rakel stood up, tightened the belt on her dressing gown and went to open the door.

6

FOR THE FIRST time since Eva's disappearance, Börje had slept at Junibacken. He tied his shoelaces, felt the nagging ache in his lower back and straightened up. He placed his palms where the pain was, grimaced and pushed his hip forward until it clicked.

He left Junibacken, took a last look back at what had been his and Eva's and walked slowly down the path.

She was alive. He knew it.

The last thing to leave him would be hope. He wasn't going to rest until he'd found Eva. It hadn't felt right, sleeping at Junibacken without her. Empty. Because it was *their* place. For the most part, he'd been lying there awake, tossing and turning. Trying to find a position that let him relax. In the little snatches of sleep he had managed, he had dreamt about Eva. That she had finally come back. It was summer, they went swimming, shared an ice cream.

This wasn't how things were supposed to turn out. They had survived a cold, tough, grim winter. And now Eva was gone. On the bright side, it was better that she'd disappeared at this time of year than during the coldest months. She could have frozen to death then, got run over in the darkness, found herself on a frozen lake and ended up going through the ice.

"Stop it now," he said to himself.

He shook off the discomfiting thoughts. Eva was alive. Soon, he would find her and whatever state she was in, he would get her fit and healthy. He'd be there at her side. Carrying her, if that was what it took. There were no alternatives.

He noticed he was sweating, stopped and took off his jacket. Inside Oscar Sjölander's garden, he saw someone moving. A man walking towards the front door. He looked around several times before ringing the doorbell.

Börje stood still behind the bushes, following what was going on.

Eventually, the door was opened by a brunette wearing a blue dressing gown. Börje squinted. The distance made the man's outline look blurred. The woman really didn't look like Oscar's wife Therese.

The woman in the doorway exchanged a few words with the man, then stepped to one side to let him in and closed the door.

Börje stood there for a moment before he continued. There was something about the man's clothes, his mannerisms, that aroused his curiosity. But he couldn't put his finger on what.

7

VANESSA WALKED ALONG Sveavägen. The sun was beating down. Thermometers showed twenty-two degrees in the shade, and the forecasters had said it was going to get even hotter. Since the warm front came from the east, it was dubbed 'Russian Heat' by the tabloids.

Her head was still pounding after yesterday's meeting with Nicolas. She'd spent two hours wandering around town trying to get rid of her headache, but it hadn't helped. She was devastated that Nicolas was moving. Yet she knew she was being unreasonable.

Over on the other side of Sveavägen, the green, inviting spaces of the Observatory Park. A few kids were skateboarding in the drained fountain basin. People at the bottom of the hill were sitting on colourful blankets. By the steps to the City Library, a dealer stood waiting for customers. On Sveavägen, groups of runners ran down the pavement. Vanessa bought an ice-cold frappé from a café and continued homewards.

As she approached Roslagsgatan 13, she saw a woman with long curly locks and round glasses waiting under the scaffolding. To Vanessa's surprise, the woman started walking straight towards her.

"Vanessa Frank?" she said.

"Yes?"

"Have you got a few minutes?"

"That depends on what it's about."

The woman cleared her throat. "One of your cases."

Upon reflection, the face in front of her wasn't completely unfamiliar. Vanessa wondered where she'd seen her. A witness in some old case?

"Why do I recognise you?"

"My name is Jasmina Kovac. I'm a journalist. *Kvällspressen*."

Vanessa raised her eyebrows.

"If you want an interview, you'll have to turn to the police's media team," she said, took a step to the side and headed towards the entrance to her building. Jasmina Kovac reached out with one hand, touching Vanessa's arm, but immediately withdrew it when Vanessa responded with a murderous stare.

"I am not here as a journalist," she said. "Please, just give me a couple of minutes. It's important."

Vanessa glanced back over her shoulder. Being seen with a journalist wasn't good. A tabloid journalist, even worse. It might look like she was leaking information. But there was something in the young woman's desperate expression that aroused Vanessa's curiosity. And empathy.

"Please," Jasmina repeated.

Vanessa pointed towards Monica Zetterlund Park. They crossed Roslagsgatan, Vanessa first, Jasmina just behind her. They sat down on the wooden bench that played the jazz legend's songs around the clock and Vanessa put the straw to her lips.

"I sought you out because you're the only female detective on this case," Jasmina said, squirming. "What I'm going to tell you… I wonder if you can keep it secret?"

"If you want to talk to someone with a vow of silence, then you should find a psychologist or a priest," Vanessa said but immediately regretted it when she saw the look on Jasmina's face.

She slurped up the last of her frappé, half stood up and put the empty plastic cup in the bin.

"Karim Laimani did not murder Emelie Rydén." Jasmina exhaled. Vanessa turned to face her, taken aback.

"What makes you so sure of that?"

"I just know it."

"With all due respect, the forensic evidence says something different."

"On the 21st of April, I was at Hotel Anglais, by Stureplan. A man approached me, and we got talking. He bought me a coffee. Said his name was Thomas. There was nothing much wrong with him at first, but he soon turned creepy. When I went to stand up, everything started spinning. My body just stopped obeying. He took me out to a waiting car. While we were driving, I lost consciousness."

Jasmina was talking quietly. Vanessa moved closer.

"When I came round, I was in an apartment. I don't know where. But… they raped me. The man who'd said his name was Thomas, and two others."

"And that man was…"

"Karim Laimani."

Vanessa stared at Jasmina as she ran a trembling hand through her thick hair. Her eyes looked glazed and empty.

"May I ask why you haven't told anyone about this?" Vanessa asked gently. Jasmina gave her a sad, crooked smile.

"I didn't know who he was."

"Why are you so sure of it now?"

"Because I was in court for the remand hearing. I was there to report on proceedings, and I saw him walking into the courtroom." Jasmina sighed, shaking her head. "I've written loads of articles about women who have been raped and I know that the right thing to do is to report it. But I didn't dare. They threatened me. They know my name, and where I live. It's also my mum… I… I don't want her to find out about it."

Vanessa carefully put her arm around Jasmina. She wanted to feel rage, but she just felt weary. How many women were carrying around similar secrets? Three men had destroyed Jasmina's life and she might never feel safe again.

Jasmina leaned against her and let the tears come. Vanessa pulled her closer and searched in vain for some comforting words to say.

8

OSCAR SJÖLANDER WAS standing at Hjorthagen football ground, watching his oldest daughter's third match that day. Laura had scored twice and Brommapojkarna were leading Djurgården 3-1. Oscar, though, was struggling to concentrate on the game and feel any joy at his daughter's goals.

Rakel's news – that she was pregnant – had turned everything upside down.

The more it sank in, the more it felt wrong. Rakel was his safe haven, the one who broke up the daily grind. He didn't want to start again. Start another family. Change nappies. Be kept awake at night by baby's screams. At the same time, he felt bad. Of course Rakel wanted kids. A family of her own. She was young. He'd let it go too far. And he hadn't been able to face having the discussion with her there and then. Instead, he'd pretended to be happy, or at least not expressed any objections. He'd heard himself promise yet again that he was going to leave Therese.

The ref blew for half-time and a dad from the opposing team started heading over towards him. Oscar knew the type: some bighead who wanted to chat, talk football or hockey in the belief he had something worth saying. To show off. Then, in passing, suggest that they should have a beer together some day.

Oscar pretended not to have seen him and headed for the café to get himself a hotdog. By the car park, a car pulled up.

Two well-built men got out and walked towards the sports ground. They then headed towards the café, and to Oscar's great surprise, they asked him if they could have a quick word.

His first reaction was one of irritation. Did these idiots want a selfie? Now? People were getting more and more daft.

The men briefly exchanged glances.

"We need to speak to you," said one of them, pulling out a police badge.

Maybe it was *Candid Camera*. Some stupid TV3 programme that was based on winding up celebrities. In that case, it was best to keep up appearances. The police led him back towards the car park. The parents in Laura's team started whispering to each other.

"Okay. What do you want?" Oscar asked, flinging his arms wide.

"You are acquainted with a Rakel Sjödin?"

That was the last thing he expected. If this was a joke, it was seriously over the line. Oscar glanced at the policemen's stony faces in turn. How did they know about Rakel?

"She's missing," said one of the officers.

Oscar's thoughts were tumbling around his head.

"What do you mean?"

"She has been reported missing. Her friend claims that you met last night and that you spent the night together."

Oscar felt the rage flaring up inside him. Fucking pigs. People were being shot all over the place in this town, yet they were spending Saturday afternoon coming here?

"I am married. What the hell are you playing at, turning up and insinuating that I'm having an affair? Haven't you got anything better to do?"

"Calm down."

The policeman took a step towards him.

"Don't you tell me what to do!" Oscar said angrily. He heard a whistle and realised that the referee had started the second half. "If you'll excuse me, I want to see my daughter's match. I know Rakel, but I have no idea where she is."

He turned around to walk back, but the policeman grabbed his arm.

"You stay here."

"Let me go!"

Oscar's first instinct was to pull away, but the policeman's grip tightened. His colleague was now blocking his path and seemed prepared to get involved. Oscar calmed down. It would be disastrous if someone pulled out their phone and started filming. The policeman let go and Oscar rubbed his upper arm. At that moment, the police radios crackled. The second officer, the one who had stayed in the background, went a bit further away. Oscar couldn't hear what was being said. The policeman mumbled something into the radio, nodded, and came back over.

"We're going to have to ask you to come with us."

Oscar opened his mouth to protest, but the policeman interrupted him.

"Now. Right now."

There was something in the grimness of his face that made Oscar realise this was serious. The terror struck him like a clenched fist in his solar plexus. A dread he hadn't felt since #metoo. Had something else come out? Some old conquest who wanted to get famous? Made out he'd forced them into sex? Maybe they were just making it up about Rakel, as a way of getting him to go with them. No, that sounded ridiculous. Besides, there was nothing he could do. He could hardly try and escape. He was innocent. It would be best to get it out of the way.

"I'll come with you," he said.

9

JASMINA MADE STRAIGHT for the coffee machine when she got into the newsroom. Her body felt lighter since she'd told Vanessa Frank about the rape. Jasmina had trusted her straight away, and she appreciated Vanessa not having told her she ought to report it.

When the cup was full, Jasmina spun around and came close to spilling her scalding hot coffee onto Max Lewenhaupt.

"Oops," she said.

She wondered how long he'd been standing there.

"Have you got time for a quick chat?"

He led her into the conference room named *The Kiss*, after King Carl XVI Gustaf and Queen Silvia's wedding kiss from 1976. The single biggest-selling edition *Kvällspressen* had ever produced: 957,000 copies.

The normally so self-assured Max struggled to look Jasmina in the eye as he closed the door. Jasmina felt torn. Max was a bully. A spoiled brat who'd grown up with a silver spoon in his mouth and without the nous to realise that not everyone had had it so easy. She couldn't, however, discount the fact that he was a competent reporter.

"I want to apologise to you for... well, what I did. It was idiotic."

Jasmina nodded but stayed silent.

"Sorry."

Jasmina wondered if he really meant that, or whether he was

there because his continued presence on the paper depended on it. Probably the latter. But that didn't matter. She wanted to move on. Forget. Tuva Algotsson had asked whether it was okay to keep Max on and Jasmina had promised to keep schtum about what had happened. She didn't want anyone losing their job thanks to her.

She took Max's outstretched hand. She actually wanted to ask him to explain why he'd stolen the text, but she couldn't face it. Not now.

"It's okay," she said.

He smiled crookedly.

"If you're going to steal, you steal from the best."

"Thanks, I think."

Max's phone rang. He let go of Jasmina's hand, wrestled it out of his back pocket and stared at the screen. "I have to take this."

Max walked along the long table and went and stood by the whiteboard at the end of the room. Jasmina peered out into the newsroom and wondered whether she should leave the room, but Max held up his hand in a gesture which she took to mean that he wanted her to stay.

Jasmina walked over to the window and looked out at the functionalist buildings of Marieberg. She didn't want to be persuaded to report. Didn't want to sit through a trial. Be interrogated. Have to answer questions. She wanted to move on. Jasmina had told someone that Karim Laimani was not guilty of murder. Maybe that meant that the police could find the person who had killed Emelie Rydén. She was going to forget Karim and what he'd done to her.

"Okay," Max said behind her back.

He knocked twice on the tabletop with his knuckles.

"Are you completely sure?"

Half a minute later, he hung up.

"A police source." Max's brow furrowed. "Oscar Sjölander has been picked up by police from his daughter's football match. Apparently it's all going off at his summer house in Tyresö."

"*The* Oscar Sjölander?"

Max nodded.

"You tell Bengt," said Max. "It's the least I can do."

Jasmina shook her head.

"No more lies. But thank you."

She returned to her laptop. Four new emails. She opened the most recent, sent from an anonymous Hotmail address just minutes before. It was a picture of her face. The sender had photoshopped it onto a naked woman's body. She lay between two men, both penetrating her.

I know you like this, it read underneath the image.

Jasmina went cold and slammed the computer shut. Her hands were shaking. Karim Laimani's disgusting sneer flickered past. She rubbed her palm over her face. They couldn't possibly know that she'd spoken to Vanessa Frank. Could they? She glanced over at Tuva Algotsson's office. Thought about going over. The newspaper's policy was that all threats must be reported, but then Jasmina would have to tell them about the rape.

10

VANESSA GOT CHANGED into her sports clothes, grabbed a water bottle and left the apartment. She checked her phone, but neither her boss Mikael Kask nor Ove had called back.

Karim Laimani was a domestic abuser, but he had not murdered Emelie – not if Jasmina Kovac's account was accurate. And Vanessa could see no reason to doubt it. Karim Laimani was going to be walking off remand and back to Åkersberga. He would soon be a free man, unless Jasmina changed her mind and decided to report him. Vanessa could understand her reluctance. Only four per cent of reported rapes in Sweden lead to a conviction. And forensic evidence would be missing. As well as witnesses. No, Jasmina wouldn't have a hope in court.

Vanessa found a free treadmill, plugged her headphones in and started running to the strains of Queen's 'Bohemian Rhapsody'. The noisy air-conditioning was pleasantly cool. After getting through 5k in twenty-five minutes, she felt pleased. Freddie Mercury sang 'Somebody to Love' as Vanessa climbed onto the rowing machine. She reached for the handle and pushed off with her legs. Mercury's voice made way for a ringtone. Vanessa checked the screen. Mikael Kask.

"Thanks for…"

"I'm sorry to call you at the weekend yet again, but we need you," he interrupted.

"Go on," said Vanessa.

She stopped rowing and slowly replaced the handle in its cradle.

"A woman has disappeared, and we have found traces of blood in the summer cottage where she had, according to her friend, spent the night. The house belongs to Oscar Sjölander, the TV presenter."

Vanessa wracked her brains for a face, but none appeared.

"The media are going to go nuts," Mikael continued. "I'll send you the coordinates. I'll see you there."

Oscar Sjölander's summer cottage lay in an isolated spot, with the nearest neighbour over three hundred metres away. The house was surrounded by trees and bushes but could be partially seen from the pathway alongside the property.

The garden comprised a large lawn and a few fruit trees, a trampoline and a white Wendy house.

In the doorway, Vanessa was handed a pair of shoe covers, a disposable overall and gloves. Mikael Kask was waiting in the hallway. He was around fifty, well over six foot, and had sparkling green eyes. In the late eighties, he'd worked as a model in New York before retraining as a policeman. Within the force, he was known as something of a ladies' man. Single. Childless. But he was a good detective, and Vanessa respected him. After six months at Riksmord, she was pretty confident that the feeling was mutual.

"What do we know?" she asked.

"I'll do a proper run-down with everyone later. But thus far: not an awful lot. According to Katja Tillberg, Rakel Sjödin's friend, Oscar Sjölander and Rakel were in a relationship. They came out here together yesterday. Spent the night here. Katja got a text from Rakel this morning. She wrote that she was scared of Oscar. Katja tried to call, but there was no answer. She called 112, who sent a police car. The door was unlocked. They went inside and discovered flecks of blood on the sofa. Oscar Sjölander is being interviewed as we speak."

Vanessa walked over to the sofa. Two bloodstains the size of clenched fists shone out from the white upholstery.

"What's he saying?"

"That he hasn't got a clue where she is. He says that there are junkies living out in the woods there who have behaved threateningly towards him and his family. They hang around down by the water's edge, if you follow the path and bear right. Can you take a forensic technician and go and investigate?"

"So she's only been missing a few hours, but we've pulled out all the stops?"

"The chiefs want it that way, given the circumstances."

"The celebrity factor, you mean?"

Vanessa waved over Trude Hovland – the technician who'd attended Emelie Rydén's murder scene – and relayed Mikael's instructions. They followed the path down toward the water. The sun was no longer blazing, but the air was muggy. Trude had her hood down, and her face mask hung like a bib around her neck.

It was incredible that she could be so attractive, regardless of her get-up. Vanessa tried to spot a ring under her thin plastic gloves but couldn't see one.

"I know this isn't a PC question, but where are you from?" asked Vanessa.

"We're not as jumpy about those things in Norway as you Swedes are," Trude said, unfazed. "Dad's Indian, Mum's Norwegian. I grew up in New Delhi and Oslo."

Twenty metres from the water, the path forked. They kept right, as Mikael had said. The forest closed in around them. The air felt more moist, almost cool.

"Isn't it usually the other way round?"

"How do you mean?"

"That we Swedes go to Norway to steal your jobs," Vanessa said with a smirk. "You think we pay subsistence wages, don't you?"

"I fell in love with a Swede and moved here years ago. That didn't last, but I ended up staying."

"I'm sorry."

Trude shrugged.

"Don't be. I like my job and I enjoy living in Stockholm. Besides, it was me who was unfaithful, so it was only right that he dumped me."

Between a couple of trees, Vanessa spotted a green tarpaulin. Trude went first and they walked away from the path. In a clearing, they found an old fire and a log that seemed to have served as a seat. Under the tarp were piles of old newspapers, and next to them two black bin bags. Trude pulled up her mask and quickly investigated them.

"Sleeping bags, an old loaf, a cassette player, clothes."

Vanessa crouched down by the papers, most of which were copies of the free daily *Metro*. She pulled on a new pair of gloves and flipped through them. The newest one was *Aftonposten*, a week old.

"Did Sjölander say they were drug addicts?" asked Trude. "Feels a little bit too well organised, don't you think? Look, they've even got a washing line."

A worn, pale-blue cord was suspended between two birch trees. On it, about a dozen clothes pegs.

Vanessa heard footsteps, spun around and saw Ove Dahlberg walking down the path towards them.

"They wanted as many people in as possible."

"Have the journalists started ringing already?"

"No, but it's only a matter of time. You and I are going to Blackeberg to meet a Katja Tillberg. She was the first one to call us when she was worried. Kask wants us to establish the nature of the relationship between Oscar Sjölander and the victim."

"Isn't that pretty obvious?" said Vanessa.

Ove shrugged.

"The parents?"

"We've got people there already," said Ove. "And with Oscar Sjölander's wife."

Vanessa felt relieved. No one liked telling parents that something had happened to their children. But she hated it the most. She knew better than anyone what losing a child meant.

Vanessa turned to Trude, who by now had pulled out a camera.

"Go on, off you go, I'll be fine," the Norwegian said with her eyes firmly fixed on the little screen in front of her.

11

OSCAR SJÖLANDER WAS sitting waiting for the two interviewers who had left the room for a break. He closed his eyes, put his elbows on the table and his head in his hands.

What the hell was going on?

He couldn't grasp any of it. Rakel had disappeared. Somehow, they knew that she had spent the night with him. There must have been a misunderstanding. To begin with, he had, of course, lied, saying that they were friends, and colleagues. Attempted to save his marriage. Eventually, though, he told it like it was. Told them about their nights together, their meetings. The child in Rakel's belly. They asked whether he'd argued with Rakel, and he denied it, even if he did admit that the pregnancy had changed his view of the relationship's prospects.

Surely they had to understand that he didn't have a clue where Rakel was. He'd driven from there, home to Bromma, picked up Laura and then driven to the sports ground.

The door opened and the stern-faced detectives sat down opposite him. The female lead interviewer – an ugly, short-haired woman in her mid-forties – folded her arms. The man, who was wearing a green corduroy blazer, pressed the Dictaphone once more.

"Alice Lundberg and Niklas Samuelsson resuming the interview with Oscar Sjölander," he said, then leant back in his chair.

Oscar straightened up and gulped.

"You've got to fucking believe me," he said.

He could hear how he sounded. Desperate. Volatile. Why weren't they saying anything? Why were they just staring at him? He was telling the bloody truth.

"We were seeing each other, yes. We saw each other yesterday. But I left her this morning and she was fine. There was no blood on the sofa. We were going to meet up during the week. I would never hurt Rakel and I'm just as anxious as you are about her having disappeared."

He looked at them in turn. It was obvious that they didn't believe him.

"About fifty metres from your home in Bromma, a black plastic bag has been recovered from a litter bin," said the woman.

"And?"

"Inside it was a jumper and a knife. Both bloodied. Your wife has confirmed that the jumper is yours. And that the knife came from your home. Can you explain that?"

"The tramps. The junkies. The ones I told you about. It must have been those bastards. I've been there and I haven't always been very nice. I've told them I don't want them there and they must've attacked Rakel in revenge. Have you found their fucking... den?"

"We have asked our colleagues at the scene to keep an eye out," replied Alice Lundberg. She went quiet and anchored her stare on a point on Oscar's forehead. "Information has emerged suggesting that you have been violent before. Towards women."

Oscar was convinced that she was one of those rabid, man-hating feminists. Probably got the job thanks to some quota. She certainly didn't look like she'd have been able to fuck her way to promotion.

"Where the fuck have you got that from? *Flashback*?" he said with a truculent stare.

"It doesn't matter where it comes from. We want you

to answer this question. Have you ever used force against Rakel Sjödin?"

"No!" he exclaimed. "Never!"

"Against other women?"

Oscar clenched his teeth. Breathed through his nose. His speech was juddering. "I would never hurt Rakel," he said, attempting to keep his voice steady. "I don't know where she is. I want to go now. I need to talk to my wife. This... this could ruin my marriage and I have to explain to her. Ask forgiveness."

12

THEY DROVE BACK to the city centre in separate cars. Vanessa pulled into the garage under Norra Real and left her BMW there. Ove was waiting outside Café Nero with the engine running and he handed Vanessa a takeaway coffee.

She took a gulp and put the cup in the drinks holder.

"There's something I need to tell you," she said. "It's about Karim Laimani."

"That bastard. Okay. Shoot."

"A woman tracked me down earlier today. She gave him an alibi for the night in question."

Ove took his eyes off the road and gave Vanessa a surprised look.

"What the hell are you saying? Who's the woman?"

"She wants to remain anonymous. And I promised her that she could. She has good reasons for wanting to."

They turned onto S:t Eriksgatan towards Fridhemsplan. Ove had an anxious furrow across his brow. He looked like he wanted to object, ask questions, demand more detail.

"Okay," he said. "If you think she's credible, I have no reason to doubt your judgement. The question is, what do we do now? What do we say to the prosecutor?"

Vanessa turned her face towards the street outside and smiled. "Thanks," she muttered.

Her colleague looked at her, confused.

"For what?"

"For trusting me."

Katja Tillberg was pacing back and forth across the living room. Washing-up, packaging, clothes, jewellery and spirit bottles lay strewn across the sofa, lined the window sills and the light parquet floor of the little one-bed apartment. There were several framed photographs on top of a chest of drawers.

While Ove tried to persuade Katja to sit down and tell them about her last contact with Rakel Sjödin, Vanessa moved an empty wine bottle to get a better look at the photos. One, in particular, caught her attention. A picture taken on a holiday in warmer climes. A younger version of Katja and a person Vanessa understood was Rakel lay floating on a pink lilo somewhere in the Med. They were both holding up cocktails complete with little umbrellas and laughing at the photographer.

The other pictures were different. Like they'd been taken by a professional. Katja, a few years older, jumping on a trampoline. The photographer must've been lying on their back, on the trampoline itself.

"Vanessa?"

She spun around. Katja was now slumped in the sofa. Ove had pulled a kitchen chair over and put it on the other side of the table. Vanessa moved a pizza box off another chair and put the chair next to Ove's.

"So we understand that Rakel texted you this morning?" said Ove.

Katja felt her way through the chaos on the coffee table. Found her phone, unlocked it and showed it to Vanessa and Ove, who were leaning in to read what was on the screen.

He is really fucking angry. I'm afraid he's going to hurt me, it read. Ove leaned back.

"And by *he*, she means Oscar Sjölander?"

"Yes."

"What makes you think that?"

"Because she met him last night. They were going to sleep in his summer place – they usually do when they meet up at the weekend. Rakel was anxious. She was going to tell him that she's pregnant."

Vanessa and Ove exchanged a brief glance.

"Can you tell us about their relationship?" Vanessa asked gently. "Starting with how long it's been going on."

"I suppose about a year. They met when Rakel was working on his talk show. They flirted a bit. To begin with, it was mostly him going after her. All the guys like Rakel – you know what she looks like. She was flattered, thought it was exciting that he was so much older. And famous. Even if she isn't that type of girl."

"What do you mean?" asked Vanessa. "What type of girl?"

"The type who get impressed by celebrity. She is not shallow. On the contrary. But recently it's been as if she's falling in love with him. Meeting up more and more regularly. She didn't admit it, not even to me, but of course I noticed. It was like she was planning a life together with him. Or hoping for it at least."

"How did you feel about that?"

"That it was stupid. Of course it was a bit of fun to begin with. Exciting, given who he is. But he's married, with a family. There was just no chance of it being the two of them. Besides, everyone knows he's a pig."

"What makes you say that?"

"*Flashback*. It's all there, what he's done to his wife. And Rakel herself said that everyone in the industry knows he cheats. All the time."

"Was he violent towards her?"

"Not that I know of."

Vanessa, who had been leaning forward throughout, straightened her back.

"Would she have told you, do you think?"

Katja thought about it for a moment.

"Maybe not. She already knew that I really didn't like him."

An hour later, Ove double-parked by the row of cars outside Vanessa's block. On the way into town, they had called the officer in charge of the investigation and confirmed that they were not needed in Tyresö. Ove turned off the engine and they ended up sitting there in silence for a while.

"I'll get the conversation with Katja transcribed and then send it in," said Vanessa.

"Thanks."

Ove drummed his fingers on the steering wheel.

"I'll talk to the prosecutor about Karim Laimani. Try and get her to give us a few days to try and find an alternative suspect. Do you have any ideas?"

"Not really. We have fingerprints on that pen, from the rape attempt. But that might not have anything to do with it. We'll have to dig a bit deeper into her background. Find another motive."

"Sounds good."

Ove opened the storage between the seats, dug around and fished up a Snickers. He tore open the wrapper and took a big bite.

"What about chance?" he asked through a mouthful of chocolate.

"What do you mean?"

"A mad man. He sees her through the window, gets inside and stabs her to death. Then disappears."

"You're forgetting that Emelie's blood was found in Karim's cell. That does suggest a link. And why would she have let some unknown person in?"

"Could he have sent someone to murder her? Someone she knows, and trusts, since she opened the door?"

Vanessa shrugged. Ove grunted and stuffed more chocolate into his mouth. "What are your thoughts about Rakel? Still alive?"

"I don't know." Vanessa sighed. "I don't bloody know."

13

HENRIETTA WALKED BRISKLY with music in her headphones and her stare fixed straight ahead. Tom kept a distance of thirty metres – there was no reason to risk being noticed. After crossing S:t Erik Bridge, she continued towards the supermarket on the corner of Rörstrandsgatan, where she took a left. He put his hand in his jacket pocket, drew strength from the match ticket from Stockholm Stadium, where he'd been earlier that day.

The pubs and restaurants were full, and music escaped through their windows. Behind them sat happy, successful people. In couples, and in larger groups.

When he was younger, Tom had been convinced that he'd be one of them. That everything would work out: somehow he'd meet a woman, start a family. But the years had passed. He ended up getting further and further away from all that, became increasingly isolated. Nowadays it didn't even feel like he belonged to the same species as the people he shared a city with.

He was so absorbed in thoughts of what might have been that he realised too late that Henrietta had disappeared. She was probably on her way home, but he couldn't know that for sure.

Tom picked up his pace and made it to Norrbackagatan where he breathed a sigh of relief as he spotted her back. He was too far behind. He stretched his strides, closed in on her.

The distance shrank. Five metres. Four metres. Sure enough, she went into the entrance to Norrbackagatan 36. Tom crouched down, pretending to tie his shoelace as he peered over at the entry keypad. One, seven, eight... he missed the last digit. Henrietta opened the door and disappeared. Her steps echoed from the stairwell before the door slammed shut. Tom craned his neck. Another door opened. So she lived in the annexe. Tom walked over to the other side of the road to get a better view. The building's frontage was painted beige, probably built at the turn of the twentieth century.

Tom had work in the morning. He really ought to have gone home. The walk was at least half an hour, but he didn't feel ready yet.

He walked over to the keypad, looked around and tried four combinations before the little lamp flashed green. The last digit was nine. 1789. Tom smiled. The French Revolution. He liked entry codes that were easy to remember.

He snuck into the stairwell, pushed open the door leading out to the annexe. Outside, he snuck into another stairwell. He stopped and made sure he was alone before he carried on up the stairs.

Erlandsson/Bucht read a brass sign on the door. Tom could hear the hum of a television set. At home, on his computer, he had sound files of secretly recorded conversations, voices, quarrels and sex. He enjoyed spying on people, finding out the sorts of things they didn't put on their social media. At night, when he couldn't sleep, he would listen to them, recall the women he had followed, studied, got to know, masturbated over and dreamt about living with.

Behind him was a window that overlooked the courtyard where the annexe was located. Tom looked at the façade opposite. On the outside of the stairwell were a number of small balconies. From there, it ought to be possible to see right into Henrietta and Douglas' apartment.

Tom crossed the courtyard once again and heard a rustling

in the bushes. He spotted the rat's tail before it disappeared to safety.

He felt an affinity with rats. From birth, they were up against a war of extermination. Yet still they reproduced, found a way to live. They were everywhere in society, living in their little underground tunnels. Only the weakest individuals were visible to people. The ones looking for food in daylight were the ones with the lowest standing in the group. The most comfortable were living overweight and contentedly in safe hiding places. When rats weren't eating, they were fucking. The males were insatiable, able to have sex up to twenty times a day. Sometimes he'd wondered if he would have had a more successful life, been happier, if he'd been born a rat.

Tom opened the door carefully and stood there for a moment to make sure no one was on their way down. He climbed the stairs to the top balcony, on the fourth floor. He tried the handle and discovered it was unlocked. He stepped out and was able to see Henrietta lying on the sofa under a blanket and with her hair wrapped in a towel.

Tom closed the door behind himself. The space was large enough that he would be able to lie down on his front. If he brought a blanket to cover his head, he would be able to take photographs undisturbed.

14

NICOLAS HEARD A scraping sound from outside. The balcony door was open. He went out, stood with his hands on the railing and looked out at the concrete buildings in front of him.

It was a beautiful, warm, cloudless night. Once again, he heard that same sound – coming from Celine's balcony.

"Celine, are you there?"

"No."

Celine's voice. He smirked, leaned over the railing and tried to see in behind the metal screen. She poked her head up.

"What are you doing?" he asked.

"Camping." She got to her feet. Her body was swaddled in a sleeping bag. "See? Can you keep the noise down now. You're spoiling the illusion of wilderness."

"Sorry," said Nicolas. "But are you going to sleep out here?"

"Am I disturbing you?"

"Not at all," he said with a smile. "Just be careful, so the wolves don't get you." He slid down with his back against the railing, tipped his head backwards and looked up at the stars.

"Thanks for helping my friend when she was here."

"Vanessa? Well, she's cool. For a cop."

It went quiet. From one of the neighbouring flats, the sound of a hip-hop beat over which a man was bellowing his hatred of society. Nicolas' meeting with Magnus Örn had gone well. He had explained AOS security, how their operatives comprised former soldiers from all over the world. And that Nicolas, with his Special Operations Group background, would be welcomed with open arms.

The missions ranged from bodyguard duty to assisting British and American troops in war zones – in everything from battle to patrol work and training. Nicolas was offered a basic wage of ninety thousand crowns a month, and an apartment in London. Generous allowances for overseas duty. His mouth had dropped, and he'd said yes on the spot. It was the only way to go.

And yet, he still felt torn. Maria was here. And Vanessa, who was, aside from his sister, the only person he trusted. On top of that, he'd miss Celine. She would be left alone when he went.

"Nicolas, what do you actually do?"

"I used to be a soldier."

He thought about telling Celine about the job in London, that he was going to disappear, but decided not to. Not yet.

"Have you killed anyone?"

"I shot a man last week," said Nicolas. "In the pizza place."

"So that was you? Is that why the police were here?"

"Yes."

The true answer was that he had killed many people, even if he didn't know an exact number. Probably over twenty. Almost ten years in SOG and Special Protection Group. Action in Afghanistan, Mali, Nigeria. Covert operations the world over. Situations in which Swedish lives had been in peril. Last year: with Vanessa in southern Chile. At the pizzeria the other week. In self-defence. But still. He was, in all probability, one of the biggest killers amongst all living Swedes. More than any feared gangland boss. Yet he wasn't seen as a murderer. At least not in the eyes of the law. Now his talent for extinguishing life had landed him a well-paid job.

The world was strange. Certain people's motives for killing were deemed legitimate, while others were punished.

Just moving over an invisible border between countries could mean the difference. In certain places, it was okay to stone a woman who had been raped or kill a homosexual man for the love he had for someone else.

"But you're not going to prison?"

The anxiety he thought he could detect in her voice made him feel warm. "No."

"Why did you kill him?"

Nicolas sighed. Not because he was irritated at the question, but because he didn't know how to formulate his response.

"Because he was going to kill someone else."

"Who you cared about?"

"Not really. But she wasn't involved. She didn't deserve to die."

He could hear Celine squirm in her sleeping bag.

"Would you kill someone who wanted to hurt me?" she asked quietly.

At first he laughed, before realising that she was being serious.

"Yes, Celine. I would."

"Good."

PART V

Genocide against women would be perfectly warranted, that is my humble opinion.

Signed Saint Marc Lepine.

1

BÖRJE TRUDGED UP the stairwell. His legs felt heavy; his head was pounding with exhaustion. He had to have an answer. And the only way of getting it was to ring on Nina's door again. Over the past few days, something had changed inside him. He'd carried on his search. Mechanically. To keep himself busy. But he had stopped hoping. It was now Monday, and she had been missing since the Sunday before.

Everyone had given up on Eva. Börje wasn't going to let her down. He was going to keep searching until he found an answer. He owed it to her, after all she'd done for him.

He stopped outside her door and rang the bell. He didn't bother fixing his hair, didn't care if he was dirty. Footsteps approached on the other side of the door. The handle was pushed down, and Nina stared out at him. She was so much like Eva it hurt.

"Have you heard anything about your moth... about Eva?" said Börje.

Nina didn't move a muscle.

"Please. All I want is to know, so that I can stop looking."

A tear pushed its way out, ran down his cheek before being absorbed into his beard. Nina stepped to one side. He stayed put, unsure of what to do. "Do you want me to... may I come in?"

Börje could smell home cooking. A dishwasher whirred.

"My son is asleep," Nina whispered.

Börje undid his shoes. Placed them together carefully on the doormat. Nina sat down on a chair in the kitchen. Börje stayed on his feet by the sink. He didn't want to get the cushions dirty. Nina did her best not to reveal how bad he smelled. He avoided looking at her. Not because he was ashamed, but because she reminded him so much of her mother.

"You can stop looking," she said. "They found her two days ago."

He was winded. His legs went from under him, and he grabbed the table for support before sinking onto his haunches.

"She took her own life," Nina said as she ran her fingers over the tablecloth.

"Why?" whispered Börje. "I don't understand. She was feeling better. We'd put the winter behind us. We were going to…"

The chair legs scraped as Nina stood up and pulled him to his feet. With one hand she pulled out a chair and guided him gently onto it with the other.

"She wrote you a letter."

Nina went out of the kitchen. Returned with a white envelope. It read *Börje*, in Eva's handwriting. He sobbed. He could not hold back. He pressed the envelope to his chest as if he were afraid Nina was going to demand it back at any second. Tears dripped onto his thighs.

"Sorry," he said after a while.

"It's okay. I've been crying too. I didn't think I would. But I did."

She walked over to the sink and ran the tap cold before filling a glass and placing it in front of Börje. She tore off a bit of kitchen roll and passed it to him.

"You loved her," she said.

He nodded.

"She was my best friend. The best I've had. The kind you can never even imagine until you meet them."

Nina's expression darkened momentarily.

"It is weird," she said, "how someone can be a dreadful mother to one person and a good friend to another."

Börje didn't know what to say. He took a sip. He put the glass back on the table with a trembling hand.

"You… She talked about you. Every day. She loved you above all else."

Börje sniffled.

"What did she say?" Nina whispered.

He searched his memories.

"She told me about the time you saved another girl from drowning. And when you dressed up as Ronja Robbersdaughter and escaped into the woods. About how you'd pretend to be asleep, and turn the light off when she knocked, even though she knew that you were lying there reading stories under the covers. She told me that you'd wanted to be a train driver at first. Then a fisherman. About how you cried when you lost your first tooth because you were afraid of the tooth fairy. And about that Christmas when…"

A child's cry came from across the apartment. Nina shuddered and stood up. She was gone for a while. She returned with a little child in her arms. The baby was cooing. Börje leaned over. He had Eva's nose.

"Edvin," Nina said with a smile. "His name is Edvin."

2

VANESSA ATE LUNCH at Dino's, a simple Italian restaurant on Kronobergsgatan. She kept her stare fixed on the open newspaper next to her, twirled the spaghetti onto her fork, dipped it in the tomato sauce and put it in her mouth.

Mikael Kask had cancelled her trip to Halmstad. Instead, Vanessa and Ove were to assist the Rakel Sjödin investigation together. The bosses were demanding results. Not least because Oscar Sjölander had attracted attention during #metoo.

For the second day running, *Kvällspressen* went with her disappearance on the front page, news bills and four inside pages. Missing women sold papers. Not as well as chopped-up or mangled women, but almost. So far, no paper had named Oscar Sjölander. The reporters switched between calling him *the TV-star* and *the presenter*.

Rakel was *his lover* or *young mistress*. Correspondents never failed to mention the age gap and they had dug up innocent-looking, beautiful pictures of Rakel. In his interviews, Sjölander was still denying having anything to do with her disappearance, even if he'd admitted their sexual relations. Several people with knowledge of the entertainment industry commented anonymously on *the TV star*'s appetite for young women. A picture series showed the police technicians combing the street outside Oscar Sjölander's Bromma home.

It was probably just a matter of time until he cracked and admitted his guilt.

The door of the restaurant opened, and a warm wind found its way inside. Vanessa looked up from the newspaper to see Ove Dahlberg wiping his forehead with the palm of his hand.

"We've got the green light to start looking for another suspect in the Emelie Rydén case," he said, sitting himself down opposite her. Ove asked a passing waiter for a glass of water. His face was flushed. New beads of sweat gathered on his brow. "The question is, where do we start?"

Vanessa passed him a paper serviette. He took it gratefully.

"We'll retrace Emelie's final twenty-four hours again," she said. "There must be something we've missed. We'll go through the forensic evidence and find out how she got that pen."

"Why is the pen significant?"

"I don't know whether or not it is yet."

Ove looked longingly at her plate. She smiled and pushed it over.

"Yes, you can have a taste."

"Frikadeller in tomato sauce?"

She nodded.

"Would you like me to leave you alone with them?"

"As long as you don't film us. My wife would get jealous."

While Ove was eating up the leftovers, Trude Hovland called Vanessa's mobile.

"I'll get straight to the point," said Trude.

Vanessa had always thought that Norwegians couldn't sound serious. Instead, their intonation always seemed to make them sound surprised. Trude was an exception.

"The lean-to has given us a match in the criminal records. Fingerprints and DNA matching a Börje Rohdén. Convicted of manslaughter. Assault. Grievous bodily harm. Drink-driving. I've emailed you a summary."

"Last known address?"

"That's the tricky part. He doesn't have one. After his release, he went up in smoke. No arrests, nothing with the tax authorities. Nothing. But I've also sent you contact information for his children and ex-wife."

Vanessa relayed what Trude had told her to Ove, who added a drop of olive oil to the tomato sauce and wiped up what was left with a piece of bread.

After returning to the police station, Vanessa added a call-out with the name Börje Rohdén in connection with Rakel Sjödin's disappearance, so that colleagues would contact her if he was found.

She turned on her computer and skimmed through Trude's email.

Börje Rohdén was born in 1968, in Sala in Västmanland. In his youth, he had been booked on a number of occasions for minor violent crimes. After that, everything seemed to have sorted itself out. He established a building company in his hometown, started a family – two kids – and for a number of years, his tax returns recorded annual incomes of over a million crowns.

Five years ago, Börje Rohdén had got into his car and then hit and killed two people. A father, with his ten-year-old son. Börje fled the scene but was apprehended by a patrol shortly afterwards, since one of the witnesses had seen his car's registration. The breathalyser showed an alcohol level of over 1.7mg/l and he was convicted of aggravated drink-driving and manslaughter. His wife divorced him. Trude was conscientious – she had even attached a scan of the divorce papers. After Börje Rohdén had served his two-year sentence in Salberga, he disappeared. And now his fingerprints appeared in a lean-to, three hundred metres from the house where Rakel disappeared. In interviews, Oscar Sjölander had reported that Börje Rohdén had threatened him. Abused drugs. Stolen things.

Vanessa took off her shoes and put her feet up on the desk.

Could he have anything to do with Rakel's disappearance?

A bloody knife and jumper belonging to Oscar Sjölander had been found outside his home in Bromma. The police's theory had been that the presenter had panicked when Rakel told him she was pregnant. Assaulted her. Hidden the body.

But where? An inexperienced criminal, who, furthermore, was acting in panic, ought to have left some tracks. The perpetrator had been inside the summer house. The bloodstains on the sofa matched Rakel's blood type. Oscar Sjölander's wife Therese had stated that they had not been there earlier.

Surely Rakel wouldn't have let in an unknown man, just like that? Vanessa took her feet off the table and put her shoes back on. Her mobile rang. Ove. She pressed answer.

"Miss me already?" she said.

"They've found Rakel Sjödin."

3

BÖRJE WOKE UP in the recovery position on Elvis' sofa. His fringe was in his eyes. He swept the hair to one side and slowly straightened his large frame. His head was pounding. His mouth tasted of vomit and alcohol.

"GOOD MORNING, FARSTA," Elvis muttered hoarsely from his mobility scooter, which he'd fallen asleep on.

They were separated by a table strewn with spirit bottles, a dismantled old radio, kitchen towel, red bills, various tools and a large photo of an old woman who Börje assumed was Elvis' late mother. And there, amongst all the crap – Eva's letter. Still unopened. Börje wiped the letter against his thigh and put it on the sofa's armrest. Did it matter what she'd written? She was gone. She had abandoned him.

With some effort, Börje got to his feet and opened the balcony door to let some air in. His body wanted more booze.

Elvis' stare was burning into his neck. It was like Plura Jonsson once sang:

You can have all the fun you like in life. If you're prepared to pay the price.

Börje wasn't. The price was too high. The thought of living without Eva too unbearable. After he left Nina the day before, Börje had pounded on Elvis' door to ask him if he had anything to drink.

"Have you got any more?" muttered Börje.

"No."

Elvis grimaced, then leaned forward to massage his stump.

"Shit. Did we drink it all?"

Elvis shook his head.

"Bring it out then. I need a drink."

His friend rolled across the living room and parked himself next to Börje.

"I poured what was left away, while you were asleep."

Börje stared at Elvis, who was looking out at the neighbouring high-rise blocks.

"Why'd you do that?"

"For your sake. Listen. I know you relapsed yesterday. But if you're going to drink yourself to death, I don't plan to watch you doing it. Eva would have been cross with me."

Börje felt that familiar rage rush through his body. He stormed into the kitchen, flinging open cupboard doors and pulling out drawers. Throwing things onto the floor. When he failed to find anything potable, he went into the bedroom. He chucked the mattress of the single bed to one side. In a drawer in the bedside table, he found two hundred crowns, which he stuffed into the pocket of his jeans.

He returned to the living room, put his hands on the scooter's armrest and leaned forward menacingly.

"You're lying. You would never pour booze away. Tell me where your stuff is."

Elvis met his stare calmly. Shook his head slowly.

"Give over, fuck's sake," he said bitterly. "I did it with you in mind. Because I'm your mate."

Börje smiled mockingly as he straightened his back.

"Mate? What the fuck would I want you for? You're a fucking cripple."

Fuck him, Börje thought. Fuck the pathetic benefit dependents and the long-term sick. He wasn't one of them. He didn't need them. He needed booze. Comfort. A last proper drink to make him fearless. After that, death.

"And by the way, I know you weren't pushed onto the

tracks. You were trying to kill yourself. Everyone knows it. But you were too thick to manage that."

He enjoyed the sensation of watching Elvis' eyes burning with shame.

Börje stuffed Eva's letter into a pocket. Kicked the coffee table and sent it crashing into the radiator. The things on top of it shuddered and fell.

"Börje. Where are you going?"

"Where the hell do you think?" he replied, slamming the door of the flat behind him.

4

TOM SAT AT his kitchen table, swathed in the red dressing gown that had once belonged to his mother. Food crumbs, stains and burn marks from the thousands of cigarettes she smoked in her dismal life covered the coarse fabric.

She had basically lived in it. Despite years having passed since her death, he had never washed it. He couldn't really understand why he'd held onto it. He hated her. Shuddered at the mere thought of her pale, soft body and the dark, fuzzy pubic hair peeking out of her dressing gown.

The night time crying. How she, since there was no husband in the picture, would snuggle down in Tom's narrow bed – and push his face into her swelling, hideous breasts as she sobbed.

"My darling boy. What will become of us?"

Tom shook off those images and stared out of the window. He didn't want to hate women, but not doing so was getting more and more difficult. Society had given them so many advantages, privileges that he, as a man, could only dream of. Women were indispensable for society, for the survival of the species. A man was only required in conception itself. After that, he might as well die. If only a single woman had wanted Tom. Wanted to give herself to him and make him feel like a person, not like a genetic aberration.

A couple of years earlier, Tom had had well-advanced plans about hiring a man to assault a woman. He could see the scene in front of him. The woman was to be beautiful and young. Walking in the woods. The man would launch himself at her, and she would realise how perilous her situation was.

Then Tom would come to her rescue. Beat the man off and save her. Afterwards, she would be unable to resist falling in love with him. They would get married, and at the wedding, she would tell people how they'd met. And Tom would be bashful, explain that he'd just acted on instinct, like a man.

Those, though, had been childish fantasies. He was ashamed of having been so naive.

Be yourself.

Beauty is in the eye of the beholder.

Everyone has a soulmate. You just need to keep looking.

Throughout his childhood and early teens, Tom had hoped and believed that that was the way things were. He'd seen others pairing off in school corridors, holding hands, seen colleagues getting drunk at conferences and work dos, then disappear together, giggling. Fucking. Giving themselves to each other. On the metro, he'd heard beautiful men with sharp jawlines and broad shoulders talking about their one-night stands. Complaining about the women who contacted them.

Slowly, Tom had been worn down. He had seen through the lies. Women were all around him. At work, in the corner shop, on the pavement, at the gym. So close. But with time, he learned that every attempt at approaching a woman led to humiliation. Disgusted grimaces. Threats of involving the police if he didn't leave them alone. He was never going to be able to get a woman to love him. He was never even going to get a woman to touch him voluntarily.

Tom clenched his teeth, forced out the self-loathing, and concentrated on the grainy images on his computer screen. Henrietta Bucht.

He was going to ruin her life, the way she and other women ruined his on a daily basis.

Unfortunately, he still didn't have any pictures of her naked. He had, however, mapped out her life in more detail. She worked at PR agency Ronander, by Stureplan. Her boyfriend Douglas was on the books of the same firm. The first posts of the two of them had appeared on her Instagram a year and a half earlier. As recently as December, she'd proudly announced that they'd bought an apartment on Norrbackagatan.

He chose four pictures, quickly edited them and then shut down his computer.

Tom's pay-as-you-go phone buzzed. Yesterday, he'd sent an encrypted message using the app *Telegram*, to the one and only person he counted as a friend.

I need to think about it, read the reply.

Tom smiled. He knew he'd be able to talk him round.

Claws scratched on the parquet floor and the rats' squeaks grew louder. Tom went to the fridge, took out a raw chicken breast fillet and came back. He stood over by the half-metre-high plastic board that screened off part of his study. They went berserk at the smell. Shot in all directions. He threw down the pink flesh, heard the thud. They rushed at it. Fighting. Squealing. Less than a minute later, there was nothing left of the chicken breast.

He changed into his gym clothes.

Black pants, black hoody and Adidas runners. It was going to be a long day; he would have to do his workout in the morning. After an hour's parkour, he was going to go to work. At the end of his working day, he was going to see what Henrietta and Douglas were up to.

5

JASMINA SAT WEDGED behind a corner table at Le Café in Sture shopping mall. She was surrounded by wealthy housewives drinking low-calorie drinks through straws so as not to damage their teeth. Two suit-wearing salesman types laughed loudly from a couple of tables away.

Her body felt weary. The sleep deprivation pricked her eyes. She was already onto the day's sixth coffee. She was waiting for Simona Strand, a twenty-seven-year-old woman who worked as a receptionist for production company TLZ in Frihamnen, who had contacted Jasmina claiming to have had a brief relationship with Oscar Sjölander a few years earlier.

The last twenty-four hours had been the most hectic of Jasmina's career. Since Oscar Sjölander's arrest, she had only been at home to grab a few hours' sleep and then returned to the newsroom.

On one of the two days since the disappearance, Jasmina's article had made the front page, and been highly praised by both Bengt and Tuva Algotsson. Yet Jasmina still couldn't enjoy it. She spent the whole time looking over her shoulder, terrified that at any moment she was going to see one of the men who had raped her. She ran through the stairwell, up to her front door. She hated Karim. Hated herself, for having helped to free him. She knew that he had been sent back to Åkersberga but was soon going to be released. Once he was out, she didn't know whether she would dare to stay in Stockholm.

Jasmina recognised Simona Strand from her Facebook profile picture and she stood up. Simona, who had been heading for a table on the other side of the room with a smoothie in her hand, turned and walked towards Jasmina's table.

She was even more attractive than her photos. Summery, in a skirt and vest top. Plump, shiny lips that were probably not as nature intended. Blonde, billowing hair that hung around her shoulders.

"Thanks for agreeing to meet."

"You cannot print my name or the production company I work for. I've got a boyfriend."

Jasmina would never, ever, expose an informant who had requested anonymity. Not to anyone. Once again she assured Simona that she would remain anonymous. She pushed her coffee cup to one side and put her Dictaphone on the table.

"How did you meet?"

Simona rolled a few strands of hair around her index finger.

"At a Christmas party four years ago. TLZ produced that football show that Oscar fronted."

Jasmina noted that she'd called him *Oscar*. Not *Sjölander*. Not *Oscar Sjölander*.

"He used to come in, say hi, be friendly. A bit flirty, perhaps. I was new and I didn't know about his reputation. I knew he had a wife and kids. But at that Christmas do, he was wasted. Me too. We snuck off to the basement, and snogged."

Simona put her straw to her lips. Her neck muscles flexed. Jasmina still hadn't decided what she made of her.

"A few days later, I got a text. He wondered if I'd like to meet up. It was midweek. We went out to his summer place, that house that Rakel Sjödin disappeared from. There... well, how much detail do you want?"

Jasmina felt herself blushing.

"Tell me whatever you think is relevant. I'll ask questions if need be," she rushed to say.

"We had sex."

Thus far, Simona hadn't said anything startling. That

Oscar Sjödin was notoriously unfaithful was no secret if one had read the tabloids recently.

"Was it… violent?"

Jasmina had never posed such an intimate question before. She generally disliked talking about sex. She had never had close friends but had kept herself to herself. Jasmina realised at that point that her curiosity extended beyond her interest as a reporter. She peered anxiously at Simona, who, to her great relief, didn't seem to mind.

"A bit. But that's how I like it, so it was no problem. We met regularly. I started liking him more and more. He said that he was beginning to have feelings for me and that he was considering leaving his wife. With hindsight… I'm ashamed that I believed him. But I kept grinning and bearing it. Hoped against hope. Didn't ask any more questions. I noticed that he would get annoyed if it ever did come up."

Simona bit her lip. Jasmina pictured the scene, Oscar Sjölander on top, behind her. She realised that she was thinking about sex for the first time since the rape.

"All of a sudden – silence," Simona said in a hushed voice. "He stopped answering calls, texts, everything. I got worried. Went down to TV4 HQ after work, waited outside and then confronted him. He told me to get into his car. We drove out to some deserted woodland on Djurgården. He screamed. Grabbed me by the throat. Told me that if I breathed a word of it to anyone, or contacted him again, he would put a group of biker thugs onto me. Get me sacked. Make sure I never worked in the industry again. I thought he was going to kill me."

Jasmina pushed the Dictaphone closer to Simona, who was now leaning back. "What did you do?"

"As he said. I was terrified. You have no idea how many similar stories I've heard about him. He's a fucking psychopath. I don't get how he didn't get caught during #metoo. Well, actually, I do."

A short, joyless laugh escaped Simona's mouth. Jasmina swallowed. She could understand her horror.

"He rang every woman he's bedded since he came to Stockholm. Threatened. Pleaded. Asked forgiveness. He's so fucking manipulative. Talking about his daughters, his wife, saying that he'd changed. I know you shouldn't believe everything you read online. But a lot of those stories are true, I know that."

Jasmina pushed her glasses back up her nose.

"So how come you're telling me this?"

"I want everyone to know what a wretch he is. I should have told someone before now. Then this wouldn't have happened."

"You mean Rakel Sjödin's disappearance?"

"Yes."

Jasmina didn't know what to say. She had no idea whether Oscar Sjölander had hurt Rakel Sjödin – even if most things pointed to that. As a journalist, she was supposed to be objective, and present the facts. Not speculate about whether a crime could have been averted.

The screen on Jasmina's phone lit up. She feared it was another anonymous threat. Since Saturday, she had received another one. But in that, her face had lain alongside a decapitated female body, probably from war-torn Syria.

Now though, it was a text message from Max.

Hurry back, they've found Rakel Sjödin's body.

Jasmina stood up.

"I have to go," she said, and hurriedly gathered her belongings.

6

VANESSA WAS SITTING at the window table at McLarens. The sun's last desperate rays clung to the frontage. She'd turned down Kjell-Arne's offer of food, sticking with a large beer, which was untouched.

The photos of Rakel Sjödin's naked, pale body appeared on her retinas once again. She had seen dead people before, but Rakel's death hit Vanessa in a way she wasn't prepared for. Maybe it was easier to understand a murderer who came from the underclass? One who'd had a tough childhood, sabotaged his future with drugs, been alone, vulnerable, bullied. But Oscar Sjölander was a celebrated TV personality with a seven-figure salary, two daughters and a wife. A country house in easy reach of the city. A stable upbringing. Parents still married and alive.

Vanessa wasn't the only one affected. The murder shook Sweden. Oscar Sjölander's double life was discussed everywhere. Anonymous women spoke out in the papers and on websites about what he had done to them. Polemicists became hoarse hotel drunkards, banging on every door. On social media, people competed to invent the cruellest, most creative punishments. Vanessa couldn't decide whether this was a way a healthy society *ought* to react. With rage. Frustration. But what was the alternative? Apathy?

The evidence against Oscar Sjölander continued to stack up. The bloody jumper, as well as a knife presumed to be the murder weapon, had been recovered twenty metres from his house in Bromma. A motive: he didn't want to have kids with Rakel. A well-documented history of violence in the form of stories told by women he had threatened. Grabbed by the throat. Rakel's text message to her friend Katja. Now even his wife, Therese, admitted that he had hit her.

Oscar Sjölander denied it. Although he did so, judging by the recordings Vanessa had heard, with ever-dwindling conviction. He continued to blame the rough-sleeper.

After examining Rakel, the pathologists would be able to ascertain an approximate time of death. From that, it would be possible to check the movements of Oscar Sjölander's black 4x4 as it passed traffic cameras on the way from Tyresö to Bromma.

Vanessa heard a knock on the window and squinted towards the shadow outside. Trude Hovland waved and made a gesture that Vanessa interpreted as a request to join her. She nodded, but immediately regretted doing so. Most of all, she wanted to be alone with her thoughts.

Trude ordered a beer and sat down.

"What a day," she said, taking a sip. "I had to go for a walk."

"Do you live nearby?"

Trude nodded. "Markvardsgatan."

With her thumb, Vanessa gestured towards her own building.

"Roslagsgatan. By Monica Zetterlund Park."

"What's that?"

Trude pointed to a list of companies that had visited Rosersbergs Slotts Hotel that was sticking out of Vanessa's bag.

"Me and Ove are trying to identify an alternative suspect in the Emelie Rydén case. At least we were. Rakel Sjödin got in the way."

"Is this to do with the prints on the pen from Rosersbergs?"

Vanessa nodded slowly as she took a sip of her beer, which was now flat and warm.

"Do you have any ideas?" asked Trude.

Vanessa turned around, looking for Kjell-Arne. She wanted a gin and tonic. To relax. Sleep without dreaming. Without seeing images of stabbed female bodies.

"Emelie Rydén lets the murderer in. She knows him. Or at least recognises him. Above all, *he* knows that she's home alone that night. Maybe he's a customer from the salon?"

"Well, Swedish men might be vain, but there can't have been many male customers there in the past six months."

"Fifteen."

"Have you checked them out?"

Kjell-Arne looked at Vanessa. She formed her fingers into a 'G' and 'T'. Received a thumbs-up in response.

"I've checked for criminal records," she said, turning to Trude. "Nothing out of the ordinary."

"Customers who paid cash in hand?"

Vanessa shrugged. Of course some of Emelie's customers could have paid that way, but then they would not be listed in the booking system that the detectives had searched.

"The statistics..." Trude began.

"Say that it's Karim," Vanessa cut in. "Around twenty-seven women are murdered in Sweden each year. The perpetrator is unknown to the victim in only six per cent of resolved cases. What is the first thing we do when investigating a woman's death? Check out her partner. Number two? Other men in her life. We do so routinely – because the statistics tell us to do so. Most of the time it leads us to the right place. This time, it led us straight to Karim. A history of assaulting women. He had threatened Emelie. He is a wretch, but he did not murder her."

"How do you know that?"

"He has an alibi."

"That mate of his?"

"No, someone else. A woman."

"What about the blood on his shoes?"

Vanessa nodded. She placed the two-page list of Rosersbergs conference guests in front of Trude, who gave her a quizzical look. "Next page."

Trude hurried to turn the page. Her eyes widened. She was staring at the line that Vanessa had highlighted in yellow marker pen.

"So, there's your connection."

7

THE SKY BAR was empty, but Börjc had managed to borrow the money for yet another bottle of vodka and was sitting alone on the bench as the thoughts floated through his murky, stupefied brain. He had drunk himself brave enough to die. His head slumped onto his chest, and he almost fell asleep. His mouth had a life of its own. He was wheezing. Talking incoherently to himself.

After being released from Salberga, he'd had no choice. What was left for him in Sala? His kids hated him. As did their mother. He had never been much of a father. When he was sentenced, his oldest son was beaten up at school, and they shouted murderer at him in the corridors. During the trial, Börje hadn't even had the decency to apologise to the widow. A lisping popinjay of a lawyer had instructed him to remain silent.

When Börje got out, he'd made straight for the railway station and jumped on the first train to Stockholm. In the capital, he'd slept in metro carriages. Fearing the city's youth gangs, he'd prowled the streets at night. Had a few beatings. That, somehow, had felt good too. As though he deserved it. Twenty-four months in prison – no fucking way was that atonement for taking the lives of two human beings.

Eva's death was his real punishment. God or not. You didn't just get away with hitting and killing two people while drunk.

Börje stood up, his legs unsteady. He took a sideways step and stood still for a minute to get his balance. Walked along the platform. The people waiting for the train moved out of the way.

That's right. Just despise me.

Two minutes until the next arrival.

He ought to throw himself in front of the train. Dodge months of drinking. Angst. Abstinence. Misery. It was unavoidable that he was going to die before the year was out, whether he wanted to or not. He was better off deciding how himself. Get it out of the way. Stop feeling sorry for himself. Now that Eva was gone, no one made him happy. He felt guilt over what he'd said to Elvis. How he'd treated him. His friend had done nothing wrong, was only trying to help. To pull Börje upwards, keep his head above water. To do what he'd failed to do for Eva.

One minute.

Passengers stood up from the benches. The driving cab's headlights came into view in the distance. Came closer. Swept down the platform. Long shadows danced along the walls. Börje grunted and barged his way forward. He longed to take that leap. He stumbled. Dropped the bottle, which smashed. The spirit ran across the concrete. Anxious looks. A teenage girl stared daggers.

"Look where you're going," said a woman with a pushchair.

Börje grunted again. He focused on what lay ahead. A leap, then he would be a bloody carcass. He wouldn't have to miss Eva every single moment. He wouldn't have to feel guilt and shame. He had nothing left to fill the voids with.

The brakes squealed. The glare of the headlights blinded him, and he raised his hand to protect his eyes.

"Little Eva. I'm coming," he slurred.

8

THE NEWSROOM WAS a hive of activity. Jasmina's eyes met Bengt's and he walked over and leaned in towards her desk.

"Kovac. What a bloody piece. That's going to sell loads!"

He thumped the desk twice, did a quick shuffle to one side, and danced on his way.

"When the pizzas arrive, we'll have a meeting by the big desk," he called out to the room. "Well done, everyone."

Next to Jasmina, Max Lewenhaupt was clattering away, huddled over his laptop. His tongue poked from the corner of his mouth. His usually so well groomed hair was all over the place.

"Can you read this before I send it off?" he said without looking up.

"Sure."

"Give me a couple of minutes. I'm just going to polish the last bit," he said and continued hammering at the keys.

Since Rakel Sjödin had been found dead, the story stayed alive by itself. Reader interest was sky high. Each new article broke records. Contrary to what people believed, it wasn't quick clicks the editorial team were after, but loyalty. Returning visitors, the ones who pay for content. That meant having to deliver quality.

The number of digital subscribers was increasing by three hundred a day.

"Right then," Max exclaimed then leaned back and turned the computer towards Jasmina.

She rolled her chair closer. Their elbows touched. She pulled hers in. The article was a longer piece about developments in the Rakel case throughout the day, beginning with a short summary of the detention of *the TV presenter.*

Afterwards, Max proceeded to recount what had leaked from Police HQ about the interviews with Oscar Sjölander. According to an anonymous informant close to the investigation, the presenter had started crying when he was told that the body had been found. They had had to suspend the interview. And, in a concise statement, Oscar Sjölander's lawyer had stated that his client was in a bad way. Rakel's family had been informed.

After a sub-heading came what was probably going to be tomorrow's news bill. The police had confirmed – for the first time – that the bloody knife found outside the presenter's villa in Bromma was the murder weapon.

Jasmina could feel Max staring at her expectantly.

The last part was a dutiful statement from a senior figure at TV4, explaining that they did not wish to comment on the allegations.

"Good," she said once she'd finished reading.

"Good? Is that it?"

He seemed disappointed.

"It's very good, Max. But you already know that," Jasmina said and stood up.

"You sure?"

"Yes, Max. I'm sure," she said with a smile.

Bengt gathered the remaining reporters by the news desk. Jasmina took a slice of pineapple pizza, a plastic glass of Fanta and joined the semicircle of reporters who had lined up around Bengt. He thanked them for their hard work over the past few days of intensive reporting. Jasmina longed to go home to her bed. She realised that this was the first time she'd thought about the little apartment on Valhallavägen as *home.*

She actually wanted to stay there. Karim Laimani shouldn't be allowed to ruin that. Every time she thought about him having been inside her, she was filled with revulsion. It was unfair. He was going to go free; she would remember him for the rest of her life.

Bengt started distributing the next day's assignments. Jasmina was asked to report at one o'clock.

"It's just a matter of time until we go public with the fact that it is Oscar Sjölander. I want you to put together an in-depth piece about his life. Use the contacts you have in Växjö to get hold of childhood friends and people that knew him growing up. How does that sound, Kovac?"

"Sure. No problem."

Jasmina returned to her desk to collect her things. Max was still lolling at his desk, yawning as he packed away his laptop.

"Do you fancy a drink?" he asked. "I have such trouble sleeping after days like today."

She hesitated, since she wanted to be well-rested for tomorrow. At the same time, she did need to relax. She too found it difficult to come back down after news-intensive days. On top of that, she ought to get better at socialising. Since arriving in Stockholm, Jasmina had been alone.

"Come on. A cocktail will do you good."

9

THE TRAIN WAS a dozen or so metres from Börje. Its brakes squealing. He took a step towards the edge. The next step would be his last, the one that took him down onto the tracks. In front of the train. Under its wheels. He was just about to leap when he felt a hand on his shoulder.

The person, who he still could not see, was holding him back. Börje spun around and stared angrily at a familiar face.

It was Jörgen, the security guard, the one who used to wind up Börje and Elvis and the others in the Sky Bar. His close-set eyes studied Börje belligerently, then moved to the broken vodka bottle on the ground and then back to Börje. The carriages rushed past.

"So you're having a little party on my platform?"

"Let me go," Börje said, attempting to struggle free.

Around them, people were stepping off the train. Börje felt furious. Clenched his fists.

"Calm yourself down, otherwise I'll have to use the truncheon," said Jörgen. His colleague took a step forward. Börje aimed a blow at Jörgen, who was still holding his shoulder. But he was too drunk. His clenched fist missed its target by some margin but signalled to the guards to draw their batons.

Börje roared and threw himself towards Jörgen. They tumbled against the side of the train with a loud bang. People around them started screaming. Inside the train, people got to their feet to see the tumult. Börje lay on top of his adversary, who was struggling to take control. His colleague raised his truncheon and slammed it onto Börje's back. Something in there broke. The pain made his head crackle.

Börje fell to one side. Took another blow, to his upper arm, before they threw themselves over him and between them managed to hold him down. His face was pressed against the platform. He bawled at them, unable to catch his breath. Kicking his legs and squirming his torso as he tried to break free.

After a while, the movements eased off. The guards dragged him towards the centre of the platform. Jörgen had his knee pressed in Börje's back and made him lie still on his belly.

The doors closed. Börje could feel the tarmac vibrating against his cheek as the train pulled away.

"You fucking freak," Jörgen muttered, wiping his bloodied lip. He spat onto the ground.

"Shall we take him into the room?" his colleague asked.

Börje knew what the room was – a soundproofed space underneath the platform which the guards used to detain people while waiting for the police to arrive. There were no windows or CCTV cameras. The guards would usually claim that the detainee had been violent and had to be calmed down while they waited. In those circumstances, it was easy for a head to bang into a wall or an arm to get broken. Börje didn't care. They could kick him in. He could take a beating, and he was a dead man no matter what.

"Pussies," he snarled, and the pressure from the knee in his back increased.

He tried to swing his arm backwards, but this resulted in Jörgen grabbing hold of his hand and pushing it up tight against his back.

Börje screamed.

"Jesus you stink, you homeless gorilla. What the fuck does that hag you usually hang around with have to say about that? But then maybe she doesn't give a shit, being an old whore and all," said Jörgen.

"Don't talk about her like that," Börje panted.

The guard laughed mockingly.

"Whore."

Börje pressed his face to his shoulder, didn't want them to see that he was crying. They went through his pocket. Jörgen's colleague found the letter and held it up to the light between his thumb and index finger.

"Don't throw it away. Whatever you do, don't throw that letter away," Börje muttered.

"What would you pay for a session with his old bag?" Jörgen asked, ignoring Börje's protests.

"Not much," his colleague replied, pinching Börje's upper arm hard. He clenched his teeth so as not to make a sound. "You'd have to search far and wide to find an uglier bitch."

They slotted handcuffs around Börje's wrists and led him roughly towards the escalator.

"This should be fun, boss," the other guard said with a laugh that sounded like a hyena.

"You know we've got a big stock of telephone books down there?" Jörgen whispered in Börje's ear as they walked. "Not like we fucking use them when we need a number these days. No, even you can grasp that, despite being a stinky tramp of a clown. The thing is that if you hit – let's say a thigh – with a truncheon, you get these ugly marks. Then the police who come to pick you up will end up getting cross with us. But… you put a phone book in between. And ta-da, no bruises. The pain is the same though. I promise you that."

10

IT WAS HALF-PAST eight in the evening when Tom took up his position on the balcony on Norrbackagatan.

His bag contained blankets, a flask of coffee, dark hat, a Sudoku book and a camera with two different lenses. The apartment looked empty. Maybe she was having dinner out with a friend?

He rolled onto his back and studied the silvery cloud formations that were gliding in over Stockholm.

He took out his phone, checked Henrietta's Instagram. Her only post was a couple of hours old. Tomorrow, she and Douglas and their friends had booked a table at Taverna Brillo to celebrate her birthday.

Douglas, meanwhile, had made more regular updates that evening. He was in Copenhagen, and Henrietta was not with him. If Tom knew her, she would never have passed up the opportunity to brag on social media. He pulled out the Sudoku book, solved three of the advanced puzzles in a matter of minutes and then put it down. He was bored. He thought about heading home.

He logged into the forum that he spent most time on. User *Wacko* was online. Then again, he almost always was. He just sat there in his bedroom, smoking his cigarettes and staring down the lens. They'd written to each other a few times. Soothed each other's angst. Joked. Talked about suicide.

What you doing? wrote Wacko.

Waiting for a hottie, replied Tom.

What are you going to do with her?

Tom sniggered and was putting his thumbs to the screen when he heard the main door opening.

Two people crossed the courtyard. He recognised Henrietta immediately. The man too. Broad-shouldered, with a Neanderthal jaw. His hair was brown and close-cropped. It was one of the guys from the gym. Tom had seen Henrietta chatting to him on a couple of occasions and been filled with jealousy.

Tom's hands expertly rigged up the camera, removed the lens cap and assumed the position. A moment later, the lights came on in the living room.

The man stood with his back to the window. Henrietta had taken off her coat, revealing the short black dress underneath. She was dancing around with a bottle of spirits in her hand. Her foot didn't seem to be bothering her any more. She tried to get the guy to join in and he danced a few steps but then slumped onto the sofa.

The man pulled a zippy bag from his trouser pocket, held it in the air and waved it around. Henrietta disappeared, then came back a few seconds later carrying a silver tray. As they made their way into the living room, she turned the dimmer. The lighting softened. Tom adjusted the camera's settings. Henrietta put the tray on the coffee table. The guy carefully emptied the bag's white contents and then scraped sideways lines with a credit card.

As he zoomed in and adjusted the camera's focus, Tom could feel his pulse rising.

11

JASMINA HAD ONLY seen the Grand Hôtel in photographs. A green-uniformed porter nodded and held the door. Max pretended to bow and let her go first.

After leaving the newsroom, they had gone to Lemon Bar, close to Police HQ, with a couple of colleagues. They'd drunk watery beer for twenty-five crowns a pop.

There, they'd talked about the news events of the past twenty-four hours, shared gossip about their bosses, and discussed article ideas. Jasmina had enjoyed it. Felt relaxed. Included. After both their colleagues had gone home, Max suggested that they go on. At first she'd thought he was joking when he mentioned the Grand Hôtel. She was wearing jeans and an old white shirt that had been embellished with a coffee stain that day.

Max had laughingly dismissed her concerns and flagged down a taxi.

"The bar is this way," he said, pointing to the right.

A couple of tourists sat drinking beer while watching football on telly. A mental image from Hotel Anglais popped up – from when Karim had moved closer to her on the sofa. Jasmina batted it away.

They walked on into a narrow, beautifully decorated room. Tanned businessmen with loose ties stood around drinking cocktails. Waiters dressed all in white swanned around taking orders. Through the pillars, Jasmina could see the palace on the other side of the water. The city's lights shimmered on the dark waters beneath the quayside as shadows moved along it. A sorrowful melody was coming from the grand piano, which somehow resembled a large black spider in the far corner. Jasmina recognised it but couldn't recall the name. A couple of people were sitting on high stools close to the piano, and had their cocktails perched on its top.

"The veranda?" asked Max.

"I'd rather be close to the pianist."

"I'm with you."

Jasmina let Max order them cocktails – she thought it was best not to reveal how clueless she was – and leaned back.

"Do you come here often?" she asked once the waiter had moved on.

Something in his eyes lit up.

"When I first started dreaming about becoming a journalist, I used to get dressed up in a suit and come down here with a notepad. I used to pretend to be a war correspondent, recuperating after a long day in the field. But you mustn't say that to anyone."

"I promise," Jasmina said with a smile. "Actually, I used to do something similar."

"Do tell."

"I used to force Mum to let me interview her. She had to play different characters. One day she was a film star who'd just won an Oscar, the next she played a politician who'd been caught lying. And I used to make news bills that I hung up in my room."

Max laughed out loud.

"She's supported you then?"

"Always."

Max gulped. Then nodded slowly. Jasmina's head felt comfortably muffled. She looked straight at him.

"Why did you pinch my article?"

He thought about it for a moment. Scratched his chin. Jasmina noticed that his fingernails were bitten to the quick.

"Because it was bloody good. But I am ashamed. It was dishonourable. I was getting desperate. I was worried you were the one who was going to get to stay on at the paper."

His answer took her by surprise.

"What on earth made you think that?"

"Because there's something about you – even if you don't talk much – something that means people understand that you're competent. People listen to you, whenever you do say something. Call it charisma, if you like."

No one had ever told Jasmina that she was charismatic. She studied him intently, trying to work out if he was winding her up.

"Excuse me," he said and got to his feet. "Back shortly."

Max disappeared towards the toilets. In the meantime, the waiter came over with their cocktails. They looked identical, both garnished with a slice of pineapple and a cherry. Jasmina said thanks, the waiter nodded in reply, and she lifted the cocktail to her lips.

Max returned and pointed to her glass. "Singapore Sling. Do you like it?"

"I prefer beer."

Max smiled.

"Me too, really. But listen, about me nicking the article. Are we cool now?"

"Yes."

Max twirled his glass thoughtfully before putting it down again.

"This might sound silly, but success is very important to me. My family – my dad in particular – are against the whole business. Journalism is a dying industry. We earn fuck all. He wants me to work in finance, like he does. That's why… shit, I want to show him that I can take care of myself. Not getting my contract extended would have been a failure. And in my family, we do not fail."

12

TOM DIDN'T ACTUALLY know anything about drugs, but he guessed that the white powder was cocaine. Henrietta put a candlestick on the coffee table and lit the candles. The gym guy waved her over, said something that made her laugh and pointed at the tray.

Tom zoomed in yet further, and he could clearly see the four separate lines.

He switched to film mode and captured every expression that crossed Henrietta's face as she snorted the powder. Afterwards, she leaned back, touched her nose and passed the snipped drinking straw to the man. They then laid down side by side on the sofa, their faces close together. Their mouths joined. It looked like they couldn't stop talking. This was amongst the most intimate things Tom had ever experienced. The guy stroked Henrietta with his finger, running it across her tummy. She curled up, giggled and played along. There was no doubt what was about to happen.

"Prim little Henrietta, you're just demonstrating what little whores you are, the lot of you," Tom muttered.

They did another line and got shakily to their feet.

Henrietta turned a knob on the speaker by the TV cabinet. Their bodies swayed, and Tom wondered what they were listening to. Henrietta pulled her black dress over her head. She was dancing in her knickers, with her arms aloft. The man took off his T-shirt. His torso was muscular, and his arms rippled with veins.

Henrietta stroked his chest, pressing her breasts against him, and her honed back glowed in the candlelight. Tom observed the mating dance as his penis filled with blood.

Tom hated her with a passion, yet at the same time he had never been so turned on.

She should never have humiliated him. He could not let that sort of thing go unpunished. Sure, it was rough on Douglas, but he was better off finding out what a treacherous slut he was living with.

They kissed. Henrietta extricated herself and pointed to the table. She put the candlestick on the window sill, forcing Tom to adjust the camera settings once more.

Henrietta banged on the tabletop with her hand. Her eyes were misty, lustful, excited. The man took off his trousers and pants and threw them onto the floor. Then he laid himself, naked, on the table.

Henrietta picked up the bag and knelt down by his feet. The guy raised his head, watching as she tapped cocaine along the length of his penis, straightened it out with the credit card and then sucked it through the straw up her nose. After that, she licked up any leftovers.

Henrietta swapped places with him, but lay on her front, waving her bottom in the air. The guy snorted from her right buttock and then peeled off her knickers.

Tom had an idea. He quickly adjusted the camera and propped it on the blankets so that it continued filming the apartment while he looked for the microphone case. He stood up carefully, opened the balcony door and listened. The stairwell was silent and empty. He jogged across the courtyard and up the steps leading to the annexe. Then he crouched down, opened the letter box and lowered the mic in. He heard them panting and moaning.

"This is how you like to be fucked, isn't it?"

Henrietta moaned. A hoarse, submissive whimper. Like a porn film, Tom thought to himself as he grew hard once again and moved his hand down towards his groin.

"Yes, yes. Harder!"

Tom smiled.

The main door opened and the light in the stairwell came on. Tom reeled in the cable and carefully closed the letter box. He got to his feet and walked calmly down the steps with the microphone hidden in his hand. Halfway down, he nodded to a woman who was on her way up with a pizza in her arms.

He would really have liked some more audio material, but that was enough for a film that would ruin Henrietta's life.

Tom unlocked the door to the flat at Essinge Brogata 18 and hung up his jacket. He walked mechanically into the study, moved the mouse and checked the surveillance camera he had secretly installed in the stairwell. Nothing untoward had happened in the hours he'd been away.

He went into the kitchen, took a fresh head of broccoli out of the fridge, put it on a plate and took it into the study. He put the plate down on his desk, dropped to the floor and did fifty push-ups. He then turned over and did a hundred sit-ups.

When he was finished, he sat himself down at the computer, breathing heavily from the exertion, and took a bite of the broccoli.

Because he suffered from anosmia, Tom had no sense of smell, which meant he couldn't taste anything either. Tom ate vegetarian and fish as often as he could, because he wanted to live a long life. Puberty had been a living hell, since no one had ever told him that he smelled bad. In ninth grade, his PE teacher had taken him to one side and explained that he ought to wash more regularly. Since then, Tom showered every single day.

He surfed between a few of his favourite forums. In the dark window behind the computer screen, Tom's thin face and shaved head reflected in a cold, bluish light. He quickly pulled down the blinds to avoid having to look at it. Some days, he couldn't look at himself in the mirror without hearing the abuse thrown at him in the schoolyard.

Tom put his feet up on the desk, leaned back on his chair

and ate the rest of the broccoli. He opened the top drawer and pulled out one of the testosterone injections that he'd bought on the dark web and opened the packaging. He went into the bathroom, pulled down his trousers and leaned against the sink as he injected the fluid into his buttock. Sound poured through the wall.

His eighty-nine-year-old neighbour Greta had left the telly on.

Tom went out into the hall where the keys to her apartment hung. Greta's self-important idiot of a son had left them with Tom. The front door locked itself and occasionally the dippy old bag would knock on Tom's door so he could let her in.

In the flickering light cast by the TV, Greta was sleeping with her head on her chest. The remote was lying on the coffee table. Tom turned it down. She was sitting, legs apart, in a nightdress that reached halfway down her thighs. He crouched down, attempting to catch a glimpse of her genitals.

Tom stood up and went into the kitchen to inspect the fridge. He spotted a saucepan, lifted the lid and saw that it contained a fish stew. He fished a Tupperware box out of a drawer, filled it and took it out into the hall.

Tom searched the pockets of her jacket. Where did the biddy keep her purse? He usually pilfered a few notes during his visits. She only had herself to blame, and besides, Tom needed the money more than she did.

He squinted in the weird light and thought to himself that he should've brought a torch. Eventually he found the purse, in a bag hanging from a hook next to the hall mirror. He opened the notes compartment. Four hundred crowns. He stuffed three hundred into the back pocket of his jeans. He found himself suddenly transfixed by the black-and-white portraits hanging on the wall.

He put his finger to his lips.

"Shh," he hissed.

They were probably all long-dead. All that was left of them was yellowing photographs in the home of a half-senile pensioner. Taking the lunchbox with him, he left and locked the door behind him. Back in his own flat, he noticed that he'd got a message.

I'm in.

Tom smiled.

13

VANESSA AND OVE were driving back towards Åkersberga Prison to meet Karim Laimani again. On the cliffs and beaches of Brunnsviken, day trippers in swimming costumes jostled past each other. A couple were paddling a canoe. On the radio, a news anchor was recounting how two masked men had stolen an ambulance the night before, from a call-out in Fittja.

"Idiots," muttered Ove.

A colleague on a motorbike passed them in the outside lane.

"Have you heard the one about Gorbachev?" Vanessa asked him.

Ove shook his head.

"Moscow. Sometime in the eighties. Reagan is there on a state visit, Gorbachev is late for their meeting. The driver is driving fast, but not fast enough according to Gorbachev. He asks to drive himself and they swap places. Manage a few miles. Two motorcycle cops at the roadside. They see the limousine race past at top speed. One of them jumps on his bike and gives chase. He soon comes back though."

"Right?"

"His colleague asks him if he wrote a ticket. The officer shakes his head. 'There was a very powerful person in the car.' His colleague answers: 'Oh right, who was that then?' to which the first officer replied: 'I don't know. But Gorbachev was his driver.'"

Ove grunted.

On the motorway, the traffic tightened at first before eventually grinding to a complete standstill.

"Open the glovebox," she said.

Ove leaned in. The Volvo in front of them rolled forward slightly. Vanessa accelerated gently. Managed a few metres before gently pressing the brake.

"What am I looking for?"

"A plastic wallet."

Ove held it up.

"What's this?"

"The list of names of companies that have visited Rosersbergs Slotts Hotel in the past six months. Check the yellow highlighting on the next page."

Ove turned the page.

"Prison Service," he muttered, turning to Vanessa. "So they had a conference there. Did Emelie get the pen from the prison?"

"We ought to have a look at the surveillance footage from the visit, now that we know what we're looking for."

"I'll do that when we get back to the station," said Ove.

Vanessa and Ove approached the uniformed guard behind the front desk at Åkersberga and explained the purpose of their visit. He made a phone call, asked them to hand over their phones before they walked through the metal detector.

"What did you do yesterday?" asked Ove.

"I met Trude."

Ove raised his eyebrows.

"By chance," said Vanessa. "She was out for a walk, passed by my local and then she ended up coming in and having a few beers."

"You know what they say about her, right?" asked Ove. He glanced at the prison guard a few metres in front of them and lowered his voice. "She's a sex addict."

"A what?"

Ove nodded.

"That's why she split up with her ex. She was unfaithful. With men and women. She's supposed to have had a fling with your boss, Kask, since then. But he's by no means the only one."

Vanessa couldn't help picturing her boss with Trude. Naked, beautiful, writhing. She liked that image.

"Get out of it, Ove."

"I'm just reporting what I've heard. Neutral. Balanced. *Public Service.*"

"More like a spotty kid sitting in the basement of his mum's house with sticky kitchen roll in the bin, spewing nasty words onto *flashback.org.*"

The guard stopped in front of a door, explained that the prisoner was being brought up and unlocked it. Vanessa and Ove sat down. Vanessa crossed her legs and leaned back against the chair's hard backrest.

A key turned in the lock and Karim Laimani entered, flanked by two warders. His mouth formed into a mocking sneer. The man in front of them had not murdered Emelie Rydén, but he had drugged and raped Jasmina Kovac.

Karim walked slowly over to the empty chair. He looked shamelessly at Vanessa and licked his lips. She held his stare. Remembered Jasmina's face. The tears. Her shuddering body.

Ove nodded to the warders, who left the room. Vanessa and Karim were still staring hatefully at one another. Ove cleared his throat.

"We're here to find out whether you have any thoughts about who murdered your ex-girlfriend, Emelie Rydén."

Karim didn't answer. He formed a V with his index and middle fingers and stuck his tongue out between them. Vanessa reacted instinctively, drilling her heel into his crotch. Hard. Ground it around.

Karim screamed, grimacing with the pain. He got halfway to his feet, clenched his fists. Vanessa smiled with her lips pressed together.

"You're too old for my tastes anyway, pig cunt," said

Karim, bending over and rubbing the palm of his hand against the point of impact.

"And you're too small for mine," Vanessa shot back, wagging her little finger.

"Can we all calm down," said Ove, who had himself got to his feet in readiness to throw himself at Karim if he tried to start on Vanessa.

Vanessa held her palms up and gave her colleague an apologetic look. She slumped back onto her chair.

"Karim, we are investigating the murder of your daughter's mother. We know that you didn't do it, but we wonder whether you have any thoughts about who might have wanted to kill her?" said Ove.

"Why would I help you, fatty?"

"Because it's your daughter's mother who's been killed," Ove said calmly.

Vanessa noted that Karim's neck was blotchy red. She guessed that wasn't because of the heat.

"She wasn't much of a mother. Or a girlfriend for that matter." Ove sighed.

"Did she seem afraid, the last time she was here? Was there a particular reason that had made her contact you?"

Karim closed his mouth tightly and folded his arms.

"For Christ's sake. Help us, for your daughter Nova's sake." Now Karim sighed.

"She gave me a drawing, said it was over and then she left."

"That was it?"

Karim nodded.

"Do you know if she had a pen with her?" asked Ove.

"How would I remember that?"

Vanessa leaned forward.

"Emelie's blood was found in your cell. Someone planted it there and led us to you. Do you have enemies in this prison? Someone who could have hurt her to get at you?"

Karim sniggered.

"Isn't a man with no enemies no man at all?"

"Four other inmates were on parole at the same time as you," Vanessa said, then listed their names. "Could any of them be involved?"

"If they were, I wouldn't be grassing to you. I'd be sorting it out myself."

Vanessa rolled her eyes as Karim Laimani called the warders and stood up. Before he turned around, he gave her one last glance.

"I'll see you when I get out, Vanessa Frank."

Vanessa raised her little finger as a goodbye. "I'll be waiting, dwarf cock."

An hour later, Vanessa and Ove drove past the Natural History Museum, where school groups gathered on the steps. Vanessa's phone vibrated. Unknown number. She pressed her phone between her ear and her shoulder.

"Frank?"

The conversation lasted exactly one minute and twenty-seven seconds. As she hung up, she turned left onto Norrtullsrondellen.

"I'll drop you off at the police station. I have to go somewhere." Ove looked at her, taken aback.

"What's this about?"

"Rakel Sjödin."

14

NICOLAS PAREDES HEARD a loud scream from Celine's apartment. He stood up from the sofa and put his head to the wall. More screams. His first thought was that Celine's dad had attacked her, but the sounds coming from in there lacked both fear and pain. She sounded furious. He checked the time, 10.30. She should have been at school.

Nicolas went out onto the balcony. The cloudless sky was light blue. The sun was beating down. Celine's apartment door was open. He called her name and she emerged wearing an enormous headset.

"Why are you screaming?" asked Nicolas.

"I'm playing *Fortnite*."

"What's that?"

"It's a game, Grandad."

"It's Wednesday. Why aren't you at school?"

"I just told you."

"Because you're playing computer games?"

Nicolas was in a good mood. He didn't feel like being cooped up in his stuffy apartment. In three days' time, he would be boarding the plane to London. He might as well go to school with Celine if that's what it was going to take to get her there.

"What school do you go to?" he asked.

Celine didn't answer.

"Where is it? I'll go with you," he said.

"Can't."

"Why not?"

"My class is at Eriksdal Baths."

Celine closed the door, and he watched through the glass as she slumped onto the sofa.

Nicolas stood there, not knowing what to do next. Was he imagining it, or had he just seen a crack in her normally so confident façade? He felt sorry for her. And Celine had no one to talk to. Not only that, he owed her a favour after she'd helped Vanessa to get his holdall out.

He stepped up onto the railing, hopped over to her side and knocked on the window.

She stared at him in surprise from the sofa, then got up.

"What do you want?" she mimed through the window.

Nicolas felt unsure. He exaggerated his pronunciation so that she'd be able to make out what he was saying through the glass.

"I just have to ask… well, it's not that… Is it that you don't like wearing a swimming costume?"

She studied him for a couple of seconds before she slid open the door. "Swimming costume?"

It felt like a sensitive subject. Nicolas shrugged.

"Yes. Or a bikini, perhaps. I don't know."

"Are you deaf? I just don't want to go. And anyway, the chlorine makes my hair yellow."

Nicolas studied her green mop and thought to himself that a bit of chlorine would do the bacterial cultures in there good. But at the same time he realised that neither chlorine nor bodily insecurities were the reason Celine didn't want to go swimming.

"What?" she asked irritably.

"Can you swim, Celine?"

The air was still, and small, gentle waves sloshed against the rocks. Celine was standing knee-deep in the water and looking terrified. In front of them, across the water, lay the island of Fläsket.

"Can't we just sod this and sunbathe instead?" she pleaded. "It's bloody freezing."

Once Nicolas had finally persuaded her to change into swimwear and leave the flat, Celine had refused to go anywhere someone might see her. They'd taken a right by the beach at Mälarhöjden and followed the shoreline.

"You can't have a rubber ring all your life."

"There's no law that says you have to be able to swim. I can just not go in the water."

"Like this," he said, demonstrating a swimming stroke. She hesitantly copied his movement. "Lie down here, in the shallows. Try it. I'll be standing next to you. The whole time."

Celine knelt down. Then she lay flat on the bottom and took a stroke.

"That looks good."

"I feel really fucking silly."

"Come on. We'll try a bit further out."

They waded out a couple of metres in the shallow waters.

"I'll keep my hand underneath you, so you won't sink."

Celine rolled her eyes but did as he said. Nicolas walked alongside, holding her up. He pulled his hand away. It wasn't pretty, but she managed to keep herself afloat.

"Look, Nicolas, I'm swimming!" she called out.

Her mouth filled with water. She started coughing and flailing her arms about. He picked her up.

"Did you see?" she spluttered happily, clinging onto him.

"I did." He laughed. "Try again."

A while later, they were drying themselves with their towels in the sun. Strips of Celine's green hair were plastered across her cheeks, and she had a smile on her lips. "It's quite fun, learning to swim, you know," she said.

"Good," Nicolas said, squinting at her.

"My fingers are like crinkle-cut crisps."

Nicolas examined her hand.

"That's to make gripping tools easier in wet environments.

Way back, we humans used to work and trap animals around water courses and lakes."

"Did you learn that in school?"

"No, military service. We did a bit of diving."

"Can you teach me?"

"Sure. When you can keep yourself above the surface."

"I think I'd like to do military service too. What was it called, what you did?"

"Coastal Ranger Company. Then attack diver."

"Do you think I can do it?"

"I think you can do anything. If you put your mind to it."

Celine turned her face away. She rolled onto her side and leaned her head against the palm of her hand. "Thanks," she muttered.

She lay down on the towel again and closed her eyes in the sunshine.

Nicolas' phone started vibrating. He shielded the screen with his hand. Vanessa. He stood up and walked a little way away. He had been planning to call her, see how things were between them.

"I want you to go and see Ivan again," she said without further ado. "He knows who Karim Laimani's enemies within the prison are. Which of the other inmates would have been able to put the forensic evidence there that made us believe he was behind Emelie's murder."

Nicolas wanted to stay as far away as possible from his childhood friend. But Vanessa wouldn't have asked if it wasn't important. If he could help her investigation in any way, he would of course do his best.

15

VANESSA PEERED INTO the cell through the hatch. It comprised a barred window and a bunk. The man lying on his back on the bed had a grey beard flecked with black. He was thin, verging on skinny. His face was swollen and bruised, his clothes were hanging off him, and his hair was dirty.

"Where did you find him?" Vanessa asked the officer standing behind her.

"He was picked up by security guards on the platform at Farsta metro station but resisted arrest. He was screaming and bawling, so we brought him in to sober up. Then, a couple of hours ago, once he was responsive, we discovered that there was a warrant out for him," she replied.

This, then, was the Börje Rohdén whose fingerprints and DNA had been found in the lean-to close to Oscar Sjölander's summer house. Violent past. Convicted of manslaughter. In the car on the way to Västberga, Vanessa had tried to call Mikael Kask but got no answer. When he returned the call half an hour later, she was already there. Vanessa explained that Börje Rohdén was in custody and wondered whether they wanted to send interrogators. Her boss, though, responded that there was no need; there was too much evidence pointing to Oscar Sjölander.

"Is he well known to our colleagues?"

"He's never been here. But since I got curious when I saw you were looking for him, I started asking around. He usually hangs out at the Sky Bar."

"Sky Bar?"

"Farsta's metro platform gets called that by the alkies. Because of the view, they say. I think that's quite sweet. They're pretty harmless, even if one or two of them have occasionally overdone it and had to spend the night here sobering up."

The woman turned the key in the lock, pushed open the door, and Vanessa stepped inside. She sniffed the air. Boozy vomit. Ajax. Börje Rohdén hardly seemed to notice that she was in the cell.

"My name is Vanessa Frank." No reaction. "I'm a detective at the National Homicide Unit."

Börje Rohdén folded his arms and carried on staring up at the ceiling.

"May I ask what happened to your face?"

"Ask the security guards about that," he growled. "They took me into a room and beat the shit out of me out of spite. But they're going to tell you I fell head-first into a wall."

"Table. They said you hit your head on a table."

"Idiots."

"I'm sorry," said Vanessa. "I'll ask the staff to make sure you get those wounds dressed."

Börje Rohdén lay on his side, grimacing in pain. He was still avoiding looking Vanessa in the eye. He stared stubbornly past her, straight at the wall.

"Where were you on Saturday morning?"

"Dunno."

"Come off it. It's four days ago."

No reply.

"You're not suspected of any crime."

His stare was blank. Indifferent.

"I don't know if you've been partying the last few days but…"

He flew up from the bed and straightened up to full stretch. Only now did Vanessa realise how tall he was. The eyes that were looking down at her were black with rage.

"Partying?" he screamed.

Vanessa braced herself to avoid stepping backwards. So as not to reveal that she'd been taken by surprise by his sudden aggressiveness. The situation was about to get out of hand. She wouldn't have a hope in that little space. She thought about calling out to a colleague but then decided that for now, she was okay. He pressed his jaws together.

"You don't have a fucking clue what you are talking about."

"Enlighten me."

Börje Rohdén gave a hollow laugh. Shook his head. His shoulders dropped, and his posture became less hostile. His belligerence disappeared, replaced by weariness. He slumped onto the bed. Vanessa could feel herself breathing out. There was something about this crumpled, sad figure in front of her that aroused her sympathy.

She took a step forward and then sat down next to him.

"I'm investigating the murder of Rakel Sjödin and…"

"Who?" asked Börje.

Vanessa was taken aback. Not even a homeless person could have missed the headlines over the past few days.

"Oscar Sjölander," she said. "Do you know who that is?"

"Yes, a bully."

Vanessa noticed that he was angry again, his voice tense and hard once more.

"He used to run up to me and Eva and accuse us of stealing things. He is not fucking right in the head. Is he the reason you're here?"

"In a way."

Börje Rohdén looked baffled. Vanessa went quiet. Let him wonder. Get curious. Just as she'd hoped, he softened.

"What's he accusing me of now?"

"Murder. Rakel Sjödin, a young woman he had a relationship with, was found dead after being missing since Saturday. He was the last person to see her alive. Then, when interviewed, he pointed to you as a potential suspect."

Börje opened his mouth, was about to say something but got a truculent look on his face and sealed his lips.

"I have nothing to do with that, so if you don't mind, I would like you to leave now."

"Where is Eva?" asked Vanessa.

"How do you know who Eva is?"

"You just said Eva. That Oscar Sjölander had accused you and Eva of stealing things."

Börje looked at her calmly. He knew something. Vanessa could tell by looking at him.

"There is a letter I want to get back. Those fucking security guards took it. If you get it for me, I'll tell you what I saw."

16

TOM WALKED IN to Taverna Brillo. He passed the kitchen on his left. Chefs in their whites clattered saucepans and barked instructions at each other.

He suddenly remembered that he'd been here before. Once, when he was still in the early stages of his awakening and had created a profile on a dating site. He used pictures of an American man he'd found on Facebook. He'd called himself Christoffer and claimed to be a photographer, with the world as his workplace. Shuttling between Los Angeles, New York, Milan, Paris and Stockholm. The response was overwhelming. Women wanted to meet up. Beautiful women. Tom was consumed with chatting to them, giving them compliments, inventing little stories about Christoffer's life.

One of the women, Rebecca, happened to be a colleague of his, a reporter at *Kvällspressen*. Young, overbearing and successful. Tom was always friendly towards her, but she was almost dismissive. She was only friendly towards bosses and the big-name reporters. The ones that could give her a leg-up. Rebecca was dazzled by her own beauty and excellence. Tom had arranged for Christoffer to meet Rebecca here, at Taverna Brillo. He'd taken a seat at the bar and taken pleasure in watching her wait in vain. Watching her otherwise so confident façade cracking in front of him.

Perhaps it was those months spent playing Christoffer that made Tom realise that women only cared about looks, status and money. No matter what impression they tried to give. In his eagerness to understand them, he had exposed them. And now, once he'd started seeing the pattern, that he'd stay alone because he was ugly, there was no way back.

To his right was the dining area where large groups and couples were eating dinner. On the left was a large bar, lined with groups clutching cocktails or beers in their hands. Tom felt awkward in the midst of the well-dressed, inebriated crowd. He went to the bar and ordered a tonic water with ice.

"Slice of lemon?" asked the barman.

Tom nodded. Not that he could taste it, but it looked nice.

He turned his back to the bar and surveyed the dining area. He took a sip, put down his glass just as he spotted Henrietta and Douglas a dozen or so metres away. The party comprised seven people. They must have arrived only minutes before Tom because they were still looking at the menu. Henrietta was so self-absorbed that he wasn't the slightest bit worried that she would notice him.

A waiter arrived with two bottles of fizz which he served and then left the remainder in shiny champagne buckets. The party raised a toast, turning towards Henrietta, who smiled, drank, and put down her glass. She stood up, revealing a black strapless dress. Tom got turned on at the thought of her naked. She said a few words, chinked her glass again and sat down.

What if he could blackmail her with the film instead – force her to satisfy him sexually. It was a lovely, titillating thought. But the risks were too great. Not given what lay ahead. She was nothing but a personal vendetta.

He was going to destroy her life, humiliate her in front of her boyfriend, colleagues and friends. She would never be able to trace it to him, even if he wished there was some way of telling her that it was him, Tom, who had defeated her.

The waiter took their order and Tom decided he might as well get it out of the way.

He pulled out his phone, put his headphones on and covered

the screen with his hand as he clicked on the forty-second-long film. As a soundtrack, he had chosen Vivaldi's *Four Seasons*.

The dramatic strings began to play. Henrietta and the man from the gym, dancing out of time. It looked comical. Tom smiled. The white lines appeared on screen. Cut to a close-up of Henrietta's face as she snorted off the guy's penis. She licked up the leftovers. The music got more and more dramatic. They swapped places. Henrietta arched her back on the coffee table. The music got quieter. Henrietta's screaming and moaning drowned out Vivaldi. The film concluded with the text *Happy Birthday, Henrietta! PS. Say hi to Douglas.*

Tom summoned the email addresses of her colleagues which he'd obtained from the PR company's website and sent them the film from an anonymous email address. After that, he logged into the Facebook account he'd created earlier, posted the film on Henrietta and Douglas' walls and tagged them.

All he had to do now was wait.

He put his phone in his back pocket and propped himself up against the bar. Tom watched as Henrietta reached for her mobile and put her finger on the screen. The next second, she shot the phone underneath the table. Douglas turned to her and asked her something.

Henrietta stood up without answering.

She stormed off towards the toilets with her phone in her hand. Tom wanted to see Douglas' reaction, but her boyfriend was still to discover the film. Douglas loosened his tie and leaned over towards the guy on the other side of the table.

Oh well. It was just a matter of time. Henrietta had still not returned.

Douglas peered over towards the toilets, seemingly bewildered by his girlfriend's sudden disappearance. He started fiddling with his phone. Tom guessed he was texting Henrietta, to ask what was taking so long.

The other guests didn't seem to have noticed anything and carried on chatting happily to each other.

Douglas shot up from the table. His mouth fell open as

he stared at his phone and then made for the toilets. Tom followed him.

Douglas squeezed past two women and called out to Henrietta. Tom pretended to be washing his hands, and in the mirror, he could see Douglas banging on the cubicle door.

"Come out here and explain to me what the fuck this is," Douglas screamed.

The door was slowly opened, and Henrietta's face came into view: red and swollen from crying.

Tom took a couple of steps back to get out of sight. Henrietta tried to soothe Douglas, but he was too upset. He pushed her aside and swept past Tom, leaving Taverna Brillo without saying goodbye to anyone.

17

JÖRGEN OLSÉN CROSSED the square at Liljeholmstorget with a takeaway beef Madras in a carrier bag. The evening air was still warm. Sweat trickled down the small of his back.

There weren't many people about. From somewhere came the sound of a dog barking.

A car was parked in the middle of the square. A black, shiny BMW with tinted windows. Definitely a dealer's, Jörgen thought to himself.

That was the problem with Sweden. Ordinary, honest people got nowhere. The only things you had to look forward to as a hard-working taxpayer were the weekends, summer holiday and the obligatory two weeks in Thailand in January. As a security guard, he could entertain himself by roughing up the odd alky or junkie, but that was nowhere near enough.

He ought to emigrate. Open a bar, get himself a sweet Thai girl who could cook, clean and satisfy his cock. He'd come close last winter. Not the stuff about the bar, but the woman.

At Showroom in Pattaya, he had met Lucy, at least that's what she called herself. Small and cute like a doll. Good in bed. Funny. Decent English. Jörgen usually had a rule about not fucking the same pro more than once during those two weeks. But then the next day, when he was back at Showroom and saw Lucy again, he couldn't resist. Without understanding how it had happened, he found himself sitting eating breakfast with her on a café terrace the next morning. For the remainder of his trip, he stuck with Lucy. She moved into his hotel room. She woke him with her lips around his cobra, like that Swedish Hollywood hag Anna Anka, who had said on TV that she usually woke her husband up that way. The stuff of dreams. Jörgen felt like James Bond.

On the last night, he had suggested that she should move to Sweden with him.

To his great delight, she said yes. But of course there were a number of practical things that had to be sorted out first.

Jörgen flew home. Deeply in love. He called her after work every day. Acted like a lovesick teen. After a week, Lucy needed money. Something to do with the rent. He happily sent two thousand crowns. The week after that, one of her aunts fell ill. What the hell, thought Jörgen, Lucy is family now, so there's no dilemma.

The aunt recovered, but then it was Lucy's turn to go under the knife. She explained that she wanted to look her best for her husband-to-be. And she had realised that Swedish men appreciate a substantial bust. Could he send her twenty thousand for a breast augmentation? Jörgen was over the moon. Sent the money. After the operation, they talked on Skype and Lucy had bandages over her breasts. They didn't look much bigger, but Lucy assured him that the camera was deceiving him. Jörgen begged and pleaded to see her tits, but Lucy refused. She wanted to wait until they finally met to show him.

Yet something didn't feel right. Something nagged away inside Jörgen.

Almost two months had passed since he left Pattaya. When was she going to come to Sweden? Each and every time, something got in the way. Eventually, he put her on the spot. Lucy cried. She explained that she longed for him, for Sweden and their new life together. But that now she owed a bar owner money. Five thousand crowns. After that, she could travel. Jörgen sold some of his shares and sent the money over.

After that, silence.

It took a couple of weeks for it to dawn on Jörgen that he'd been ripped off. A friend had recommended a Facebook page called *Thai Sluts Pattaya*, where Swedish men warned each other of fraudsters. One of the women was Lucy.

What kind of people got fooled like that?

Jörgen punched in the door code and stepped into the entrance hall. The door didn't close; a blonde woman had stuck her foot in the door. Snootily dressed, in blue suit trousers and a white blouse. She was attractive. A MILF. Bulging breasts beneath her blouse buttons.

"Jörgen Olsén?"

He was taken aback. Did he know her?

"Can I help you?"

"My name is Vanessa Frank and I'm a police officer. I need to talk to you."

What the fuck was this about? He had read an article in *Aftonposten* about some man-hating feminist's proposal to allow Swedish men to be prosecuted for paying for sex abroad. Was that why she was here? Shit. There he was, doing his bit to tidy up all the vagrants and other scum, keeping the streets safe for ordinary citizens. Surely he was allowed a bit of fun while he was recuperating?

"Can we talk up in your flat?" she asked.

"What is this about?"

"I'd rather discuss this somewhere a bit more private," she said as she pointed to the lift.

Jörgen studied her. She was too attractive for a policewoman. He, if anyone, knew that. The policewomen he'd met through work tended to weigh at least twenty kilos more. They were broad-shouldered, moved like men, spoke like men. This woman was nearly as skinny as Lucy.

Could the boys be behind this? Jörgen was turning forty the following week. Maybe they'd booked him an escort to keep his spirits up? Maybe decided to have a bit of fun first?

"What do you say, have you got time?" the blonde said.

Jörgen sniggered and stepped to one side so that she could

enter the waiting lift. He put the takeaway in the kitchen before sitting down, legs spread, on the sofa.

The blonde woman was left standing in the middle of the living room. She didn't appear to be in any hurry, and let her eyes wander around the room. They settled on the posters of bikini-clad suntanned beauties and sports cars that hung on the walls.

"Interesting decor," she said. "It's like going into my teenage boyfriend's place in 1989. The only thing missing is the bits of scrunched-up kitchen towel on the coffee table."

What a cheeky bitch, coming here and insulting him. Once he'd got her clothes off, she was going to be punished with the fleshy truncheon. She probably liked it rough. And if she didn't, that would make it even more fun. But then when she took off her blazer to reveal both a holster and pistol, he suddenly felt unsure. If it was a dummy, it was an unusually accurate one. Had he got the whole thing wrong?

"You and your colleague picked up a Börje Rohdén in Farsta," she said.

Shit. The woman really was a cop. That filthy tramp had reported him. Next time he saw him, there'd be no holding back. That alky had just signed his own death warrant.

"We felt that he was a danger to the public. Unfortunately the gloves had to come off when we were dealing with him. It is never enjoyable, but I'm afraid it's part of the job," he said mechanically.

She nodded. Gave her nose a quick scratch, without taking her eyes off him. Something about her had changed. Those eyes of hers were giving him the shivers.

"Listen here, Jörgen. I know that he didn't trip into the wall or hit his head on the table or whatever you put in the report. But today's your lucky day. The only thing I care about right now is the letter."

"What letter?"

Shit. What had they done with the letter? It must still be in the room by the platform.

"He had a letter on him. You or your colleague took it. And if you don't want *me* to have to invent a story about how you ended up with a bullet in your stomach after hitting your head on the table, then you'd better pull it out now."

Bluff, he needed to bluff her. Not give her anything to use against him. His brain went into overdrive, but without managing to come up with anything remotely useful. Jesus, she terrified him. But how did she do that? She was just standing there looking at him with her X-ray eyes.

"Ask your two brain cells to speed up their communication," she said, placing her fingers on her weapon. "Now…"

She took a step towards him. Felt for the pistol. He had a bad feeling about this.

"He must've dropped it."

"You can do better than that. Where might he have dropped it, do you think?"

"In the room. I mean where we detain them while we wait for your colleagues."

"Great. Let's go there then."

18

TOM CHOSE THE route via Kungsgatan. He drove slowly. The women were skimpily dressed and inviting. Bulging bodies in figure-hugging tops and tight jeans. Lots of them were wearing skirts. Tom wasn't sure what he preferred. Sure, he was egged on by the warmer months, yet there was also frustration because he knew that he would never get anywhere near that tanned, smooth skin.

Maybe countries like Saudi Arabia had a point. Women there had to cover up to avoid attracting men. Tom dreamed about emigrating from Sweden. It was like living in quicksand, and every day was a struggle to keep his head above the surface.

He stopped at a pedestrian crossing to let four women over. They didn't thank him or even look at him. How easy it would be to just floor the accelerator and plough into them. Scythe them down. See their bodies bounce off the bonnet.

"Nasty cunts," he said.

They reached the pavement on the other side, and Tom drove on. He didn't want to hate women. He just couldn't help it. Perhaps it had all started with his own mother – weak, depressive and obnoxious. She would invite home all kinds of men who she would spread her legs for. They hit both her and Tom, drank for days at a time, fucked her with the door open as he came home from school. And then they'd disappear. Always. His mother would cry, and come to his room at night, get into bed and look for comfort.

You have to promise me to always be kind to girls, Tom.

He shuddered. He hated the echo of her shrill, pitiful voice that was still alive inside him. Defining. Destructive.

At the end of ninth grade, he had called a landline. Jenny, the most popular girl in the class. The one who smoked, drank shit mixes of whatever drinks she could get her hands on and who was rumoured to have had sex with a high-school student on the climbing frame a couple of blocks down. She asked Tom if he wanted to meet up. Have an ice cream.

He got dressed up. Showered. Put on aftershave. Put on the graduation suit his mother had bought him. His mum was proud of him. She helped him comb his hair and gave him some money to buy some flowers. Tom arrived at the arranged meeting place – a bench down in Farsta precinct – in good time. The sun was shining. Blue skies. Pollen in the air. His heart was pounding, and his sweaty hands stuck to the cellophane wrapper.

The first water balloon landed a little way away from his shoes. The second was a direct hit, on the back of his head. Yellow, teenage urine ran down his shirt and blazer. The boys in his class came running towards him. Tom looked around in panic for an escape route, but they were coming from every direction. Like a giant, screaming creature, they captured him and took him to a multi-storey car park. He pissed himself. Thought he was going to die. They were punching and kicking him. Pulled down his trousers and rammed an empty bottle into his rectum.

Did you really think Jenny wanted to go on a date with you, you freak?

Look at his suit. I bet his nasty mum sewed it for him.

He was probably planning to rape her.

Once the echoes of their laughter had ebbed away, he was left lying there, panting.

His suit was ruined. His mother tore her hair out at the sight of him, crying as she locked herself away in her room. Tom rolled the suit and shirt into a ball and threw them down the rubbish chute.

In spite of that, he wanted to change. He'd assumed that it was his own fault. Now though, he understood. It was the fault of Western civilisation. He was one of the losers. A white, worthless man who was mocked and ridiculed on a daily basis by the female columnists in the papers. The media whores, the high priestesses. Couldn't people grasp what was going on? They switched things around and wrote as if they were coming from a position of weakness. Who, though, had the most power? Tom was a white man. Society expected him to succeed. He had never had a chance. With his single mother, the bullying, his unusual appearance. He didn't have a degree. Earned just over twenty-six thousand a month, before tax. How could they have the nerve to call him privileged? Those people, with their platforms in nationwide newspapers, their social media accounts with thousands of followers, their dinners with powerful people and politicians.

Tom's entire life had been a desperate cry for help, one drowned out by their voices.

He slowed to a stop by the traffic lights on Kungsgatan. The phone rang. Tom looked at the screen in surprise before he answered.

"I knew it," sobbed Katja. "I knew he was going to hurt her." She sounded drunk.

"I can't believe Rakel's dead."

"Have the police interviewed you?"

"Yes."

"What did you say to them?"

"I told it like it is, that she was pregnant and was about to tell him. She texted me saying she was scared."

Tom was too angry to be bothered with talking to her.

"I'm at work," he said. "I have to go now. Let me know if I can help, Katja, whenever you like. I'm here." They hung up.

He didn't direct the rage he felt over the car park incident towards the guys who'd assaulted him. No, he was cleverer than that. Jenny was the one who'd lured him down there. She was the one that Stefan, Max, Jonny and his other classmates were trying to impress. It was Jenny and the promise of her cunt that were the poison that had unleashed it all. Even as children, boys judge each other by their ability to attract girls. If the girls in his class hadn't pulled faces at Tom, wafted the air in disgust as he passed and laughed at his clothes, the boys would've left him alone.

Anyone who couldn't see that was an idiot.

Behind him, a car beeped its horn. The lights had changed.

Tom took a right, off Sveavägen, and took the back roads towards Malmskillnadsgatan. Dark-skinned women in short skirts walked the pavements and hung around the street corners. Cars slowed and windows wound down. The women leant in, to negotiate the price of their bodies.

Tom parked up in an empty loading bay.

He fantasised about what it would be like to buy himself a dark-skinned whore. He'd read online that a fuck cost a thousand. It wasn't that he couldn't afford it. But he didn't want to humiliate himself. That would be like kneeling, giving in to the system. And there were certainly men in some of the cars who really didn't need to pay for sex but did it for the thrill.

Tom, though, was not like them. For him, the only way to get sex was to pay for a whore. And even then, he was breaking the law. Society – the politicians and the feminists – had removed that right. From him and thousands of other men. What did society want them to do?

One of the whores noticed him and waddled over towards his car, pouting her lips. Fat thighs under a tight neon-yellow dress. *No, thanks*. Tom shook his head and shooed her away.

Women hated him. Men mocked him. He was denied what everyone else took for granted.

Love.

Physical contact.

He was a ghost that no one saw, that no one wanted anything to do with. Occasionally he had fantasised about luring one of the women into his car, driving off and then raping her. Strangling or stabbing her. Leaving the body to rot in a ditch. No one would care. No one beyond her Gambian family anyway. The police would not work themselves to death looking for a dead whore who almost certainly wasn't even supposed to be in the country. Her pimp probably wouldn't bother to report it. And that was the problem. If he was going to strike, he wanted to do it properly. Bring about change through blood and terror.

Tom parked in the garage, pulled the tarp over his car and went up to his stuffy apartment.

He checked the CCTV. Then he opened the fridge and stood there for a moment to cool off before picking up the plastic container in which he stored his own semen. In a few days' time, it would be worth loads. But, if he'd got this right, he had to replace it every week for it to be usable. This might be the last time.

He rubbed the washing-up brush against the plastic and then rinsed. Removing his trousers and pulling down his pants as he went, he returned to his desk. He chose a couple of images of dead and bloodied women that he'd printed from the internet and filled the little tub with his sperm.

Afterwards, he opened all the windows to get a cross-draught. He went out onto the balcony. He felt cleansed, and able to think about something besides his throbbing cock.

19

VANESSA HAD HER heart in her mouth as she parked her BMW outside the police station in Västberga.

She could feel that she was getting close to a breakthrough. Börje Rohdén was sitting on his bunk, right where she'd left him two and a half hours earlier.

"Have you got it?"

Vanessa, who'd been holding the letter behind her back, was now waving it in the air.

"I've kept my part of the bargain."

Börje nodded, keeping his eyes firmly on the letter.

"What did you see, Börje?"

"A man knocked on the door at Oscar Sjölander's."

Vanessa held her breath.

"Are you sure? You hadn't been..." She went quiet, grabbed an imaginary bottle and lifted it to her mouth.

"I was sober. This was before they found Eva."

Vanessa could tell by the way Börje said 'found' that Eva was no longer alive. She couldn't stay on the subject though; that would risk him breaking down and stopping talking.

"What happened then?"

"The door was opened by a brown-haired woman. That stuck in my head because it wasn't Oscar's wife Therese. She's nice; there's nothing wrong with her. When Oscar wasn't there, she even used to say hello to us."

Vanessa showed him a picture of Rakel on her phone.

"That could have been her," said Börje. "She let him in."

"Was Oscar Sjölander's car there?"

"It was not."

What Börje was saying put the whole investigation in a new light. A man had been let into the house by Rakel Sjödin the same morning that she disappeared. What's more, that was after Oscar Sjölander had driven off.

"Can you describe this man?" asked Vanessa. Börje shook his head.

"'Fraid not."

"Did he have a car?"

"If he did, I didn't see it. But I can tell you one thing – he was wearing a uniform."

Vanessa stared at Börje.

"Uniform?"

"A uniform of some sort. Blue? Grey? Not unlike the one that you and your colleagues wear."

"A police uniform?" said Vanessa, glancing towards the door.

"Perhaps."

Vanessa put a card bearing her phone number on top of the letter in Börje's lap.

"Thanks for telling me this," she said, looking him straight in the eye.

He nodded. Vanessa stopped, halfway to the door.

"Jörgen Olsén withdrew his complaint against you."

Börje stayed quiet. Continued stroking the letter with his palm.

"You've been carrying that letter around, but you haven't read it?" she asked.

"You think I should read it?"

"Eva chose to write it. However difficult it might be to read, I promise you it was harder to write."

Vanessa put a hand on his shoulder and smiled briefly before she turned around and left the cell. She got into the car and started the engine but ended up sitting there with her hands resting on the wheel.

What Börje had told her changed everything. Earlier that day, Vanessa had called Nicolas and asked him to visit Ivan Tomic in prison as soon as possible, to find out what Karim had refused to tell her and Ove: who Karim's enemies were, and, by extension, which of the other inmates might have planted evidence in Karim's cell. Nicolas would have a better chance of getting something out of Ivan. Criminals don't like talking to the police if it doesn't benefit them.

There were indisputably similarities between the murders of Emelie and Rakel – not between the victims, besides their age and gender, but between the men suspected of killing them. They were violent towards women, which made them potential suspects in any investigation. More than that. Vanessa could feel the hair on her arms stand on end when she let her imagination run wild. A person with knowledge of how the police work when a woman is killed would be able to point to a perpetrator. Send the investigation in the wrong direction. Even if the evidence was insufficient, it could give them enough time to get away, destroy evidence.

Emelie Rydén and Rakel Sjödin might not have been chosen for themselves – but for the violent men in their lives, who made them suitable victims.

PART VI

There will be many more mass shootings.

Red Pill Robert.

1

THE SMELL OF freshly baked bread, coffee and crepes perked Vanessa up as she pushed open the door of Mellqvists on Rörstrandsgatan. It was a few minutes past seven in the morning and trendy Stockholmers were drinking their cappuccinos, wearing sportswear. Mikael Kask and Ove Dahlberg, both of whom were wearing jeans, waved at her.

Vanessa ordered a croissant with Serrano ham and cheese before filling her coffee cup from the black urn and sitting down with her colleagues.

"So Oscar Sjölander could be innocent?" Mikael Kask said, scratching at his carefully groomed three-day stubble.

Vanessa thought about what Ove had told her about Kask and Trude.

"I've also got something to say, but about the Emelie Rydén case," said Ove. "I went through the CCTV of Emelie's last visit to Åkersberga. She asks for a pen in reception. From what I can see, she never returns it."

Mikael Kask ran his hand through his hair.

"Alright," he said. "Let's take Emelie Rydén first. The perpetrator must have been in Åkersberga. A visitor, perhaps. Another group that wanted to hurt Karim, so they've gone after Emelie. What's he saying?"

Vanessa glanced up at the clock. In a couple of hours' time, Nicolas would be at the prison, to find out via Ivan

Tomic who Karim's enemies at Åkersberga were. But Vanessa couldn't tell them that.

"He's saying nothing," said Ove. "We've tried."

"How would you like to proceed?" asked Mikael.

"I would like to explore possible connections between the two murders," said Vanessa.

Ove and Mikael both just stared at her. She'd expected them to react like that and she took a bite of her croissant. Flaky crumbs fell into her lap.

"There are no similarities whatsoever, apart from both the victims being women of around the same age," said Mikael.

"Not between them. But between the men who've been named as the perpetrators. Both are known for using violence against women, to varying degrees. We investigated the victims' social circles, came across Oscar Sjölander and Karim Laimani and got stuck there. Karim turned out to be wrong. And now Oscar too."

"You're forgetting…" said Ove.

"The forensic evidence? In Karim's case, I'm certain that it was planted in his cell. In Oscar's, the murder weapon and a jumper were found in a plastic bag around fifty metres from his house. I would suggest that there's a connection."

"That feels like a long shot."

Vanessa looked pleadingly at her boss.

"Give us a couple of days. We need to establish who else knew about Oscar and Rakel's relationship."

"I can talk to Katja again," said Ove, looking at Mikael Kask for approval. "She might think of someone else who knew about them."

The boss of the National Homicide Unit sighed and raised his palms in the air.

"Vanessa?"

"I'm going to meet Therese Sjölander."

"What for?"

"Because in one interview, she mentioned that their daughter had been woken by someone standing in her bedroom. We didn't investigate it though, because everything pointed to Oscar Sjölander."

Mikael raised his cup to his lips and took a sip. "Go for it," he said resignedly.

2

IVAN TOMIC GOT to his feet as Nicolas entered the visiting room. His clothes were the same as last time. Grey top, grey trousers. Black slippers. His hair had grown a bit, which made him look younger, more like the boy who had been Nicolas' best friend.

"I was surprised you wanted to see me again," said Ivan. He held out his hand; Nicolas took it. "But happy."

They sat down. Nicolas reminded himself what he was doing there. He despised Ivan. Everything about his macho posturing. The constant references to being an alpha male. But now Vanessa needed his help, in the hunt for Emelie Rydén's murderer. A final favour, before London. If it hadn't been important, she wouldn't have asked him.

He was going to miss Vanessa. Her dry, understated humour. Her sarcasm. She was one of the most unique people he had met. Full of contradictions. Completely ruthless towards her enemies. But beneath that armour was a soft, wounded and lonely person who was unfailingly loyal towards him.

Ivan looked expectantly at Nicolas, waiting for him to say something.

"Maria says hi," Nicolas lied.

"How is she?"

"Good."

"And you?"

"I'm leaving Sweden on Saturday to take a job in London.

You look like you're doing better." Nicolas laid a finger under his eye so that Ivan would understand that he was referring to Ivan's black eye, which had acquired a purple-yellow hue. "Who did that?"

He had planned out roughly what he was going to say. How he was going to lure him into talking.

Ivan leaned across the table. He said in a quiet voice, accompanied by a conspiratorial wink:

"Karim. You know, the guy who is suspected of murdering his ex in Täby."

Nicolas concealed his surprise.

"Do you know him?"

"He's a mug. Goes around boasting about how dangerous he is. All mouth. Someone's going to do him in as soon as he gets out. He's wound too many people up in here."

"Who?"

Ivan studied him.

"No one you know."

Ivan interlaced his fingers and put his hands on the table.

"But it was weird that the same thing happened to him as happened to Eyup."

Nicolas wracked his brains. The conversation was supposed to be about Karim; that was what Vanessa wanted. But his curiosity was aroused. "Eyup?"

"The guy I told you about last time. We hung out a bit in here and he came to see me once he'd got out. A couple of weeks later, the police picked him up again. They thought he'd murdered his missus."

"Had he?"

Ivan clicked his tongue and quickly shook his head.

"Victoria looked like a porn star. Probably wanted to be one too. She used to visit him a lot. You know, relationships usually break down when you go inside. But between them – not a bit of it. The opposite. She was here at least once a week, used to send him nudes. He used to let me sniff his fingers after... well, you know. I would never have been able to put up with a girlfriend of mine being such a whore."

Ivan sniffed, showing his teeth. Nicolas forced himself to smirk. Play along with the banter he hated so much. It occurred to him that men who had grown up without sisters – as Ivan had done – could probably never fully understand what it meant to be a girl or a woman.

"Victoria was special, I'm telling you. Some of the visiting rooms have surveillance cameras. No one wants them, except Eyup and Victoria. The guards loved it when Eyup had a visit; they used to watch him fucking on the CCTV. She got turned on by it, and so did he. People are more fucked up than you'd think."

After half an hour, they said their goodbyes. Nicolas walked slowly down the corridor, got back his belongings from the guard at reception and left the prison.

Once he'd stepped out of the gates, he turned around and looked at the bleak building, and the high fence that surrounded it. Nicolas felt like nothing that would be of interest to Vanessa had turned up. But Eyup, his friend, had also been suspected of murdering his girlfriend just after being released. The similarities with Karim were striking.

Nicolas pulled out his phone. He dialled the number that Vanessa used for her informants. She didn't answer. He hung up without leaving a message and continued towards the bus stop.

3

A SHRILL SIGNAL sounded from inside the large building. There was a keypad above the lock. Vanessa backed away a couple of steps. The blinds at the front of the Sjölander family's home were down. Vanessa noticed movement in the next-door house. An elderly woman was watching her, half-hidden behind a curtain. When the curious neighbour realised she'd been seen, she quickly retreated.

Vanessa rang the bell again.

"Who is it?"

A female voice. Hoarse. Hollow. It didn't match the images of Therese on the internet, pictures taken on red carpets and at gala premieres.

"Vanessa Frank. Detective with National Homicide." She raised her hand holding her police badge to the spyhole, but nothing happened. "Can you open the door?"

"I've already said everything I know. I want to be left alone."

Vanessa felt sorry for Therese Sjölander. In the space of a few days, her life had been turned upside down. Even if the traditional media had not named her spouse, everyone knew who *the TV star* was. Details of her life, her husband's infidelity, affairs and violence had been dragged out for public consumption.

"It's important," Vanessa said, and to her relief, she heard the lock turn.

Therese Sjölander had dark half-moons under her eyes; her

hair was unwashed, her T-shirt stained. She stank of booze. Cigarette smoke. The gloom inside the house was a sharp contrast to the bright sunshine out on the street. Therese turned around and walked ahead of Vanessa into an expensively equipped kitchen.

On the wall behind the dining table was a rectangle where the colour was darker than the rest of the blue wallpaper.

"There was a framed picture of 'the family' there," Therese said when she noticed where Vanessa was looking. "What do you want to know? How it felt when he hit me? Show me a picture of some twenty-year-old he's shagged? Ask whether I knew?"

The remains of the frame, shards of wood and glass, lay strewn underneath the table.

"I understand that you…"

"You don't understand a fucking thing," Therese screamed. She upended a chair. "You don't know what it's like, having your life exposed like that. Ask your bloody questions and then leave me alone."

Therese walked over to a kitchen drawer and pulled out a bottle of whisky. She reached into the sink. She placed a wet glass on the table with a bang. Poured.

"You're right," said Vanessa. "I don't understand."

Therese lifted the glass stiffly to her lips and sipped carefully. Her hand was shaking.

"You said in an interview that your daughter had dreamt about a man standing in her bedroom?"

"Yes?"

"Do you remember when that was?"

"Two days before we went to the filming where we met that whor… her, the one my husband had an affair with."

Therese got up from her chair, fished a packet of Marlboro out of her tracksuit bottoms and lit one with trembling hands.

Vanessa checked the date on her phone. To her surprise, she noticed she barely had a signal. The early hours of Thursday the 2nd of May. Three days later, Rakel disappeared.

"Is there anything to suggest that Josephine was telling the truth? That it wasn't a dream?"

Therese shook her head and sat down slowly on a chair.

"Nothing went missing?" asked Vanessa.

"No."

Therese took a drag. The ash tip was battling with gravity, but she made no attempt to flip it.

"Who could have known that Oscar was going to meet Rakel Sjödin after the broadcast?"

Therese stared at her as the ash tumbled onto the tabletop.

"You mean, did he go around bragging about the fact he was shagging a twenty-year-old? He didn't say anything to me about it at any rate."

The IT technicians hadn't found any communications that suggested that Oscar had discussed meeting Rakel with anyone else, neither in his computer nor in either of his two mobile phones. He seemed to have handled the affair discreetly.

"Why are you asking me this stuff?"

Her voice, which had been thin, now cracked. Therese stubbed the cigarette out on the table and coughed.

"I don't even smoke. I was a nurse before I sacrificed my career so I could take care of Oscar's business. Dealing with invoices, booking public speaking engagements, looking after the kids. All of this while he was shining, being the nice guy in the eyes of the Swedish public."

"You might think I'm trying to ingratiate myself, but I do understand what you mean. I used to be with a famous man. I know how people get blinded by the glare. Everyone does. Including us, the ones closest to the star. And we..."

"Are standing so close to the light that we see the least. Who?"

"Svante Lidén. The director. Or 'dramatist', as he likes to call himself."

Therese picked up the cigarette packet, gave it a shake, and established that it was empty.

"I'll just... I've got another pack out there."

Vanessa opened the communications app *Signal*, to see whether Ove had been in touch. The reception was too poor.

"Could I use your Wi-Fi?" Vanessa called after Therese.

"The password is under the router. Here, in the living room."

Therese was standing at the window. She had pulled the blind halfway up and was looking out at the street. She pointed towards a TV stand in dark wood upon which green lights flickered on a white router.

Vanessa reached out her hand to turn the router over but withdrew it halfway through the movement. She suddenly recalled Celine, and how the girl had said that she usually used Nicolas' Wi-Fi.

"Has anyone been in the house since the search?" asked Vanessa.

Therese was now standing behind her.

"No."

After Vanessa had called Trude from Therese's phone and asked her to send an IT technician out to Bromma as soon as possible, they sat down in the kitchen again. Vanessa pointed to the cigarette packet that was laying on the table and Therese slid the lighter towards her. She got the cig burning, stood up, took a saucer out of the sink and put it on the table between them.

"Will Oscar be convicted?" asked Therese. She seemed less belligerent. "I mean, you read about men who get away with this sort of thing. In spite of the evidence."

Vanessa exhaled thick smoke. It didn't taste as good as she'd imagined. Things usually don't, once you give them a bit of time.

"Does it make any difference? For you, I mean?"

"I don't think so."

Therese gave the makeshift ashtray a surprised glance, as though she hadn't noticed Vanessa putting it down there.

"The worst thing is, I haven't given Rakel a second thought. I know that they found her body out in the water, and that she'd been stabbed."

White smoke tumbled out of Therese's nose in puffs. "She was beautiful. Young. Oscar is a wretch. If nothing else, I've realised that. But I don't think he murdered her. He could knock out, he could punch, but stab someone? Again. And again…" Therese shook her head.

Trude Hovland placed the laptop on the wooden floor and crouched down next to Vanessa by the TV bench. She pulled on a pair of plastic gloves and carefully turned the router over.

"Turn the lights on," Trude said to Therese Sjölander, who was standing behind them.

Trude sat down in a lotus position with the computer in her lap and asked Vanessa to read out the network key. The technician tapped frenetically away at her keyboard.

"Is it possible to see anything?" Vanessa asked.

Therese Sjölander lit another cigarette. Trude sniffed the air disapprovingly but continued working on the computer.

"Between the 1st and 2nd of May?" mumbled Trude. She stopped, mid-movement, and stared at the screen. "Blow me."

Vanessa leaned over Trude's shoulder to try and grasp what had made her react. White background. Little black letters. Vanessa had no idea.

"At 03:02 in the early hours of Thursday, a new device connected to the router," said Trude. "A computer with the name *Blackpill*."

"What else can you see?"

"Nothing, apart from that. But I'm not an IT technician. He'll be here soon."

4

OVE DAHLBERG STARED at Katja Tillberg. The window was open, and down on the street below, two dogs were barking at each other.

"Could you repeat that?"

He moved his phone closer to Katja, checked for the fifth time that the conversation was being recorded.

"My uncle Tom works as a screw."

"Where?"

He had to strain to keep his voice calm, not betray how excited he was.

"Åkersberga Prison."

The connection. Vanessa was right. Shrewd woman. Beautiful. Funny. But above all, she was shrewd. That was something he'd immediately understood when they introduced themselves to each other. Fuck those nasty bastards at Police HQ who badmouthed her. She was better than all of them.

"And your uncle knew that Rakel Sjödin was in a relationship with Oscar Sjölander?"

"Yes, I told him. I tell Tom everything. We're very close. But what has he got to do with this?"

They had been focusing on the inmates, and their relatives and friends who'd visited them in prison. Perhaps Tom was the one who'd greeted Emelie on her final visit, and handed her the pen?

"What is his full name and where does he live?" Ove said in one breath. Katja frowned.

"Tom Lindbeck," she said. "He lives on Essinge Brogata. But listen, he has nothing to do with this. He's shy. Kind. When Mum died, he was the one who looked after me. He would never hurt anyone."

Ove's gaze settled on the half bun loaf on the plate in between them. Surely he could treat himself to a little bit? He reached for a slice and stuffed it into his mouth.

"Do you have a picture of him?"

Ove swallowed, then wiped the crumbs from the corners of his mouth.

Katja nodded, pulled out her phone, tapped a few strokes and then handed it to Ove. It was the guard who usually sat on the front desk at Åkersberga. He had taken care of the signing-in on the visits they'd made to interrogate Karim Laimani. And, just as Ove suspected, he was the one on the CCTV footage who'd handed Emelie Rydén the pen. He was the man from the attempted rape in Rålambshov Park.

Ove gave her back the iPhone.

"Is your uncle techie?"

"How do you mean?"

"Is he good with computers and stuff?"

Katja laughed. "He's a real computer nerd. That's his big hobby, alongside photography. He used to work as a photographer. He's the one who took those pictures," Katja said, pointing towards some framed photographs.

Friends and family visiting inmates had to hand over their phones and tablets. All valuables were put in lockers by reception. Tom Lindbeck could have jacked Emelie's phone. That's how he knew that Emelie was going to be home alone on the evening she was murdered. She'd recognised him and let him in. Tom Lindbeck took control of the mobile phones. Was able to track his victims. Tap their phone calls. Read their texts.

Ove stared down at his own phone.

Police officers were not exempt from the requirement to hand in their possessions when visiting the prison. Was Tom

Lindbeck in his phone too? And Vanessa's? In that case, they would both be in danger. He knew that they were closing in.

Ove stood up and stretched out his hand towards Katja.

"Thanks for your help. We'll be in touch."

He closed the front door and worked his way down the stairwell.

His phone felt sinister in his hand. Ove was sweating. He was just going to go to HQ. Sort out another phone. Ring Vanessa. Telephone boxes were long-gone from the streets of Stockholm, and he had never missed them before now. Ove was dying to tell Vanessa. He loved to make her happy.

Ove turned the door handle and was about to push open the door when he heard a noise behind him.

5

VANESSA PARKED IN department store Nordiska Kompaniet's multi-storey, stepped out and leant against the car while she waited. She pulled a face. Her mouth tasted like ash. After Nicolas, she was going to meet Trude Hovland and Ove in Police HQ. She felt tense. Their discovery – that someone had accessed the Sjölanders' Wi-Fi just two days before Rakel Sjödin was murdered – changed everything. Hopefully Trude would have more to say about the computer that had logged in. Earlier, without going into detail, Trude had explained that once you got inside someone's wireless network, it wasn't particularly difficult to get inside the other devices. Mobiles, tablets, computers. That could explain how the man Börje Rohdén had seen Rakel let in had known that she was going to be there. But why her?

Vanessa saw Nicolas approaching past the line of parked luxury cars. She waved and got in the passenger seat. He opened the driver's door.

"Did you meet him?"

"He and Karim are not friends. Quite the opposite. They hate each other. Apparently, Karim is not well-liked."

"Who'd have thought it," Vanessa said sarcastically.

She felt her confidence drain. Glanced at the clock. Ove and Trude were waiting for her at HQ.

"But he did say something else that I think might interest you. Does the name Eyup Rüstü mean anything to you?"

Vanessa thought for a second, then shook her head.

"He was inside at the same time as Ivan," said Nicolas. "Got out last summer. A short time later, he was arrested on suspicion of murdering his girlfriend. He was released. The murder remains unsolved."

"There's something about this that scares me," said Vanessa. "The usual thing is men murdering women they have or have had a relationship with. Jealousy, break-ups, arguments about the kids. We often identify them quickly. Karim Laimani is the typical perpetrator. Violent. Criminal. He had previously made death threats to Emelie. Her blood on his shoe. The strand of hair. But it wasn't him."

"How do you know that?"

She could trust Nicolas, as much as she trusted herself. If not more.

"An alibi. When he was out on parole, he raped a woman at the time Emelie Rydén was murdered. Karim and two other men."

Nicolas stared at her.

"Why…"

"Because she doesn't want it to come out. I don't agree, but it's up to her. I haven't said anything to my colleagues about who she is."

A well-dressed woman passed the bonnet carrying shopping bags. Vanessa went quiet and watched her.

"Yesterday, a witness came forward who had seen a man in uniform being let in by Rakel Sjödin. Today, we discovered that someone had accessed the Sjölanders' router. That person has presumably been able to follow Oscar and Rakel's communication. Known that they were in the summer house on Tyresö."

Nicolas looked pensive.

"Oscar Sjölander didn't murder her?"

"It doesn't look like it."

"Do you think there's a connection between Emelie and Rakel?"

"I don't know. The two of them don't have anything in common. They were young, beautiful, but beyond that – nothing. Apart from the fact that we've had a cast-iron suspect in both cases and no longer do in either."

After the discovery in the Sjölanders' home, Vanessa had asked the technicians to examine Emelie Rydén's router as well. Thus far, however, they hadn't found any outsider attempts to connect to it.

"There's a connection between Eyup and Karim," said Nicolas. "Both of them were doing time in Åkersberga."

Vanessa looked down at her clothes, at her blue trousers and her white shirt. Suddenly, she slammed her palm against the steering wheel.

"The uniform."

"What do you mean?"

"The man Rakel Sjödin let in was wearing a uniform. I thought policeman, maybe a security guard. But prison warders have a uniform similar to ours. Emelie would definitely let someone wearing a prison uniform in. And Rakel might have mistaken her assailant for a policeman."

Vanessa started the engine. Looked left and then right in quick succession and rolled out of the parking space. They'd been close all along. The guards at the prison. The Prison Service had attended a conference at Rosersbergs. A screw had handed the pen to Emelie Rydén. Vanessa had stared herself blind at the inmates, which perhaps wasn't that strange. The chances of finding a perpetrator were higher among them than among those who worked in keeping them in line.

"I'll drop you off on the way," she said.

Nicolas pulled on his seatbelt while they flew past row after row of parked luxury cars at high speed.

They drove out of the multi-storey, turned right twice and passed the modernist expanse of Sergels Torg. Vanessa got her phone out and called Ove. No answer. She passed the phone to Nicolas.

"Call him again."

He did as she said. Put it on speaker and held the phone up. Voicemail.

"Call Trude Hovland."

"She's calling you now," said Nicolas.

"Eh?"

Nicolas put the phone to her ear.

"I was just about to call you," said Vanessa. "Are you with Ove?"

"No. He…"

"I need to speak to him."

"Vanessa. Ove's been shot."

6

VANESSA PUT HER foot down. Ove had been found seriously injured in Katja Tillberg's lobby and rushed to Karolinska Hospital where he was now in theatre. How close had he got? She had no doubt that it was Rakel and Emelie's murderer who had shot him.

"Is there anything I can do?" Nicolas asked.

She had almost forgotten that he was sitting next to her.

"No."

"Is he going to make it?"

"I don't know. I'll drop you here."

Vanessa turned left by 7-Eleven on Scheelegatan and then pulled up. Nicolas got out. He leaned into the car. "Be careful, Vanessa."

She nodded. Nicolas pushed the door shut and the car tore off. A car behind beeped angrily.

Mikael Kask sent a message that he was on his way to Police HQ. Vanessa decided to wait down in the garage. She drove down into the catacombs beneath the building. After a couple of minutes, Mikael's car arrived. He parked a couple of spaces away and jumped out.

"I was on my way to a birthday meal," he said, pulling off his tie and stuffing it into his blazer pocket. He was pale, seemed shaken.

"What's the latest on Ove?" Vanessa asked.

"The hospital haven't said any more than that he's in theatre."

"We need to check his mobile."

"Why?"

"Because he records his interviews on it. We need to know what Katja Tillberg said."

"But Vanessa, if someone was waiting for him, that was hardly because of what she'd said. How would the perpetrator know that so quickly?"

Mikael was heading for the lift. Vanessa put a hand on his shoulder, stopping him.

"I might have found the connection between the murders of Rakel Sjödin and Emelie Rydén. Börje Rohdén said that the man he saw Rakel letting in was in uniform. What if it was a Prison Service uniform?"

"Vanessa... not now."

"Another former inmate, one Eyup Rüstü, was suspected last summer of murdering his girlfriend two weeks after his release. He was later freed."

Mikael Kask ran his fingers through his flawless hair.

"Someone planted evidence in Karim's cell," Vanessa went on. "And outside Oscar Sjölander's house. Yesterday we got to hear about the man Rakel let in. Today we found out that someone had logged into the Sjölanders' router."

Mikael pressed the lift call button. The doors, which had closed while they were speaking, now slid open again.

"You mean there's a serial killer at work here?"

"Yes."

Mikael Kask scoffed.

"Apart from Peter Mangs and John Ausonius, we haven't had a serial killer in Sweden since 1979. The victims have nothing in common, apart from being women."

Mikael stepped into the lift, and Vanessa followed.

"No, but their men do. Karim Laimani, Eyup Rüstü and to some extent Oscar Sjölander are the obvious suspects. Emelie Rydén let her murderer in. We've assumed from the outset that she recognised him. Imagine if she recognised him from the prison. She'd received death threats from Karim just weeks earlier. And the blood in Karim's cell. Who has access to the inmates' cells? The warders, Mikael."

The lift jolted into action.

"Can you hear how that sounds?" He shook his head. "A serial murderer, working as a prison warder. You've been watching too much TV. What would the motive be?"

"I don't know."

The doors opened. Trude Hovland was waiting for them.

"I need to talk to you," she said.

"You'll have to wait," Mikael Kask said as he tried to pass her.

"Katja Tillberg's uncle works as a prison guard. At Åkersberga."

7

TOM OPENED THE weapons cabinet and put his three handguns into the black rucksack on his bed. It was just a matter of hours, perhaps minutes, until the police were going to turn up. Everything was under threat. He had panicked. Acted in anger. When Katja called to tell him that detectives were going to interview her again, he'd hidden out in her stairwell. Shot the fat investigator in the back.

Everything was under threat.

He chucked the sports bag over his shoulder and walked into his study. He packed up his laptop. Looked around. What else? Everything had been prepared. His hideout was a long way from Stockholm and had no links with anything in his life. He was going to really become the shadow he had always been. Everything he needed was there. As long as he could make it there. The uprising would spread across the world.

Canadian Alek Minassian and American Elliot Rodger looked back at him from their frames on the window sill. He was going to make them proud.

"Gentlemen."

He nodded to the portraits.

Tom was just about to turn around and leave the room when the screen of his desktop computer flickered green. The camera in the stairwell. He maximised the window to see police with automatic weapons streaming in through the main entrance.

Vanessa stared at the screen. The SWAT team were equipped with night-vision cameras attached to their helmets, so that she and the others could follow their every step. They had just entered the stairwell. The details revealed themselves in a greenish fluorescent colour. The dark van she was sitting in was parked at one end of the Marieberg Bridge, on Lilla Essingen. The atmosphere was tense. Mikael Kask's breathing was irregular, and he was drinking frantically from a paper cup. The rim had been chewed.

The island of Lilla Essingen was on lockdown. No traffic was let in, bus routes had been diverted, police with armed reinforcements had been posted to strategic locations. Tom Lindbeck had been sighted inside the apartment.

There was nowhere to go.

Soon, it would all be over and Lindbeck would be captured.

The murders of Rakel Sjödin and Emelie Rydén would be solved. Maybe Victoria Ahlberg's too. If she and Ove had known from the outset what they were looking for, they would've been able to make the connection between the murders earlier. They would now re-examine every unsolved murder in the country from the past few years. There were still lots of leads they hadn't had time to pursue. And at Karolinska, Ove was fighting for his life with his wife and his two kids at his side.

Behind Vanessa, the door opened and Trude climbed into the van.

"How's it going?"

"They're on their way up," Mikael Kask said grimly. "We'll soon have him."

Something was nagging away inside Vanessa. She couldn't put her finger on what.

The feeling that they'd overlooked something was growing all the time. How long had Tom Lindbeck managed to evade the police? Surely it wasn't going to be this easy? They were proceeding too quickly. Perhaps they should've waited, put him under surveillance.

"Can you stop doing that?"

Mikael Kask stared at her, nodding towards her fingers, which were drumming against the inside of the van. She stopped. Clenched her fist and put it in her lap.

The SWAT team continued their advance.

"Third floor," mumbled Mikael Kask. "Come on."

On the screen, Vanessa could see black-clad figures regrouping. She counted eight of them. A battering ram was brought out. The lead officer raised his fist. Gave the signal. The front of the ram struck the door.

After that, everything went black.

The wind tore at Tom's clothes. He pulled up the rope and couldn't help but cast a glance out over Stockholm, over the motorway and the black waters surrounding him. He ran. He knew this roof like the back of his hand. How many times had he fled across it with imaginary police chasing him? But this was reality. The real deal. They had just stepped into Tom's world and were playing by his rules. His feet drummed against the metal roof. When the police did finally realise how he'd managed to get away, it would be too late. They would hunt him throughout Sweden, throughout Europe, but would have to acknowledge that they had met their match.

No one would find him until he himself wanted to be found. He would become famous across the world. Women would dream about being inseminated with his sperm. To carry his genes. He would be able to pick and choose. Behind him, the explosion thundered out. Muffled. Distant. He stopped. Listened to the silence that followed before picking up his pace once more.

Inside the van, it went completely silent. Mikael Kask leaned in, staring at the dark screen. Trude reacted first. She tore off her headset, opened the doors and flung herself out. Vanessa was a stride behind. They rushed down Essinge Brogata. In front of her, behind her: police running everywhere. All around her, windows were opened, lights switched on. Curious onlookers peering out into the street. Tom Lindbeck had blown himself up and taken the SWAT team with him. From the smashed windows on the third floor, silvery smoke poured upwards into the heavens.

The entrance to the building was open. The stairwell echoed with the screams of the injured. Vanessa followed Trude's back up the stairs. Those officers with minor injuries were making their own way down and supporting their colleagues.

"How many dead?" screamed Vanessa.

Tom opened the heavy metal door on the lift, dug out his torch from his rucksack and shone its beam at his feet. He loved the sound of chaos. The wailing sirens, the desperate screams from the streets below. He felt like a conductor who finally had an orchestra in front of him. Finally, he was able to make music from the hate that had been trapped inside him for so long.

He was able to get down to the first floor unhindered. Then open the window and haul himself out. He landed gently on the lawn, straightened his legs and then peered into the darkness. Not a single car passed by on Gamla Essinge Brovåg. He peeled off to the left, half-jogging along the deserted street. He looked at the concrete pillars supporting the viaduct. The traffic thundered above him. He slowed his pace, turned onto Primusgatan, caught sight of the wine-red Police HQ building through the trees.

Yesterday, no one in there had known who Tom Lindbeck was. Tomorrow, their whole day, the next few weeks, would be spent talking about him. Not least after what was going to happen on Saturday. He had been just around the corner the whole time, had fooled the lot of them. Journalists – his former colleagues – would lose it. Perhaps he'd offer one of them an exclusive interview, if that could be arranged safely. It would be quoted the world over. It would wake others. Get them to act. He slowed to a walking pace and walked down to the water and Essinge boat club.

He held the fob to the reader, the red light turned green, and the lock clicked open.

When Tom had been on the jetty in the autumn, being shown how the boat worked, he'd been told that the boat club smelled of diesel and tar. He wondered what that smelled like.

The little waves chopped. The boats rocked. On the other side of the little channel, large, dark cliffs towered above the water. On Marieberg Bridge, to his right, blue lights flickered. He stopped to enjoy the scene.

They were there for him. He'd done this.

The boat was moored in the berth second from the end. White. Unassuming. He climbed aboard. The little motor in the stern started almost immediately. He didn't even have time to get anxious. Tom calmly steered the boat past the cliffs of Fredhäll, reaching Kristineberg, from where he could see Pampas Marina lit up. He didn't meet a single boat.

Around him, the city played its signature sounds. But out there, on the water, it was another world. Calm. Dark. Lonely.

He felt invincible.

What had happened in the apartment was necessary; what was about to follow was revenge. On the women who had refused to give him access to their bodies, on the weak men who had mocked him, on Sweden, on the world.

First though, before he regrouped and readied himself, the person who had come so close to ruining everything was going to die.

8

ONE DEAD, THREE seriously injured. It was eleven o'clock, and Tom Lindbeck's neighbours had been evacuated. The bomb squad were searching the two-bed apartment for further devices. The devastation was not as great as first feared. It seemed the explosion was probably the result of a hand grenade, which was detonated when the door was forced open. Tom had not been found inside.

Mikael Kask was sitting perched on top of an electricity junction box. His legs were dangling above the pavement. His eyes were glazed. Introspective. The press had arrived. *Kvällspressen* first, of course. Their newsroom was only a couple of hundred metres from the scene. Photographers jostled outside the cordon; reporters screamed their questions at emergency services personnel who were moving around inside the blue-and-white incident tape.

Vanessa went and stood next to Mikael. He looked at her glumly. "We're going to get him," he said.

Vanessa nodded.

"The question is, at what price?"

"Every police officer in Stockholm is looking for him; the routes out are blocked. He cannot get away."

"Ove?"

"I don't know. Go home and get some sleep, Vanessa. There's nothing more you can do. I'll need you tomorrow. Rested."

"Hopefully you won't."

Mikael Kask gave her a quizzical look.

"If we get him tonight, I mean."

Mikael flashed a smile with his lips tightly pressed together.

"You've been fantastic. I'm sorry I didn't trust you straight away. Without you, we would never have found him."

Vanessa bent under the tapes, straightened her back and ignored the questions being flung at her by the excited reporters. The skyscraper that was home to *Dagens Nyheter* was illuminated against the sky. Police cars were shuttling back and forth alongside her. A helicopter whirred overhead.

She recalled the hunt for the terrorist whose name she refused to remember, the one who had ploughed into people on Drottninggatan in his lorry. A city in terror. A city in controlled uproar. Stockholmers walked home in long columns. Scared but defiant. That time, the terrorist's hate had been directed at the Western world, at open society, at all of them. In the midst of the sorrow and the chaos, Vanessa had been able to spot something beautiful in the camaraderie. A feeling of love for one's fellow humans. Now all she felt was emptiness. Loneliness. Perhaps something reminiscent of fear. Tom Lindbeck didn't want to die. He was far from beaten.

Her car was parked in the police station by Kronoberg. Getting a taxi from anywhere near Lilla Essingen was going to be impossible – all traffic was being stopped and checked. But perhaps it might work from over by Västerbron.

Otherwise she'd have to walk to Fridhemsplan and stop a taxi. She could collect the car tomorrow. The fresh air would do her good.

As Vanessa opened the door to her apartment, she was wide awake. She took off her clothes, which were flecked with dust, blood and dirt. She unbuckled her holster. She piled everything onto the sofa before getting into the shower.

As the warm jets washed over her, she thought of Ove. He was probably lying in a hospital ward, hooked up to tubes and machines. She hoped he was going to make it, that his kids wouldn't grow up with him as only a fading memory. She saw Tom Lindbeck's pale, bird-like face in front of her. They'd got a picture from the Prison Service. She shuddered at the thought that she'd met him at the prison, spoken to him. He had fooled them. Exactly how remained to be seen. Tomorrow would see a lot of things becoming clearer.

Rakel. Emelie. Maybe Victoria Ahlberg. The police on Essinge Brogata. The man who had his stomach slashed open and bled to death, the ones now fighting for their lives. How many lives had he taken? And how many more would he manage before they stopped him?

Vanessa turned off the water, shivered in the cool air and reached for her towel. She dried herself slowly. Back in the living room, she turned on the telly. A late news bulletin was showing footage from Lilla Essingen.

"The explosion has been linked to a raid on a property," said the news anchor. "What caused the explosion – which has already claimed a life – was not something the police spokesman wished to discuss."

Sleep felt a long way off. Her brain was working in overdrive. Vanessa got to her feet and poured herself a large whisky. Outside the window, high winds tugged at the scaffolding. The plastic screens over the windows were gone.

Whisky glass in hand, Vanessa returned to the sofa and turned over.

The difference between her and most of her colleagues was that they had families, something to come home to that got them thinking about other things. Another context.

After the terror attack, Svante had stayed up waiting for her. Their relationship had been bad for a couple of years, and he was probably already sleeping with Johanna Ek, but he'd been there. Held her. Had a thousand questions which she'd asked him to wait with. Instead, he told some funny anecdote about his day. Once they'd got into bed, they'd made love. Not roughly, like they usually would, but gently. Solemnly.

The scaffolding creaked. Vanessa looked up, caught a

glimpse of a movement outside the window. Her first thought was that it must be morning already, and that the builders were starting early. A man was looking straight at her. Before she'd had the chance to realise that something was wrong, he raised a weapon. Vanessa stared straight down the barrel, put her feet on the floor, and pushed off, flinging herself and the sofa backwards.

The shot rang out. Lying on the floor, with the sofa between her and the man, she felt a stinging pain in her side and realised that she'd been hit.

9

KVÄLLSPRESSEN'S EDITORIAL TEAM found themselves in the state of organised chaos that always emerged
when a major news event hit. Reporters who'd been called
in during the evening stopping briefly at the desk, receiving
spit-flecked orders from Bengt and hurrying onwards to their
desks. Jasmina had already managed to visit the site of the
explosion and had secured two interesting pieces of information from neighbours. She pressed play on her Dictaphone.

The one who was being carried down was a policeman.

Are you sure? She heard her own voice cut through the
noise of screams, flashbulbs and police officers ordering
them back.

*Yes. He had a helmet, black clothes. Two of the other
officers were hauling him down the stairs. His whole abdomen
was torn open. It was the worst thing I've ever seen.*

Sirens wailed in the background. A policeman started
tugging at the witness Jasmina was speaking to, asking him
to accompany him.

Wait. Who lived in the apartment?

It was the one above mine. Tom, his name was.

Before speaking to Bengt, she wanted to find out as much
as possible by herself.

She entered Tom's name and address into an online
telephone directory and got his surname. After that, she
logged in to Facebook. Tom Lindbeck's profile was locked.

No details were public. Only his profile pic was visible. A selfie. He was staring into the camera with his eyes wide open. His face expressionless, mouth closed.

Jasmina googled his name. To her surprise, on page two she found a number of hits linking to articles in *Kvällspressen*. The articles were several years old. She clicked one of them and immediately understood the context. Tom Lindbeck had been a photographer at *Kvällspressen*. She stood up and hurried over to the desk where Bengt was sitting with his phone to his ear as he typed on his laptop. He told whoever he was talking to to hold on.

"Yes?" he said, staring at Jasmina.

"Tom Lindbeck."

Bengt's forehead crumpled. "What about him?"

"It was his apartment."

"That was blown up?"

"Yes."

"Come with me."

Bengt grabbed his phone, hung up without saying a word to the person on the other end and headed for Tuva Algotsson's office. Jasmina had to jog to keep up. He walked in without knocking and Tuva looked up from behind her desk.

"Tom Lindbeck," Bengt said, and gestured to Jasmina to close the door behind her.

"The photographer? What about him?" Tuva asked, pushing her laptop shut.

"It was his apartment that got blown up on Lilla Essingen. Do you know where he went after leaving here?"

"No idea, but this gives us an enormous advantage over our competitors. Tom Lindbeck was a really creepy character."

Jasmina, who had been standing just behind Bengt, took a step forward. "In what way?"

Tuva folded her arms and leaned back in her chair.

"He was… an oddball. We all thought so, from the off. But he was a good photographer. Loyal. Always turned up when we called him, no matter what time or day it was. After a couple of months, we noticed a disturbing pattern. Female reporters were receiving scary messages, threats, sexual questions, dick-pics and all sorts. It always happened after they'd been working with Tom. He was confronted, denied it all of course, but he was sacked."

"And the women?"

"None of them wanted to make official complaints. Things were different then."

There was a knock on the glass door. Max stepped in, burning with excitement.

"My police source is saying that the police operation on Lilla Essingen had to do with the Oscar Sjölander case. Not only that. The woman who was killed in Täby too. And the policeman who was shot earlier today, in Blackeberg."

10

VANESSA WAS LYING face down behind the tipped sofa, pressing herself against the floor. Another shot was fired. The bullet perforated the upholstery and drilled into the floorboards.

Fragments of shattered glass rained down.

Vanessa realised that the man was trying to get inside. Get closer. Who the hell was he? She couldn't stay put. Unarmed, she was defenceless. Yet another shot. Even if he couldn't see her behind the sofa, one of his bullets would hit her sooner or later. Where had the holster got to?

A fourth shot.

Time was running out. The hole in the window pane had to be getting to the size where he could climb through it.

Somewhere under the upturned sofa was her Sig Sauer revolver. She squirmed to her right. Her body was still damp after her shower, and it slid easily across the floor. Her rib was burning where the bullet had hit. Blood was staining her white towel red, but it couldn't be too serious. If it had been, she wouldn't have been able to move around the way she was. She stretched her arm under the sofa, tugged at her blue trousers and felt the leather holster underneath them.

Vanessa took the safety off. She held the pistol over the top of the sofa and fired blind. Turned her wrist to the left. Pulled the trigger again. The man returned fire, but he'd stopped working on the window, apparently having given up his attempt to enter now that she was armed.

Vanessa quickly peered over the top of the sofa and immediately flung herself back down. The bullet passed a few centimetres above her head and struck the living room wall. She could hear steps on the scaffolding. He was fleeing.

Vanessa was barefoot and had only a towel wrapped around her. She pushed the sofa in front of her so as not to have to trample on the sharp shards of glass. She stopped half a metre from the window and balanced on the edge of the sofa. Then she grabbed a cushion and placed it in the hole in the window so that she could climb out.

She ducked, placed the cushion over the shards and took a leap. She landed on the planks where the man had been standing moments earlier. The pain almost caused her to lose her balance, but she managed to grab hold of a metal joist. Her gaze fell towards the ground, and she felt dizzy. She hated heights.

Two storeys below, the back of the man's head was visible. Vanessa ran towards the steps. The scaffolding was rocking violently. She grabbed hold of a handrail and rushed forwards, trying to keep her focus ahead of her rather than below. He was almost at ground level. She stopped. Held up her pistol in a two-handed grip, aimed towards the street and waited for him to run a few metres and give her a clear shot.

He glanced up briefly before he threw himself out onto the pavement. He ran along, hugging the frontages, in the direction of Odengatan. Vanessa fired. She saw the bullet hit a paving stone a few centimetres away from him. Fired again. Hoping to see him crumple, fall, and stay down. He would soon reach Surbrunnsgatan, turn off round the corner and be out of sight.

In the apartment next to hers, a light came on. She quickly squeezed the trigger, twice, but both shots missed, and the man's back disappeared from view.

11

AFTER MOORING UP at the marine filling station next to Pampas Marina, Tom grabbed his rucksack and walked along the jetty. All he could do was wait. Vanessa Frank's apartment on Roslagsgatan wasn't far from the small harbour. Tom slumped onto a bench by the water's edge, looked around, pulled out his laptop and got online. Her telephone was in the apartment. Perhaps she was already dead. He hoped so. He truly hated her.

Tom thought about calling to find out how he'd got on but didn't want to disturb him. Not now. Besides, he liked this spot. It was calm, peaceful. Before too long, he'd arrive, and they would get on their way. Tomorrow they would rest, and go through everything one last time, before returning to Stockholm on Saturday.

At first, he hadn't wanted to be involved. Of course nothing pointed to him being uncovered or linked to Tom. The last few days had changed things. Vanessa Frank and Ove Dahlberg had come frighteningly close.

Tom looked at his computer and plugged in his headphones, opened mass-murderer Elliot Rodgers' farewell message – recorded days before he took revenge on the world. The American was sitting in a sports car with black leather seats. The sun, which was setting over California, gave his thin, boyish face a yellowish tinge.

"The popular guys have lived hedonistic lives while I have

had to rot in my loneliness. All of them have looked down on me. On those occasions I have tried to socialise with them, they have treated me like a mouse. Now I am going to become a god in comparison with you. You are animals. And I am going to slaughter you like animals."

Every single word seemed as if it could have come from Tom, plucked from the innermost reaches of his being.

He felt comforted by the twenty-two-year-old American's determined face and wished that he had got to know him while he was still alive.

Two headlights swept down the little road towards him. Tom stood up slowly. He put the computer away and went to meet the car. As soon as he opened the door on the driver's side, he could tell that things had not gone according to plan.

"She got away?"

The man nodded.

"It doesn't matter," said Tom. "She's not important. Not really."

"I know."

Tom gave him a friendly pat on the shoulder and rounded the Land Rover. He opened the boot. The man switched off the engine and joined him. Tom clambered into the boot, feeling for the little lever with his fingers. A click. He pulled off the panel hiding the secret compartment and lay down. The man passed him his rucksack and Tom curled up with it over his stomach.

"See you in a couple of hours," he said.

12

AFTER SHE HAD called Mikael Kask and given him the sketchy description of the man, medics had managed to persuade Vanessa to let herself be taken to Karolinska Hospital. There, they had explained that the bullet had just grazed a rib and bandaged her up. She waited in a little room for the doctor who had examined her to return.

There was a knock on the door and Trude Hovland and Mikael Kask walked in. Their faces were solemn, and their stares swept anxiously up Vanessa's body, from head to toe.

"Did you get him?"

"'Fraid not," said Mikael Kask.

They sat down in unison on separate chairs and pulled them forwards so that they ended up a metre or so from the bed.

"Do you think this had anything to do with Tom?" Mikael asked tentatively.

"I don't know," said Vanessa. She felt confused. The only thing she was sure of was that it wasn't Tom who'd shown up on the scaffolding. The idea that The Legion or Södertälje Network would strike on that particular night seemed far-fetched. "But probably."

There was a moment of silence.

"Vanessa, do you have a next of kin you'd like us to call?"

The question came out of nowhere. Took her by surprise. Vanessa pressed her lips together and shook her head. Trude seemed to notice the change in her mood, and she rushed to cut in.

"We've found a number of interesting objects in Tom Lindbeck's apartment. Amongst other things, photographs of Alek Minassian and Elliot Rodger. We believe Tom is an Incel. Or at least heavily influenced by them."

"What's an Incel?"

Her throat felt dry. Vanessa coughed and gestured towards the sink. Mikael Kask stood up and opened the tap.

"Incel stands for involuntary celibacy," said Trude. "An online movement of tens of thousands of men, united by misogyny. Members with links to the movement have been behind at least forty-five murders in the USA. Alek Minassian and Elliot Rodger are icons of the Incel world. Mass murderers."

"Not serial murderers?"

"No."

Mikael held a plastic cup out towards Vanessa. She drank carefully so as not to spill. A few drops ran down her chin, onto her hospital gown.

"We're still mapping out Tom's social circle. But it seems to be restricted to his niece. We'll find out more tomorrow."

Mikael shuffled on his seat.

"What we're wondering is how they found you so quickly."

"And Ove," Trude filled in. "Have you noticed anyone following you?"

"No," said Vanessa. She put the water down on the bedside table.

"There's another thing too," said Mikael. He looked uncomfortable. "There's a risk that you'll be taken off the case, given the situation as it is. I will of course resist such a move. If it hadn't been for you... Oscar Sjölander would still be a suspect. Probably Karim too. I want you to stay on. If you've got the energy. But the decision will be taken over my head."

Once they'd gone, Vanessa stretched out in bed.

She could hear footsteps beyond the door, and the hushed voices of the nurses. Illuminated by the screen of her phone, she read about the Incel movement. She watched the farewell video recorded by Elliot Rodger, before he went on to murder six and injure fourteen in California. Then the arrest of Alek Minassian, after he had used his van to mow down twenty-six people, killing ten of them, in Toronto. They were not alone though; there were others. On Reddit, one group had over forty thousand members. Forty-five extinguished lives could be linked to the movement in North America.

Tom Lindbeck had been exposed; he would not be able to act undisturbed any longer. But Vanessa was convinced that he wasn't just going to disappear, give up. Something else was waiting. Something bigger. But what?

She closed her eyes and tried to go to sleep. After twenty minutes, she gave up. She called a taxi, got up, gathered her clothes together and headed out into the corridor.

13

AFTER LYING CURLED up in the reconfigured space beneath the passenger seats for two hours, Tom stretched out. He wound down the window a couple of centimetres, enjoying the fresh night air that was pushed into the car.

They drove on, passing small, forgotten communities along the E20 trunk road. They hadn't managed to kill the police bitch, but they had scared her. Shown that they could strike at any time. Tom felt invincible, almost like a *Chad*. In Incel terminology, the Chads comprise twenty per cent of the male population, but sleep with eighty per cent of the women. That was the equation that meant men like Tom were left without sexual partners. He had even seen graphs demonstrating that twenty-five per cent of men would be Incels within a decade.

Thirty kilometres left to Eskilstuna. Tom was going to continue along the E18, change direction, and head northwards.

"How did you come up with the idea of customising the car?" the man next to him asked.

"East Berliners fleeing to the West often did something similar in their cars," said Tom. "Do you know what I was feeling, lying back there? Freedom."

He saw a little green larva crawling across the dashboard, and he leaned towards it. He picked it up. For a moment he thought about crushing it between his nails.

"When I was a kid, the boys in my class used to drag me off into the woods behind the school. At first they just used to hit me and spit on me, but after a while they got bored of that. Instead, they used to dig up beetles and insects and make me eat them."

He flicked the insect out of the car and wound up the window.

"But then one day, after they'd been at it for about a week, I realised something – that the worst thing wasn't eating them but being forced to do so. Instead of laying low and trying to hide when the bell rang, I ran up into the woods. Dug up the fattest worms I could find. With my hands full, I would wave and scream at them. When they got there, I'd stuff the worms in my mouth and eat them."

The man winced.

"Did they stop bullying you?"

Tom shook his head slowly.

"For a while. A few days, perhaps."

The man coughed. Silence fell once more. Outside, yet another forgotten town, like an illuminated island in a sea of darkness.

"Pull in here," said Tom. "I'm hungry."

They were alone in the petrol station. Tom asked for two veggie hotdogs and a bottle of water. He stayed in the car so as not to risk getting caught on CCTV.

He missed the rats. They would probably be put down. If he'd had time, he would've let them go before he left.

A woman of around forty climbed out of a grey Peugeot. Their eyes met briefly before she quickly turned her head away. Never again would anyone do that. His face was going to be everywhere; his name would be on everyone's lips. He already knew what he was going to say; he'd polished his lines as he lay in the void under the seats. That, though, was going to have to wait. Until they'd struck, he had to avoid doing anything that could jeopardise their mission.

The door on the passenger side opened. Tom took the sausages, wound down the window and dropped the buns onto the tarmac. The engine coughed into life.

"Wait a sec," said Tom.

"For what?"

Tom bit off a large chunk of sausage. Even if he couldn't taste it, he liked the texture. He let his teeth slowly grind through the warm mass. He had time for another two bites before the woman returned to her car. Tom's eyes followed her all the way.

"What was that about?"

"She's the last woman who will ever ignore me," said Tom.

On Incel forums, there was a lot of talk about how once you'd swallowed the black pill – and realised that there was no remaining hope of meeting a woman – there were only three ways out. To accept it, to kill yourself, or to do what Elliot Rodger did. *Going E.R.*, as it was known. The man next to him, however, had claimed that there was a fourth choice. A low-intensity war on society. Victoria Ahlberg, Emelie Rydén and Rakel Sjödin. All three were *Staceys*. Sex-goddesses. Genetic jackpots.

Tom had watched Victoria Ahlberg and Emelie Rydén since he first saw them at Åkersberga, where they'd come to let themselves be fucked by their alpha males. Even if Tom had chosen Rodger's way, he would have wanted to help. When the femoids handed over their phones at reception, he took control of them. He fixed them so that he could track Victoria and Emelie's data use, listen to their calls, see where they were. Neither Tom nor the man he had helped had held out any hope of Eyup Rüstü or Karim Laimani being convicted. What they did know, however, was that by the time detectives realised their mistake, it would be too late. The police always looked for violent men in the murdered women's everyday lives.

It was the perfect crime.

The murder of Rakel Sjödin had been different. A bonus, that had presented itself when Katja told him about the woman's relationship with Oscar Sjölander. More improvised.

It also included the chance to destroy a real Chad's life. Deep down though, Tom didn't believe in low-intensity warfare. Rodger and Minassian's way was better. Far more effective. Another way many Incels were talking about was acid attacks. Dissolving the faces of carefully selected Staceys to show them what true suffering was.

They left the petrol station and pulled out onto the main road again.

"Your niece, Katja, do you hate her too?"

Tom shrugged. Recalled Katja's face. She was a *Becky*. An ordinary-looking woman, but they too strove to be fucked by Chads.

"She would never have hung out with me if we weren't related. And despite me being her uncle, she can't help despising me, even if she probably doesn't realise it herself."

14

NICOLAS OPENED THE door when he saw that it was
Vanessa waiting outside. He stuck his head out into the
stairwell, checked it was empty before locking his door again.

Vanessa slumped onto the sofa.

"I'm sorry to turn up like this, but I didn't have anywhere
else to go," she said. "I couldn't face lying there alone in the
hospital."

"What's happened?" Nicolas asked anxiously as he stroked
her forehead. Her skin was pale.

"I was attacked. At home, in my flat."

She recounted the last few hours, what had happened
since she dropped him outside 7-Eleven on Scheelegatan. The
explosion on Lilla Essingen. The walk home. The unknown
man's sudden appearance on the balcony. The exchange of
fire. Words poured out of her. Incoherent. Shuddering. Perhaps
it was the morphine she'd probably been given. Maybe it was
because of him. That she knew he understood her anyway. He
hoped so. Vanessa pulled up her crumpled shirt and showed
him the bandage.

"And your colleague, the one who'd been shot?"

She shook her head.

"He was hit in the back. He's hovering between life and
death."

"I'm glad you're okay, anyway."

Nicolas clasped her hand and rubbed his thumb across

the back of it before quickly letting go. He straightened up and looked anxiously at Vanessa, trying to decipher whether he'd made her feel uncomfortable, but her face remained expressionless.

"Would you like anything? Water? Tea?" he asked. Vanessa nodded.

"Tea would be nice."

As he set about boiling the water, she smiled weakly at him.

"I'm sorry I got cross when you told me about London," she said. "That was childish of me. I'm happy, for your sake."

"You don't have to say sorry. I'm going to miss you."

"Are you?" she asked.

"Yes."

Her anxiety began to wane. She was here now. At his. He was pleased that she'd come. If something were to happen to Vanessa... no, he couldn't let that thought develop. He glanced towards her. She was leaning back on the sofa, her eyes closed.

Nicolas returned with two steaming mugs.

He found himself standing in the middle of the room for a moment, looking at her peaceful sleeping face. He put the mugs down on the coffee table, bent down and carefully picked her up.

Nicolas carried Vanessa through the apartment and laid her on the bed in the neighbouring room.

She looked up at him, eyes half-open.

"Thanks," she mumbled.

She reached towards him and stroked his upper arm. Her touch burned his skin, warmed him to the core. Nicolas pulled the duvet over Vanessa and turned the lights out before lying down next to her, interlocking his fingers behind his head and staring up at the ceiling.

PART VII

I will raise a beer to every victim who turns out to be a woman between eighteen and thirty-five.

An anonymous man.

1

THROUGH A GLASS pane, Vanessa could see the man who the nurse had claimed was Ove. He was lying in the gloomy hospital room with a mask over the bottom half of his face. Equipment towered around his bed, keeping death away.

She touched the door handle but wasn't able to make up her mind. Eventually she did walk in, and stood at the foot of his bed, unsure what to do. Her gaze swept up his body to his covered face. In her mind, he was a large, powerful man – but in here he looked small and wretched.

A stinging in her eye. Vanessa hurried to wipe her cheek and glanced quickly into the corridor to make sure the policeman outside hadn't seen. She pulled up the chair, keeping well away from the machines to make sure she didn't bump into them.

People didn't often trust her. They often found her awkward and difficult to understand. Ove did too, presumably. But right from the start, he had shown, in his own boisterous way, that he had faith in her.

"Don't die," she whispered.

If he'd known she was sitting there talking to herself, he'd have laughed at her. Vanessa wracked her brains, trying to recall whether she'd ever said how much she appreciated him. Probably not. That wasn't her style – in the same way she couldn't tell Nicolas how much he meant to her. But something told her Ove knew it anyway. If he knew anything now, lying there.

She wanted to talk to him. Didn't care if it was silly, that he couldn't hear her.

"What I'm wondering is why he shot you," she said in a voice so quiet it was barely audible. "It is not like him. He doesn't murder men; he murders women. I understand that Katja said something that made him nervous. But he could have disappeared. Fled. Maybe it was personal, and he was angry that we were getting so close. I don't think so though. I think he knew what he was doing."

Vanessa took her phone out and held it in her hand. She looked straight into the camera as she switched on the voice memo function and held the microphone to her mouth.

"I know that you can hear this, Tom Lindbeck. I know that you've been in my phone, in my life, since the second time we interrogated Karim Laimani at the prison. Or was it the first? That's the way you operate. You are a cowardly wretch."

She stamped the phone to pieces.

"I like you, Ove," she said, nodding slowly. "You are a good person. Someone who means well, who doesn't judge others. When you're feeling better, we can eat hotdog wraps in my car."

The taxi crawled through the city at a standstill. At first, the driver tried to make small talk, but went quiet once he'd noticed that Vanessa was not making any attempt to keep the conversation going. He turned the radio up and muttered about his fellow road users.

Tom Lindbeck could be anywhere in Sweden. Either alone, or with an accomplice. Vanessa was inclined to think the latter. She didn't think that the man who'd attempted to kill her was working with anyone other than Tom Lindbeck.

The search for him had grown into the largest police operation since the Drottninggatan terror attacks. Vanessa, though, was sure that he was no longer in Stockholm. Not for the time being.

A press conference was planned for after lunch, where the Chief Constable, flanked by a press officer, was going to go public with Tom Lindbeck's name and description. He was to be described as extremely dangerous and almost certainly armed.

Vanessa had woken up in Nicolas' bed with his arm over her. Despite them lying so close together that she could feel his calm breaths against her neck, she pushed her back up against him. Waited to get out of bed. Ran her fingers over his forearms. Put her hand on his. Eventually she did throw herself out of bed, had a quick shower and ran down to the waiting taxi.

Tomorrow, Nicolas was leaving for London. That was for the best, for both of them. She wouldn't have to wonder about it any more. He could apply himself to doing something meaningful. Without that, he would go under. He needed a context. To fill the voids that she knew were there. That was something Vanessa would never be able to do. She had her own voids inside her. And even if she had been able to, Nicolas probably wouldn't have wanted it. Vanessa knew that he liked her, but probably not enough to give up his own life.

And she respected that. Life wasn't like the movies.

Outside the window, Kungsholmen swished past. Her other phone, the one she usually used for informants, rang.

"When will you be here?"

"In a couple of minutes," said Vanessa.

2

BENGT STOOD IN front of the reporters, who had formed a semicircle around him. He folded his arms and cleared his throat. The journalists fell silent, put down the newspapers they'd been reading while they waited for the meeting to get underway. Without a word, he wandered slowly down the line. After giving each one of them a stare, he stopped. Stretched his back.

"Well done, you lot." He held up a copy of *Aftonposten*. "We're crushing them. They've got nothing to counter with. Nothing!"

He threw the paper into the air so that it opened up and sailed down and was left lying on the floor.

"Making papers is a team activity of course, I'd be the first to say that, but... Max Lewenhaupt," Bengt said, pointing at Max. "Front page *and* the news bills. A round of applause."

Jasmina joined in the clapping. Perhaps she was imagining it, but did Max seem not quite as arrogant as he usually did when he was being praised? He bowed his head, and once the applause had finished, he glanced at Jasmina.

"Today we'll pick up where we left off. Everyone already knows what to do," said Bengt.

Jasmina turned on her heels to return to her desk, but Bengt stopped her. "Have you got a minute?"

He led her over towards Tuva Algotsson's room and let her enter ahead of him. Tuva greeted them with a friendly smile.

The door behind Jasmina was pulled shut and the hum of the newsroom died away.

"Well done, Jasmina. Quick and effective. As I imagine you're aware, we're examining the possibility of naming Tom. Telling the story of his life. His apartment is being searched today and there will be details leaked from that. Max is responsible for getting hold of the details, and once he has, I want you to help him get the article together. Okay?"

"Yes."

It would be the following day's most important piece. The fact that Tuva wanted Jasmina to have a role in writing it indicated that she appreciated her.

"Good."

Tuva reached for her coffee. Jasmina noticed that it was a takeaway, from the Italian place across the road.

"The important thing is that we don't forget the *whole* story. Oscar Sjölander was released last night. I want you to try and get him to talk. He's likely to disappear out of Sweden in the next few days, so it's important that you track him down as soon as possible."

Bengt, who'd been sitting engrossed in his phone, thrust a handwritten note towards Jasmina.

"We've received information suggesting that he's holed up at this hotel."

Jasmina examined the squiggly handwriting. The informant had even supplied a room number. The porter? Receptionist? Oscar Sjölander had been in custody, accused of killing Rakel Sjödin. Even if he was innocent, his TV career was over. The witness statements about his violence towards women were common knowledge. No channel would touch him with a bargepole.

Jasmina took the note and stood up. "I'll go straight away."

3

TRUDE HOVLAND PLACED the IKEA box on top of the folding table which the technicians had brought with them and were using to sort through the items they'd found in the apartment.

There were hundreds of photographs inside it. Each photo was neatly indexed on the reverse with date and location. The forensic technicians wore white overalls as they worked through Tom Lindbeck's home, just hours after the bomb disposal squad had secured the apartment and granted them access. There was a sweet smell of decomposition and ingrained dirt in the air. Vanessa breathed through her mouth to avoid retching.

"How could he stand the smell?"

"According to his niece, he has anosmia," said Trude. "He lacks a sense of taste and cannot smell anything."

Vanessa grabbed a clutch of photos.

"So if I've got this right," she said as she studied them, "the explosion was a hand grenade. When the door opened, the pin was pulled out. Tom saw the SWAT team via the CCTV he'd installed in the stairwell. He then opened a window, where a rope was hanging down, and he climbed up onto the roof. He then ran in the direction of the bridge."

"Correct. The last door on the roof, the one closest to the bridge, was unlocked. He made his way down through that stairwell. We do not know how he got off the island."

Almost all of the photographs portrayed scantily clad women in public places. Presumably unaware that Tom was snapping them.

"It gets worse," said Trude.

She passed a thick A4 envelope to Vanessa, who then weighed it in her hand. Opened it. At first she couldn't grasp what she was looking at. Unlike the others, these pictures were dark and blurry. The top one had been taken at night, through a window. Three people lying naked in a bed. Two men and a woman. Intertwined. Another showed a couple taking coke while having sex.

"Documenting people's private lives seems to have been a sort of perverted hobby of his. We found some recordings on an old hard drive."

"Recordings?"

Trude nodded.

"Films, and sound. He has recorded people in their own homes. Conversations. Sex. Rows. Edited the films together and put music over the top."

Vanessa put the envelope down and stared out into the living room. The furniture was all heavy and outdated. If she hadn't already known that Tom Lindbeck was thirty-three, she would have guessed that this was home to a much older person.

She suddenly recalled what Ivan had told Nicolas – about the guards watching Victoria Ahlberg having sex with her boyfriend.

"Were there films from the prison?"

"I don't know yet. We haven't had time to go through all the material. Every single cupboard is full of old drawers, papers, junk and boxes. What were you thinking?"

"Victoria Ahlberg."

"We are yet to find anything that ties him to her. Then again, we haven't found anything tying him to the murders of Rakel and Emelie either. I would expect us to do so in the next few hours though. Now I'd like to show you something else."

They walked into a study. The stench got worse. By one wall, part of the floor was partitioned off with a fifty-centimetre-high plastic screen, behind which eight large rats jostled amongst rotting leftovers, gnawed chicken bones and droppings. Vanessa took a couple of steps towards them. Six of the rats were tied together by their tails. They could not move unless the others went along. The animals were squealing and scratching against the plastic screen.

Trude stood next to Vanessa.

"It's what is known as a 'Rat King'," she said. "It sometimes occurs in nature, when tails get stuck in blood and droppings. This one he has created himself, with the help of some steel wire. There were lots of books about rats in the bedroom. Almost as many as there were about sex and masculinity."

Trude walked over to the desk and returned with a notepad which she flipped open.

"He has studied them carefully. Look here," she said.

The Rat King and the loose rats were sorted into separate columns. He had noted their weight, length and colour. Neat diagrams and tables.

"Where did he get the rats from?"

"Parks, the basement, who knows... We have found cage traps, presumably the ones he used to capture them."

Vanessa turned around and walked over to the window.

Traffic on Essingeleden was heavy and proceeding only slowly. People on their way to work, to their country places, romantic meetings. Each one of them in their own universe of forbidden thoughts, angst, broken families, sexual fantasies. Just like Tom. This was his world. He had been alone in it. Had no idea how to meet people outside of it. That was why he'd become obsessed with getting into other people's lives. Finding out their secrets. But why was he happy to observe certain women, yet murder others? Perhaps it was as simple as him believing that he'd found a way to get away with it?

There was a strip of paper lying on the window sill. Vanessa leaned over. A match ticket for a top-flight women's football match, between Djurgården and Linköping at Stockholm Stadium. She stared at the date: Saturday 4th of May. Kick-off 11.30. Her heart started racing. That was surely enough time for Tom Lindbeck to drive from Tyresö to the match? But in between, he had to have moved Rakel's body from the cottage and down to the water, gone to Oscar Sjölander's house in Bromma and planted the murder weapon and the jumper in the bin. No, the timings didn't fit.

Tom Lindbeck hadn't killed Rakel Sjödin.

"Trude?" A male technician stuck his head round the door. "We've found something weird in the fridge. Come and see."

Vanessa slowly followed them into the kitchen. One of the technicians was holding up a little plastic receptacle. Vanessa couldn't see its contents.

"What is it?" asked Trude.

"We think it's semen," said the man.

4

NICOLAS HEARD A whistle from behind and spun around. Celine waved. Her rucksack bounced as she picked up the pace. He held the door open with his foot. He was going to have to tell her now, tell her that he was moving.

"Are you coming into town?" she asked.

"Not today." He couldn't keep it in any longer. It wasn't going to end with him disappearing without saying goodbye. "Have you got time to talk?"

"If it's quick. I'm just dropping my bag off, then I'm going into town to buy some clothes. I'm going to Pussy Power tomorrow."

"It'll be quick."

Celine gave him a suspicious look.

"Have I done something wrong?"

For a second, he glimpsed insecurity in her otherwise so confident face.

"No," he rushed to say.

She shrugged.

"Okay."

Nicolas pointed to a bench in the yard. Before he sat down, he brushed off the seat. Celine put her bag in her lap and wrapped her arms around it.

"Do you need to borrow money, or what?"

She giggled. Nicolas smiled. Shook his head. He steeled himself, but Celine got in first.

"I've been practising. Holding my breath."

Nicolas looked at her, confused.

"In the bath. So that I can do military service. You said I can do anything, if I really put my mind to it. I can hold my breath for forty-seven seconds now. Good, eh?" She looked at him expectantly.

"I'm moving away. To London."

Celine didn't flinch.

"When?"

A magpie hopped two-footed past a rubbish bin. "Tomorrow." Small twitches multiplied themselves around her eyes.

"Oh right. See you then. Now I've got to go."

"Don't you want to know why?"

She flung her rucksack onto her back and started walking. Nicolas got to his feet, caught up with her and carefully placed a hand on her shoulder.

"Celine, wait. I am sorry, but I have to."

He turned her around carefully, and to his surprise, he saw that she was crying.

"I'll come home now and then and say hi. Then we can go swimming. Or diving. I promise."

She didn't answer. A tear rolled slowly down her cheek. Nicolas reached towards her, but she parried his hand. "It won't be the same."

He wasn't about to lie by contradicting her. He gently pulled her head against his chest. She let herself be embraced. Her breath made the fabric of his T-shirt damp. Nicolas ran his fingers through her knotty hair as he held her.

"It will be like before you moved in," she sobbed. "Don't you understand that? I had no friends. You're the only one who understands me. Likes me. Please, Nicolas, don't leave me."

"I have to," he said quietly. "I'm sorry, but I have to."

He gulped. Held back.

"No, Nicolas. Please. You mustn't."

She tore herself away, started hitting him.

"You mustn't," she screamed. "You mustn't. You hear me? You mustn't leave me."

5

JASMINA LOWERED HER hand and waited. She wasn't looking forward to barging in, but she knew it was part of the job. She pressed her ear to the door, listening for any signs of life, but it was completely silent. All jobs have their drawbacks, even being a tabloid reporter.

She knocked again. Harder. For a couple of seconds, she visualised Oscar Sjölander lying dead in there, wrists slashed in the bath or hanging from a noose.

The door to room 1316 opened and a bearded face appeared in the crack. "Yes?" He was squinting into the light of the corridor. His lips were quivering as he waited for her to say something.

"My name is Jasmina Kovac. I'm a reporter from *Kvällspressen*. Can I talk to you for a moment?"

The relief she'd felt at finding him alive disappeared. She tensed up, prepared herself for a rollicking, but he just looked at her calmly.

"What time is it?" he asked groggily.

"Twenty to one."

Oscar opened the door fully and turned around. He was wearing a white hotel robe, over underpants and a T-shirt. The curtains were closed. Jasmina stepped in and found herself standing outside the bathroom door. By the window was an armchair and a little coffee table. Oscar opened the curtains a chink, and a narrow beam of light found its way into the room.

"Why did they send you and not someone else?" he asked.

His voice was slurred. Jasmina glanced over at his bedside table. Tablets, and miniature bottles from the minibar.

The situation didn't feel good. The paper's policy was that interview subjects had to be sober. The man in front of her was clearly intoxicated on something and had far from full control of his faculties.

"Is it because you're a young woman, do you think? Because I like young women?"

His jaw was moving as he studied her intently.

The room was hot. Damp. Stuffy. The bed or the desk? Jasmina pulled out the desk chair and turned it around so it was facing Oscar.

"Maybe," she said frankly. "Or because we're both from Växjö."

Oscar burst into a joyless cackle.

"You don't even believe that yourself," he said, suddenly serious. "Well, I'll give you a few quotes, Jasmina from Växjö."

He was pacing back and forth between the bed and the armchair. The belt of his dressing gown trailed on the floor.

He looked like a tormented, wounded animal.

"My wife has left me," he said, stopping in front of her. "She didn't want anything to do with me and I can't blame her. I've behaved like a pig."

Jasmina put her Dictaphone on her thigh, pressed record.

This was surreal. The words Oscar Sjölander was now uttering would be read by hundreds of thousands, if not millions of people. The text was going to be quoted everywhere. It would make her famous throughout Sweden. She wouldn't have to worry about finding work for the next ten years. But she had to stay focused on what he was saying and stick around for as long as possible. At any moment, he could call off the interview and chuck her out.

"The only thing I want to ask is that people leave Therese and my daughters alone. Keep them out of this."

Silence.

"What are you going to do now?" Jasmina asked tentatively.

"My career is over. Everything I worked for was in vain. Don't get me wrong. This is my fault. Mine alone. No viewer will ever be able to watch me without thinking of me as an unfaithful pig. What am I going to do? I don't know. Travel somewhere far away to begin with perhaps? Avoid the stares, and the hate."

He slumped into the armchair. Put the knuckle of his index finger between his lips and sucked it.

"Nothing means anything," he said quietly. "You know? It doesn't matter what happens to me. The fact that I'm no longer suspected of Rakel's murder; that's... it doesn't change anything. Everything that meant anything is gone. I might as well die."

Oscar buried his head in his hands. Then suddenly, he looked up. His eyes were misty and hostile.

"Maybe *Kvällspressen* would like to stream my suicide? That would be great for the page hits. Then you can buy the rights to the funeral too. Complete the circle."

He shook his head.

"I want you to leave now."

To her great surprise, Jasmina realised that she felt sorry for him. Sitting in front of her was a person whose life had been demolished. She – if anyone – knew what it meant to have your dignity taken away. To fall to pieces. To be reduced to a stressed animal. She switched her attention to the tablets, as she wondered whether there were enough there to take his life. She forced herself to focus.

"One last thing. Is there anything you'd like to say to Rakel Sjödin's family?"

He clutched his hands in his lap.

"Just that she was a wonderful person who didn't deserve what happened to her," he mumbled.

Jasmina stood up. She wanted to get out. Away. She pushed the chair back under the desk and gathered up her things.

On the way out, she stopped and turned around. Oscar Sjölander looked up in surprise.

"I was gang-raped," she said. "Three men drugged me, raped and assaulted me so badly that I could barely stand up. I didn't report it, and at first I didn't tell anyone. Because I was ashamed. Because I was scared. I'm still terrified. Constant nightmares. But I decided to survive. Not because life is that much of a hoot, but because otherwise they win, and the rapes continue. Every day, every hour. Do something worthwhile with your life. That's what I'm going to do."

On her way out through the lobby, Jasmina checked her phone. A missed call from an unknown number. She was studying the digits when the phone started ringing.

"How did it go? Did you get him?" Bengt asked excitedly.

The sliding doors opened in front of her.

"He wasn't there," she lied.

Jasmina was a journalist, and she wanted to progress, to become someone, but above all, she was a human being. She should never have interviewed Oscar Sjölander, who had barely been aware of what he was saying. His brain was not capable of making rational decisions.

It was a headline Sweden could do without.

She wasn't about to put Oscar Sjölander's family through this. They had suffered enough. Someone else was going to have to do the dirty work.

6

AFTER SIGNING FOR a new firearm, Vanessa went into her office and closed the door. She needed to be left alone. She placed the new pistol on the desk, pulled down the blinds and found herself standing there with her arms hanging by her sides.

The stench from the flat was still clinging to her clothes. She wanted a shower, to get clean. She wasn't, however, going to be allowed back into her apartment until later in the evening. If she wanted a wash, she was going to have to go to the police gym or check in to a hotel.

Every officer in the area was looking for Tom Lindbeck. But the match ticket suggested that he wasn't the one who had murdered Rakel Sjödin. That's if he'd been to the match. Why would a man who hates women go to a top-flight women's match? Had he been trying to trick them into thinking he had an alibi? No, he almost certainly knew that it would take a lot more than that. She thought about the man who had shot at her. Was he the one who had murdered Rakel?

Vanessa fired up her computer. An internal memo had been sent to all detectives with the sketchy details that had so far been collated about Tom Lindbeck's background.

Born in 1986, in Trelleborg. Father unknown. When Tom was four, his mother Agata Lindbeck moved with him and his twelve-year-older half-sister Ingela to Farsta in Stockholm. Both his mother and Ingela were dead. Apart from his job with the Prison Service, where he'd started four years earlier, he had worked as a freelance photographer, with *Kvällspressen* his only client.

During the course of the day, the memo would be fleshed out with further information, as fourteen detectives were busy interviewing people in Tom Lindbeck's life – colleagues, neighbours, his niece – to get a clearer picture of Sweden's most wanted man.

After the press conference, all the major papers had published his name. Footage of the Chief Constable's statement was played on the TV.

The phone rang. It was Mikael Kask. Vanessa could tell immediately that it wasn't good news.

"I'm sorry, Vanessa. The bosses are worried that journalists are going to start digging the dirt around that drink-driving case that saw you suspended last year. They want you to rest, considering what you went through in your apartment as well. I think this is so bloody unfair. I know what you and Ove have meant to this investigation."

He sounded tense, probably expected Vanessa to get angry. She just felt apathetic. "It's okay, Mikael. Thanks for trying."

"Are you sure?" he said, surprised.

She hesitated.

"Yes. I know this sounds mad, but I'm no longer sure that Tom murdered Rakel Sjödin."

"What are you talking about?"

Mikael's voice had shifted from being apologetic to irritated.

"There was a match ticket in his apartment. The game kicked off at half-past eleven on the 4th of May. If he was there, there's no way he'd have had time to move Rakel's body and make it out to Bromma."

"He could have got hold of that ticket from anywhere. He could've found it on the street and kept it. He could've bought it and not gone. Right?"

"Maybe. But I thought you should know. Check the stadium's CCTV, at least."

"We are working on the assumption that Tom murdered Rakel. Everything points to that."

"Do as you please, but you should be looking for an alternative suspect too. At least for Rakel's murder."

She hung up.

Without her and Ove, no one would've even heard of Tom Lindbeck. And he was involved, somehow. But there was another person out there. She was convinced of that now. Had it been a couple of years earlier, she would've been on the phone to every boss. Bawling. Screaming. Trying to get put back on the case. Now though, she started gathering her things together.

Her eyes settled on her new police issue handgun. Vanessa weighed it in her hand. She was no weapons fetishist, but there were situations she faced in carrying out her duties which required her to be armed. Like in South America last year. Or yesterday. She put the pistol into her bag and zipped it up.

Vanessa left the police station, left the car in the garage and walked towards Rådhuset metro station.

7

BÖRJE TOOK THE escalator up to the platform in Farsta. It was almost empty. At the far end, he spotted Elvis, who was sitting on his mobility scooter with a green can of beer in his hand. He didn't know how Elvis would respond to his apology. Whether he would even accept it. Börje had already lost Eva and the thought of also losing his only friend did not bear thinking about.

Elvis looked out over the high-rise blocks with an empty stare. Only once Börje was right next to him did he turn his head with a jolt.

Börje squirmed.

"Did I scare you?"

Elvis shook his head slowly.

"I saw you coming," he said, gesturing towards his eye with his stump. "Hawk eyes. I take after my mum there."

"I want to say sorry, Elvis. I called you things that… Jesus, I'm ashamed. You're my only mate. You do know that, right? I know you only meant well when you hid the booze."

Elvis nodded, without taking his eyes off Börje. Then he revealed his brown stained teeth as he cracked a smile.

"Apology accepted. Big heart and forgiving soul – I get that from Mum too. But listen, what have you done to your face?"

"I was going to jump in front of a train. Instead, I ended up in the Room, with the security guards."

"You got a proper pasting, I see. You had that coming,"

Elvis said with a wink. "That makes two of us who've failed to do ourselves in here."

The outbound train braked behind them. A couple of dozen passengers got off. One by one, they headed for the escalators. But then a blonde woman broke away from the huddle and started walking towards Börje and Elvis instead. When she came closer, Börje recognised her. Vanessa Frank.

"I've been calling you."

Börje held up his phone. The screen was black. Dead.

Elvis swung in next to him and pointed to the basket on his scooter.

"Will the lady have a beer?"

"I'm fine, thanks," Vanessa replied. She turned to Börje once more. "I need your help."

She managed to retrieve a printed-out photo from her bag. Börje took the piece of A4 and squinted at the photo of the bald-headed man. "Is that who Rakel let into the cottage?"

Börje handed the sheet back.

"I've never seen that one before."

A tinge flushed across Vanessa's face. For some reason, his answer had annoyed her.

"Are you sure?"

He nodded.

8

JASMINA KNEW THAT she was in trouble. If anyone at the paper got word of the fact that she'd lied about Oscar Sjölander, she'd be out. Loyalty to your paper was everything. Maybe Tuva Algotsson would've decided that the interview was not to be published if Jasmina had told her that the presenter had been high at the time. She didn't dare take that risk though.

Max sat down next to her. He stared at the computer screen, pretending to read the article about Karim. Apparently he was to be given custody of his daughter.

"I just spoke to my police mole," said Max. "They're in Tom Lindbeck's apartment. You know what they've found?"

She didn't reply.

"Big rats. And sex films. He has stalked people, recorded them in their apartments. Insane. We need a good name for him for the news bills. You know the way they do, 'Jack the Ripper', 'the Kindly Killer'. Ratman? No, too... Shit, I've got it. The Rat King. What do you think?"

Jasmina turned around slowly on her chair.

"I understand that you see this as a scoop," she said grimly. "But for me and all other women, it's more than that. It is us he hates. Us he wants to kill."

She could feel her face getting flushed. Jasmina never raised her voice, never got angry. But now she was fuming. She could happily have smacked him.

"He has killed two women my age, perhaps more. Do you think this is a game? Do you think he's alone? What we are writing about here is reality. And if you re-write reality too often, in the end it becomes unreal. That's what has happened to you."

And me, she'd been about to add. But for her, the opposite was true. Karim had made sure of that.

"Jasmina, I don't understand what I've done wrong or why you are angry with me."

She took a deep breath, calmed herself.

"You are an idiot, Max. This is serious."

"Of course I enjoy it. But it's my job," Max said, throwing his hands up.

She stared him out. Gulped. His phone started ringing. Max looked dejectedly at the screen. "I have to take this," he said.

He looked around for his Dictaphone but soon gave up. Instead, he grabbed Jasmina's and fiddled with the cable while he put the earpiece into his ear and headed for the corridor where he could talk undisturbed.

"THE RAT KING," Bengt said, illustrating a news bill with his fingers. "There we go." Jasmina folded her arms and leaned back on her chair in Tuva Algotsson's room.

She couldn't play this game any longer.

Bengt, who'd been standing and leaning over the Editor-in-Chief's neatly arranged desk, started walking in circles.

"Tomorrow's edition is basically finished. Well, unless they get him of course. So we've got your two articles, Max, about the police's discoveries in the apartment and the slightly longer one which we're calling *The Story of the Rat King*. I've got another two reporters ringing round to people in Tom Lindbeck's life, but I want you to write it, Max."

He stopped. Scratched his chin.

"Shit. Could really have done with an Oscar Sjölander interview. We could've led with it. Have you got any idea where he's holed up, Jasmina? Or what his plans are?"

"No. He wasn't at the hotel. And quite honestly, I don't think he really feels like talking."

Max gave her a quizzical look. Or was she imagining it? The interview with Oscar Sjölander was on her Dictaphone, but surely Max wouldn't have gone through it? He knew that she could have informants on there. Sources who wanted to remain anonymous. On the other hand, Max had stolen an article from her three weeks before.

"What about his wife, Therese?" Bengt asked, glancing at Tuva.

The Editor-in-Chief thought about it for a moment but then shook her head. "Too early," she said forcefully. "Keep her out of this."

Tuva fixed Jasmina with her stare. "Everything alright? You seem a bit down."

9

THE BLACK CABIN bag that Nicolas had bought from Hötorget Market lay open on the bed. What little he wanted to take with him to London fitted in there easily. He only had three photographs, which he kept in a plastic wallet. One was of him and his comrades in SOG on exercise in northern Sweden. They stood holding their skis like happy alpine tourists in front of a frozen white forest. Since their identities were to be kept a secret, they were not to be recorded on film, and for that reason, they were all wearing balaclavas.

The other was a picture of him and Maria, taken on Christmas Eve, in the apartment in Sollentuna. Nicolas was five years old and dressed in a white shirt and red bow tie. Alongside him was Maria, with an expressionless face and a crooked gnome hat.

At the bottom was the photograph of their mother. In all the years since her death, he had never been able to look at it. He put the plastic wallet and his green beret into the suitcase, zipped it up and put it on the floor. He then stretched out on the bed and stared up at the ceiling.

The farewell with Celine had not gone as he'd hoped. She was special. Intelligent. Funny. But he couldn't pass up the job in London, and his own life, to be her friend.

She'd get over it.

The phone rang: Vanessa.

"Hi," he said.

"What are you up to?"

"Packing."

Vanessa went quiet.

"I've been thinking a lot about Karim," said Nicolas. "It's terrible that he's going to be set free. There must be something we can do."

"Like what?"

Vanessa went quiet again. Seemed to steel herself. There was the sound of a car engine in the background.

"I was thinking... tomorrow. How are you getting to the airport?"

"On the train, I guess."

"Would you like me to come along?" she asked neutrally.

He smiled.

"To Arlanda? Have you got time?"

"Given what happened yesterday, they want me to take a step back," said Vanessa.

Nicolas could hear that she was straining to sound unmoved. How could they treat her like this? Without her, they would still be fumbling around in the dark, with two wrongly charged suspects. Nicolas losing his temper wasn't going to help things though. And if he knew Vanessa, she wouldn't want it either. It was enough to know that he was angry. That he was on her side.

"Well in that case," he said calmly. "See you tomorrow."

They hung up.

Something had changed between them. Nicolas didn't know how, or when, but it was indisputable.

He cast his mind back to the night before. He had never seen her like that, so vulnerable. On the contrary, Vanessa had always gone to great lengths to show that she didn't need help.

There was a part of him that was pleased – even if he would never admit as much – that it was him and not someone else that she'd come to. In the same way as he'd felt happy when he and Maria were small, those times his sister had come to him for comfort when she felt sad. He wanted to be important for Vanessa. Nicolas couldn't get to grips with his feelings. Didn't know what he wanted. Or what she wanted.

From the first moment, there had been something unspoken and charged between them. Sure, he was attracted to Vanessa. Not just physically – she was clearly beautiful in a way that was appealing. But above all, it was Vanessa Frank the person that Nicolas couldn't think about without feeling... well, what was it? Something that troubled his system and would not leave him alone.

10

JASMINA SLUMPED ONTO her bed with her phone in her hand. Her body was wrapped in a towel and her hair was wet. Bengt's angry voice was ringing in her ears. *You lied; you had talked to him. Do you realise the damage you've done?* They had found out that she'd interviewed Oscar Sjölander. Max, of course. He was the only one who could have known. Bengt had informed her that she'd been moved to the entertainment desk for the remainder of her contract. And even if he hadn't said as much, it was a given that she had no future at *Kvällspressen*.

She was going to be sent to cover a festival, Pussy Power, at Stockholm Stadium the next day.

"Shit," she muttered.

Jasmina was convinced she'd done the right thing, Oscar Sjölander had not been compos mentis – no one should be interviewed with their body full of tablets and booze. Tuva Algotsson might have decided not to publish the interview if she had told them, but she hadn't dared to take that risk. She'd made her own decision. And it had cost her her career.

But Oscar Sjölander's family shouldn't be made to suffer because he was a pig. She wanted to call Max and give him what for. In a way though, she was glad he'd caught her out. Her meeting with Oscar Sjölander had made her rethink all sorts of things.

Jasmina didn't want to be a tabloid journalist, but she

wasn't about to compromise what she believed in. Didn't want to sacrifice others so that she could move upwards. She would work the last few weeks on the entertainment desk, then she'd go home to Växjö. Beg to get her old job back. And if that didn't work, she'd find something else.

Jasmina got out of bed. She needed to get out, get some fresh air, clear her head. She'd put on her bra and was pulling on her jeans when the doorbell rang. She looked through the peephole and saw that it was Vanessa Frank.

They found a bench by the fountain in Tessin Park. The sun stained the fleeing clouds orange. A couple took a selfie in front of the column of water before walking off into the park, hand in hand. On the grass, a couple of teenagers lay on a blanket, listening to Avicii and smoking weed.

Vanessa got out her vape and took a puff.

"I just wanted to see how you were getting on," she said, turning her face away to exhale the vapour.

"Okay." Jasmina laughed. "Well, shit actually. I won't be getting my contract extended and tomorrow I'll be collating surveys from Pussy Power."

"What's that?"

"A man-free festival."

"Right."

A football headed for the fountain, bounced over the rim and down into the water. Some dad rolled up his trouser legs. His daughter squealed with laughter as he waded out to retrieve it.

"Did you really come here just to see how I was getting on?" Jasmina asked cautiously.

Vanessa nodded.

"Don't take this the wrong way, but you seem like a pretty lonely person."

"I am," Jasmina admitted with a smile.

"I just wanted to make sure you were keeping it together after what happened. Why aren't you being kept on at *Kvällspressen*?"

In the fountain, the man had picked up the football and

was making his way back. He splashed water at the girl sitting on the rim.

"I interviewed Oscar Sjölander today."

"So your bosses should be pleased?"

A gull squawked hoarsely above them.

"I told them I couldn't get hold of him. He wasn't with it. But it wasn't actually for his sake that I lied, but for his wife and kids. Anyway, my bosses found out about it. One of my colleagues, Max, heard the recording which was on my Dictaphone."

The gull circled above them before folding in its wings as it landed on a lamp post.

"Karim," said Jasmina. "Is it true that he'll be getting custody of Emelie Rydén's... their daughter when he gets out?"

Vanessa looked away. It looked like she was ashamed, Jasmina thought. Then she made eye contact again.

"You haven't changed your mind about reporting it?"

Jasmina slowly shook her head.

A beep from Vanessa's bag. She apologised and pulled out her phone. Her whole body went stiff, and she stared blankly into space. She put the phone away.

"Everything okay?" Jasmina asked.

Vanessa bowed her head. Her lip started quivering. She turned away so Jasmina didn't have time to notice that she was crying.

"My colleague, Ove, is dead."

PART VIII

Mass-shootings are all about revenge, enjoying getting your enemies to suffer. Of course they will never fundamentally change society.

An anonymous man.

1

VANESSA STOPPED IN front of the newsagent at Central Station, outside which *Aftonposten* and *Kvällspressen*'s news bills glared yellow.

Hunted man suspected of four murders, blazoned *Aftonposten*'s, accompanied by a picture of Tom Lindbeck.

The Rat King's double life – and hatred of women, *Kvällspressen* countered, using the same photograph.

The Rat King, then. Someone from Police HQ was leaking details from the forensic examination of Tom Lindbeck's apartment. Four women in identical red T-shirts walked past with beer bottles in hand, house music streaming from a little speaker that one of them was carrying. The backs of their T-shirts bore the words *Man-Free – no gropes, no gripes*.

"There you are."

Nicolas was wearing a long-sleeved black T-shirt, black jeans, and was pulling a cabin trolley behind him. Her rib stung as he embraced her.

"Are you still in pain?"

"Not too bad," she said. "Shall we get going?"

They followed the signs for the Airport Express.

Nicolas was about to build up a new life, meet other, younger women. She didn't begrudge him that. He deserved to be happy. Vanessa, though, hated change. She was going to stay here. Alone. Go home to her shot-up apartment, to be sent out into the country in a few days' time to go and spend her evenings in empty hotel bars. Next time they were in touch, everything would be different.

"You can come and visit me. London isn't that far away," he said encouragingly.

"Sure."

She was being selfish. She ought to make the effort, pretend to be happy. Otherwise, he was going to remember her as a bitter old hag. She stopped.

"I hate farewells, Nicolas."

He smiled and stroked her cheek.

"I know."

Nicolas' penetrating stare locked on hers. Shaking her. Stirring up.

"You… you mean something to me," said Vanessa. "Do you understand? There aren't many people that do."

The music echoed over the brick walls, through the black gates and out across Valhallavägen. Outside, hundreds of women of all ages jostled along the fencing. Drinking beer and wine from plastic cups. Portaloos and merchandise stalls lined the avenue in the middle of Valhallavägen. Girls sat in groups, like little islands dotted around the grass, listening appreciatively to songs that Jasmina had never heard.

Between the trees, above her head, someone had put up a large banner carrying the festival's motto: *Love. Sisterhood. Music.* Political groups were also represented. Volunteers from the main parties handed out flyers as more and more festival-goers arrived at the site. They came on foot from all directions and joined the dancing, rolling sea of humanity. Security guards surveyed the crowd. Inside the fence, a couple of medics were leaning, arms folded, against an ambulance. The gates had opened, but most of the festival-goers were still milling around outside the venue.

Jasmina and twenty-something freelance photographer Freja Kjellberg walked among the women, introducing themselves and asking two questions: which artist have you come to see, and why are man-free festivals necessary?

Jasmina allowed herself to get caught up in the buzz, and quickly forgot that she'd been demoted and had no future career.

Once they'd done the interviews, they headed towards the press entrance on Drottning Sofias Väg, past two parked ambulances before showing their press credentials to a steward in an orange vest. They were each given accreditation passes on lanyards and were shown to a small backstage area. It consisted of a couple of folding tables, a few flimsy plastic chairs and a TV screen on which the journalists could follow events inside the arena.

Jasmina grabbed an apple from a fruit bowl and said hi to a couple of colleagues. On the screen, they could see the expectant crowd gradually filling the stadium. She wanted to get out there and feel the atmosphere.

There was a pain in her side, and Vanessa felt the bandage on her ribs with her fingertips. It was moist.

"I just need to check the wound," she said.

"I'll get the train tickets in the meantime. I'll see you on the platform."

Vanessa headed back towards the departure hall, and down the escalators to the toilets. A couple of dozen women stood in a huddle, singing Robyn's 'Dancing On My Own' with hands outstretched. A few passers-by stopped, pulled out their phones and filmed the scene. In front of the mirror, Vanessa unbuttoned her white shirt and peeled off the surgical tape that was holding her bloody bandage in place. She replaced it with a new one.

Behind her, cubicle doors were opening and closing.

"Where is the stadium anyway?" a woman with a Malmö accent asked as she washed her hands.

Vanessa looked at her in the mirror. She was one of the ones who'd been singing the Robyn song.

"Take the metro red line towards Mörby," another woman answered.

"Thanks."

Vanessa buttoned up her shirt and ran her hand across it to flatten out the creases. She checked her reflection. *Not long to go*, she thought. *Nicolas is going and you'll be able to go back to your uneventful life of solo drinking, Animal Planet shows and repeats of reality TV.*

She took a step towards the exit but then stopped suddenly. A chilling terror pulsed through her body. The man-free festival was the subject of lots of debate. It was like a red rag, especially for anti-feminists. Personally, Vanessa felt torn about the idea, even if she could well understand women's desire to listen to music without getting groped.

She pulled out her phone as she jogged towards the escalators.

"Vanessa, how are things?" enquired Mikael Kask.

"Listen here. I don't know where you think Tom Lindbeck might be right now or how close you're getting, but you need to send people to Stockholm Stadium."

"What for?"

"Pussy Power. The man-free festival."

"Don't worry. We've got the situation under control. He's no longer in Stockholm. We have…"

Vanessa hung up, pushed past a couple of stationary travellers on the escalator and reached the departure hall. She ran through the food court, out of the sliding doors and emerged onto the platform, where a yellow Arlanda Express train was steadily filling up with passengers.

Jasmina and Freja were standing in the middle of the crowd. The speakers crackled into life at the same time as a figure in a black cape with the hood up took to the stage at the northern end of the stadium and climbed into the DJ booth.

"Alright, girls. Are you ready for love, sisterhood and music?"

The women in the crowd chorused *Yes!* in unison, and the

next moment, the music was streaming over them. It came from all directions, transforming the women into a dancing, singing body. The artist threw off her cape, raised a fist into the air and started moving rhythmically. The bass was so heavy that Jasmina could feel it in her stomach. Her organs were vibrating. She got caught up in it, started bouncing up and down. Freja laughed and joined in.

The track died away, but the DJ didn't give them a chance to catch their breath. A new melody. Freja grabbed her by the arm, leaned in and shouted something. She pointed towards the press area; Jasmina nodded and followed her.

They held up their passes and were let in. They opened the door, went down the corridor and the music quickly quietened.

"I need to send in some pictures," said Freja. "The entertainment editor wants the surveys as soon as possible."

"Then I'll write up the interviews."

Jasmina pulled her phone out. Three missed calls. Two from an unknown number at *Kvällspressen*, which she presumed was the ents editor. One from Max.

In the press room, her colleagues sat hunched over their laptops. Almost all of them were women, even if there were a couple of men there. The papers had been given permission to send male reporters, even if the organisers had made it clear that they preferred female ones. The air was stuffy. Still, Jasmina took a mineral water, got the cap off and sat down at an empty desk.

She opened up her laptop and entered her password. She launched *Newspilot*, the writing programme used by most Swedish newspapers, and connected to Wi-Fi.

The door opened, and the music got momentarily louder before disappearing again. Jasmina turned around to see who had come in. Hans Hoffman. He walked over to the fruit bowl, picked up an apple and took a bite. He looked around the room. Jasmina stopped writing and pushed her chair back.

"Hans," she called out. "What are you doing here?" He seemed surprised to see her.

"Same as you. Aren't you on news?" he asked.

She shook her head.

"Are you in the bad books?"

His tone was playful, but he went serious as soon as he saw Jasmina's expression.

"You could say that," she said. "But I didn't know you were going to be here. Am I glad to see you."

She leaned in to hug him and felt his prickly chin against her cheek.

"One of the other reporters pulled out, so they called me in at short notice. But listen, I have to interview the artists. Got to shoot backstage."

"The festival," said Vanessa. "The man-free festival at the stadium."

"What about it?"

She breathed out and tried to synchronise her speech with her breathing.

"I think they are going to attack it. There was a ticket to a football match in Tom's apartment. I think he was there on reconnaissance."

Nicolas stared at her.

"Celine is there."

He stood up and started running along the platform with the bag. In front of the doors to the main hall, he turned left, out towards the taxi rank. Vanessa saw him push in front of a group and over to the first taxi. The driver was busy putting an older man's suitcase into the boot of his Volvo V70. Nicolas ripped it out of his hands and put it down on the pavement. The driver was furious. Started shouting. Vanessa flashed her police badge.

"We need this car. Now."

The taxi driver threw his hands up.

"You can't just take my car!"

The old man was looking at them quizzically. Nicolas

chucked in his own bag, rounded the car and opened the driver's door. Vanessa got into the passenger seat.

"How sure are you about this?" he asked without looking at Vanessa.

"Very," she said.

He zigzagged his way down to Kungsgatan, where he turned right.

"Call 112," said Nicolas. "Say there's been gunfire at the festival."

Jasmina returned to her computer, plugged in the headphones so she could listen to her Dictaphone, put her phone on the table and started hammering away at the keyboard. She was interrupted by a call from Max. She rejected it. Pushed her hand through her hair irritably and carried on writing up the survey responses. It rang again. She sighed, got up and took the phone out with her into the corridor.

"What is it?"

"I heard about what happened, and I just wanted to say that it wasn't me who talked to Bengt."

"Stop lying, Max. For once in your life, stop lying. Do you have to be a liar as well as a thief?"

"Oscar Sjölander called the newsroom yesterday, trying to stop publication. He was put through to Bengt, who worked out that you'd spoken to him."

If Oscar Sjölander had got cold feet after their conversation, he knew enough about how tabloids work to try and contact them and ask them not to publish the interview. Once Jasmina had left his hotel room, he could not have known that she had had a change of heart.

"Hello?" said Max.

"Yes?"

"You have to believe me."

She sighed. Stared at the brick wall. Further down the

corridor, a door opened. The music found its way inside. Approaching footsteps. "I have to work now."

"How's the festival?"

"Good. Hoffman is here."

"Hans Hoffman?"

"Yes. He got called in this morning."

Max went quiet for a moment.

"Hoffman's been sacked. He sent threatening messages to female journalists and politicians. For obvious reasons, Tuva hasn't wanted to go public about it. But I know, because I was the one who exposed him. That was why I got to come back, if I promised not to tell anyone."

The traffic on Kungsgatan was at a standstill. Nicolas put on his hazard lights, beeped the horn and proceeded with his right-hand wheels on the pavement. Pedestrians flung themselves out of his path, squeezed against buildings, screaming and gesticulating as they passed.

"What did they say?"

"They don't believe me. There are police there and they have not reported any gunfire."

"If we're lucky, we'll find them before there is."

Nicolas slammed on the horn and an elderly woman jumped out of the way just in time. Vanessa recognised the focused look on his face. Grim determination. Inhuman. She had seen it before. On the way to Täby, in the middle of the night. Another car. Another life. That time, they had arrived too late.

At Stureplan, a blue bus blocked the whole carriageway. Nicolas pulled out into the oncoming traffic. Somehow glided along, inches from the bus, without losing speed.

"Are you sure that Celine is there?" asked Vanessa.

Nicolas nodded.

They drove past Humlegården Park. Frontages a blur outside the car. She glanced at the speedometer: a hundred kilometres per hour. She craned her neck. Wondered where on Valhallavägen the road closures would start. How many were there? A thousand? Two thousand? Exclusively women. They could fire blind and still be sure of hitting. All women were targets. But the fact that it was a purely female audience would also make it more difficult to hide.

On Karlavägen, the lights turned red. Nicolas slowed down. Looked left, then right, pulled out in front of a red Porsche and sped off. Came close to hitting a Peugeot approaching from the direction of Östermalm but spun the wheel, sent the car swerving off, and for a moment, Vanessa was certain it was going to tip over, before Nicolas managed to straighten up.

They reached Valhallavägen. Nicolas pulled up. Just music. No gunfire, no cries for help. Just happy, dancing people standing in long queues as they waited to be let in.

2

TOM SAT ON the stretcher inside the ambulance, which was parked on the side of the stadium closest to Drottning Sofias Väg. Outside, women were laughing, singing and cheering. He clenched his right fist until his wrist hurt. Relaxed. Clenched it again. He was dying to get out. To spread death around him. To see the blood run. To hear the screams. Finally, he was going to take revenge for everything they'd put him through.

Hans Hoffman was to take the first shot, towards the artist on stage. Some feminist with tattoos and rainbow-coloured hair, no doubt. When the crowd started running for the exits, Tom would take over. Sweep his weapon through the crowd. He had seven fully loaded magazines for his Glock. A hundred and nineteen bullets in all.

Tom wished he'd had more, that he'd had time to line them up against the wall one by one and pull the trigger. He was going to kill as many as possible. Age was of no significance. None were innocent. Only man-haters would go to a place where men were not welcome. This was a war. He was a soldier, and the singing femoids out there were the enemy. They wanted to obliterate him. They had come close to succeeding. How many Incels ended up taking their own lives? Slashed their wrists, filled their bodies with pills, threw themselves from bridges?

He was there for their sakes.

Tom grabbed a couple of eyelashes between his finger and thumb and plucked them out. It stung. He studied the black strands of hair before letting them fall to the floor. Through the tinted windows, he could see the women.

"You little whores," he said. "I'm going to slaughter you."

He checked his watch and pushed open the door. Looked out. Fat, thin, old, young. Beckys and Staceys. Hideous. They didn't notice him. The green-yellow paramedic's uniform and the brown wig made him invisible. He climbed a couple of steps, through the concourse. He looked out across the sea of people. Worked his way down through the grandstand.

The music stopped.

He hadn't heard the shot; it had been drowned out by the din. Two loud bangs followed. Screams came from the people in the front, close to the stage. The cries spread as more and more women realised what had happened. Tom raised his weapon. A woman of around forty, in a purple vest top, boots and leather trousers, screamed as she stared down the barrel. The fat whore held her hands up; two straggly clumps of hair stuck out of her armpits. Her lips moved. Tom took his time, aimed calmly and pulled the trigger.

At that moment, she turned her head, and the bullet forced its way into her temple. Tom laughed and looked around for his next victim.

Vanessa and Nicolas approached a woman in an orange vest who was directing people in through the marathon entrance at the end of the stadium by Valhallavägen. Vanessa showed her police ID. The woman examined it indifferently and then turned her attention to Nicolas. The music was deafening. From where they were, they could see the stage through the stone concourse.

"He is with me."

The woman shook her head.

"No men."

Behind her, the music stopped abruptly. The woman who had refused Nicolas entry turned around and peered into the crowd. Two shots rang out. For a brief second, everything went deadly silent, before the desperate screams of the crowd reached them. A wall of people was rushing towards them.

The sniper's position was impossible to determine because the sound echoed around within the high walls. Vanessa barged the woman out of the way, forced her way in and pulled out her weapon. Complete chaos reigned as hundreds of festival-goers pushed for the exits. The iron fence, over a metre and a half tall, became a death trap. Some stumbled to the ground and were trampled by those behind. Vanessa and Nicolas ran in the opposite direction, towards the stage, sticking close to the walls to force their way forward.

Another volley of gunfire. More screams.

"Down," roared Vanessa. "Get down on the ground."

The crush got worse. Crying, despairing women screamed in desperation. Nicolas and Vanessa managed to get past the first human wall and onto the pitch, which had been covered by white plastic flooring for the concert. The women had dropped whatever they were holding when the gunfire started. Nicolas ran past Vanessa and swerved to the right, sticking close to the stands' concrete foundations to avoid the worst of the crowd. He raised his hands and hauled himself up.

"Can you see them?" Vanessa called out, but her voice was lost among the screams.

Nicolas climbed higher; Vanessa followed him upwards. It was impossible to get a grasp of the situation until more people had left the arena. The exits were surrounded by complete chaos as the bottlenecks backed up. Women were climbing over each other and tearing at clothes to get themselves out.

Even if Vanessa couldn't see Tom Lindbeck and his helper, she was going to show them that they weren't alone. She aimed her Sig Sauer skywards, towards the blue, and shot. She waited a couple of seconds before firing off a second shot.

Jasmina slumped into her chair, pushed her specs up her nose and put her earphones in. What was Hans Hoffman doing here? The song died abruptly. Instinctively, Jasmina looked towards the screen. The woman, who had just been standing up and dancing energetically, was lying next to her discarded cape. The murmuring and the sound of fingers on keyboards stopped. Chair legs scraped across the floor as reporters got to their feet and approached the screen to get a better view.

Hoffman ran out onto the stage. He raised a weapon and started shooting into the crowd.

"No!" she heard herself scream.

She pulled out her phone. Her hands were shaking. Her fingers didn't want to obey as she tried to enter her code to unlock it. After what felt like an eternity, she managed to press Max's name. The ringing tone dragged itself down the line while Jasmina stared at the screen, hypnotised.

"He's shooting," she screamed when he answered.

"Eh?"

"Hoffman. He... he's shooting."

A young woman had curled up next to one of the stands. Tom crouched down and stared her straight in the eye as he raised the gun to her forehead.

"One, two, three," he counted.

She screwed her eyes shut. Tom fired. He recoiled as warm blood spattered onto his clothes and face. One bullet per woman. No waste. He wiped his face with his sleeve and spun around. His wig fell off. That didn't matter now.

In the middle of the arena, a number of bodies lay strewn on the ground; some of them were moving weakly. Hoffman was standing on the other side, by one of the exits, picking off women as they tried desperately to escape. It looked like fun. They should have arranged a couple of hand grenades to chuck in there.

Tom felt alive, elated. Like a captive animal released into the wild for the first time. A murder machine. He fired off two shots at a couple of escaping women, missing one and felling the other mid-stride.

A shot was fired, and another.

It didn't sound like it had come from Hoffman, but from the grandstand by Lidingövägen. Tom looked in that direction. At the same time, he spotted a man in the stand, looking at him. Their eyes met. Was he a cop? In front of the man was a blonde woman. Tom squinted at her familiar face. Vanessa Frank. The police whore. He stifled an impulse to rush over.

The woman he had just shot was inching forward. Tom caught up with her, walked alongside her crawling body, and put a bullet in her back.

Tom called to Hoffman, but his voice was drowned out by the noise.

"Hans. Over here."

Even if the crush had eased somewhat, there were still hundreds of femoids still inside the arena. He actually wanted to keep going, but he couldn't do that when Vanessa Frank was there. It was time to move on to phase two. The getaway. When Hans didn't respond, Tom rushed over. His eyes were wild, glaring.

"We've got to go."

"Now?" said Hoffman as he fired a shot towards a huddle of women.

Tom did not take his eyes off him, didn't know whether he'd hit or not. They started running towards the ambulance.

Jasmina tried to call 112 to give them Hans Hoffman's name, but it rang and rang without being answered.

"Barricade the doors!" roared a woman inside the press room.

Journalists got up from the tables, grabbed the furniture and dragged it across the room.

Jasmina could not stay. She had to give Hoffman's name to the police at the scene. She threw a chair out of the way and pulled at the door. Someone screamed after her, but Jasmina got out into the empty corridor and rushed towards the performance area.

The guard who'd been supervising the press entrance had disappeared. The stage was over to her left. She avoided looking at the bodies in the centre of the arena. No police anywhere. Jasmina ran through the stands towards the exit on Valhallavägen. There ought to be police there.

The gunfire had stopped. Screaming could still be heard. Jasmina steeled herself. She rushed through the high-ceilinged concourse and had to stop almost straight away. A wall of women's backs was pushing towards the exit. Prevented her from going forwards. What if they show up here? Start shooting again? Jasmina was hyperventilating, battling not to be overcome with panic. She looked around. Then rushed back into the arena. In the centre of the field, a man and a woman were standing amongst the bodies. Vanessa Frank. Jasmina tried to avoid seeing the corpses at Vanessa's feet.

"One of the shooters is a colleague of mine. His name is Hans Hoffman," she panted.

"Picture?"

Jasmina held up her phone towards Vanessa.

"Send it to my email. I'll make sure it gets to my colleagues. Run over to the ambulances. Get the medics in here."

The photo Jasmina had shown her was the same man who had attacked Vanessa in her apartment.

The banner, bearing the words *Love. Sisterhood. Music.* was stained red with blood.

Vanessa was breathing heavily; she could feel the adrenaline rushing through her body in waves. The smell of gunpowder prickled in her nose. She pressed her clenched fists to her temples, gritted her teeth and stifled a scream. Beneath the banner was a police officer. Her body was twisted; she'd been shot in the head. The blood that hadn't ended up on the banner was pumping out of her skull and onto the ground. Strewn in a semicircle lay another four women. Some of them were still moving weakly, others were screaming in pain. Calling out to their mothers, to God, to their children.

By the exit, women were trying to force their way out of the festival. Police and ambulance sirens came closer, squealing, as if they too were panicking. Vanessa felt a movement by her side. Nicolas was pulling at her arm. She stared at him in confusion. Squinted. His mouth was moving, but Vanessa couldn't hear what he was saying.

Suddenly he ran over to one of the girls and threw himself down next to her. The girl was small and slight.

Dyed-green hair.

Vanessa took a step towards them, but her legs wouldn't carry her. She stumbled. Almost fell. She managed to stay on her feet and approached Nicolas and the little girl. He was holding her head in his hands. Her hair fell between his fingers. He screamed and pressed his forehead against hers.

Only now did Vanessa realise who the girl was. She let her eyes trace their way down the girl's body. There was a gaping hole in her stomach. Nicholas had let go of her head and was now pushing his hands onto the wound to stop the blood from leaving her body.

"Is she alive?" Vanessa screamed.

Most of the women had now made it outside the black gates. It was chaos out there. In the avenue of trees of Valhallavägen, some of them stopped, caught their breath, lay with their backs towards the parked cars and wailed out their terror. Others hobbled around with empty, dead eyes. Looking for friends. Screaming questions that no one yet had the answers to.

Jasmina turned off to the right, to the place where she'd noticed the ambulances earlier. Perhaps even the medics had panicked. Hidden away. The vehicles seemed abandoned, standing there behind the empty western grandstand. They were parked close to the gates on Drottning Sofias Väg and were not visible from Valhallavägen or the main entrance. Jasmina tried the door of the one parked closest. Locked. She banged on the side and tried to peer in through the tinted windows.

"There are casualties over here," she screamed.

At that moment, the back door of the second ambulance swung open. Hans Hoffman jumped out, wearing a green paramedic's uniform. She tried to curl up, make herself small, but he'd already seen her. Hoffman raised his pistol. Behind him was another man, Tom Lindbeck. He too was wearing medics' clothing. Jasmina realised it was over, that she was going to die.

"Don't shoot, Hans," she said. "Please."

She raised her hands, as if to protect herself as she backed away.

Hans Hoffman's face was expressionless. Indifferent. Tom Lindbeck said something to him. He lowered the barrel and, as Jasmina screamed in despair, he fired a shot. She felt the bullet smashing something inside her thigh and she fell to the ground. They ran over and dragged her across the ground towards the ambulance.

Celine's lips were moving weakly. Her body was wracked with convulsions. Vanessa looked towards the southern entrance where the ambulances had been posted.

"The medics will help her. We've got to chase Tom."

Nicolas gave Vanessa a blank stare. She turned his face towards her own.

"I need you," she screamed.

Vanessa went over to the dead policewoman to get her

firearm. She avoided the empty eyes as she turned the body over, pulled out the pistol and ran back to Nicolas. She wiped the handle against her trousers before placing it firmly in his hand.

The gunfire had stopped. Tom Lindbeck and his accomplice had finished murdering. For now. She had already had one chance at stopping him. She wasn't going to fail again. Vanessa looked around. Wondered which route they would have chosen. Her colleagues ought to be in position around the outside of the stadium by now. Two men would not be able to slip out unnoticed and disappear. Jasmina had gone round a corner and was out of sight.

Vanessa got out her phone, logged in to *Signal* and sent the image off to her colleagues. The stadium would soon be cordoned off. Only medics and police would be able to enter or leave the site or pass the roadblocks.

"Shit," she screamed.

The ambulance that had been stolen in Fittja. It must have been Tom Lindbeck and Hans Hoffman.

Vanessa ran off across the athletics track.

The silence was broken by a gunshot. If things were as she suspected – that they were going to attempt to escape disguised as medics – she had sent Jasmina Kovac straight to her death. She rounded the corner and was met with the sight of police cars and ambulances outside the gates attempting to make their way through the sea of people outside. When she reached the back of the stand, she realised that she was right. The gates were open. Further along Drottning Sofias Väg, the rear lights of an ambulance were disappearing up the hill.

She called the control room to tell them which way the suspects were fleeing. No answer. They had to be completely swamped with calls. She rang Mikael Kask, but it went straight to voicemail.

Jasmina was lying on the stretcher inside the ambulance as it bounced along. The windows were tinted; she could see treetops and buildings rushing past. She was strapped down, unable to move her arms or legs. Her right hand was strapped to the stretcher with a cable tie. On a seat, alongside her, was Tom Lindbeck. Her thigh was burning. Jasmina lifted her head. Her jeans were sticky with blood. The bullet had hit her right thigh, and for a brief moment, she had lost consciousness. She was freezing; her teeth were chattering. Life was running out of her.

Tom noticed that she'd come round.

"Hans has told me about you. Sweet old Hans. Who helped you out so much," Tom said with a sneer.

Jasmina didn't answer. What difference would it make? She didn't need to understand any more; she was soon going to die. Bleed to death from the bullet wound or be executed with a shot in the head as soon as they no longer needed her.

"Your article about unsolved murders of women, which included Victoria Ahlberg, meant that Hans had to keep an extra close eye on you. Particularly when that fucking Tuva Algotsson started listening to you. I've been following you a long time, Jasmina. You quota-filling little slut."

Nicolas lifted Celine in his arms and rushed after Vanessa. The girl would not last many more minutes. It would take too long for the ambulances to make their way through the crowds on Valhallavägen. Next door to the stadium was a hospital, Sophiahemmet. That was Celine's only hope. As he ran, he tried to keep talking to her so that she wouldn't lose consciousness. Her face was pale, her eyelids half-closed, her head hanging limply.

"Stay awake. Please, Celine, stay awake."

Outside the hospital, white-clad staff rushed down the slope. They were carrying stretchers and kitbags. Nicolas caught sight of Vanessa, who was standing by an abandoned ambulance inside the fence.

"Just hold on a little bit longer. Celine, can you hear me? You'll get help soon."

He pushed his way out through the gate and over the tarmacked road towards the car park as he screamed to attract the attention of the medical staff. A nurse noticed Nicolas, grabbed a colleague by the arm and headed towards them. When Nicolas reached the lawn on the far side of Drottning Sofias Väg, he stopped and carefully placed Celine down on the grass. The women crouched down beside her.

"Gunshot wound to the abdomen. No exit wound," he panted.

"Get a stretcher over here," screamed one of the nurses.

Vanessa appeared.

"We have to go after them. There's nothing more you can do. If they disappear now, we've lost them."

He patted Celine on the cheek before he turned and ran after Vanessa towards the car park. A man hunkered behind a black Volvo XC90. Next to him, on the ground, was a car seat with a baby in it.

"Is this your car?" Vanessa said, pointing at the 4x4.

The man glanced back and forth between the car and Vanessa. He hesitated, opened his mouth to reply, but Vanessa raised her pistol towards him.

"Give me the keys."

The man felt in his pockets, retrieved the keys and Vanessa handed them straight to Nicolas, who jumped into the driver's seat and started the engine. He hit the accelerator and drove straight through the flimsy fence separating the car park from the roadway.

3

"TURN OFF THE SIRENS," said Tom. "They're attracting unnecessary attention."

They finally left Drottning Sofias Väg, and the cycle path they'd driven down led out onto a road with two lanes. The ambulance bounced down from the pavement and out onto Södra Fiskartorpsvägen.

Hans Hoffman felt his way across the dashboard and the wailing suddenly ceased. He turned around and glanced at Tom. To the left, Lill-Jans woodland. On the right, a Porsche showroom. Behind that, Östermalm Sports Grounds. On the far side of the artificial pitch, Lidingövägen was just visible.

Tom clutched the handle and stifled the urge to put a bullet in Jasmina Kovac's skull. He wasn't going to have to wait very much longer. Part of the plan had been to get hold of a woman in case the police had time to put out roadblocks. That way, they could pretend they were on their way to Karolinska. Vanessa Frank's sudden appearance had meant time ran out.

As soon as they reached the boat, Jasmina would die.

"How could they get there so quickly?" Hans Hoffman asked, his eyes firmly fixed on the road.

Tom didn't need to give directions. If they carried straight on, they would get to Ropsten. From there, they could cross the bridge to Lidingö, where the boat was waiting.

"I don't know," Tom said, shaking his head. "How many did you get?"

"Six, I think. You?"

"About the same. We took more than both Rodger and Minassian."

"We made it," Hoffman said, banging his fist against the roof. "Jesus, we made it!"

A police car came speeding towards them in the other direction, passing them with sirens blaring. Tom laughed, and Hoffman joined in.

"I'm glad you persuaded me to choose life," said Hoffman. They had discussed what was more impactful – surviving, or letting themselves be killed by police inside the stadium. Hoffman had advocated *suicide by cop* – but Tom had refused. Their escape plan was going to work, as long as they made it to the boat. After that, they'd lie low for a month, before leaving the country on the fake passports they'd obtained via the dark web. Other Incels would protect them. Keep them hidden. The movement and its members were everywhere, hiding in the sewers of major cities, where ordinary, functioning citizens never ventured.

Tom wanted to write a manifesto. To get more people to notice the madness, the genocide against men, that was underway. At worst, they'd be arrested within a couple of months. Then convicted. But in Sweden, a life sentence was the maximum punishment available.

They had to get through the next few hours. Tom knew how the police operated. If they were to surrender now, the police would invent some story about how they'd resisted, violently, how they'd been armed and had been shot dead as a result. Tom wasn't planning to die. He wanted to live. A long life. Jasmina Kovac stared up at him. That annoyed Tom, who raised his pistol and struck her with the handle in the middle of her forehead.

They drove through the forest, along the perimeter of the Athletics College. A helicopter circled above them. Vanessa wound down the window and stuck her head out. The word *Polis* was emblazoned on its undercarriage. She dialled Mikael Kask's number again, and this time it rang.

"They disappeared northwards in an ambulance, but they may turn off and drive back towards the city centre. Don't they have GPS in their vehicles?"

"They should do. I'll find out. How do you know that they've got an ambulance?"

"I saw them leaving the stadium. I'm three or four minutes behind them. The helicopter over the stadium, can you put me in touch with it?"

"I'll try and sort that out."

"Good."

"Are you alone?"

Vanessa glanced at Nicolas, who was steering the 4x4 down the little woodland track with grim determination.

"Yes, I'm alone."

"I'm sorry I didn't listen to you."

Vanessa didn't feel annoyed at not having been believed, only grief at the horrific scenes they had witnessed.

"So am I, Mikael."

"I'll get the co-pilot of the helicopter to call you. Vanessa, be careful."

Nicolas drove straight out of the woods and avoided crushing an approaching cyclist by the narrowest of margins.

"She's tough, Nicolas. She'll pull through."

"You can't know that."

"No, I can't."

He went quiet and turned off towards Lidingövägen. The car's speed showed a hundred and forty kilometres per hour. As they reached Tegeluddsvägen, Vanessa's phone rang. A loud voice attempted to make itself heard above the background noise.

"Can you see anything?"

"An ambulance heading towards the eastern side of the island, along Norra Kungsvägen."

"That's them. Place yourselves upwind. Keep your distance. And let me know where they head," Vanessa screamed.

Jasmina slowly regained consciousness. The ambulance was travelling at high speed, surrounded by woodland on both sides. Tom Lindbeck's stare was fixed on the road ahead, through the windscreen. While she'd been unconscious, he had tied her even more tightly to the stretcher. She couldn't move her upper body. Her head was pounding, and blood was running from her forehead into her eyes. Her thigh was burning. Pulsating. Each bend in the road almost made her throw up. Yet Jasmina wanted the journey to continue. As soon as Tom Lindberg and Hans no longer needed to worry about roadblocks, they would kill her.

The ambulance slowed down. Proceeded on a bumpier road surface. Should she talk to Tom Lindbeck, plead, negotiate for her life? No, she wasn't about to give him that, wasn't going to let him play God. Death would come quickly. A bullet in the head, then it would be over. Throughout history, billions of people had coped with dying. Jasmina would do the same. She just wished that she could say farewell to her mother. She decided not to ask for mercy. No one would know how she died, but it was important to her that she didn't let them win. Her mother always spoke about living with dignity. Now Jasmina was going to die with dignity.

The ambulance stopped. Complete silence. No sirens, no traffic. She tried to get her bearings but then closed her eyes so that Tom wouldn't see that she was awake. He gathered his things together. Opened the back door and jumped out. The driver's door opened. Jasmina raised her head carefully, to see what was happening. Everything was blurred. Without contours. She caught a glimpse of his back. Something green beyond it. Treetops? A forest? Where were they? Had they changed their minds? Were they going to let her live?

"Got everything?" asked Hoffman.

"Yes."

"What are we going to do with her?"

"Up to you."

They threw the ambulance crew jackets into the back.

"Close the back doors, then…"

The doors slammed shut and the voices grew quieter. The conversation continued, but it was impossible to decipher what was being said. She looked around for something she could use to free herself. What did they mean? What was about to happen?

There was someone behind her, in the driver's seat. Suddenly the ambulance started moving, but the engine was still silent. They'd taken the handbrake off. The ambulance was rolling and gaining speed and she couldn't hold it any longer. Jasmina screamed as she writhed to tear herself free.

Vanessa was holding tight on the handle above the window. The car was juddering as Nicolas turned the wheel hard and accelerated away from Lidingö Bridge. The large homes flashed past. A petrol station. Nicolas overtook someone. An oncoming car swung out of the way into the bike lane, beeping angrily. On the left, a cluster of high-rise blocks towered above them. Vanessa looked at the tall, grey concrete buildings. She visualised Tom Lindbeck's face. She was going to kill him and his accomplice for what they'd done today. For what they'd done to Nicolas, by shooting a twelve-year-old girl. She looked over at him. He had ceased to be a person, been transformed into a tool. This fascinated and terrified her in equal measure.

"My mum," said Nicolas. "You asked me why I never mentioned her, that night on Djurgården."

Vanessa turned towards him in surprise. She remembered the bench, the whisky bottle and the ducks. Adeline's birthday.

That was when he'd told her that he'd taken the job. She had stood up and left.

"She was the most brilliant person I ever met. She could've done anything. Scientist, author, politician. Instead, she had to work herself to death, for me and Maria. Defend us. The only time Dad lifted a finger was to hit us. She sacrificed herself for us. She never got the chance to live up to her potential, just like the women still lying in the stadium never will."

Or Adeline, Vanessa thought, and her throat tightened. She searched for the right words but didn't find them.

"In here."

Nicolas slammed on the brakes and turned left. A woodland track. The gravel pinged up against the underside of the car. Between the tree trunks, she could see the water.

Vanessa hoped that they were going to get there before her colleagues.

Tom Lindbeck and Hans Hoffman were not going to be captured and tried in a Swedish court.

Jasmina screamed as the ambulance rolled downhill at high speed. Her wrist stung as she struggled to break out of the cable tie. It was impossible. The next moment, she felt the wheels lifting and the vehicle flying through the air. She closed her eyes. Braced every muscle in her body in preparation for the impact. Pushed down on the stretcher. The underside of the ambulance struck something hard. She opened her eyes and looked around.

I survived, she thought. She raised her head. Tried to see what was out there and was instantly filled with a terror so violent that she stopped breathing.

Water. Dark water.

Tom watched as the ambulance flew through the air before it struck the surface with an almighty splash. He picked up his bag and headed for the jetty where the boat was waiting. Every single police officer in Stockholm was looking for them. An abandoned ambulance would be clearly visible from the air. Sinking it was the obvious thing to do. Jasmina Kovac would meet a gruesome end. She was going to die slowly as the ambulance filled with water. And Tom had saved yet another bullet which might be needed for something else.

The boat wasn't going to attract any attention. It was to take them inland, to Lake Mälaren. Towards Råby, south of Bålsta, where the car was waiting. The car would enable them to reach the cottage, where they were to remain in hiding for a month before then leaving the country. In the meantime, Tom would start polishing his manifesto.

Finally, they were going to listen. Understand what they had done to him.

Tom heard the sound of an engine on the track. He turned around to see two white headlights coming through the trees.

"There!" yelled Nicolas.

Two dark-clad men, heading out onto a jetty where a boat was waiting. He looked to the left. The ambulance they had escaped in was floating, about to be pulled down by the mass of water.

He drove out onto the little grassy patch by the jetty and pushed the brake. The car skidded as the tyres ripped up the grass and it stopped about fifty metres away from the men.

Tom Lindbeck and Hans Hoffman noticed them and opened fire. The windscreen was hit, and the bullet passed through the car and out through the rear window. Nicolas opened the door with his weapon ready and took cover. Bullets pinged into the car. He heard screaming from the water. Nicolas stuck his head out and looked towards the boat. He couldn't see anyone other than the two men.

"The ambulance!" shouted Vanessa. "She's in the ambulance!"

Vanessa climbed into the driver's seat and curled up. She sat, bent double, with one hand on the wheel.

"What are you doing?"

She took the handbrake off.

"We need to get closer."

The intensity of the shooting increased as Nicolas ducked behind the rolling car.

Tom was confused. It had looked like everything was going so well. They'd managed to get away unnoticed, and suddenly they'd been tracked down. He recognised the woman who threw herself out of the Volvo. It was police slut Vanessa Frank. The one who had come close to ruining everything before, the one who should've been dead. He shot wildly at the car, mostly to stop them coming any closer.

What had he done with the ammo? He pushed himself against the ground and rooted around in the bag but couldn't find it.

"Start the engine," he screamed at Hoffman. "We'll get over to the other side and continue on foot."

The magazine on his Glock was empty.

Tom regretted not having taken Jasmina on board. They could have held her hostage. Negotiated her life for their free passage.

Hoffman hesitated, his eyes darting between the rapidly approaching car and the outboard motor.

"Now!" screamed Tom.

Hoffman stood up. Took a couple of steps. Was hit and fell. Tom roared. The car had almost reached the start of the jetty, where it stopped. Only one headlight beam; the other one had been shot out. He couldn't see Vanessa Frank in the driving seat. Regardless, she was safe behind the engine. Nine-millimetre rounds would not penetrate it.

Hans Hoffman was lying on his side. Shot in the chest. Blood poured from his comrade's body. He was trying to say something. His lips were moving slowly, reminiscent of a landed fish, gasping for air.

"No," Tom wailed. "No!"

They had stopped shooting.

Tom felt down his leg with his fingers, towards his ankle, where he kept his knife.

He was going to do anything to survive.

If Vanessa had counted correctly, he had four bullets left. Only the roof of the ambulance was now visible. The boat was eerily silent.

"One down," said Nicolas. "I've got one bullet left."

He handed his weapon over and Vanessa immediately realised what he was planning to do. She stuffed the second Sig Sauer into her waistband, got carefully to her feet and went out onto the jetty holding her weapon in front of her.

The bodywork was creaking, weird noises, echoes. Jasmina was hyperventilating. Couldn't scream any more. Her lungs ached. She could feel how she was being dragged down. Towards the bottom. When the water had filled the driver's cab, the pressure would smash the little window and the water would cascade in. She was going to drown. Unable to move as the water slowly rose. She wondered whether she would have time to hit the bottom, feel the impact, before she fell unconscious.

4

AS A MILITARY diver, Nicolas had once held his breath for four minutes. But that time he had been lying still, not moving so that his muscles did not use any oxygen. He had been able to free-dive to depths of up to thirty metres and keep moving for three minutes. That was when he was younger though, fitter, and practising several times a week.

As he moved towards the water, hunched over, he filled his lungs for seven seconds, then held his breath for the same length of time, before pressing it out. He really ought to spend five minutes preparing his body, to completely rid it of old oxygen and replace it with new inside the cells. There was no time though. Twenty-one seconds would have to do.

As long as he found the ambulance quickly, it might be possible to save Jasmina.

Nicolas took a deep breath. Could feel his lungs swelling beneath his ribs. Holding his breath, he threw himself out. He broke the surface. Let the momentum of the dive propel him downwards. The darkness enveloped him. After a couple of strokes, he spotted the fluorescent yellow ambulance. It was sinking like an apparition. No screaming could be heard. Air bubbles surged upwards in clutches.

He swam another few strokes, tried to see the bottom beneath him, but it was too dark. The back doors were out of the question. The water pressure on the outside was too great.

He swam past the tinted windows, towards the front doors, where the windows were down. Nicolas was by the bonnet. He peered in. The cab was full of water. Between the cab and the back was a pane of glass.

The windows around the back of the ambulance gave way. The air was pushed out in an enormous bubble, and he heard a scream from inside.

Vanessa snuck towards the boat. She supressed her desire to turn around and look in Nicolas' direction. He was a simple target. She had to be ready to cover him.

A splash made her realise that he'd dived in. Was out of the firing line.

Vanessa breathed out. Stopped. Listened. The boat was bobbing against the jetty. Could Nicolas have got it wrong? Had he hit them both?

She traced the length of the boat with her gun before hopping on board. She almost lost her balance but managed to stay upright. Slowly, she proceeded towards the stern. The sound of police sirens could be heard coming from the road. She had to get a move on. Check that they were dead. Tom wasn't going to get the chance to defend himself in a trial. Put out propaganda. Pound his chest. Terrorists did that, regardless of their motives. Murdering innocent people, women, young children – they called war. Wanting to make it sound heroic. No mean feat.

Tom Lindbeck was going to die for what he'd done to the women at the festival. Vanessa took two quick steps forward and peered around the corner. Saw a body. It was the other one, Hoffman. He was lying on his side in a pool of dark blood, which was still pumping from his body. There was a black holdall by his feet. She rolled the body over in a synchronised movement along with her weapon, ready to shoot into the cabin.

Empty.

She glanced towards the road and saw the blue lights approaching through the trees and bushes.

The footsteps came closer. Tom was clinging onto a white fender on the port side. His whole body was in the water, except his head. He pushed himself tight against the hull of the boat, so that he couldn't be seen from above. The sirens grew louder still. He was going to have to act, and quickly.

He carefully pulled himself up and caught sight of Vanessa Frank's back.

She was looking inside the cabin, with her weapon in front of her. She hadn't seen him. Had no idea that he'd tricked her. He was going to enjoy stabbing her to death. At the same time as she took a step down the ladder, he flexed his arms and hauled himself over the edge.

He bent over, took up his knife, and snuck after her.

Jasmina screamed as the windows exploded in a cascade of shattered glass and the water rushed towards her. The quicker she filled her lungs with water, the quicker she would be dead. She didn't want to be tortured. Just cease to exist. Stop being afraid.

The water was splashing up onto her arms.

The fact that she'd decided not to resist a couple of seconds earlier was of no consequence. Her body reacted automatically. Desperately wanted to survive. She gasped for air, and as the water reached her face, she closed her mouth.

Nicolas made himself wait a couple of seconds while the back of the ambulance filled with water. He stayed still, hovering just above the sinking ambulance, so that his muscles would not use more oxygen than necessary. Fewer and fewer air bubbles were being forced out. A pocket of air remained, just under the roof, but he could wait no longer. He pushed off with his legs, got hold of the frame where the glass pane had sat, and stuck in his head.

It was dark. He could barely see his hand in front of his face, because the roof of the ambulance was blocking out what little light there was. He kicked his legs to get inside, feeling his way to the middle. He whacked his knee.

His hands grabbed hold of something soft, human tissue, in the form of a leg. Nicolas clamped onto the leg and moved so that he was parallel with Jasmina's body. There was still some air left by the roof. If he breathed in though, he would start panting, wanting more; it would do him more harm than good. Nicolas shut the thought out. Forced himself to focus. He moved the palms of his hands over Jasmina. Two thick straps were strained across her body. That was why she hadn't been able to get out.

He pulled at the straps, but they weren't going to budge. He let his hand feel along the edge of the stretcher, felt for the buckle and released the first strap. Moved backwards. Got the other one off. He tried to feel whether she was responding to his touch, whether she was conscious.

Nicolas tugged at Jasmina. But she was still stuck. Something was holding her there. Her body felt heavy, had to be unconscious. Perhaps she was already dead. He pulled harder. His muscles were screaming. Her right arm.

His fingers found the hard plastic strap around her wrist – a cable tie binding her to the stretcher. He didn't have a knife, had nothing sharp to cut her loose with. There ought to be scalpels in one of the cabinets, but there was no time. His head was splitting, and his pulse was pounding by his temples.

Nicolas couldn't get her off the stretcher. It was over. She was going to die.

Vanessa only had time to register how something moved in the opening behind her, realise it was Tom and throw herself headlong out of the way. In the corner of her eye, she saw the shiny knife blade swish past. She landed hard at the bottom of the ladder, felt her foot give way beneath her. She raised her weapon towards Tom's chest. Squeezed the trigger. Nothing happened. Tom, who had stopped, ready to die, came to life. Threw himself towards her. She pulled the trigger again. The same deafening click.

Whispering panic tried to seduce him. Nicolas, though, knew that if he gave in to it, he would die.

He had to get out now. He couldn't take any more.

But the stretcher. Wasn't that removable? It had to be. Nicolas fought off the pain and the protest of his muscles, looking for the release mechanism he hoped was somewhere underneath the stretcher. Did it matter?

She was probably already dead.

He could take no more. He had to give up. There wasn't a single oxygen molecule left for him to call on. The dizziness had him almost passing out. If he stayed any longer, he'd be staying in the ambulance as it descended to the bottom. Tom Lindbeck would win. Another person dead.

Nicolas took hold of the stretcher to push himself out, and as he did so felt a metal lever, not much bigger than a thumb. His strength returned. Just another few seconds. He tugged. Rocked. Jasmina's hair floated into his face.

He pulled on the stretcher. It was loose. It moved as he pulled in. She was still attached to it, but it would be possible to bring up. Nicolas spun around and swam towards the back doors.

There was no longer any air left under the roof.

The world was dark, thick and murky. The back doors ought to open. He pushed. His muscles protested, but in the end, the doors gave. Nicolas stared out into the light. The ambulance was almost on the bottom. He reached backwards, grabbed hold of the stretcher and tore it out. Pushed off. Upwards. Soon, soon. Air. Oxygen. Light. Life.

Tom landed on top of Vanessa. His knee hit her diaphragm, but she barely felt it. All her energy was focused on preventing him from pushing the knife blade into her. She got hold of his left wrist and held it in her right hand. He was too strong.

"You're going to die now, you whore!" he screamed.

Tom tried to straighten up, get his whole body weight behind the blade. The floor was slippery though, and he couldn't pull himself up.

"Die. Die. Die."

Vanessa was squirming back and forth. Flailing. Feeling desperation. How life, and time, were running through her fingers. The blade inched closer. She wasn't going to be able to resist much longer. Her throat. Her chest. That's what he was going for. That was where death could be found. If he stuck the knife into her arm, it would give her some respite. Half a second. Maybe more. It was her only chance. She desperately hoped Nicolas had kept count. That there was still a bullet in the chamber. Otherwise, she was going to die.

Become Tom's last victim.

Vanessa looked him straight in the eye. She turned her body to protect her vital organs, put her right upper arm against the tip of the knife and let go of his wrist with her left hand. Tom pushed. She screamed with pain and saw the triumphant look in Tom's eyes.

Vanessa felt along her back with her left hand. Tom pulled out the blade. The muscle in her arm was torn apart. Vanessa roared. With rage, with pain, with hatred. Blood squirted from her arm, and over their faces. He raised the knife. Her eyes were wide open, and wild. Vanessa put the barrel under his chin, pulled the trigger and felt the explosion that sent the nine-millimetre round into his brain.

* * *

Nicolas gasped and filled his lungs with fresh air. He pulled Jasmina up, holding her head above the surface. He just needed to breathe a bit more, then he could make it to the shore. Police cars were pulling up at the edge of the woodland. He tried to spot Vanessa by the boat, but there was no sign of her. Had a shot been fired as he came up, or was that his oxygen-starved imagination? No, Nicolas was sure he'd heard the bang.

He turned onto his back, held Jasmina's head against his chest and paddled with his legs. The stretcher dragged behind them, sinking. Twenty metres to the shore. Two policemen spotted them and rushed to the quayside. Threw themselves in and swam out to help. Nicolas looked at Jasmina's lifeless face. She wasn't breathing. Eyes closed. Water was trickling from her mouth. The policemen reached them and took over.

"I can manage," he grunted when one of them started tugging at him.

Land under his feet. He waded towards the shore. Turned around, looking towards the jetty and the boat. Where was Vanessa? The police on the jetty looked at a loss. He hobbled over. He tried to pick up the pace, lift his feet, but his soles kept dragging along the ground.

"Stop!" shouted one of the policemen.

Nicolas ignored him and reached the boat. Clambered on board. He saw the man he'd killed. Where was Vanessa? The door to the cabin was open. Nicolas peered into the gloom and wiped his eyes. They were stinging, and itching. Two bodies. Tom Lindbeck was lying on top of Vanessa. Nicolas stopped halfway down. Didn't want to go any closer. Didn't want to see, didn't want to know. He grabbed the handrail to keep himself upright.

"Vanessa?"

He heard a weak murmur. Nicolas threw himself down the last rungs, flung Tom out of the way and slumped down next to Vanessa. In her right arm was a deep wound that was bleeding heavily, but that looked to be her only injury.

Vanessa, who'd had her eyes closed, opened them and smiled drowsily.

EPILOGUE

VANESSA STOOD UP from the pew, then bowed her head before casting one last glance at the coffin on the altar.

The organ woke into life, and the tune of Astrid Lindgren's 'Poor Farmhand' echoed between the walls of the church while the dozen or so mourners slowly proceeded out down the aisle. Outside, they huddled, red-eyed, in little groups. Vanessa felt like she didn't belong in any of them.

After the attack on Stockholm Stadium almost a month ago, Sweden had recovered. The dead were buried. Daily life had resumed. People were on holiday, talking about the weather, and the papers were reviewing the best bag-in-box wines.

Eleven women had been killed in the arena. Had Vanessa and Nicolas not managed to interrupt the shooting, it would probably have been more. A further fourteen had been injured but survived, mostly thanks to the stadium's location next to Sophiahemmet Hospital, where medics had saved the lives of many of the injured.

The investigation into Tom Lindbeck and Hans Hoffman was ongoing and was due to be presented in the autumn. Thus far, it had only been established that both were part of the growing and increasingly misogynistic Incel movement. But it turned out as Vanessa had suspected: Tom Lindbeck had not killed Rakel Sjödin, Victoria Ahlberg or Emelie Rydén. His involvement revolved around his work as a prison warder, which had enabled him to map out the women and give Hans Hoffman access to their mobile phones. Tom was the one who had broken into the Sjölanders' home in Bromma. Tom's goal appeared to have always been the attack on Stockholm Stadium.

That was why he had been gripped by panic and killed Ove, when the murder investigation had turned in his direction just a couple of days before the attack. He could not allow himself to be detained or put under surveillance, thereby losing his revenge project. His fingerprints also matched those of the attempted rapist in the Klara Möller case.

Hans Hoffman's radicalisation remained a mystery. On his computer, which had been found in the farmhouse near Sala that they'd used as a hideout, technicians had found hundreds of threats sent to women in positions of power – primarily journalists and politicians. He seemed to have blamed women for his original sacking from *Kvällspressen*. Their exact escape plan had still not been uncovered. Detectives suspected that they were planning to stay in hiding for a while before leaving Sweden on false passports – the house was stocked with weeks' worth of food.

Vanessa's phone vibrated in her bag. She pulled it out, checked the screen and smiled.

"Are you almost here? We mustn't arrive too late. It's his first trip home. What if the plane's early, he comes out and there's no one waiting? Can you imagine how upset Nicolas will be?"

"I'll be at yours in twenty minutes. Don't worry, we'll make it," said Vanessa.

"Good."

"See you soon."

"So long, sucker," Celine said and hung up.

Vanessa popped a painkiller in her mouth and wandered over towards her BMW. The wound in her arm tightened. She pulled out her keys and pushed the button to unlock the doors.

"Vanessa."

Börje Rohdén's hair was combed; his suit trousers reached halfway down his calves. His shirt was crumpled.

"You scrub up well," said Vanessa.

She raised her hand to screen her eyes from the blazing June sun.

"I don't know how to thank you for helping me to give her this send-off."

"Don't mention it." She placed her hand on his shoulder. "I'm sorry for your loss."

"I hope she's at peace now," Börje muttered, staring at the ground. "There's a few of us heading up to Sky Bar to pay our respects, if you'd like to join us?"

Vanessa shook her head.

"I'm afraid I don't have time. Besides, I'm not allowed to mix the painkillers with alcohol, however tempting that is."

"I'll be sticking to coffee myself," said Börje.

"Good choice."

She gave him a hug, got behind the wheel and started the engine. Börje stayed where he was. Vanessa opened the window.

"Eva's letter. Did you get any answers?"

Börje nodded.

"Good."

A moment later, Vanessa pulled off the motorway and drove past the pizzeria in Bredäng. The shot-out window had been replaced. A family were sitting eating pizza at one of the outside tables. She carried on, onto Ålgrytevägen. Her phone rang. Vanessa assumed it was Celine again and pressed answer.

"I'm outsi…"

"Did you hear about Karim?"

Vanessa smiled.

"No," she lied.

Jasmina Kovac laughed.

"The police pulled him up in a routine traffic patrol the day he was released. On the back seat, he had a black holdall containing fifty thousand in cash and a firearm. He's going back inside."

"So careless of him. That means he won't get custody of Nova," said Vanessa.

The entrance to Celine's building flew open. Beneath a far-too-big green beret, her hair shone bright pink.

"Jasmina, I've got to go. But I'm glad Karim's getting some kind of punishment, even if I wish it was more than two or three years in prison. Get in touch if you'd like to meet up next time you're in Stockholm."

Celine flung open the passenger door. It was hard to believe she'd been shot in the stomach a few weeks before. A wall of perfume slammed into Vanessa as she leaned over to hug the girl.

"Open the window, dear," she said, stifling a cough.

"Did I put too much on?"

"Oh no."

Vanessa put the car into gear and turned it around. "Nice beret."

"It's a Coastal Ranger beret," Celine said proudly. "It was in my hospital bed when I woke up."

Vanessa smiled.

"Have you missed him?" she asked, glancing towards Celine, who had folded down the car's sunshield and was adjusting her beret in the rectangular mirror.

"Yes."

"So have I."